PRIMAL Reckoning

Book 1 in the Redemption Trilogy

JACK SILKSTONE

Published by Jack Silkstone

www.primalunleashed.com

ISBN-13: 978-1533548818
ISBN-10: 1533548811

BOOKS BY JACK SILKSTONE

PRIMAL Inception
PRIMAL Mirza
PRIMAL Origin
PRIMAL Unleashed
PRIMAL Vengeance
PRIMAL Fury
PRIMAL Reckoning
PRIMAL Nemesis
PRIMAL Redemption
PRIMAL Compendium
PRIMAL Renegade
SEAL of Approval

PRIMAL Reckoning is dedicated to Eric,
Frederick, and Cyril.
Men of a different era who give their all for
those they loved.

PROLOGUE

CHIHUAHUA, MEXICO

Christina Munoz balanced her notebook on the thigh of her khaki trousers and glanced down at the shaggy black and white collie that had thrust his head onto her lap. She gave the dog a pat and looked back at the man she was interviewing. "So, Roberto, when did the expansion start?"

"Not long after they started mining," the Mexican Rancher replied. "Started small. Small trucks, small mine, not much digging. But then, then they brought in bigger trucks and the hole grew." His voice sounded exactly as he looked, rugged.

Christina listened intently to Roberto Soto's story. He had lived his entire life on the land. Inheriting his father's property at the age of twenty, he was the sixth generation of the Sotos to do so. It was all he knew, and all he wanted to know. His thick mustache and salt and pepper hair were tinged with dust, his brown eyes deep set in leathery skin. He was not a tall man but had broad shoulders and muscular arms.

"They lied to us. When we all voted we gave permission for a small mine. Now it has become monstruo, the beast that eats everything it touches."

Christina was conducting the interview on the front porch of the Soto Ranch farmhouse. Nestled within the eastern edge of the Sierra Madre Occidental mountain range, it was set in a landscape of rolling dusty hills and stunted vegetation. The farmhouse itself was centuries old; hand-built from local stone with a corrugated iron roof. It sat on a clearing with three other buildings: a kitchen, bunkhouse, and a small shed stacked with firewood. Together they formed a square in the middle of which two trucks were parked, dogs slept, and children played. A track led away from the buildings, past a cattle corral, before linking with the dirt road that ran into the town, Barrio Del Rancho.

"How many farms have been destroyed?" Christina asked.

"Three so far." He gestured to the bunkhouse where a huddle of people was watching them. The men and women were dressed like Roberto: jeans, flannel shirts, and worn leather boots. They wore a look of desperation that Christina had seen before, on the faces of refugees in war zones. Two young boys chased the shaggy farm dog between pickups loaded with belongings. To them it was a grand adventure.

"This is just the start," continued Roberto. "They've poisoned our water, and now they're stealing our land, one ranch at a time."

"What about the authorities? Won't they do anything?"

He spat into the dust. "Who do you think pushed these people off their land? The only person who wants to help is a pretty journalist from New York."

Christina blushed. She had arrived only a few days prior, and already felt a part of the Soto family. They'd welcomed her into their home and their lives. She wasn't naive; she knew Roberto wanted her to tell their story to the world. It didn't change the fact that these people had so little, yet gave so much. Roberto had also taken in the families made homeless by the mine. He provided them with food, water, and a warm place to sleep.

His youngest son dashed into the clearing and skidded to a halt in front the trucks. "They're coming. They're coming."

Roberto issued sharp commands and everyone scrambled into action. Women and children were ushered into the bunkhouse. Shotguns and hunting rifles appeared in the hands of the men.

"You'll need to hide," said Roberto as he checked the breech of a double-barrel shotgun he'd retrieved from his truck.

"Who's coming?" Christina slung her camera over her shoulder and stuffed the notebook in her daypack.

"The men from monstruo." Robert led her around the bunkhouse and behind the shed. "Stay here until they leave. You can see through the back of the shed." He showed her where she could hide behind the wood but still see through a hole in the rusted iron. "If something happens, go down the hill to the stream and follow it to the next farm."

Perched on the wood, Christina aimed her camera through the rusted hole and zoomed in across the clearing and up the road. Her finger depressed the shutter release, snapping half a dozen shots of the approaching vehicles. Two black SUVs were following a white police pickup. The SUVs stopped at the fence as the police truck continued. It pulled up a dozen yards from the farmers' heavily laden vehicles.

Roberto strode across and spoke to the policemen through the open window. She struggled to hear what was being said but it sounded heated. Roberto pointed back up the hill. His stance sent a clear message; get off my property.

She tracked the police truck as it turned around and headed back to where the black SUVs were parked. When it stopped the doors on the two vehicles opened and half a dozen men stepped out. They were dressed in a uniform of sorts: jeans, shiny black jacket, and an assault rifle.

Christina snapped more shots as a tall man wearing a Stetson hat appeared from the back of one of the vehicles. She zoomed in to the limit of the lens and photographed his face. He was dressed in a dark blue suit with a white shirt open at the collar. She watched as he listened to the two officers then spoke to one of the Black Jackets, all the while sipping from a disposable cup. Christina took a dozen more photos before her camera emitted a beep. "Damn!" The card was full. She rummaged inside her backpack, found a spare and replaced it. She slipped the full card into the back pocket of her pants.

When she repositioned the camera, the Black Jackets and a policeman were advancing along the drive. They held their weapons at the ready. The man in the suit stayed with the vehicles. He leaned calmly against his SUV, still sipping his drink.

Christina's heart pounded as the men got closer. They spread out aiming their weapons at Roberto, who was standing on the porch with his double-barrel shotgun. The black and white collie stood before him, its hackles raised.

"That's close enough," Roberto's voice boomed.

The men stopped. The policeman lifted his hand to his mouth. "Are you going to leave?"

The shaggy dog growled, baring its teeth.

"Why should we? This is my land, it was my father's land, and it will be my children's land when I'm gone."

"That might be sooner rather than later," one of the Black Jackets snarled, his eyes hidden behind mirrored sunglasses. He was younger-looking than the others and wore a pistol on his hip. Christina knew that the sidearm meant he was in charge, a trusted lieutenant of the cartel boss. Given his age, it was likely he was related to someone in power.

Roberto ignored the comment. "This is illegal. You have no right."

The collie positioned itself between the intruders and Roberto, baring its teeth and growling. The cartel lieutenant drew his pistol and fired. The dog gave a heart-wrenching yelp and its hind legs collapsed. Wailing in agony, it dragged itself under one of the trucks.

Tears formed in Christina's eyes and she willed Roberto to shoot back. But the broad-shouldered rancher did not move. He met the cartel lieutenant's glare, the barrel of his shotgun still pointed at the ground.

The Black Jacket holstered his pistol. "You've got thirty minutes to finish packing your shit, dirt farmer. Get your people out of here or I'm going burn it all down. You don't want them getting all crispy."

Roberto's shoulders slumped. He turned back to the buildings and cupped a hand to his mouth. "Finish loading the trucks. We're leaving."

The Black Jacket grinned at the policeman standing beside him. "See, they're not so tough." He walked toward the house waving his men forward. "Make sure they don't try anything sneaky, and someone shut that fucking dog up."

Christina stuffed her camera into her backpack and wiped the tears from her eyes. She sat quietly for a minute before deciding it was time to leave. Trying her best not to disturb the wood, she clambered over it.

"And who are you, guerrita zorra?" a voice hissed.

She screamed as she was yanked out of the shed by her hair and thrown on the ground.

"Get off me!" she yelled as the attacker straddled her. She slapped him hard, knocking the sunglasses from his face. It was the boy-faced cartel lieutenant.

He grabbed her by the throat and pushed his pistol against her cheek. "Shut your mouth, puta. You make another noise and I'll blow your brains out."

She whimpered as he traced the muzzle of the pistol over the rose tattoo on her neck. "That's a pretty little flower." He slid a hand inside her shirt and squeezed her breast. "And nice firm tits."

"No." She squirmed under him.

"What the fuck did I tell you, bitch?" He thumbed back the hammer on his pistol as he tugged at her belt and tried to force his hand down her pants.

She caught a glimpse of movement. There was a dull thud and the Black Jacket fell sideways.

Roberto dropped the piece of wood. Effortlessly he tossed the unconscious would-be rapist into the woodshed. "Run downstream. You'll hit the Chavez ranch. They'll make sure you are safe."

She sniffed, trying to hide her tears. "If I go they'll kill you."

He helped her to her feet. "No, we'll be well gone before he wakes up. There's a meeting at the church in Barrio Del Rancho tonight. I'll meet you there. Now go."

Christina scrambled down the slope that led from the back of the ranch house to the creek. She ran as fast as she could over the rocky terrain, not slowing until she hit the creek line. It was then she realized she'd left her backpack in the shed. It was too risky to go back for it. She needed to get as far away from the Black Jackets as possible.

***

George Henry Pershing leaned against his armored Chevy Suburban and watched as the ranchers finished loading their trucks. He stopped eating from a bag of dry-roasted almonds and tipped his Stetson as Roberto drove past. The F250 rode low on its axles, the bed jam-packed to the brim. Two more pickups, overflowing with women, children, and possessions followed. "Not a bad morning's work, if I do say so myself."

The farmer gripped the wheel and stared straight ahead. Dust lingered in the air as the pathetic convoy disappeared down the dirt road.

"I guess he doesn't feel the same way." Pershing offered the bag to one of the policemen. "You see, the key thing to understand about people is what motivates them. Everyone has a motivator. In the case of these ranchers here, it's fear. No amount of money will make them move, but if you throw in some fear they mosey right along."

The cop nodded and took some of the almonds.

"We nearly done here, boys, or are y'all gonna screw around all day?" Pershing asked.

"The farmers are all gone," replied one of the Black Jackets.

"Good, now where the hell is Burro?"

The man shrugged. "He was right here."

"Goddamn it, do I have to babysit that idiot twenty-four seven?" Pershing pushed back his jacket revealing a chrome 1911 holstered on his hip. The belt buckle on his pants was emblazoned with an enameled Texan flag. He unconsciously tapped his leather holster as he walked down the drive.

The men in the black jackets were members of the Chaquetas Negras, a local gang that Pershing had hired as muscle for the mining project. In return for a small cut of the profits, they ensured the security of the mine and took care of any dirty work. They weren't exactly the consummate professionals that the security consultant was used to dealing with, but they were ruthless and that in itself was useful.

"Burro, where the hell you at?" he drawled.

"He's here, Mr. Pershing," said one of the Chaquetas. He was supporting the dazed lieutenant as they walked slowly toward him.

Burro had blood running down from a lump on the side of his head.

"What the hell happened to you, son?"

"I found some gringa bitch behind the shed then bang! One of those filthy dirt farmers must have hit me."

Pershing folded the top of his bag of almonds and slid it inside his suit. "A gringo bitch? Do you mean an albino hound or an actual woman?"

"A woman, Mr. Pershing. Pretty, with brown hair and a hot body."

His eyes narrowed. "Burro, you need to keep that dick of yours in your pants."

The lieutenant smirked. "It doesn't fit, that's why they call me Burro."

"Really, and here's me thinking it's because you're dumb as a mule." He pointed to the backpack the other man was carrying. "Is that hers?"

"She must have dumped it."

"Show me." Pershing took the bag and peered inside. He pulled out a camera, powered it on, and scrolled through the pictures. There were only a few shots saved, pictures of him and the Black Jackets. Who the hell was this woman? He stuffed the camera back into the bag and searched through the woman's other belongings. One by one he dropped them in the dirt. Sunscreen, face-wipes, lip-balm, pens, a bottle of water, and other random items piled up before he found a notebook. He flicked through the pages. The writing was scribbled in shorthand. He turned it on its side and a white business card fell out. He stooped, examined it, and slid it in his pocket. He handed the backpack to Burro. "Put it in the truck."

"What do you want to do with the farmhouse?"

"Burn it." Pershing turned his back on the farm and walked to his SUV. Once he was inside he pulled out a black satellite phone and dialed a number. As he waited for it to establish a secure connection he re-examined the business card. "It's me. Find out everything you can on a Christina Munoz." He read the phone number and email address off the card.

"Got it. Now I've also got some intel you might be interested in." The voice on the other end of the phone was casual. "All your buddies are going to be having a little support group in town tonight. It's at the church. You might want to drop by."

"How do you know that?" Pershing asked.

"Hey man, you live in the Stone Age, you heard of social media?"

"Is that all?"

"That's it."

Pershing terminated the call as he glanced out the window at the farmhouse. Thick black smoke was billowing out from under the tin roof. He sighed; he didn't enjoy this part of the job. When he was in the CIA he'd worked in northern Mexico for over a decade and felt a close affinity with the region. The rustic architecture and harsh terrain reminded him of his hometown in Texas.

A knock on the window interrupted his thoughts and he lowered the heavy armored glass.

"What are we doing now, Mr. Pershing?" Burro seemed to have recovered, at least partially.

"Back to the mine. There's a meeting at the church tonight in Barrio Del Rancho. It might be a good opportunity to deal with some more of the trouble makers."

Burro grinned. "Fuck their shit right up."

He closed the window and took off his Stetson revealing a receding hairline and ears that stuck out from the side of his head. "Goddamn animals."

***

Roberto parked his truck outside the small church that serviced the parish of Barrio Del Rancho. He'd spent all afternoon driving his family and the other refugees to his cousin's property outside of Juarez, then returned to make the meeting.

Chavez, the neighboring property owner, greeted him at the door. "Glad you made it."

Roberto crossed his heart and glanced up at the statue of Christ that hung over the altar. "Have you seen Christina?" he asked quietly as they sat on one of the wooden benches at the back of the church. The meeting had already started; a member of a non-profit organization was speaking from the pulpit. A dozen other farmers and the town mayor were seated, listening.

"The journalist?" Chavez whispered. "No. Why?"

"I sent her to your farm." Roberto was half listening to what the young activist was saying. He was advocating a campaign of demonstrations and petitions to stop the encroachment of the mine on the environment and the local ranches.

"Does anyone have anything they want to add?" asked the Mayor when the activist was finished.

There was silence as the farmers looked at each other. Many of them cast enquiring glances at Roberto. Word of what happened at the Soto ranch had spread.

Roberto stood. "You're sadly mistaken if you think you can negotiate or petition these people. They're not like us."

"You're right, they're not like you at all. But, they are a legitimate corporate entity and they have to follow rules," responded the young man. His groomed beard complemented his hip clothes and the intricate tattoos that covered both his arms. "We can raise awareness, sign petitions, generate social media interest, and force the mine to adopt cleaner, safer methods."

Roberto had taken Christina to meet with the activist the previous day. A graduate of an exclusive college, he had traveled from Mexico City to raise awareness about the pollution that monstruo was spewing into the waterways. While that was a concern for the ranchers, being forced from their land was the more pressing issue.

Roberto grimaced. "Have you heard of the Chaquetas Negras?" he asked.

The man shook his head.

"The Chaquetas Negras, the Black Jackets, are a narco cartel. If you expose them, they will kill you. Then they will skin you and hang your body for the world to see. These are the men forcing us from our lands so the Americans can dig for gold."

"Yes but—"

Roberto held up his hand. "We appreciate your help but you need to understand. The only thing the Chaquetas respect is force."

An older man, one of the wealthiest in the area, stood. "And how do you expect us to show them force, Roberto? We have shotguns and hunting rifles. They would kill us."

"We raise funds and we buy weapons. We form an autodefensa and we fight back."

The man gave an indignant laugh. "You're dreaming."

"What other option do we have?" replied Roberto.

"We could pack up and leave like you."

The broad-shouldered rancher clenched his fists and glared. He stormed outside and lit a cigarette.

Chavez joined him. "Don't listen to him. There was nothing you could do." He lit his own cigarette. "What happened to the journalist?"

Roberto breathed in the smoke and exhaled. "I'm not sure. I'm going to go try and find her. She might have made it to Emilio's farm."

Chavez shook his head. "That stubborn old fool won't leave his land, not even for this." A set of headlights appeared on the road leading to the church. "There's more people coming. Perhaps we can convince them to fight?"

"You stay. I need to go find the girl." Roberto climbed into his truck and drove down the road. A few hundred yards before the approaching headlights he turned down the track that led into the valley Christina would have followed. He missed seeing the two black SUVs and a pickup truck full of gunmen racing toward the church.

***

Christina sat on a slab of rock the size of a snooker table watching the headlights on the road below. She slipped off her shoes to rest her feet. They were swollen and tender from walking all day on the rocky ground. Laying back on the smooth rock, she licked her cracked lips. What she wouldn't give for a bottle of water. Throughout the day the sun had been unrelenting. The stunted trees that speckled the hills offered little in the way of shade. Fortunately, now the sun had dropped behind the horizon, the conditions were pleasant. There was a cool breeze rolling over the hills and the first stars were glimmering in the sky. Christina could almost forget what had happened at the ranch that morning, almost. She checked her cell phone. The time read just after seven p.m. There was no signal.

She had followed the creek as Roberto had instructed but somehow had overshot the Chavez ranch. Unsure who else to trust, she'd avoided the roads and followed a goat track toward town.

She sat up, pulled on her shoes, and continued along the track that wound along the hill. She knew the little chapel wasn't far away and Roberto would be there. He'd have water in his truck.

The track angled down out of the hills, crossing above the church before sweeping back down a ridgeline. The road would have been a lot quicker but there was the threat of being caught by the thugs from the mine.

As she scrambled down the spur she heard yelling from the church below. She stopped at a spot where she could see the old wooden building through the bushes, fifty yards away. There were trucks parked in front of it. In the light cast from the church she saw at least a dozen armed men. Her heart raced as she recognized the Black Jackets and the Stetson-wearing cowboy. Crouching, she took a photo with her camera phone. The LED flash lit up the shrubs around her. "Shit."

She crouched, fumbling with the menu to turn the flash off. After a few seconds, when there were no shouts from the men below, she rose slowly and snapped grainy pictures of the armed men blocking the ranchers from escaping the church. A blast of gunfire sent her scurrying for cover. She waited for more bullets. When none came she pushed back the leaves for another look. The Black Jackets had closed the church doors. Her legs felt like they were encased in concrete as the gunmen took cans from the back of a truck and started splashing liquid on the door and walls.

"Oh god no."

She watched in horror as the man who had tried to rape her at the farm, the young cartel lieutenant, flung a cigarette at the doors. There was a muffled whump and the church burst into flame. Tears streamed down Christina's face as it burned. She heard terrified screams from inside the church as the building took light. Within seconds it was a raging inferno.

Once the screams subsided the Stetson-wearing man gave an order and they loaded up and drove away.

She ran down the track toward the flaming pyre. The intense heat forced her back. Collapsing to her knees, she sobbed uncontrollably, failing to notice a truck pull in behind her.

Roberto ran past and tried to get to the flaming doors. He held a coat over his face but the heat was too intense.

"Who did this?" he spoke hoarsely, grabbing her by the shoulders. "Was it the men from the mine?"

"Yes," she said between sobs.

He scooped her from the ground and bundled her into his truck. They drove back down the track and turned out onto the main road.

She wiped her face with a sleeve. "Where are we going?"

"To the border. You're going back to New York. You need to write your story, Christina. You need to tell people what's happening here."

"What are you going to do?"

"I have friends in Chihuahua. I'll go there and find a way to make money to buy guns." He turned to her, his face completely emotionless. "I'm going to kill the men who stole my land and murdered my friends."

***

Pershing punched in a number on his satellite phone as he traveled in the back of the Chevy. The call connected as they turned onto the access road that wound its way through the mountains to the mine. "I don't think we're going to have any more problems with the local resistance," he drawled.

"Good. What about the journalist?" The man on the other end of the call was Charles King, the CEO of Ground Effects Services, the organization that employed Pershing to manage the mine's security.

"I've got her camera and her notes."

"That won't stop her from trying to sell the story."

"No, you're right. I've got our Agency asset looking into it. They'll put her phones and email under surveillance. We'll know exactly who she's talking to."

"Let me know how it goes. If anyone credible is even thinking about running it, we need to intervene."

"Not a problem, sir. It might also be worth having a word with her editor."

"I'll put some of the boys onto it. I want you to focus on making sure nothing stops the mine from expanding. We need to be pulling three tons of ore out of the ground a day by June."

"Understood. We've only got a handful of farms left on the southern side. It ain't gonna be a problem."

"Good to hear. Has the equipment you ordered arrived?"

"Yes, sir. I appreciate the espresso machine. That was a nice touch."

"Not a problem. Anyhow, I'm sure you have it all well in hand. Check in with me in a couple of days."

"Will do."

The line went dead. Pershing selected a number from the speed dial menu and activated it. "Where are you at with that contact I sent through?"

"I've got all her selectors on cover. She as much as farts near a device and you'll know about it."

"That's charming. You got anything else?"

"Nope, not hearing squat from any of our resistance friends from the church."

"No? That's unfortunate."

"Shit man, you've been there and dealt with them haven't you?"

"I need to go." They were nearly at the mine.

"Hey look, this isn't a one way street, bro. You need to pass me some intel or my boss is going to get suspect."

Pershing brushed dust from his Stetson. "How about something on the Sinaloa?"

"That should do it."

"I'll see what I can do." Pershing terminated the call as they drove through the security checkpoint at the mine's entrance. "Burro, get me some intel on the Sinaloa," he said to the cartel lieutenant who was sitting in the front passenger seat nursing his head. "Something good."

CHAPTER 1

LASCAR ISLAND

Bishop typed into a chat window on his laptop. Hey mate, what's up? He was communicating with his fellow PRIMAL operative, Mirza Mansoor.

His computer beeped as a response came in. I'm good, mission success. I'll be back in a day or so.

Bishop was sitting in the recreation room on the accommodation level of PRIMAL's underground facility in the southwest Pacific. Two floors above him, in PRIMAL's command center, the operations staff were running covert missions across the globe. Only a few days earlier, the Bunker, as it was known, was supporting his own operation against a Yakuza sex-trafficking clan in Japan.

The laptop beeped again. Sorry to hear about Kurtz.

He had tried to push the former German policeman from his mind. A member of his team in Japan, Kurtz had gone AWOL after a particularly traumatic mission. Bishop blamed himself. He had been forced to shoot a young girl who Kurtz had cared for. The incident cost them a PRIMAL operative and, although he was loathe to admit it, a friend he cared about.

He kept typing. How about that trip to New York? I've already cleared it with Vance. He looked forward to getting away from the island, from PRIMAL, and from the stress that came with covert operations.

When?

I'm flying today. You can meet me there.

There was a pause before Mirza responded. What is it you say… I'm in like Flynn.

He laughed as he typed. Yankees or Jets?

What about Broadway or the Guggenheim?

He fought the urge to heckle Mirza. Plenty of time to get your culture fix. As long as we hit a Yankees game, it's all good.

Bish, I have to run. Will meet you in New York. Stay safe.

He managed a smile. This trip was exactly what he needed. He opened a website and started browsing for tickets to the Yankees. He ignored the sound of the door opening as he searched for the best seats.

Chen Chua, PRIMAL's chief of intelligence, walked to the fridge and helped himself to a can of energy drink. The slightly-built Chinese American had a folder tucked under one arm. "Planning the trip?"

"Yep. Mirza's coming, he's pretty excited."

"He should be, New York is the greatest city on earth."

"I thought you were an aloha kind of guy."

"I'm a bit over tropical islands. Give me the bright lights of New York over the humidity and mosquitoes any day." He gestured to the seat next to Bishop. "Do you mind?"

"Not at all. But you're a mountain biker now, why would you be into New York. You're not a closet Williamsburg, soy-latte drinking, fixie-riding, hipster are you?'

Chua snorted into his drink. "No, I love New York because it never sleeps. It's a city that pulses with energy." He gave a wry smile. "And the women are amazing: beautiful, well-dressed, and independent."

Bishop chuckled. "Didn't realize we had so much in common."

"Guy like you in New York, rugged and outdoorsy, with the Aussie accent. You'll have them eating out the palm of your hand." Chua was lost in his thoughts, the energy drink half way to his mouth.

"Mate, we got to get you off this island."

"Tell me about it." He gulped a mouthful of caffeine-laced soda. "OK, let's talk through the job in NYC."

The intelligence chief opened the folder and laid it on the table. Inside was a picture of an attractive brunette. She had long wispy hair, hazel eyes, and a button nose. Bishop noticed the rose tattoo on her neck. He was not into ink, but something about the simple design appealed to him. "If you think I'm going to play valentine for you, you are most definitely barking up the wrong tree."

Chua laughed. "No, she's the journalist I told you about, Christina Munoz."

"The one writing about covert ops?"

"That's her. She's a freelance journalist working through an independent editor in New York." Chua flipped her photo over to reveal a number of articles. "This is all her work. She's got a real bee in her bonnet with regards to covert ops. Written a couple of pieces on jobs we've done, one in Kiev, and another in the Sudan. She's got this theory that a covert arm of the US government is running round the world targeting bad guys."

"That's a little close for comfort."

"My thoughts exactly. I know she's been working on an article that pieces it all together…"

"And you want me to check in with her and find out how close to the truth she's getting."

"Exactly."

"And what happens if she's all over it?"

"I don't think that's the case, but if it is I'm sure we can come up with a plan to convince her otherwise."

"Non-lethal of course."

"Of course. I've already worked up a cover story for you." He handed Bishop another document. "You are Mr. Aden Barnes, an investigator from the UN's Office on Drugs and Crime. She's been trying to sell a story about corruption and terror tactics being employed by a mining company operating in Mexico. You've got wind of it and you're interested in checking the story out. I've got a friend in the UN office in Manhattan who'll sort out the details. The meeting will be organized through her editor."

"And all I need to do is subtly question Ms. Munoz on what she knows about us?"

"That's it. Oh and it would be good if you didn't fall in love with her."

"Very funny."

"The file is uploaded to your iPRIMAL so you can read it

on the plane," Chua said referring to the custom smartphone issued to all PRIMAL operatives. He rose from the table and made for the door. "Your movements sorted?"

"Yeah, Mitch is dropping me in Hawaii. Flights from there are booked. What about you? Not taking any time off?"

"No, Vance and I need to plan the next few jobs." Chua referred to PRIMAL's director of operations, a behemoth of a man who seemed to have equally as much energy as the caffeine-fuelled intelligence chief.

"Man, you guys are suckers for punishment. You know we're not chasing KPI's?"

"You just make sure you enjoy yourself and get some down time. I'll see you in two weeks." He pushed through the door and left the room.

Bishop glanced at his watch. It was almost time to fly out. He left his laptop in his room, grabbed his worn leather travel bag, and followed the corridor to the elevator.

The walls of the passageway were raw volcanic rock, constructed during the Japanese occupation of the Pacific islands. They contrasted with the modern stainless-steel elevator. He punched the button for the bottom level of the underground facility where the shooting ranges, equipment workshops, and ammunition storage magazine were located. When the doors opened he walked through Warmart, a cavernous space filled with racks and shelves stacked with every piece of equipment or weapon that a covert operative could possibly need. A pair of swinging doors gave him access to a workshop where he spotted Mitch hunched over a bench. "Hey, brother."

PRIMAL's resident tech guru, scientist, and pilot, looked up from what he was doing and gave a broad smile. "Hey Bish, you good to go?" he asked in his British accent.

With his beard, receding hairline, wing-nut ears, and infectious grin, Mitch looked every part the crazy scientist. That was until you noticed the bulging muscles that stressed his cargo shorts and T-shirt. They often trained together and the man was a wrecking ball in the gym. He out-lifted Bishop in almost every discipline.

"I'm good to go when you are, mate." He leaned forward to see what Mitch was working on. "What's this?"

On the bench was a sniper rifle mounted with a bulky scope that resembled a video camera.

"It's a precision-guided sniper rifle."

"Guided?"

"Yep, fires .50 cal smart rounds. I'm trying to work out how to integrate it into the iPRIMAL fire control system. Not sure it's going to work though."

"Maybe then you can finally out shoot Mirza."

Mitch laughed. "I'm an area weapon, Bish, not a surgical instrument." Mitch wiped his hands on a rag and pulled open one of the drawers under the bench. "I've got something here I thought you might like." He rummaged around, found a black cylindrical device, and tossed it to Bishop.

"You got me a torch." He switched it on. A bright spot appeared on the wall. "You do know we've got night vision goggles, yeah?"

"Got rocket launchers too, but you still carry a knife. This is a pretty specky bit of kit. Got a supercapacitor in it." Mitch showed him how to twist the lens and it clicked into place. "That turns safe-mode off. Now, you press that button and nail someone in the looking gear, they'll cop 7000 lumens to the retina."

"And that's bad, right?" He pointed it at Mitch.

"Put it this way, they'll get a little more than just a tan. I've tested it on some of the monkeys up top. They don't like it. Anyway, thought it might come in handy seeing as you can't carry your Beretta in NYC."

"I'm going on a holiday, not banging in. The mission's token."

"You never know with you, Bish. By the way, it's a one-shot wonder, so use the low-power light sparingly."

He twisted the lens back to safe-mode and slid it into his pocket. "Thanks. So you ready for this crazy dog sled race you've been harping on about?"

"It's called the Iditarod, and it's going to be killer." Mitch grabbed his bag off a bench and led them back through Warmart to the elevator.

"You sure you don't want to come hang out in New York? Mirza and I would love you to come along." Bishop hit the button for the hangar.

"Wouldn't want to bust in on your little bromance, old man."

The elevator ascended. "Do you know what everyone else is up to over the break?"

"Aleks is somewhere in South East Asia looking for Kurtz. The other lads mentioned something about beaches and birds in Spain."

"Aleks has taken this pretty hard."

"Kurtz is his oppo, mate. What would you do if Mirza suddenly wigged out and legged it?"

"I'd go after him."

"That big boof-head of a Russian is just doing the same thing we all would."

"Do you think I should have gone after him?"

Mitch gave him a sideways look. "No mate, give it some time."

"Yeah, you're right. What's Saneh up to?"

Afsaneh Ebadi had been Bishop's lover. The former Iranian intelligence operative had fallen out with him over Kurtz's decision to leave PRIMAL, and the death of a teenage girl. The change in their relationship was something he was still coming to terms with.

"She's in Bali on a health retreat finding herself. Two weeks of clean eating and yoga. Sounds bloody awful if you ask me."

The doors of the elevator opened and they walked out into an enormous cave that served as PRIMAL's hangar. There were a number of aircraft in the open space including a massive vulture-winged Ilyushin Il-76 transporter, a couple of helicopters, a tiltrotor, and a Gulfstream G650 business jet. The airframes had been purchased by a boutique high-risk air transport and logistics company known as Priority Movements

Airlift, or PRIMAL. Their tail numbers and markings changed regularly as they flew the organization's field operatives around the globe.

"You get the engines on the Pain Train fixed?" asked Bishop as they strode under the wing of the Ilyushin. The huge cargo plane was a highly-modified special operations support aircraft that enabled PRIMAL to deliver their unique brand of justice almost anywhere around the globe.

"Waiting on parts. Russians aren't big on customer service. She's going to be out of action for at least another two weeks." He unlocked the door and lowered the stairs on the G650 executive transport. "Sleek is good to go, though. All new systems are installed and green lighting across the board."

They walked around the business jet as Mitch conducted his preflight checks.

"New systems? That countermeasures suite you've been going on about?"

"Yep, and a few other mods." Mitch ran his hand back along the smooth fuselage and pointed out a section under the tail. "This hatch is new. We can free-fall from it, or drop an equipment delivery pod."

"I'm going to stick to the front door," Bishop said as he walked up the stairs into the luxurious cabin.

Mitch followed, dropped into the pilot's seat and powered up the aircraft systems.

Bishop strapped himself into the co-pilot's seat.

"You know, you really should learn to fly. Mirza has logged over a hundred hours on the sim." Mitch flicked a number of switches, checked the instruments, and spooled up the engines. He nosed the jet toward the floor-to-ceiling blast doors that hid PRIMAL's lair from the outside world.

"I'll get round to it one day."

"That's what they all say, mate. Then before you know it, you're pushing a Zimmer frame and worrying about staying regular." Mitch pressed a button and the gigantic doors rolled open with a rumble. They taxied through into a regular hangar and waited for the doors to close behind them. In the tail camera he watched the faux-rock face slide back in place. He checked the iPRIMAL interface built into the aircraft's systems and confirmed that the skies above them were clear of spy satellites. Another button opened the rusty hangar door to their front, slowly revealing a runway lined with palm trees, and the crystal blue waters of the Pacific.

Bishop slid on his Ray-Ban aviators. "Say goodbye to blue waters and hello to bleak white ice and dog shit," he said as they taxied onto the runway.

Mitch nodded at Bishop's Yankees baseball cap. "You play nice or I'll forget to drop you in Hawaii and you'll never get to that game. And it's husky shit not dog shit!"

He laughed. "I'm sure it all smells the same."

CHAPTER 2

NEW YORK CITY

Christina placed a bunch of flowers on the desk and sat in the chair opposite. "How are you feeling, David?"

David Collins had been her freelance editor for over five years. The gray-haired media veteran was one of her closest friends, a mentor, and father figure. He was the only truly solid foundation in her life of chasing stories across the globe.

The editor of the Global Independent News Agency lifted his arm cast out of his lap. "As good as can be expected." He feigned a smile. "Thanks for the flowers." The sixty-year-old had been mugged on his way home two days earlier. Two thugs had beaten him before stealing his wallet and leaving him semi-conscious on the street. That was what the official police report stated. What David hadn't told them was the shorthaired, muscle-bound assailants had also delivered a message along with the beating. If the RED mining story was ever published, he was a dead man.

"We can't run scared from these people, David. This story needs to be told," she said softly.

"That's easy for you to say, you haven't had your arm broken in three places. These people scare the shit out of me, Chris."

"I know what they're capable of. I watched them burn a Church filled with innocent people. But, if we don't do something about it, then who will?"

David stared out the window at the people in the opposite office building. They were going about their mundane lives with no thought for the people of Mexico or anyone else for that matter. "Fine, but so far the only publications interested in your article have been left-wing rubbish that no one reads. The big boys aren't going to be interested unless we have something more substantial. We need better pictures for a start."

"What about the shots from the ranch and the church?"

He shook his head. "The photos you took with your phone aren't good enough, and the ones from the ranch just show a bunch of punks standing around. You didn't even get a shot of the mine."

Christina slumped back in the chair. "I'm going to have to go back."

"You might not have to. Like I said on the phone, some guy from the UN wants to talk to you. If you're lucky they might run the article in the UN Chronicle. As far as drawing attention to the corruption, you can't do any better than that."

"True, did you check him out?"

"I rang a UN buddy of mine. Says he's legit, works for the Office on Drugs and Crime."

"I wonder how he knows about the article?"

"He might have read that piece you put in REMA." David referred to the Mexican Anti-Mining Networks newsletter. It was the only publication so far that had printed any of Christina's work regarding the mine.

"He must be one of four people who read that thing."

"So are you OK to meet this guy?"

"Of course. If I can convince him to help us we might be able to hit back at the assholes who broke your arm."

***

CHIHUAHUA

Pershing leaned against his black Chevy. "I really do love Mexican mornings in spring." His take-out coffee was sitting on the hood. "The air just feels so damn crisp and fresh."

Burro, the Chaquetas lieutenant, kept glancing at the ranch two hundred yards further down the dirt track. A police pickup was parked in front of it. "Whatever you say, Mr. Pershing. Now can we go down and sort these dogs out?"

"Patience junior, you'll have your chance." The ranch was one of the last still standing in the area. They had been busy in the two weeks since burning the church.

The boom of a shotgun sent Burro scurrying for cover.

Pershing chuckled and picked up his coffee, sipped it, and grimaced. Goddamn, he hated percolated crap. The sooner he got his new espresso machine running the better. He tossed the cup into the grass as the police truck reversed at high speed toward them.

The truck wobbled back along the road as the sound of more single shots rolled up the hill. Rounds hissed through the air a few feet over Pershing's head.

"Well, I'll be damned, if we haven't finally found someone with some balls."

Burro pulled his pistol and fired back at the ranch. "Motherfuckers!" he screamed as his men piled out of their truck and joined him, shooting randomly down the hill with assault rifles.

"Hold your damn fire!" Pershing yelled.

Burro lowered his weapon and screamed out for his men to do the same.

The police pickup roared up alongside Pershing's Chevy and came to a halt in a cloud of dust. One of the cops jumped out, walked to the other side of the truck, and wrenched open the passenger door. "Those idiots shot my partner."

The other police officer was clutching his leg, face screwed up in pain.

Pershing stepped over to take a look. "Show me."

The cop pulled back his hands. There was a single tiny hole in his pants the size of a match head.

"Harden up, sunshine. It's just a BB. Hell, I've seen ducks fly away with more lead in them than that."

Burro waved his pistol. "We can take them now. Me and my boys will go down there and kill them all."

Pershing gave the motley crew of cartel gunmen a once over. They'd proven capable of intimidating farmers but he wasn't sure they were up to the task of rooting out ranchers who were experienced hunters. At least not without taking casualties. He had a much safer option.

"No, we've got some new toys back at the mine. I'm keen to make an example of these boys. We'll come back later and blow them out."

Burro smiled. "Yeah, let's blow these motherfuckers up."

"What about my partner's leg?" the police officer objected. "Nobody said anything about getting shot. We're going to need extra dinero."

"Fine." Pershing took a wad of US currency out of his jacket and tossed it to the policeman.

***

Roberto stared out the shattered window of the house as he reloaded his shotgun. "They'll be back."

"And we will fight them off again. Narcos and corrupt cops are all cowards," said Emilio, the ranch-owner. He was a weathered old man with fine white hair who'd been working his land for nearly fifty years. His property was only a few miles from what was left of Roberto's hacienda.

"I'm not so sure, Emilio."

There were half a dozen of them in the small farmhouse. Roberto had brought two volunteers to help out the farmer, his wife, and his teenage son, Carlos. The burning of the church had scared the locals and no one wanted to join his newly formed autodefensa. Many were willing to demonstrate, petition, and provide shelter, but his small group seemed to be the only ones willing to make a stand.

Roberto turned away from the window. "We need to go now. We need better weapons before we can hit them again."

The weather-beaten rancher folded his arms across his chest and jutted out his leathery chin. "We're not leaving. This farm is all we have."

"Emilio, they're going to take it one way or another, and if you're here, they're going to kill you. Remember what happened at the chapel."

The rancher looked at his family. His son was standing protectively in front of his mother, holding a pick handle. The skinny youth was barely fourteen and yet to shave. He wouldn't stand a chance against cartel gunmen. The ancient bolt-action rifle in his own hands, Roberto's shotgun, and the two hunting rifles wielded by his men were the only firearms they had.

"Come on, Emilio, we could really use your help to fight back. But this is not the time and place. We need to get your wife to safety."

"Where will we go?"

"I have friends in Chihuahua who'll provide beds for as long as you need them."

Emilio put his hand on his son's shoulder. "My wife will need a place to stay, but Carlos and I will join your autodefensa."

"Good, we're staging a demonstration in the city tomorrow. You'll see that there are many others who want to help. Some have even promised money to buy weapons."

"I hope so," said Emilio, "because we need to punish these criminals."

Roberto and his men helped load the family's belongings in the back of Emilio's red F250 truck. He watched as his friend shut the door of his family home for the last time.

CHAPTER 3

NEW YORK CITY

An attractive middle-aged woman gave Bishop a coy smile as he stepped out of the subway onto Sixth Avenue. He gave her a nod and smiled as she passed. Chua was right. The women of New York really seemed to appreciate the outdoors type. He guessed he was a bit of a novelty in a city full of tourists, bankers, and hipsters.

His stomach grumbled as he walked past a diner on his way to the intersection with West 16th. The crisp morning air carried the smell of coffee and pizza dough out to the street and straight into his nostrils. Damn he loved New York. The streets were alive with people. It was almost as if the city had a pulse and you felt it beat as you flowed along her veins.

His thoughts turned to Saneh and he felt a little melancholy. New York was a city they had planned to explore together. He caught his reflection in the glass of a shop front. The face that looked back at him was tired, bags under bloodshot eyes, and a semi-permanent frown.

He exhaled and relaxed the muscles in his jaw and forehead. This trip was about taking time out and that's what he needed to do. Forget about Saneh, forget about the ghosts of his past, and clear his head. First, he needed to get the meeting with the journalist out of the way.

He glanced at his watch; he needed to find The Gray Duck café in the next ten minutes. Stepping off down the avenue he turned onto West 16th. Almost immediately, the city's pace eased. Low-level apartment buildings and a leafy aspect replaced the shop fronts and offices of high-rises.

His phone vibrated and he pulled it from his jeans. The iPRIMAL looked exactly like any other smartphone and appeared to have the same functionality. That is, unless you knew how to unlock its secrets. A hidden menu gave access to the powerful intelligence and communications tools that PRIMAL operatives used in the field.

The message was from Mirza. He was in Dallas and his flight would arrive in a few hours. Perfect timing. He'd be done with the meeting in time to meet Mirza for lunch.

The Gray Duck was exactly where his mapping app said it would be. A quaint café nestled in the basement of a renovated warehouse. It was filled with funky-looking hipster types and Bishop hoped like hell they served something other than kale smoothies and soy-lattes.

He picked a table in the corner of the room and flicked through a magazine as he waited. He glanced up as two men entered the café and sat at a table close to the door. If he were in a different city and on a real job, he would have been concerned. Fit and alert, they looked like plain-clothed police or security personnel. He turned his attention back to the magazine.

***

Christina chained her bike to a pole outside the café and ducked inside. She looked around and realized she had no idea what the UN investigator looked like. She spied the only male sitting by himself. A second later he looked up from his magazine, spotted her, and smiled. She waved. He was surprisingly handsome, in a rugged way, with sincere brown eyes and an easy smile.

"Christina?" he asked as he rose from his chair and shook her hand.

He was tall with broad shoulders and strong hands. A man who looked like he knew how to handle himself in a fight. She guessed he was either ex-military or police.

"Aden," she replied.

"Pleasure to meet you."

She sat in the chair he offered, placing her bag on a spare seat.

He waved the waiter over. "I haven't had my morning

coffee yet, and I'm a little jet-lagged. Will you have one?"

"Sure." She ordered a soy latte and cocked her head inquisitively. "You've got an interesting accent. Australian?"

"Yeah. It's a bit of a mix though. Been living overseas for a while."

"And you just flew in today?"

He nodded. "Haven't been to Manhattan for a while but had some meetings at our headquarters here. Just wrapped up a sex trafficking case in Europe."

"I wrote an article on that last year."

"Yes, an interesting read."

"You read it?"

"Of course, I've read most of your work. You've got a good nose for digging up corruption and crime."

"Don't tell me, you're here to offer me a job," she said with a laugh.

"Trust me, you don't want to work for the UN." He flashed a smile. "Enough red tape to patch up the Titanic."

"That must suck."

"It does. Most of my time is spent trying to convince corrupt authorities to take action against the criminals operating directly under their noses. It's frustrating work."

"So the UN doesn't have a Special Forces team running around arresting bad guys?"

"No, my office consists of a group of investigators who build a case then hand it over to local law enforcement."

"What if they don't do anything? Can you give it to the US government so they can get the CIA to take care of it?"

Bishop thanked the waiter when she delivered their drinks. "God no. Even if I was allowed to share the information with the CIA, most of the time they couldn't do anything."

"Why is that?"

"Because even they have to seek authority from their masters and Washington doesn't want to piss off all its friends."

"But someone's doing something," Christina said between sips of coffee. "Have you read my article on South Sudan?"

"The one about Chinese influence in the region?"

"That's it. But, more importantly, it was about a team that helped balance the conflict. I found witnesses near the border who had seen strange aircraft and well-equipped soldiers."

"And you think they were an element from within the CIA?"

"Yes, villagers recognized American accents. They told me it was a small team, very capable, and very well equipped. And there's more. I've found another five actions that may have been conducted by the same group. One in the Ukraine, one in Hungary, two in Libya, and one in Russia."

"And all of them are the work of this theoretical CIA black ops unit?"

She nodded over her cup.

He scratched his chin. "Interesting theory. The CIA certainly gets involved in lots of places you don't read about in the news. Could even be JSOC, or a joint task force. Is that what you're working on at the moment?"

"No, I'm still trying to garner interest in my Mexico piece."

"Yes, I read your article in REMA and I'm interested in knowing a little more."

She placed her cup on the table. "What do you want to know?"

"You mentioned an American mining company was employing cartel gunmen to push farmers off their land."

"Yes, and they've also committed mass murder. I saw them burn down a church with people inside it." She pulled a tablet from her bag and placed it on the table. "I've got some photos. They're not great but they tell the story." She opened the tablet and brought up the images. The first few were grainy but they showed the burning church and the figures in front of it. "I know they're bad quality, but trust me, they're cartel guys."

As she swiped through photos she watched his face. He studied each one intently, his brown eyes scanning every inch. She got to the shots from the farm. They were clear and focused. "These guys came to the ranch I was staying at. They forced the farmers off their land at gunpoint." She paused on the picture of Pershing. "This is the American running the show. The little scumbag next to him is his cartel sidekick."

"This is very interesting. Can I get a copy of those photos?" He reached into his jacket and handed her a memory stick.

She considered the request. It wasn't usual for a journalist to share unpublished material, however this man might actually help Roberto and the ranchers. "Sure. I've also got other photos of the farmers I interviewed, but wasn't able to get close to the mine." She plugged the memory stick into her tablet.

While the photos copied, she continued. "The locals call it monstruo, it literally means monster. The mine operators are Resources Environmental Development Group which is a joke because not only are they forcing people off their land, but they're poisoning the waterways."

"Have you sent any of this information to the authorities? It's a US mining company, right? You could make an application to the Environmental Protection Agency. Or talk to someone in the Department of Justice. Even go to the FBI."

"No, I haven't got enough evidence. RED, that's what they call themselves, has a lot of money behind it so I need to tread carefully."

He nodded.

"I have to go back and get more information. Need more photos and witness statements." She handed him the memory stick and looked him in the eye. "Do you think the UN would be interested in sending someone with me?"

He sighed. "Seems like a worthy cause but our resources are pretty stretched right now."

"So that's it then? These bastards get to continue raping these people's lands and murdering them?"

"If you give me your email, I'll let you know if I find anyone able to help. Maybe the UN Chronicle would be interested, but I can't guarantee anything."

She put the tablet back in her bag and handed him a business card. "You can call me. Do you have a card?"

"Sorry, I was running late this morning."

She had the feeling Aden wasn't going to be much help but that wasn't surprising. The UN were a huge bureaucracy driven by political agendas. If she wanted to make a difference, she knew she would have to get back on the ground with Roberto and gather compelling evidence. An article in a world-class publication might generate enough interest for the US authorities to take notice and hold the mining company to account. As charming as Aden was, he probably wasn't going to make that happen. Still, the off-chance that he could was good enough reason to flirt with him a little.

Bishop paid for the coffees. He felt it was the least he could do all things considered. The UN was never going to see her article, at least not from him. At least Chua's bullshit task was completed. The intelligence officer's concerns she was getting close to PRIMAL were unfounded. She wasn't actively pursuing a story linking their activities and had no clue that an independent, altruistic team of operatives was actually doing the missions. Now, he was going to focus on relaxing and enjoying his holiday in New York.

As they headed for the exit, he noticed the two men sitting near the door were still at their table. One of them glanced up as he held the door open for Christina.

Bishop put on his Ray-Bans as she unchained her bicycle. "So what are your must-dos for an out-of-towner? I haven't had time off in the city in, well, in forever."

"What are you interested in? Museums? Parks? Galleries?"

"What do you suggest?"

"I could show you around." Her smile was warm. "I've got some things to do today, but I was planning on taking tomorrow off."

Bishop returned her smile. "That sounds great."

"OK, how about we meet back here at ten tomorrow?"

"Sounds good. I've got a friend coming in tonight so it will have to be the three of us."

"Oh, I don't want to impose."

"Not at all. He's a good guy, and we'd appreciate the local knowledge."

"OK, see you then."

Bishop pecked her on the cheek and walked off. As he strolled, his instincts told him to double back. He crossed to the other side of the road and swung back in Christina's direction.

He caught up quickly. She was wheeling her bike as she fiddled with a tangled set of earphones. The two guys from the café were following her.

Bishop watched them from the other side of the road. They were tailing her but there was no way they were going to keep up once she was on her bike. That meant one of two things: either they had a mobile unit they were working with, or they were going to target her before she started riding.

He scanned the road. The slow moving traffic included two vans and half a dozen cars. Any of them might be working with the guys following her. He pulled the brim of his cap down low and ducked between a van and a cab. The men had almost caught Christina and he was still a dozen yards away.

A white tradesman's van caught his attention. It was parked a few car-lengths down the road from Christina. He felt strangely vulnerable, missing the pistol usually holstered on his hip. The only weapon he had was the single-shot flashlight Mitch had given him. He pulled out the stubby cylinder and increased his pace.

The men made their move as Christina jumped on the bike. One of them wrapped his arms around her and the other wrenched open the door on the van. Her bike hit the pavement with a crash.

Bishop grabbed the hair of the man who held her and wrenched his head back. He slammed his fist into his temple, dropping him with a single punch.

Christina stumbled to her knees. The second man turned to face Bishop and was blasted with a blinding light. He grunted, covering his eyes with his hands.

"Nighty night!" Bishop said as he jabbed him in the temple with the stubby tube and shouldered him through the open van door. The dazed thug collapsed onto a third man who'd been waiting in the van.

Bishop grabbed Christina's hand and hauled her off the ground. "Run!" They sprinted down the street and around the corner.

"Who are they?" she asked between breaths.

"I was going to ask you the same thing."

They ran along the sidewalk, weaving between the crowds until they hit a crossing. The pedestrian light was red. "We need to get off the street." Across the road Bishop spotted one of the green signs to a subway entrance.

He glanced back. Two of the thugs were in pursuit. He grabbed Christina by the hand and dragged her into the busy morning traffic. Horns blared and tires screeched as they dodged cars. A yellow cab missed Bishop by an inch. The driver hurled an insult through his open window.

They reached the other side as the crossing light changed, giving their pursuers a clear run. "Into the subway." He pulled Christina around the railing and down the steps.

"Shit." There was a queue at the ticket booth and no way through the wall to ceiling turnstiles. Behind them the two heavies shoved people out of the way as they barreled down the stairs.

Bishop looked for a transit cop. Aside from the geriatric manning the ticket booth there was no one else in uniform.

"You coming or what?" Christina was on the other side of the turnstile. She held a MetroCard through the bars. He grabbed it, swiped the sensor, and pushed through the rotating bars.

Someone grabbed his shoulder. Twisting back, he looked directly into the face of one of the men chasing him. He broke the man's grip as the turnstile locked with a clunk. The thug swore as he tried to shoulder the heavy gate. It didn't budge. Bishop gave him a wink and followed Christina down to the subway platform.

She led him past the waiting crowd, all the way to the end. "It won't take them long to get a ticket." She pointed at the screen that showed the arrival of the next train. One minute and thirty seconds.

Bishop watched as the subway timer counted down the final thirty seconds before the next train arrived. If the guys chasing them made it onto the platform they would have to push their way through the hundred-plus waiting people. He took off his Yankees cap and stuffed it in his jacket pocket.

Twenty-five seconds. He saw the two men charging down the steps that led to the platform.

Twenty seconds. He dragged Christina down into a crouch. "They're at the other end of the platform."

Ten seconds. A rush of wind and noise was followed by the train screaming into the tunnel. The doors opened. Bishop and Christina jostled their way in.

Seconds passed, the doors hissed shut, and the train was away. He dragged Christina to the end of the carriage.

"They're probably the same guys who beat up David," she whispered.

"Who's David?"

"My editor. He got warned not to publish my Mexican article."

"You didn't say anything about that before."

"Yeah, well it didn't seem relevant then."

"Well, it is now. The guys who tried to grab you arrived at the café before you did. That means they knew exactly where to find you."

The doors at the end of the carriage slid open and a pair of metro cops walked in. She let out a sigh of relief. "Should we tell them?"

He shook his head and put his baseball cap back on. Their two pursuers had entered directly behind the cops. They stood at the opposite end of the car glaring. Bishop took out his phone and snapped a photo.

At the next stop the doors opened and the metro cops stepped onto the platform. Bishop led Christina out behind them. He maneuvered around the police, pushed through the exit turnstile and ran through the tunnel up to the street.

Behind them the two men gave chase.

"Damn." Bishop spotted the white van as it pulled to the curb in front of them. "In here." They burst into the foyer of a twenty-four hour gymnasium. Ignoring the protesting attendant, they continued through a door marked STAFF ONLY.

"Where are we going to go now?" Christina latched onto his arm.

"We'll head out the back. But not till I've slowed these bastards down." He pulled a fire extinguisher off the wall, yanked out the pin, and turned to face the door.

As the two men entered he sprayed them with the chemical extinguisher. The stream of fine powder hit them in the face, blinding them. He threw the heavy canister. It hit the lead man in the head with a thud, knocking him to the ground.

"Let's get the hell out of here." He pushed open an emergency exit and stepped into a back alley. They walked between bags of garbage and onto the street where he hailed a cab.

"Where are we going?"

"Not to your place, that's for sure. You need to get rid of your phone and stay low."

Christina took the phone from her bag, looked at it reluctantly, and tossed it down a drain. "What else do I need to do?"

He guided her into the cab. "We can lie low at my hotel."

CHAPTER 4

Bishop opened the bottle of bourbon he had picked up at the airport and splashed some into a tumbler of ice. "Drink this, it'll calm your nerves. You'll be safe here." They were in his modest hotel room, not far from where they'd jumped into the cab.

Christina's hands were shaking. "They were trying to kidnap me, weren't they?"

"My guess is they want to scare you into dropping your story on the mine."

"David was right. These people are serious. I need to go to the police."

He poured himself a drink. "And tell them what? You've got no evidence and these people have some pretty serious assets if they've been targeting your emails. We need to do a little digging before going to the authorities."

She sat on the edge of the bed and held the glass with both hands. "Do you think they would've killed me?"

He shook his head. "No. This is New York, not Mexico. They might have hurt you, but they probably wouldn't have murdered you."

Tears welled in her eyes. "I'm not so sure. When I was in Mexico, one of the narcos tried to rape me. A farmer, my friend Roberto, he stopped it. They burned his farm to the ground." She sobbed and wiped her eyes. "Then I watched them torch a church full of people, they killed them all. That's why I have to go back. That's why this story needs to be told."

He sat next to her on the bed. "That's some serious motivation."

She tucked a loose strand of hair behind her ear and wiped her cheek. "God, I'm so sorry. You just saved my life, and I haven't even thanked you." She put her glass down on the bedside table and hugged him.

There was an awkward moment where Bishop didn't know what do. Then he wrapped his arms around her and returned the hug. "It's OK, anyone would have done the same thing."

She sighed and released him. "Most people would have panicked. You stayed calm."

"Most people don't have training to fall back on."

She gave a weak smile. "Having you around would be pretty useful in Mexico."

"Nice try." He laughed. "Alright, I've got a lunch meeting, and after that I'll do a little snooping around. I don't want you going home till I get a little more info about these RED guys. OK?"

She nodded.

"I'll come back here and we'll do dinner at seven." He downed his drink and made for the door. "I'll also sort you out a room of your own."

"Who's going to pay for the room?" Christina asked. "I can't really afford to stay here."

"Compliments of the UN. I'll see you at seven."

***

Bishop rode the elevator down to the hotel lobby and walked into the bar. He spotted Mirza waiting at a table with his bag on the floor. The former Indian Special Forces operative rose to meet him.

The pair had been friends for years, ever since they had met on a UN operation in Sierra Leone. It was Bishop who'd recruited Mirza into the covert vigilante organization and they'd been partners ever since. Despite embodying the fearsome fighting spirit of his Nepalese forefathers, Mirza was in fact the more deliberate of the two. His cool-headed demeanor balanced Bishop's hot-headedness perfectly.

"Good to see you with a beard again, mate." Bishop embraced the smaller man in a bear hug. "I didn't want to tell you, but that mustache of yours was getting a little creepy. How was Myanmar?"

Mirza had just finished a preliminary operation in the military dictatorship. His mission was focused on establishing contacts in the underground for a future operation. These contacts would be cultivated into agents, or Blades as PRIMAL's chief of intelligence called them.

"It was hot and sticky."

"Well you're not going to get any of that here. New York in the spring is like heaven compared to South East Asia."

Mirza grinned. "I've been looking forward to it. So many things I want to see."

"And see them you will. There's just one small thing we need to take care of before we hit the sights."

Mirza's smile dropped. "What are you talking about?"

They sat at the table and Bishop explained the task Chua had given him. He then outlined the series of events that led to the attempted abduction of Christina.

"I've never met anyone who attracts trouble like you do, Aden. It's like I spend my time running around with Dirk Pitt." Mirza was an avid fan of Clive Cussler's early work.

"This one isn't my fault. Chua dumped me right in the middle of it."

"But you completed the mission. The girl's problems are not yours."

"Really, is that how you feel?"

Mirza sighed. "No. What's the plan?"

Bishop pulled out his iPRIMAL and showed him the photo he had taken on the train. "I flicked this through to Flash. He ran it through the system and managed to track these bozos down on the web." Flash was PRIMAL's digital intelligence specialist. The former NSA analyst was a genius when it came to exploiting communications and computer networks. He worked in the Bunker with the rest of the PRIMAL support staff.

He tapped the screen. "Both these guys work for a private security firm called Ground Effects Services. What's interesting is they have an office in the same building as a private equity fund called Manhattan Ventures."

"And how do they fit in?"

"They're the ones bankrolling the mine Christina is

investigating in Mexico."

"It's obvious they're trying to intimidate her. Stop her from investigating further."

"That's exactly why we need to check them out."

"Before we go any further, Bish, I've got to ask one question."

"Shoot."

"Is this journalist attractive?"

Bishop laughed. "She's not ugly, mate, but it's not like that."

"Just wanted to make sure you hadn't fallen in love in the six hours you've been in New York."

"That's not even funny." He frowned. "Why does everyone think I run around with my heart on my sleeve?"

"Because you do, but that's part of your charm. Now what's your plan for getting inside? Manhattan Ventures or the security guys?"

He shook his head. "Too much risk. I want to go in through the guys running the mine. They're called Resources and Environmental Development, or RED. It'll be much easier. They'll always be looking for new opportunities." He ordered a gin and tonic from a waiter along with a lemonade for Mirza.

"It's simple. We get Flash to build an online back story that makes me out to be an investor with links to the PNG government. We make it look like I have access to the rights for the Bougainville Copper mine." Bishop referred to a massive copper and gold deposit located on a Papua New Guinean island. Thought to be the largest in the world, it had been shut down in the nineties due to civil unrest.

"Good plan, Bish, there's only one problem."

"What's that?"

Mirza gestured to the photo on the screen. "The thugs you snapped might recognize you. I'm going to have to be the one that visits RED."

"Damn, you're right. That'll work, there's a lot of Indian money in PNG. You'll have to get a suit though and put on a few pounds."

"A shiny watch might be in order."

"And a hotel more suited to a man of your stature." Bishop grinned. "Throw it on the company plastic, that's what it's for."

"Will do."

"I'll get Flash onto it. In the meantime, I'm going to take Christina out for dinner."

Mirza rolled his eyes. "It's not like that, mate," he said mimicking Bishop's Australian accent.

"Bugger off and find yourself a hotel."

CHAPTER 5

CHIHUAHUA

Pershing lowered his SUV's armored glass. "Anyone still at home?" he asked through the window.

Burro was watching the ranch through a pair of binoculars. It was the same one they'd visited the day before, except this time there was no sign of movement, let alone gunfire. "No, Mr. Pershing. They've run away."

He opened the door and stepped out onto the dusty track. "That's a pity. I really wanted them to see this. Still, I'm sure someone's watching."

He thought the ranch looked quaint in the soft afternoon sun. A little like the bed and breakfast places his parents liked to visit.

"Tell your boys to attack. Remember to do it exactly how I showed you." Pershing reached into the back of the SUV and took out a thermos. He unscrewed the top and poured himself a black coffee as Burro issued orders to his men.

The Black Jackets, as Pershing liked to call them, lined up on the barren slope above the farm. They were kneeling or lying down with their assault rifles, as he had instructed. Every second man also had a long green tube with black rubber end-caps slung over his shoulder. Supplied by Pershing's boss, the SMAW-D bunker-busting rockets were surplus from the American war in Afghanistan.

Pershing raised his coffee and used it to gesture to Burro. "Let's get this rodeo started."

Gunfire cracked and dust kicked up around the little farmhouse as they began to attack. The men moved forward in odds and evens, every second man taking turns to fire their rifles as the others walked forward half a dozen yards then kneeled. Pershing sipped his coffee as he watched. The line was a little uneven but it was a start. At least they'd stopped shooting randomly and running around like madmen.

The ranch house was soon pockmarked with bullet holes, the windows shot out, and the woodwork splintered. The Black Jackets stopped bounding forward and started unloading long bursts into the building. One of them unslung a green tube, knelt, and aimed it from the shoulder. The rocket left its tube with a thump, screamed over the building, and disappeared into the distance.

The gunfire stopped and was replaced by heckling as the gunmen screamed obscenities at the man who missed. Pershing chuckled. Boys would be boys.

The next rocket did not miss. It slammed into the front of the house and the thermobaric warhead detonated with a chest-shuddering explosion. Spurred on, they fired off the remaining rockets in a few seconds. The roof collapsed and soon the little house was a burning wreck.

Everything went quiet. Burro's men had expended all of their ammunition. Fire discipline would have to be the next lesson. Pershing finished his coffee and waved a bulldozer off the low loader parked behind his Chevy.

The dozer rumbled down the track as the Black Jackets gathered around their trucks. They cheered as the D7 lowered its blade and demolished the mortally wounded structure in a single pass.

Pershing knew the locals would come out to look at the devastation and word would spread. He smiled. When it came time to clear the next farm, he didn't expect any resistance.

***

NEW YORK CITY

The Manhattan Ventures and Investments offices were situated on the top floor of the Pulvermach building, one block from Wall Street. The bespoke private equity firm, also known as MVI, had a staff of ten and a board of four consisting of the chairman, Chief Financial Officer, and two additional directors.

With over two billion dollars in investments, it wasn't one of the wealthiest funds in New York, but it was one of the most secretive.

Today, the directors were assembled in the boardroom for an update on their latest investment, a gold mine in Mexico operated by the Resources and Environmental Development Group. At the head of a polished mahogany table sat the chairman and majority stakeholder, Jordan Pollard. A former military officer turned businessman, Pollard had been a Brigade commander in the Second Gulf war before retiring and cashing in on the lucrative security market in war-torn Iraq. But, unlike most, he'd seen the writing on the wall. As the contracts expired, he channeled his funds into MVI using his security expertise to exploit investment opportunities in emerging high threat environments. He gathered a team of ruthless bankers able to pull in enormous amounts of capital, using companies like the RED Group to implement the investment.

The mining operations officer of RED, Brian Kestrel, was briefing the Board from a screen perched over the end of the long table. He used a laser pointer to indicate the graphs on the presentation. "We're currently producing two thousand tons a month, with an additional five hundred of increased output forecasted by the end of the month." Kestrel was Canadian, a hulking bear of a man who'd been hired for his ability to establish mining projects at break-neck speed.

The gray-haired chairman clenched his chiseled jaw and fixed him with cold eyes. "Is there any way we can increase it in the subsequent months?"

"Yes we can, and we will, sir. We've recently brought two more heavy loaders online and four more dumpers. With these running twenty-four-seven we'll be able to expand and increase productivity." He clicked to a map that showed the current mine size and the anticipated areas of expansion. The pit was set to more than double in size.

"So the only thing holding us back is how quickly we can gain access to these areas?" Pollard switched his gaze to the director with a shaved head sitting opposite him. "Charles, is that going to be a problem?"

"Not at all, sir. Pershing has it well in hand." A former Special Forces officer, Charles King also ran Ground Effects Services, a company owned by Manhattan Ventures.

The miner scratched his beard. "Look, I know it's not my area of expertise, but some of the methods we're using to clear ranchers off their land seem a little… excessive."

King leaned back in his chair. "You were right the first time, it's not your area of expertise. Let my people worry about security."

Kestrel glanced at the chairman.

Pollard nodded. "You ensure the mine hits its production outputs and you'll get your bonus."

"Yes, sir." He addressed the other directors. "Are there any other questions?"

The other two board members shook their heads.

"That's all, thank you." Pollard gestured for the mining engineer to leave.

Kestrel gathered his notes and left through the opaque glass doors.

Pollard waited until he was gone before turning to MVI's Chief Financial Officer, a bespectacled accountant in his late thirties. "If we hit three thousand tons a month, how long will it take before we're cash flow positive?"

The CFO scribbled an equation on his notepad. "A little over six months."

"Good. Our rate of expansion is spot on."

Wesley Chambers, the youngest of MVI's directors, slapped the table with his palm. "What did he mean by excessive? Your man Pershing's not doing anything that'll come back to bite us later on is he? I mean, we've already had one journalist sniffing around. If we're burning ranches, and dare I say it, killing people. Well, if that gets out, it could shut us down."

King glared at him. "The security situation is under control, Wesley. You worry about your job and let my people do theirs."

"What about the journalist?" the chairman asked. "Has she

been dealt with?"

"There's been a minor setback."

"Your men had a simple task. Force the woman to drop her investigation. How in God's name did they mess that up?"

"The woman had help."

"Who?"

"The man she met with. The UN investigator. When they met–"

Wesley interrupted, "You're shitting me! She met with a UN investigator? You're burning farms in Mexico and the woman writing articles about it has already met with someone from the UN?"

"It'll be taken care of, alright," King growled.

"Not in New York," said Pollard. "The woman is tenacious, she'll return to Mexico."

"That's fantastic, maybe she'll take her UN buddy with her," said Wesley.

"Mexico is a dangerous place," said King.

"And what if she decides not to return to Mexico?" the young director continued. "What if the UN decides to send their own investigators? What then?"

King shook his head. "Without evidence, no one's going to buy her story. She'll head back to Mexico to chase her story. When she does, the gloves come off."

"Enough!" Pollard held up his hand. "The woman will be dealt with." He turned to the CFO. "Where are we with the investment for Venezuela?"

"We have over six hundred million in liquidity on hand. By the end of the week we should reach the required target of eight hundred."

"Good, and the situation with the government?" he directed the question at King.

"You're scheduled to fly in at the end of the month to finalize the rights. Team One is fully operational, and from all reports the government appreciates their work. I'm not anticipating any problems."

"Very good." Pollard rose from the table. "That concludes

the meeting, gentlemen." He left the room with King in tow.

"Mr. Chambers is starting to concern me," he said as the elevator doors closed and he pressed the button for the top floor. "I'm beginning to think he doesn't have the stomach for our investment model."

"Do you want me to take care of it?"

Pollard shook his head. "No, just watch him. We need his access to the capital markets." The elevator doors opened. The entire level was dedicated the chairman's office and apartment. "Where are we with Longreach?" He strode past his secretary and pushed open the ornate wooden doors to his office.

"First flights are scheduled for next week." King stopped at the doors.

"And we have complete deniability?" he asked as he poured himself a tumbler of scotch from a well-stocked cabinet.

"Of course."

"Good." He took a sip. "Charles, I don't want to hear any more about this journalist. Deal with it."

The former Special Forces officer nodded and spun on his heel.

***

CHIHUAHUA

Emilio glanced around the kitchen at Roberto and his two men, a confused expression on his face. "Is this it? I thought you had more men? This is our autodefensa?" His son Carlos was by his side. "And your guns." He gestured the rifles leaning against the wall. "They're old enough to have been used by Pancho Villa."

They had taken refuge in a house nestled in the urban sprawl of Chihuahua, close to the city's international airport. The single-story cinder block residence belonged to a distant cousin who had smuggled his family across the border into the US. Unoccupied and inconspicuous, the walled compound offered protection from prying eyes. A sliding back gate gave them access to a maze of narrow laneways that separated dozens of similar dwellings.

Roberto sat at the kitchen table and gestured to his two offsiders. "Miguel and Gerardo are brothers. They have been with me from the beginning. There are others, many who will be at the demonstration. Not everyone can fight, but they want to help."

Emilio sat at the table and ran his hands through his white hair "Did you hear? The Chaquetas used bazookas to blow up my house! They had bazookas, and you're talking about a demonstration. What use is a demonstration? We need to hit back at the coyotes, otherwise they'll think we are lambs."

"In time, we will, but to do so now would mean certain death. We start small and we build. Tomorrow we'll find additional supporters and perhaps money."

"When we have more guns, then we'll make the cocksuckers pay."

"That's the plan, my friend."

"So, who's organized the demonstration?"

"Do you remember the man from Mexico City who was testing the water on our ranches?"

Emilio nodded.

"The Chaquetas killed him when they burned down the chapel. The police told his family it was a tragic accident, but his amigos in Chihuahua were not fooled."

"Will they join our fight?" Emilio asked.

Roberto shook his head. "But they've spread the word. Anyone able to help will be at the rally."

"And so will the policia."

Roberto shrugged. "They won't be looking for us."

He thumped the table with his fist. "We should go to the Sinaloa. They'll give us guns if we promise to kill Chaquetas."

Roberto scowled. "You want us in debt to a cartel?"

"It would be better than letting those criminals level our farms and poison our water."

Roberto considered the old man's words. "If we cannot do this ourselves, then we'll discuss it. Let's see what the demonstration brings tomorrow."

CHAPTER 6

NEW YORK CITY

Bishop was dining with Christina at a restaurant in New York's Meatpacking district. He took a sip of wine and admired her new outfit.

She was dressed in thigh-high boots, black leggings, a gray singlet top, and a leather jacket. All newly purchased thanks to Bishop. Her hair was down and she wore a bright shade of lipstick that drew attention to her rosebud mouth.

"You think it's safe to be out?" she asked.

"New York's a big city, Christina, I think we're OK." He'd left his cap at the hotel and swapped his T-shirt for a white button-down shirt.

Together they appeared to be a good-looking professional couple out on a Friday night dinner date.

A spicy calamari dish was placed on their table and Christina eyed it hungrily. "This place is amazing. How did you know about it?"

The restaurant was outfitted to resemble a 19th century Indian tea warehouse with teak beams crossing the ceiling and raw timber floorboards.

"TripAdvisor. It has great reviews." He caught the attention of their waiter and ordered another bottle of wine.

Christina spooned some of the calamari onto her plate. "I thought you were going to keep me cooped up in that hotel all night."

The wine arrived and he sampled it before giving the waiter the OK to fill their glasses.

"So," Christina said before taking a sip, "are you going to tell me what you found out about RED?"

He tore off a piece of roti bread and used it to mop up the sauce in an empty dish. "Unfortunately, not a lot. I did find out they've got links to a security company based here."

"And you think the goons who chased us work for them?"

"It's a fair assumption." He poked the empty bowl with his fork. "I guess you liked the calamari?"

"Sorry," she said with a laugh. "I guess I was hungrier than I thought."

"A big appetite is a sign of good health. There's more on the way."

She smiled. "Aden, I want to thank you again for what you did this morning."

"Don't worry about it, you just owe me a coffee. You can get them tomorrow."

"I was kind of hoping to go back to my apartment tomorrow."

Bishop shook his head. "I'm not going to pretend that I can keep you locked up, but going home's not a good idea just yet. Do you have a friend you might be able to stay with?"

"For a few days, but then I'm thinking about going back to Mexico."

He frowned. "Even after what happened?"

"Because of what happened. These people are trying to scare me off because what they're doing is completely immoral and criminal. I need to go back and get real evidence. I need photos of the mine, the church ruins, and I need to interview more of the victims."

"These people are playing hard ball, Christina. They'll come after you in Mexico."

A waiter placed a bowl of beef curry on the table and she eyed it eagerly. "I've got a friend who'll take care of me. Although I'd feel a hell of a lot safer if you came along. You can gather your own evidence and get the UN interested."

"I can ask, but my gut feeling is my boss won't approve it. My next job is already lined up."

"There's no pressure." She reached out and placed her hand on top of his. "I'm very grateful for what you've done already. Now, let's enjoy dinner. We can talk Mexico tomorrow."

***

"Can you give me a little more room around the stomach?" Mirza asked the tailor who was marking chalk on the suit he'd ordered. "I'm going to be doing a lot of eating."

The tailor raised an eyebrow and adjusted the marks he'd placed on the back of the gray pants. His client was one of the most wiry and muscular he had ever measured up. "As you wish." He adjusted the pins he had placed in the hem. "All done, sir." He waited as Mirza removed the pants and put on a bathrobe.

"I'll have the suit and the three shirts delivered by nine in the morning."

"Excellent. Please have it put on my account along with two hundred dollars gratuity."

"Thank you very much, sir."

There was a knock at the door of the of the hotel suite. "Come in," Mirza called out.

A smartly dressed hotel staffer entered and handed him a paper bag. "These arrived for you, sir."

"Appreciated." Mirza handed him a crisp twenty-dollar bill and the attendant dipped his head as he departed.

The tailor excused himself while Mirza inspected the package. Inside he found a box of business cards, and checked the details were correct. Putting the cards aside, he peered into the bag, and pulled out an embossed leather box. The container opened with a snap, revealing a Breitling Navitimer watch. It was a striking yet functional timepiece. Crafted from the highest quality stainless steel, it was as rugged as it was handsome. He savored the weight and snapped it onto his wrist. The watchmaker had sized it perfectly. Mirza would have preferred something a little more subdued but it fit the role of an investment banker.

He adjusted the dive dial as he walked to his dresser and picked up his iPRIMAL. Accessing a hidden menu, he initiated a secure call to the intelligence team inside the Bunker.

Paul 'Flash' Gordon, PRIMAL's digital intelligence specialist, was waiting for the call. "Hey bud, you get the cards?"

"Yes, they just arrived. They're good."

Flash had generated the business cards using the logo and details of an existing India-based investment firm.

"Glad you like them. Now, I've just finished hacking the company's website and updated their contacts page to include Mr. Adir Premiji."

"So everything's in place for the cover story?"

"Yep. I've also re-routed their mail and phones through a server I control. Any calls or emails originating from New York will be routed through to us here."

"I hope you can do a convincing Indian accent."

"Good day, Mr. Premiji. How can I help you?"

Mirza laughed. "That's actually not bad."

"I'll work on it. So, you going to tell me what this is all about? You and Bishop up to something dodgy over there?"

"We're conducting an initial investigation into a mining company involved with murder, kidnapping, and environmental degradation."

"Does this have anything to do with the girl Chua sent him to see?"

"Yes."

"Enough said really. Chua's got a nose for these things. Well, Mr. Premiji, I will check in with you later. Good luck."

Mirza terminated the call and logged on to the company's website. There, under the contacts tab, were his cover name and details. Now everything was in place all he needed to do was contact RED and organize a meeting. Then he could relax for the evening and maybe order some room service for dinner. After all, he did need to fill out his new suit.

***

Bishop and Christina were in no rush when they strolled back from the restaurant. New York was alive and bustling, and the air was warm. It was midnight before they reached the hotel.

"Thanks for an amazing evening," said Christina as they reached her room. "It was nice to escape from the world for a few hours."

"A good bottle of red will do that." Bishop smiled. "Or was it two?"

"Do you want to come in for a night-cap?"

"I won't say no."

"Help yourself to the bar."

He followed her into the room and opened the mini-bar. "What are you having?"

"I think there's a Malbec in there."

Christina sat on the end of the bed as Bishop poured some wine and handed her the glass.

"Thanks. So what's your story, Aden? How's a handsome man like you single?"

He sloshed a hefty slug of scotch into a tumbler and sat in the armchair in the corner of the room. "I'm rarely in one place for longer than a week."

She sipped from her glass. "Makes it hard."

"What about you?"

"Had a boyfriend when I was researching my Sudan piece but we drifted apart"

"Yeah, I know the feeling."

Christina raised her glass. "A toast. To lonely souls wandering the earth in search of the truth."

"Cheers." He raised his tumbler and threw the rest of the scotch down his throat. "Now, if the lady permits, I'm going to turn in."

Christina intercepted him as he crossed the room, grasping his arm. "You don't have to go." She stood on her toes and kissed him.

Bishop wrapped his arms around her and held her close. He was surprised at how passionate the kiss was. Their lips stayed pressed together for what felt like a minute.

"I wanted to give you a proper thank you," Christina said when they finally broke. She looked up at him with brown eyes that said a lot more than just thank you. She lifted her singlet over her head, dropped it, and unfastened her bra in one smooth movement.

Bishop exhaled; her body was amazing. Her shoulders and neck were elegant, almost athletic. She had small, pert breasts, and a lean stomach.

"We shouldn't do this," he said.

She gave a sly smile. "If you're worried about taking advantage of me, Aden, I can assure you that's not the case."

"No, it's just I don't have a great track record when it comes to this sort of thing."

"I'm not after a relationship, just company for the night." She put her hands on her hips and cocked her head to one side. "Or are you one of these guys who falls in love at the drop of a hat?"

He smiled. "I've been accused of that before, but this is a little more complicated."

She pursed her lips. "Another woman?"

He shook his head. "Not any more. I'll see you in the morning." He kissed her gently on the cheek and made for the door. As he departed, he glanced over his shoulder. "I must be an idiot," he mumbled and walked down the corridor to his room. As he undressed he could barely keep his eyes open. Sleep came quickly.

***

Bishop focused on the unwavering barrel of the pistol pointed at his face. "Lower the weapon!" he screamed, his finger taking up the last ounce of slack in the trigger of his Tavor assault rifle. "Lower the fucking weapon!"

On the floor, Kurtz was lying on his back, blood dribbling from his mouth as he held his hands over the gunshot wounds to his chest. "Don't shoot," he mumbled. "Don't shoot." His hands slipped to his side as he passed out.

"Bish, we've got multiple hostiles following up." Mirza's voice sounded in his helmet. "I've been hit. I can't find Saneh."

Time slowed to a crawl as Bishop focused on the weapon in

front of him. The slender fingers gripping the pistol were white around the knuckles. The shooter had the gun in a death grip.

"Bishop, I can't find Saneh." Mirza's voice was slow and distant.

He squeezed the trigger once. He released until it reset then fired once more.

Time raced forward and he watched his black-clad target shudder as the high velocity rounds punched home.

Bishop lowered his weapon and stood over the fallen hostile. He looked down at the almost alien full-face helmet and realized it was exactly the same as his.

"I can't find Saneh," Mirza repeated, a distorted sound that barely registered.

Bishop reached under the jawline of the mask and unclipped it. As he pulled the visor away his heart jumped. It was Saneh. She looked up at him with tear-filled eyes and mouthed the words, "I love you." Then her eyes glazed over, fixed in a death stare.

"NO!" Bishop screamed as he sat upright in his bed, his heart racing.

It took him a second to realize it was a dream, but when he did, it didn't make it any less painful. He swung his legs out of bed, walked across to the mini-bar, and poured himself a hefty slug of bourbon. His hands shook as he lifted the glass to his lips.

According to the clock by the bedside it was three in the morning. He pulled open the curtains and stared out at the city that didn't sleep. The dazzling lights seemed to soothe his racing mind as he sipped from the glass.

This wasn't the first time he'd had this dream. Every time it was a slightly different variation but this was the first time the girl Karla had been replaced by Saneh.

Japan had changed everything. He'd killed a young girl who had posed a direct threat to his team. It was not something he was proud of, but in his mind there had been no other option. If Karla had lived she would have killed the woman he loved.

He put his drink down and reached for his bag. As he

pulled on shorts, a T-shirt, and trainers, he planned his run through the city. Physical exertion would drive the emotional pain from his body. Once again he was running from ghosts.

CHAPTER 7

CHIHUAHUA

Pershing leaned back in an office chair and watched a bank of screens in the Chihuahua police headquarters situation room. "I didn't realize we had so many fans. Appears to me half the town's out there," he drawled.

"They'll lose interest soon enough," said Felipe Guzman, the Chihuahua District Chief of Police. He pointed at one of the smaller monitors. "Bring that up on the big screen."

One of the system operators transferred the image onto the central screen. A high definition camera affixed to the Secretariat of Environment and Natural Resources building was filming the throng of demonstrators gathered on the street. They held banners declaring their anger toward RED and were demanding closure of the Barrio Del Rancho mine.

"Look how young they are, they won't last." Felipe furrowed his thick eyebrows and stroked his prominent chin. He was a career police officer and had witnessed many demonstrations. In a region beset with high unemployment, protests were inevitable. "There's a few farmers in there, but most of them are students. They'll grow bored with this."

Pershing studied the crowd intently. "Can you zoom in on that cluster there?" He pointed at a group of demonstrators.

"Yes, sir." The operator zoomed the camera in on two older looking men who were addressing the students.

"Run their faces."

Yellow squares appeared around the faces on the screen as the facial recognition software locked on to them. The system was the latest version of the C4I4 public-surveillance network that Ground Effects Services had first installed in Mexico City. CIA funded, GES had the lucrative contract for setting up duplicate systems in regional centers. It gave the police unparalleled ability to track criminals and informants across the city. What the local police did not know was the CIA maintained backdoor access to the system.

The targeted faces appeared in a bar across the bottom of the screen. Of the six faces only one was outlined with a green box.

The operator read from his monitor. "I've got a match on a Miguel Martinez. He's a student at the university. Second-level Sinaloa connections."

"So what about those two older guys?"

"They're not in the system."

The police chief turned to Pershing. "Do you know them?"

"I know that one." He pointed at Roberto. "He's a rancher we booted out a week ago. Shot one of your cops. Thinks he's a bit of a tough guy."

"Shot a police officer?"

"Relax, he winged him with a bit of buckshot. Goes by the name Roberto Soto." Pershing watched as the broad-shouldered rancher and his gray-haired associate moved through the crowd talking to the demonstrators. "Pretty obvious what he's up to, though. They're identifying smaller groups of demonstrators and pitching to them. That son-of-a-bitch is recruiting."

"Recruiting for what?"

"Resistance, another demonstration, how the hell would I know? We need to bring him in."

"No." The police chief shook his head. "The demonstration is peaceful, I want to keep it that way."

"You must have misheard me," said Pershing. "We need to bring him in."

Felipe met his gaze, then faltered and turned to the operator. "Pass a description to the riot squad and have them arrest that man."

***

The forward line of demonstrators was chanting and thrusting their banners in the air. The energy in the crowd had intensified. Roberto and Emilio pushed to the front.

One of the protesters yelled, "Policia! They're blockading the street."

Roberto climbed onto the back of a pickup to try and see what was happening. Earlier, the crowd had gathered peacefully on the road in front of the four-story government building. It had taken an hour before the police arrived. Now, the crowd was agitated, corralled by a line of helmeted riot police. The dark-blue uniformed officers were pushing the activists back with their polycarbonate shields and batons. More cops were clustered at the fringes.

He glanced back down the road; two police pickups were parked nose to nose across the street with a dozen more officers in riot gear.

Something didn't feel right. He heard a shout from the closest line of riot police and saw an officer pointing at him. Something whistled past his head and smacked into a building. He jumped down from the truck as another projectile sailed into the crowd. One of the demonstrators was struck in the head and collapsed to the ground.

The cylindrical projectiles hissed as they released gas and Roberto coughed as he dragged the unconscious man off the street. "He's alive."

Emilio grabbed a spluttering canister with a leathery hand and pitched it over the crowd back into the police line.

Yelling turned to screams as the police swung batons and beat their way through the crowd. Banners became weapons as the students retaliated. More grenades fell among them and the cloud of tear gas grew.

Roberto tore a sleeve off the wounded student's shirt and used it to bandage a deep gash on his head. "This is getting out of hand."

Emilio pointed up at the camera on the Secretariat building. It was aimed directly at them. "I think they're trying to get us. I'll call Carlos, we need to get back to my truck."

Gunshots echoed down the street and there was a shriek from the crowd. He hefted the wounded man onto his broad shoulders as one of the riot police pointed and yelled, "That's him!"

"Go, go!" screamed Emilio, coughing and stumbling through the gas.

Beanbag rounds hissed through the air as they floundered in an eye-watering haze. Roberto covered his mouth with one hand, gripped the casualty on his shoulders with the other, put his head down, and ran.

"Stop, get your hands up!" The voice was amplified through a speaker attached to a police truck. It was a roadblock, less than a hundred yards in front. Roberto skidded to a halt. Emilio tugged at his arm. "Leave the kid. Let's go. This way."

He lowered the student from his shoulder and followed the gray-haired rancher. Emilio attempted to enter a restaurant, but it was locked. He kicked the door, failing to budge it.

Roberto shoulder charged the door, splintering the wood around the deadlock. "Stop!" a voice yelled followed by a shotgun blast. As he stumbled inside, a paintball-sized nylon bag filled with lead struck him in the arm.

Emilio followed him in, slammed the door behind them, and shoved a table against it.

Roberto tried to grab another table with both hands, but his right arm hung useless by his side. The muscles were numb. "Goddamn it." He dragged the table with his good arm and Emilio helped heave it against the other.

Someone bashed at the door. "Policia!"

"That's not going to hold them for long." Roberto was clenching his fist in an attempt to work some feeling back into the muscles.

Emilio led the way to the kitchen. "There's got to be a back door."

They dashed out of a service entrance as the sound of splintering wood and crashing furniture came from the dining area.

The ranchers sprinted down an alley, the police in hot pursuit. They weaved between empty crates and piles of trash before bursting out onto a busy street. To their left was the police checkpoint, orientated away from them toward the remnants of the demonstration. A thin shroud of gas hung in the air. It stung their eyes and nostrils.

A horn sounded as an old red F250 screeched to a halt. It was Carlos, Emilio's son. "Get in!" yelled the skinny youth.

They piled into the truck as riot policemen appeared from the laneway. One of them raised his shotgun and fired. The beanbag round slammed into the tailgate with a clang.

"Jesus Christ!" yelled Carlos as he slammed his foot down on the accelerator. The truck took off like a startled gazelle.

"Watch your mouth," said Emilio.

The teenager weaved the truck through the traffic. "They killed people. They opened fire with no warning."

"They wanted us." Roberto shook his head. "They were searching for us."

"The Chaquetas have friends in high places," said Emilio.

"Not the Chaquetas. The miners."

"So now we're fighting the police as well as them? That's too much. We don't even have proper guns."

"You're right." He sighed. "Maybe for now, we just need to find a way to hurt the mine."

"How are we going to do that without guns?"

"By destroying their machines," Roberto said with conviction. "If they can't get the gold out of the ground they can't pay the Chaquetas or the policia. Without the gold they're weak. We need to go to the mine and see how we can stop them from digging."

Emilio looked thoughtful. "The mine will have explosives, we may be able to use them. But, it will also be heavily guarded by the Chaquetas."

"We can sneak past those fools. They're criminals, ill-disciplined, and soft."

They arrived at the back of the safe house and Carlos tooted the horn twice. A sliding steel door opened an inch before the man inside identified them and dragged it open.

"Perhaps it's time to go to the Sinaloa for help," said Emilio as his son parked the truck and they climbed out.

Roberto tried to flex his arm and winced. "Not yet. We hide out here till things quiet down. Then we go look at the mine." He followed Emilio through the back door of the house into the kitchen. "If we need help, after that we can go to the Sinaloa." He sat at the computer in the corner of the room and logged in to the email account that Christina had set up for him. He hit reply to the test message she had sent and started typing.

***

FORT BLISS, TEXAS

Terrance Howard scratched his crotch as he guzzled from an oversized can of energy drink. He was having a shit day. His boss, the director of Joint Task Force South, had issued him with an official warning regarding his dress and attitude. The director was a relic, he thought. A moron who believed that wearing a suit and calling everyone sir made you a better analyst.

It was the second warning he'd received this month and it meant he was not going to be promoted anytime soon. That pissed him off. He ran rings around his colleagues and yet they had all been promoted a pay grade, or even two, above him.

Despite his boss, Howard had enjoyed his two years at the Task Force. As a CIA analyst he loved his role supporting the multitude of CIA activities across Latin America. Currently the focus was on cartel activities and border control, his areas of expertise.

One of the NSA signals analysts attached to the JTF stuck his head over the partition that separated them. "Hey, Howard."

He dropped his feet off his desk and rotated his chair to face the junior analyst. "What do you want, dipshit?"

"I got a hit on that email address you put on cover."

"Well then, what are you waiting for? Flick it over."

"You sure this shit's legit, man. I mean, this chick's an

American citizen."

"Yeah but I bet the douche bag emailing her isn't. She's got herself linked in with a bunch of nasty mofos down in Chihuahua."

"I still think this should go past the director."

"We don't need to do that, Sam. Otherwise, we might have to let him know about the illegal tap you put on the guy who was banging your ex."

"You're an asshole, Howard."

"I'm the asshole who tailed the bitch and found out she was messing around on you."

"Whatever." Sam disappeared back into his own cubicle.

A few seconds later the email Roberto sent Christina appeared in his inbox. "Boom!" After scanning the email, he pried himself from his chair, grabbed a packet of cigarettes, and waddled out of the secure office. Outside in the designated smoking area he dialed the number for Source 88 as he smoked. "I just got a very interesting email on that journo's account you wanted monitored."

"What's it say?" drawled Pershing.

"That's not the way this works, George. You give me some information, then I give you some information, remember?"

"I'm already paying you…"

"Dude, stop right there. There were terms to this agreement and they were pretty simple. Information needs to flow both ways so I can justify the support you're getting."

There was a pause on the other end of the line.

"What do you want to know?"

"I want to know a lot of things. I'm more interested in what you know."

"Does the new Sinaloa plaza boss for Chihuahua state interest you?"

Mexican police had killed the Chihuahua representative of the Sinaloa Cartel eight months earlier in a raid. His successor was someone that JTF South had been unable to determine. Pershing knew very well the name was a highly valuable piece of intel.

"That would do it."

"The name I've been given is Ramon Ramirez. Now, what have you got for me?"

"Your journalist just received an email from some guy called Roberto. He gave her a heads-up on a demonstration in Chihuahua that went bad."

"That all?"

"No, she replied within a few minutes. She's coming down to Mexico. They're going to meet at an unspecified location on the outskirts of town. Somewhere she's been before."

"Can you forward me the emails?"

"That might be pushing our friendship a little far."

"Fine, keep an eye on it, and tell me if you get anything else."

The call ended. Howard stubbed out his cigarette, went back to his cubicle, and opened the file he had on Ramon Ramirez. He wanted to cross-reference Pershing's claim against what they knew. They already had him pegged as a mid to high level player, a businessman who made savvy decisions when it came to both narco-trafficking and the cartel's more legitimate operations. If he'd been promoted, it meant the Sinaloa Cartel was angling away from violent criminal activities. It also meant they might be more willing to work with the CIA against the other cartels.

Howard locked his computer and went to the change room. He hardly ever used his locker. Fumbling with the combination lock, he opened it, and found the shirt he had hung up almost a year ago. It was an off-green color and short-sleeved but at least it was a shirt. He swapped it for the Simpsons T-shirt he was wearing, wet his hair, and tucked the scraggly ends behind his ears. On his way out of the locker room he spotted a glossy red tie hanging on the towel rack next to a neatly-pressed suit. He grabbed it and managed to tie it into something resembling a Windsor knot. Then he left the locker room and knocked on his boss's door.

"Come in." Everest Palmer, the Director of JTF South, had a booming voice.

Howard pushed open the door and stepped into the spartan office of one of the most influential men in Latin America. The Director was almost completely bald. What hair he did have, at the back of his head, he kept clipped short. He had a strong beak of a nose and his forehead was constantly wrinkled with frown lines. Howard thought he looked a little like a vulture.

Palmer's gaze fell on the green shirt and bright red tie. "What can I do for you, Terrance?"

"Wanted to bring this to you straight away, sir. One of my sources has identified the new head of the Sinaloa Cartel in Chihuahua."

"That's good news. Who is it?"

"Ramon Ramirez."

Palmer rocked back in his chair. "That actually makes sense. Sinaloa has been transitioning to a more business-centric model. He's the perfect man to take that forward. Who did this come from?"

"Source 88, sir."

Palmer nodded. "That means it's pretty likely." He was aware of Howard's source in Chihuahua. In fact he had worked with Pershing when the contractor was still in the CIA.

"Yes, sir. I believe so."

"We'll convene a working group later in the week. I want you to lead it."

"Yes, sir."

"That's all."

As Howard stepped out of the office the director spoke again. "I appreciate the effort with the tie, Terrance. But in future it would be better if it wasn't one of mine."

**

CHIHUAHUA

Felipe Guzman threw a shot of tequila down his throat and slammed the glass back onto the table. "Two dead students and at least a dozen more wounded! The Mayor is screaming for answers."

Pershing was nursing a tumbler of scotch. "Tell him the narcos infiltrated the demonstration and killed the students. You control the evidence, Felipe, you can make it say whatever you want."

The two men were drinking in the Loco Poni, a dive of an establishment a few miles from the police headquarters. It was a private club the police chief frequented. It had seven types of tequila, fifteen varieties of cigars, and a stable of young women who, for the right amount of money, provided all manner of services.

Pershing thought it was a shithole. He hated the rancid stench of cigars. The scotch tasted like brake fluid, and the women were peasants dressed in cheap stockings and ill-fitting underwear. It represented everything he hated about Mexico and none of the things he loved.

Felipe chopped the end of a cigar with a knife and lit it with a match. "What about your magic cameras? They saw everything."

"Delete the footage, you idiot. Do I have to hold your hand, twenty-four-seven? Surely with the amount of money I'm paying you can take care of a few little problems." Pershing studied the liquid in his glass. "I mean, you failed to even bring me the damn rancher."

"You talk to me like a dog?" Felipe snapped and furrowed his thick brows. "Don't forget who helped you get approval for that hole you've dug."

Pershing placed the glass on the table and made a sour face. "This scotch tastes like horse piss." He looked the cop in the eye. "Listen, Felipe, I'm not ungrateful for everything you've done. I'm just saying you're not being helpful regarding this particular problem."

"Then why don't you get your Chaquetas Negras pets to sort it out for you?"

"Because, my dear friend, I don't trust them." He reached into his jacket and took out a thick wad of hundred dollar bills. "But I do trust you."

"You better watch those idiots." Felipe slid the cash into his pocket. "Before you know it they'll turn on you."

"Don't you worry about that. I've got the Black Jackets well in hand. I just need you to find the rancher and his little posse of troublemakers."

"My men will find them."

He stood and brushed the creases from his pants. "There's another ten K in it if you get him before the end of the week."

"You're not going to stay for some fun?" Felipe waved over a pair of young girls from where they were waiting at the corner of the bar.

They were dressed in knee-high stockings with lacy panties and push-up bras. Their faces were heavily plastered with makeup. Pershing judged their age at eighteen, barely legal. "No thank you, I've got work to do." He grabbed his Stetson from the hat stand at the door. "I'll see you in a few days when you've got the rancher."

Felipe already had one of the girls on his knee. "Of course, mi amigo."

Pershing waited for the bouncer to open the door and stepped out onto the street. His driver was waiting in the Chevy. "Take me to the farm," he said as he jumped into the back. He retrieved his thermos from the seat pocket and poured himself a cup of black coffee. He needed his wits about him, and more importantly, he needed to wash the taste of cheap scotch from his mouth.

CHAPTER 8

NEW YORK CITY

Brian Kestrel walked into the Resources and Environmental Development Group's reception area at exactly eight o'clock. "Mr. Premiji, sorry about the early meeting."

Mirza looked up from his phone. "No problem, I'm an early riser." He had turned up his Indian accent a notch for the benefit of the RED Group's chief of operations. The usually lean PRIMAL Operative was wearing his new suit complete with a few extra inches of padding taped around his waist. His hair was slicked back and he'd shaved his beard leaving a thin mustache.

Mirza offered his card and the broad-shouldered Canadian gave him one in return.

"If you'd like to join me in my office." Kestrel directed him down a narrow corridor into a spacious corner office with a view over the Hudson River.

Mirza sat in a plush leather armchair. "I'm so glad you found time to fit me in at such short notice."

"I made room in my schedule. Your project sounds very interesting."

"Very interesting and very lucrative."

The miner smiled. "Well, we're in the business of making money. Before we get started, would you like a drink? Coffee or tea?"

"Yes, thank you. Black tea with one sugar."

Kestrel lifted his phone and placed the order with his assistant. They made small talk until she delivered the beverage.

"Your email mentioned the old copper mine in Bougainville," said Kestrel.

"The Panguna mine. You've heard of it?"

"Of course. Not many in the industry haven't. One of the largest copper deposits on the planet. Shut down in '89 due to a civil war."

"Correct. My company has successfully negotiated the rights to re-open the mine."

"That's very interesting. I hope you don't mind but I had my assistant look into your company. She tells me you've got fingers in some very lucrative pies but nothing that approaches the complexity of Panguna. We're talking hostile elements on the ground, adverse environmental conditions, and very large-scale mining operations."

"True, this is much larger than anything we've worked on previously. That's why we want to partner with organizations that have the required experience and expertise."

"Well you've come to the right place. RED has all of the necessary skills to run a project like this. We can develop the infrastructure and our people are the some of the best when it comes to open pit mining."

"What about logistical services?"

"We can cover it top to bottom. Everything from accommodation and catering for the workers, through to the shipment of ore and on-site refining if required. If you like I can arrange for you to inspect one of our mines in Indonesia. The conditions would be similar."

"In the future, that may be a good idea. I've also done my research and your projects are impressive. The only real risk factor from my point of view is the security environment. The locals in Bougainville are unlikely to be completely compliant."

Kestrel's brow furrowed. "True, it's a significant concern considering the circumstances that shut the mine down previously. But RED has overcome similar issues before."

"So your organization is able to provide security services in addition to infrastructure, operations, and logistics?"

"Not directly but we do have a partner we work with to ensure a stable security environment. We can integrate the costs directly into the operational budget."

"And they're experienced at dealing with non-compliant indigenous elements?"

"They have a proven track record. Most of their employees

are former US Special Forces and intelligence. They've extensive experience in influencing the local population in hostile environments."

"But now they're civilians. Can a private company achieve similar outcomes?"

"I can assure you that they're an outcomes-based organization. They'll do whatever it takes to ensure the project is successful."

Mirza smiled. "That's exactly what we need."

"So, when do you expect the project to be finalized?"

"We have PNG government approval already. We're just tying in contractors and investors at the moment. I anticipate initial infrastructure development to commence early next year."

"If you're interested in international investment, there's a firm I can put you in contact with here in New York. We've worked together on a number of projects. I think you'll find them a good fit."

"I'd be grateful for the introduction."

"I tell you what. I'll give them a call today and find out if we can arrange a meeting in the next day or so."

"That works for me. Though I have to be back in India by Friday."

"I'll do my best. Now, I'm sorry this has to be short but I've got another meeting in a few minutes. I hope this has been useful for you."

"Yes, very. I think we'll have to continue talking."

"Definitely. What are you doing for the rest of the week?" Kestrel asked, leading him out of the office.

"I was hoping to see a few of the sights while I'm here."

"You've chosen the best time of the year to visit. It starts getting humid in a month."

"Humidity isn't so much a problem for me." Mirza laughed. "India and Papua New Guinea are not like Canada."

Kestrel nodded. "Indonesia damn near kills me every time I visit."

"Maybe you should start mining in Siberia?"

"Hell no. Colder than a polar bear's scrotum. Nope, New York suits me just fine." He shook Mirza's hand. "I'll have my assistant let you know the time and place for the investor meeting."

"I look forward to it."

***

Bishop paused at the entrance to the café opposite his hotel and scanned the room. He spotted Christina sitting the corner dressed in a T-shirt, with her hair in a ponytail. He dropped into the seat in front of her.

There was an awkward silence as she scrutinized him over her sunglasses. "You look worse than I feel."

Bishop smiled. "Nothing coffee won't fix."

"Did you hear about the protest?" she asked as he ordered. "No."

"There was a demonstration in Chihuahua yesterday. Three students were killed in clashes with the police. They were demonstrating against the Barrio Del Rancho mine."

"Things are getting serious down there."

Christina nodded. "My friend, the rancher, he was targeted by the police. They must be working for RED."

"How do you know all this?"

"He sent me an email last night. I'm going to fly to Chihuahua this afternoon."

Bishop shook his head. "That's too dangerous. These guys are playing rough and there are no rules in Mexico. It's the Wild West.'"

She raised her voice. "What do you want me to do? Sit on my hands while these bastards murder and steal from innocent people?"

An elderly woman one table over shot them a scowl over her breakfast.

"Christina, your emails have been compromised. If you fly in, they'll be watching the airport. If they think you're going to blow this wide open then God knows what they'll do to you."

The veins at Christina's temples were throbbing. "I'm going, Aden. I made a promise to Roberto and I'm going to make good on that promise."

"OK then, I'm coming with you." He was not about to let another woman enter his life then tragically leave it.

Her face immediately softened. "You said your boss wouldn't let you."

"I've got some leave. I'll take a week off. But here's the deal. I'm going to make all the arrangements and you're going to listen to me. You're also going to stop using any emails or social media."

She nodded.

"I'll need to head into the office and finalize a few things. I'll sort out the transport. You go out and buy whatever you need but don't go back to your apartment."

"OK."

The coffees were delivered and Bishop took a sip from his cup. "We're going to play this safe. Get you the photos and interviews you need, then get the hell out."

"I feel safer already."

He shrugged. "We'll see how safe it is when we get down there. It's got to be safer than having dinner with you."

Christina blushed. "Look, Aden, I want to apologize for last night. I came on a bit strong and I just wanted you to know it was a little out of character. With the escape and the alcohol I just…"

"Oh, so now you don't find me attractive?" He feigned indignation and gave her a cheeky smile. "It's OK, Christina, I get it. We'll just put it behind us." Bishop poured himself a glass of water and drank from it.

"I still very much want to sleep with you, though." She returned the smile.

He snorted water out of his nose and the elderly woman gave them another angry look.

Christina spoke softly. "You're a very handsome man who swooped in and saved a maiden in distress. As if I'm not going to find that desirable? The timing wasn't right. I get that."

Bishop wiped his face with a napkin. "I'm flattered and you're a very attractive woman. But for the time being let's keep this professional. You try to find trouble, and I'll try to keep you out of it."

She shook his hand. "Deal."

CHAPTER 9

Bishop knocked on room 604 of the Waldorf Astoria. Mirza opened the door and he entered the luxurious suite. "Wow, nice digs. Pity you look like a tubby douche bag."

His partner was still dressed in his Indian businessman outfit complete with a padded midriff and mustache. "At least I can take off my disguise, Aden. You're stuck with yours."

"Ouch." Bishop slapped him on the shoulder. "You get a little more like me every moment we spend together." He grabbed a fist full of cashews from a bowl on the bar.

Mirza sat on the bed. "I thought that's what this trip was about. But then you make me dress like a jerk while you hang out with your new girlfriend."

"Hey, she's just a friend. That's all."

"Really?"

"Yeah she's attractive but it's strictly professional. Look, I really appreciate you helping out. We can do the touristy stuff when I get back from Mexico."

Mirza's eyebrows shot up. "Mexico? Since when were you going to Mexico? Have you run this past Vance?"

He shook his head. "Nope. I'm on holidays and this is just a quick trip down to Mexico. Think of it as my spring break."

Mirza looked him in the eye. "Really?"

"Yeah. Christina's going back to investigate further and take some photos. I'm going to make sure she stays safe. That's it. I'm not going looking for trouble, the opposite in fact."

"Do you want me to come?"

"If you like. It's only going to be a day or two."

"I'm meeting a cousin for dinner tomorrow but I could reschedule if you need me."

"It's fine. You do your dinner and check out a few of the museums. Then, when I get back we can hit that Yankees game."

"OK, but for the record, I don't think Mexico is a good idea. What's more, no matter what you say, this is going to look like you're chasing a girl. Considering what happened in Japan with Kurtz, that's not going to go down well."

Bishop sat on a plush sofa and rested his feet on a coffee table. "I'm on holidays. As long as I stay out of trouble, HQ isn't going to care."

"They'll see you're down there on the tracker."

"Yeah, and if they ask what I'm doing, I'll tell them. Now, what did you get from your meeting with RED?"

"No new intel. What I did get was a lunch meeting with a potential investor for the Bougainville project."

"Tell me it's Manhattan Ventures."

Mirza nodded. "You were right, they must be bank rolling the Mexican operation. I spoke to Flash and he's shown me how to bug their phones. If I get the chance we'll hack their emails and see what he can find."

"And he's not going to tell Vance or Chua?"

"As long as you're not running around shooting people he's happy for us to keep this low key. But that might change when your iPRIMAL shows up south of the border."

Bishop nodded. "You know, not so long ago you would never have gone along with this."

"Not so long ago you couldn't be trusted to go down to Mexico and not get into a gunfight."

"I guess we're all growing up."

Mirza stood and smoothed out his jacket. "I think hanging out with you has made me a little reckless."

"A bit of recklessness is what keeps us sharp."

"You just stay out of trouble, Bish. I don't want to have to come running down there to pull you out of the fat."

"You mean the fire."

"I mean stay out of trouble. I've got to go; they're sending a car to take me to lunch."

***

The silver Mercedes S500 collected Mirza from the hotel foyer and whisked him around the block to another high-rise.

The doorman directed him to an elevator and up to the top floor.

"Mr. Premiji?" a security guard asked when the elevator doors opened.

"Yes." Mirza frowned as he was led down a corridor and through a set of doors into a stairwell; there wasn't a restaurant in sight.

"Mr. Kestrel is waiting for you." They climbed a short flight of stairs and the guard pushed open a door to reveal a Eurocopter Squirrel idling on the helipad.

The big Canadian waved at him from where he was sitting in the back.

Mirza grasped the sides of his jacket and ducked beneath the rotor-blades. When he climbed in, Kestrel handed him a headset as the pilot secured the hinged door.

"I hope you don't mind. The chairman of the investment company already had an engagement so he extended us an invitation," Kestrel said over the intercom.

He nodded and strapped himself in. The engines screamed and the helicopter wobbled as it lurched into the air.

"It's always a little rough but there's no better way to see the city," Kestrel added.

They climbed until they were a few hundred feet over the building. Then the pilot tipped the nose slightly and they beat their way over the city toward the Hudson River.

Mirza caught himself grinning. He looked over at Kestrel; the Canadian was doing the same. "This is amazing."

"Best view in the city."

"I thought we were having lunch," Mirza said as they swept past the Empire State building.

"We are. Just doing a little sight-seeing to work up our appetites. One of the directors owns a boat and he's going to take us along the coast to the chairman's place."

The chopper banked and descended toward a marina perched on the far bank of the river. A helipad floated among the rows of luxury cruisers and sailing boats.

They touched down with a gentle bounce. The pilot leveled

off the blades, got out, and opened the passenger door.

Mirza gave the man a nod and followed Kestrel off the helipad to the floating dock. It bobbed lightly under the big man's weight as he led them between the luxurious vessels. Mirza counted over a dozen motor cruisers, each well over sixty feet in length.

There was a white-uniformed steward waiting on one of the pontoons with a tray of champagne. Kestrel took one and headed up the gangplank. Mirza declined.

"Wow!" Mirza mouthed as he approached one of the most impressive boats he had ever seen. It looked like a cross between a stealth fighter and a massive 118-foot cabin cruiser. The hull was a deep metallic green with raked angles and gaping air intakes. As he walked up the gangplank and onto the smooth teak deck the vessel's superstructure came into view. Like the rest of the boat, it was exquisite with jet-black glass encasing a sitting area that would not be out of place in an exclusive nightclub.

"She's beautiful, isn't she?" Kestrel said as they walked between the tables on the aft deck into the main cabin.

"Magnificent." He looked around in awe. The central cabin of the vessel held another lounge and a long table complete with leather chairs. It looked like the boardroom of an architectural firm. At the far end was a control console with two men standing at it.

The taller one turned from the console. "You don't want to know what she costs to run." He looked youthful with a clean-shaven, narrow face. Mirza guessed late twenties to early thirties. His white linen shirt was open at the collar and bright blue slacks were rolled up at the ankles.

He offered a hand to Mirza. "Wes Chambers." His face was partially hidden behind black-rimmed sunglasses.

"Adir Premji. A pleasure to meet you. Are you the captain of this fine vessel?"

Wes laughed. "No, dude, I'm the owner."

"Wes is one of the directors of the investment fund," Kestrel explained.

"Make yourself comfortable, gentlemen. We're going to cast off and then the captain here will take us for a short cruise along the coast." He led them to the lounge at the back of the cabin and waved over a white-clad crew member. "Frank, make sure these men have plenty to drink and bring the ladies up." Chambers returned to the console as Mirza relaxed on one of the sofas in the cabin.

"Sir, can I offer you a drink?" the waiter asked.

"No thanks, I get a little seasick."

Kestrel sat across from him. "Not on this thing, you won't. She cuts through the waves like a knife and…" He smiled. "Wes always has good company."

On cue, two blondes appeared from below decks. Mirza almost blushed; their bikini tops barely contained their enhanced breasts.

"Hello, my name's Natasha, and this is Paulina," the tallest of the pair purred. Her sarong parted as she sat next to him.

Mirza felt the deck tremble lightly as they backed away from their mooring. The boat's engines thrummed as the waterjets pushed it out into the channel.

"Twin turbines," said Kestrel as he put his arm around the other girl. "Just like Paulina's." He laughed and the two girls giggled.

Mirza barely heard the faint whine of the gas turbines as they cruised down the Hudson between Liberty and Governor's island. They made small talk for a few minutes before Wes strolled back to check on his guests. "You sure you don't want a drink?" He had a tumbler of whiskey in his hand.

"No, I'm good for the moment."

Natasha put an arm on his thigh and squashed her breasts into his side. "It's OK, I'll take care of him."

Mirza almost laughed, if only Bishop was here to see this. He felt the bow of the boat rise as they swung into a wide bay and gathered speed. In a few minutes they were a mile offshore and the skipper began a lazy turn, sweeping around until they were heading east following the coast. The bow rose further out of the water as they gathered even more speed. Despite the choppy seas the ride was smooth, the deep V-shaped hull cutting through the waves with ease. He heard the turbines now, they howled like banshees as they propelled the sleek vessel at over fifty knots.

"Pretty amazing, isn't it," said Kestrel. "She'll do sixty five at full throttle."

He couldn't contain his grin. "What's it called? I've never been on anything like this." He'd pushed thirty-foot rigid inflatables to forty knots in similar conditions and they bounced around like a bucking bronco.

"She's a Wally 118. The only one of its type. Wes calls her Nemesis."

Mirza nodded. He would have to tell Mitch about the vessel. "So, where are we heading?"

"The Chairman has a holiday home in the Hamptons. At this speed it won't take us long to get there."

Mirza sat back and enjoyed the high-powered ride and the attention of the beautiful blonde.

Forty minutes later the skipper powered back the engines and they curved in toward the coast. They slowed to half-speed and slid through a narrow channel into a small bay.

"Natasha, show him around," said Wes as he sat next to Kestrel.

Mirza followed the model through the superstructure and out to the wooden front deck. The sun was shining, the skies were blue, and he almost forgot he was on a mission. "Are you a friend of Wes's?" he asked Natasha.

"Aren't you just the sweetest thing." She dropped her sarong and lay down on a sunbed. "Let's just say that I'm part of the crew." She gave a wink then closed her eyes.

In his bulky suit and padded midriff he felt more than a little overdressed. He tried to make himself comfortable on the adjacent lounge and occupied himself by watching the mansions on the far bank.

Five minutes later the boat pulled in against a wooden pier that extended out over the beach and onto a bank covered in manicured grass. Beyond a row of willows Mirza saw the large glazed windows of a modernist mansion.

"This way, guys." Wes led them off the boat and through the trees.

The smell of barbecuing meat greeted them as they reached a patio in front of an exquisite sparkling blue swimming pool.

"You made good time." A tall, gray-haired gentleman was drinking a beer and cooking on the most expensive looking BBQ Mirza had ever seen.

"That boat moves pretty quick," replied Kestrel.

"You know what they say about boats," said Jordan Pollard as he handed the tongs to the miner. "Best investment a man never made."

Kestrel laughed but Mirza sensed the off-hand comment annoyed Wes who seemed to avoid eye contact with his boss.

"Mr. Adir Premiji, my name's Jordan. Welcome to my home away from home." He reached into a cooler and offered Mirza a beer.

"Please call me, Adir. Is there any chance you might have some soda? That boat ride upset my stomach a little."

"Wesley always drives that damn toy of his too fast. Follow me, we'll grab a drink from the kitchen." He gestured for Mirza to follow him through the floor-to-ceiling folding glass doors into the residence's living area. "My wife's responsible for the house so I can't make any claim to having good taste."

"Well, she certainly does," said Mirza as they entered the well-appointed kitchen.

"Cola?" He pulled a bottle from the fridge and handed it over.

"Thanks."

Pollard leaned against a white marble bench top. "Brian gave me a heads-up on your project. If you've got the rights to the mine we'd be interested in investing."

Mirza cracked open the soda. "We've got the rights, what we need is capital.

"If the project is what you say it is, then money will not be a problem."

He took a sip. "Did Mr. Kestrel make you aware of the

security issues?"

"He mentioned a lack of indigenous support. We specialize in managing that sort of thing. It won't be a problem."

"You've worked on similar projects?"

"My people can provide a number of case studies."

"Food's ready!" yelled Kestrel from outside.

"Hungry?" Pollard asked, walking back to the patio.

"Starving."

"Good, because my beef ribs are the best this side of the Mason Dixon." He took a plate of food from the table setting and handed it to Mirza. "I apologize that I won't be able to stay for much longer. I've got to head out of town for business but I'm sure Brian and Wesley will keep you entertained."

They made small talk over lunch and the financiers asked more questions about Mirza's fake mining project. After half an hour Pollard excused himself, bid Mirza farewell, and went back into the house. Mirza noticed the chairman had paid scant attention to Wesley, treating the young director with an element of disdain.

"Let's ditch this place and get back to the boat," said Wes once he was gone. Kestrel licked his fingers and finished off his beer. "Good idea, should we take some food for the girls?"

"No, dude, models don't eat." Wes threw back his whiskey and they started off down the path.

Mirza followed them back on board and a few minutes later they were underway and lounging with the models in the main cabin. Wes had his arm around Natasha. "Not much of a drinker, are you?"

"Not when I'm on a boat. Makes me feel a little sick."

"I've got something that'll help." He reached into his jacket and took out a small bag of white powder.

"No, thank you."

"Well I hope you don't mind if do. Brian you in?"

"Nah, man," the big Canadian was sprawled on a couch with Paulina. "But you knock your socks off."

"Oh, I will." Wes emptied the bag on the glass table and used a credit card to chop it into lines.

Mirza watched as he rolled up a hundred-dollar bill and hoovered a line.

Kestrel shook his head. "You know if Pollard saw you doing that, he'd flip out."

"He can suck my dick. I get the money in. He needs me more than I need him. But right now, I need Natasha." He slapped her on the bottom and she giggled.

"Mr. Chambers, do you mind if I borrow your phone?" Mirza asked. "I've got a booking tonight and my battery's gone flat."

"No problems, dude." Wes reached into his jacket and pulled out his phone. He unlocked the device and tossed it over.

Mirza walked to the stern, opened the phone's browser and punched in a short URL. The device downloaded an app and automatically deleted the URL from the browser history. He opened Google and typed in a restaurant, then clicked on the number. "Hello, this is Adir Premiji. I want to confirm my appointment for tonight."

"We don't have an appointment under that name, sir."

"Very good, I'll see you at nine." Mirza hung up and returned the device back to Wes. "Thank you."

The young banker pocketed the phone and watched Natasha snort a line off the table. "You sure you don't want any of this? It's high quality shit."

"No, thank you. I'm just going to sit out back and get some fresh air."

"Be my guest."

Mirza left them inside the cabin and headed back to the stern deck. He sat on one of the lounges and did his best to look sick. The padding taped to his stomach was itchy and the suit stifling in the mid-afternoon sun. He couldn't wait to get back to the hotel and ditch the outfit.

CHAPTER 10

CHIHUAHUA

Bishop fought back a yawn and glanced across at Christina snoozing in the passenger seat of the Jeep Cherokee. Her eyes opened as they passed a sign welcoming them to the outskirts of Chihuahua City.

"Sorry, I didn't mean to doze off."

"That's OK, only been a few minutes."

The pair had flown to El Paso the day before and overnighted in a cheap motel. In the morning they'd paid cash for the second-hand Jeep and crossed the border into Ciudad Juarez. The crossing was uneventful; the customs officials had paid little attention, waving them through the security checkpoint onto Highway 45. They drove south through a barren desert for five hours before hitting the outer suburbs of the city.

"You've had a bit of experience sneaking across borders haven't you, Aden?"

"Joys of working in less than desirable locations." He checked the price of gas as they flashed past a truck stop. "Do you know exactly where we're heading?" It was just after lunch and he contemplated pulling over to get something to eat. He'd been driving non-stop and was famished.

"Roberto is staying on the other side of town near the airport. Keep following the highway, I'll let you know when to turn off."

His stomach grumbled.

She laughed. "That was subtle."

"Hey, if I don't eat soon, I'm going to pass out."

As they drove down the dual-lane highway, Bishop noted almost every vehicle was a pickup. In fact, so far the city looked like it belonged in Texas. The roads were in good condition, large industrial estates flanked both sides, and obtrusive signs advertised everything from soda to nappies.

"Can we drive through the city center?" Christina asked as the landscape transitioned from industrial warehouses to dense urban dwellings. "I wouldn't mind seeing where the riots were."

"Might be safer to avoid it."

"Just a quick look. We're a long way from the mine."

"OK, but I've got to warn you, my stomach will start eating itself soon."

"Roberto will have food for us."

They drove for another fifteen minutes through the suburbs before turning onto the road that led downtown. Bishop's first impression of the city of nearly a million Mexicans was that it was remarkably ordinary. They left the highway down an off-ramp and drove into the town center.

"We should find a park here and walk in, it can get pretty busy," said Christina. The traffic had increased noticeably with smaller cars and motorbikes adding to the lines of pickups.

He pulled the Jeep into a public parking lot and they walked toward the town center. They strolled past a few blocks of low-rise buildings before reaching a wide open plaza.

"When you get past the urban sprawl, this place is actually steeped in history." She pointed up at the gilded angel looking down on them from atop a column. "That's the Angel de la Libertad."

"Isn't the real one in Mexico City? I'm sure this one was opened in 2003."

"OK smart-ass, then what's that building?" She pointed across the road at a beautiful rectangular stone structure. It was three stories high and each level had ornate carved openings: doors across the ground level, balconies on the second, and windows on the third.

"The post office?"

"Close, it's the Government Palace. It houses the offices of the governor as well as a shrine commemorating the execution of Miguel Hidalgo. Many consider him the father of Mexico."

"You're a bit of a history buff, hey?"

"I like knowing things."

They walked another two blocks until Bishop spotted yellow crime scene tape flapping in the wind. It was tied from one side of the street through the bumper bar of a police pickup and across to the other side. A cop was sitting in the truck with the door open.

"This has to be the spot." Christina opened her bag and pulled out a compact camera. Bishop had insisted she leave her new Canon 5D in the Jeep until they were outside the city.

She walked to the tape as Bishop hung back, his baseball cap low, eyes hidden behind sunglasses. In the bright midday sun he'd caught a glimpse of cartridge cases scattered on the road. He scanned the buildings around them. They appeared to be government offices and he spotted a CCTV camera atop one of them.

"Hey, no photos," the police officer called from his vehicle.

"Christina, we're going," Bishop announced.

"Yeah OK, just a second."

"No, I mean it. We're leaving." He grabbed her by the arm, gave the officer a friendly wave and dragged her away.

"Hey, I needed pictures. That cop wasn't going to make a big deal of it."

"We don't need to draw attention to ourselves," he said as they walked back to the car. "That guy would have been babysitting the scene all day. The last thing we want to do is give him something to do."

She knew he was right. "Maybe we should go straight to Roberto's."

"That's probably a good idea. You should call him from a pay phone, there was one by the car park." Bishop glanced back over his shoulder as they walked. The police car was still parked and no one followed them.

Christina dialed Roberto's cell from the phone booth and exchanged a few words.

"He's waiting for us," she said after hanging up.

"Good, let's go and see if he's got anything to eat."

Back in the Jeep, the drive took longer than he expected.

Although the safe house was only five miles away they had to negotiate traffic and a maze of narrow streets and lanes. At one point Bishop thought he may have picked up a tail, a motor scooter, but then it was lost in the masses of cars and pickups.

Eventually they reached a cinder block walled compound. A skinny youth wearing a cowboy hat was leaning against the entrance when they arrived. He spotted the Jeep, pushed open the sliding metal gate, and waved them in. As the gate clanged shut behind them Christina jumped out of the cab. The back door to the house opened and a broad-shouldered man appeared. She threw her arms around him. Bishop assumed he was Roberto, the farmer who'd saved her from the rapist.

She waved him over. "Roberto, this is Aden. He's the one who works for the UN."

The leather-faced farmer offered him a hand. "Bueno, it's good to have you with us. Come inside. We were about to eat."

Christina grabbed him by the elbow. "See, I told you they'd have food." She turned to Roberto. "Poor guy's been on the road all day without eating."

Roberto ushered them into the kitchen and Bishop's stomach rumbled as the aromas of Mexican cuisine assailed his nose. "Damn, that smells good."

"That's Emilio's cooking. His chili is the best in Mexico. Please, take a seat."

They joined two men who were already eating at the kitchen table. A third, much older than the others, was stirring a large pot on the stove.

Roberto spoke a few words in Spanish then addressed everyone in English. "This is Aden and Christina. They're here to help get our story out to the world. Aden works for the UN and Christina is the journalist I told you about." He gestured to the two men who were still eating. "This is Miguel and Gerardo. They are brothers, and were the first to be forced off their land."

Emilio brought the pot over and spooned chili into two bowls.

"This is Emilio," continued Roberto. "He lost his farm a

few days ago." He gestured to the skinny teenager who sat beside him. "Carlos is his son."

"Hello." Bishop gave the kid a nod.

The boy looked at him inquisitively. "Is the UN going to help get our farm back?"

Carlos's grasp of English surprised Bishop. He was thankful because his Spanish was rusty at best. "I don't think they will, mate. There are so many other problems in the world that they're focused on."

The boy nodded. "Like the war in Darfur?"

He hadn't expected anyone in Mexico to have a grasp on global issues, let alone a teenage kid. "Yes, that's one place."

Emilio returned the pot to the stove and joined them at the table. "So, as we have always known, we are on our own."

Roberto shook his head. "No, there are others who may help. Look how many there were at the rally. The people of Chihuahua are on our side."

"They may be on our side, Roberto, but they are sheep. What use are sheep when we need wolves to fight the Coyote?"

The dynamic of the group was clear to Bishop. Emilio was the heavy hitter. He wanted to take up arms and hurt the men who had pushed him from his lands. He wanted justice. Roberto was more pragmatic in his approach.

Emilio continued, "We need men and we need guns. The only way we're going to get those is if we go to the Sinaloa and ask for their help."

Roberto snorted. "You think they'll help us? The Sinaloa care only about profits. They will hang us out to dry as soon as they see the glimmer of gold."

"We need guns and they have guns."

"Yes, but at what cost? We need to explore every option before we tie ourselves to a cartel. Swapping one yoke for another is no way to escape slavery." Roberto turned to Christina. "Did you have any luck with your article?"

She shook her head. "I need more photos. I need to see the mine and maybe interview a local who works there."

"First, we will get you photos."

Emilio threw his hands in the air and muttered, "Photos and newspapers, what use are they?"

Bishop sat quietly eating his chili. He really felt for Emilio, having lost his livelihood and family home to the mine. It was understandable that the elderly rancher wanted justice, something that resonated with the PRIMAL operative. He was here to keep Christina out of trouble, but that didn't mean he couldn't gather information for a potential PRIMAL mission.

***

Two black SUVs bounced along a rutted dirt track that threaded its way between the lush green crop circles of an irrigated farm. "Slow down," Pershing grunted from the back seat of the first vehicle. "You trash that coffee machine and you're fired."

The technicians at the mine had finally installed the espresso machine and he was keen to give it a test run before his meeting. "Burro, has your uncle left his hacienda yet?" he asked as they pulled up on a concrete pad in front of a hanger-sized equipment shed.

"Yes, Mr. Pershing. He just left."

"Good." He stepped out of the vehicle and waited for the driver to raise the heavy armored trunk. The dual head Segafredo was fixed to a steel tray that slid out the back of the truck. Alongside it was a small refrigerator and a stainless steel workbench.

"That sly dog wants more money, doesn't he?" Pershing asked Burro as he packed the portafilter with coffee, scraped it off, and stamped it firmly before twisting it onto the group head. He checked the pressure and temperature gauge. It was perfect.

"I don't know, Mr. Pershing."

He hit the pour button and timed the maple colored liquid as it flowed into the espresso glass. "Come on Burro, you're his nephew. You've got to know what he's up to." Twenty-two seconds, spot on. He picked up the glass and turned to look out over the farm's green wheat fields as he sipped.

"He doesn't tell me much." Burro leaned against the side of the Chevy.

He directed his attention to the mechanical irrigator working its way across the perfect circle of wheat. Like the hour hand of a clock, it inched its way around, ensuring every square foot of the field was soaked. He wondered how long it would take the desert to reclaim the fields if the machine was turned off; a week, a month? Maybe not even that long; the Mexican desert was relentless.

The sun started to sink below the horizon when the sound of vehicles caught his ear and he downed the last of the espresso. Three SUVs left a trail of dust as they approached along the track from the main road.

"Here comes Uncle Cardenas now."

The lead and rear vehicles were regular SUVs with the usual dark tinted windows. The black beast in the middle was a Conquest Knight. A six hundred thousand dollar luxury armored truck capable of withstanding an attack from a .50-cal machine gun. The angular SUV had more grills and vents than a pimped Camaro. Pershing thought it belonged in a B-grade action movie.

Once the convoy halted, a squad of black-jacketed thugs got out brandishing assault rifles. A moment later, Raphael Cardenas, the head of the Chaquetas Negras, alighted from his Conquest Knight and took in his surroundings. He gave his nephew a nod, then turned to Pershing. The brow of his spherical head wrinkled as he scowled behind his Ray-Bans. "This is how you're going to pay me? With a fucking farm? I give you my best men and you want me to grow goddamn wheat?"

Pershing laughed. "Of course not, Raph. I wouldn't waste your time with something so trivial. What I've got show you is far more profitable than grain. Follow me."

He led the cartel boss and his bodyguards into the cavernous equipment shed.

Inside, under bright lights, coverall-wearing men were

working on an assembly line. They were unpacking components from boxes and assembling what appeared to be large model aircraft.

Raphael poked a box with his designer loafers. "What the hell is this?"

"That, my friend, is the future of narcotics smuggling."

"Model airplanes?"

"No, drones."

Raphael shrugged. "Drones?"

"Come this way." Pershing took him to the end of the production line where a fully assembled aircraft sat on an angled aluminum ramp. It had a wingspan well over four yards with twin tail booms and a compact two-stroke engine that spun a rearward-facing propeller.

"This little thing is going to smuggle drugs?"

He gave one of the technicians a nod. "It certainly will."

The man used an electric screwdriver to remove the top half of the aircraft's nose and body. Another worker wheeled over a cart heaped with pound blocks of cocaine and started loading them into the compartment.

Pershing tapped the aircraft's wing. "Each of these can carry twenty-five pounds of product. That's a street value of over million dollars."

The men finished loading and refastened the fuselage hatch.

"They've got a range of eight hundred miles, they're undetectable by radar, and when they get to the other end they deploy a parachute and float softly to the ground."

The two men unlocked the wheels on the catapult ramp and wheeled it with the drone toward the shed doors. They locked it in place a few feet from the doors and slid them open.

Raphael watched closely. "How much do they cost?"

"Fifty grand. The parts are all from China, shipped here individually, and assembled in location."

A technician plugged a laptop into a port on the side of the aircraft.

"This little gal will take four hours to reach her destination in Kansas. There she'll be received by our associates and within another six hours the cargo will reach Chicago."

The other worker spun the prop on the two-stroke engine and it coughed to life. It revved to high speed, filling the shed with noise and wind. With a hiss the catapult system tossed it out through the doors into the evening sky. Within moments it was a speck on the horizon.

The cartel boss removed his sunglasses, smiling like a child at Christmas. "How many can we send a day?"

"Two or three every night. You supply the drugs and we supply the aircraft."

"And how much cut do you want?"

"Fifty percent."

Raphael laughed. "I will give you ten at most."

"Here's the deal. Fifty's the magic number. Our security contract for the mine stays the same, and I bring you in on this. There's no risk for you, only guaranteed profit."

"Who's your buyer at the other end?"

"That's need to know only. They'll pay a little over market rate to secure our loads." He took off his Stetson. "Look, Raph, I could go to one of the other cartels with this. But our partnership with the mine is strong and I want you on board."

Raphael nodded. "OK, George, fifty fifty in the profit. My people will deliver a hundred pounds tomorrow. If you can get that through by the end of the week the deal will continue."

Pershing shook his hand. "Sounds good to me."

The cartel boss turned, snapped his fingers, and walked out to his armored truck, which was now illuminated by the building's floodlights. Pershing followed, catching the pause as the cartel boss examined the espresso machine in the back of his Chevy. Raphael shook his head and climbed up into his own vehicle. With a roar the convoy sped away down the dirt track.

Burro swaggered across to him. The boy-faced killer was chewing a piece of gum. "So, Mr. Pershing, did it go good?"

"Exactly as I planned." Pershing decided to make himself another brew. "Would you like a coffee, Burro?"

"Yeah, OK, boss."

He was about to start when his local phone rang. He opened the battered Motorola with a deft flick of his wrist and checked the caller ID. It was the police chief. "Felipe, have you found the farmer?"

"No."

"Then why the hell are you wasting my time?" He took off his Stetson and cocked his head to trap the phone between his ear and shoulder.

"It's the girl. Your journalist, her face came up in the camera system. She's back in Chihuahua."

He started making a coffee. "Where?" He pulled a pen from his jacket and scribbled the address the police chief gave him onto the back of one of his business cards. Then he continued preparing an espresso.

"Do you want me to send my people?" Felipe asked. "The surveillance unit that followed her and the gringo from town are close by."

He handed an espresso shot to Burro. "Gringo? She has someone with her?"

"Yeah, a tall guy with a baseball cap and glasses. We didn't get a good look at him. Might be some kind of bodyguard."

Pershing stamped more coffee into the group head. Was it possible Christina Munoz had convinced the UN investigator to come to Mexico? Or had she hired a private security contractor?

"So, do you want my people to pick them up?" Felipe asked impatiently.

"No, I'll deal with it."

"Do I still get the cash?"

"Yes Felipe, you'll still get your money." He snapped the phone closed and turned to Burro. "How's that roast, buddy?"

The cartel killer took a sip of the espresso. "Good."

Pershing smiled as he ran the machine through. Burro was mimicking the way he drank; the little glass cupped in one hand and held daintily with the other. He shut down the machine, pushed the tray back inside, and closed the trunk. "Get your boys ready, Burro. We're going to make a house call."

CHAPTER 11

Bishop used a chunk of bread to wipe the last trace of food from his bowl. "That was the best tasting chili I've ever had." He leaned back in his chair and groaned. He'd been eating consistently for the last hour as he listened to Christina interview Roberto and his men.

Roberto dipped his head in recognition of the effort. "Three bowls is good. You've almost caught up to Carlos."

"Yeah, what's your record, champ?"

The skinny youth flashed a toothy smile. "Seven."

"Holy crap, what are you, a tape worm? I've clearly got some work to do."

Emilio brought the pot over from the stove. "Want more?"

"No, no, take it away. I can't eat another thing."

Everyone laughed.

"Do you want coffee?" asked Emilio.

"That would be great."

The silver-haired farmer handed him a steaming mug. "So what do you think, Aden?"

He sipped. "What do you mean?"

"What should we do about the mine? You're a military guy. What would you do?"

I'd gear up and take the fuckers down, is what he wanted to say. "It's difficult for me to assess it without the whole picture. I'd want to get out on the ground before I gave you any advice. I can help Christina get her photos and then maybe we can get the international community to take a closer look."

Roberto nodded. "Aden's right, we need to scout the mine and let Christina take photos. Then we can make a decision."

Emilio didn't look convinced. "Maybe we can destroy something vital? Or hit them when they ship the gold? We could force them to close the mine or at least stop expanding."

A soft knock on the front door interrupted the debate. The brothers Gerardo and Miguel reached for their rifles as Roberto held a finger to his lips.

Carlos darted into the living room and answered the front door. A few hushed words were spoken. The teenager closed it, locked the deadbolt, and returned to the kitchen. "It was the neighbor. We're being watched."

"By who?" asked Bishop.

"Policia."

Roberto grabbed his shotgun from where it was leaning against the wall. "We need to go now. Emilio, get your truck ready. Everyone meet out the back."

Carlos retrieved his backpack from the living room as the roar of a powerful engine filled air.

"Go, go, get out!" Bishop yelled, trying to shepherd everyone out the back as the bed of a pickup smashed in through the front of the building, punching a hole through the cinder block wall.

Part of the roof collapsed, knocking Carlos to the ground. Bishop dragged the dazed youth out from under the plasterboard as the truck's tires spun on the carpet. It lurched away and two men dressed in black jackets wielding AKs ducked in through the gap.

Bishop leaped forward and savagely kicked one of them in the groin. The victim doubled over as he palmed the second man in the face with one hand and pushed his weapon up with the other. The AK roared, blowing chunks out of the ceiling. He grabbed the man's hair, delivered a sharp head butt, and the thug slumped to the floor.

Bishop took one of the rifles and shoved Carlos through the back door into the yard. Emilio's truck was already facing the gate, engine running. Christina waited beside the Jeep; she didn't have the keys. The air was filled with yelling and the revving of more engines. "Go, go, go!" screamed Bishop as he pushed Carlos into the back of the Jeep. Christina followed and he jumped in the driver's seat, jamming the AK between the seat and the center console.

Emilio rammed his truck into the sliding gate, smashing it off its runner. He burst into the narrow laneway, spun the truck sideways, and roared off.

Bishop turned the ignition, and was about to stomp the accelerator when a black pickup screeched to a halt in front of them, blocking their escape. Two men pointed assault rifles at them from the bed of the truck.

"Fuck!" He dropped the shifter into reverse and spun the wheel. With a squeal of tires they rocketed backward. "Brace!" he yelled as they smashed through one of the walls and shuddered to a halt. He floored the accelerator again but the wheels spun. The Jeep was wedged in the rubble, blocking another narrow thoroughfare. The shattered remains of the cinder block wall pinned the front doors shut.

"Get out the back!" Bishop yelled as cartel men vaulted from the bed of the pickup and aimed their weapons. He lifted his AK and fired a burst through the windshield. They dived for cover as the bullets stitched the pickup.

Christina screamed and scrambled out into an alley. Bishop fired another burst and threw the weapon onto the back seat. He felt exposed as he wriggled between the front seats and slid out through the open door. Grabbing the AK, he spotted Carlos on the other side of the Jeep.

There was a screech of tires and yelling as another truck drove into the lane on the skinny youth's side of the car.

"Carlos, get over here."

Rounds smashed into the Jeep, and a blast of gunfire echoed off the walls. Bishop struggled to find a clean shot. Carlos was frozen, his face a mask of fear. He screamed and collapsed as a bullet clipped his leg. More gunmen appeared from the house and Bishop fired through the back of the Jeep, hitting one of them.

"Crawl under!" he ordered. The weight of return fire pinned Bishop behind the car.

"Aden, we've got to go!" Christina screamed over the shots.

Carlos was down and wasn't moving. "FUCK!" Bishop punched the car door. He grabbed Christina and they sprinted away from the Jeep up the laneway.

They hit a T-intersection and turned onto a street. The road was hemmed in on one side by a tall chain fence of a parking

JACK SILKSTONE

lot, and more cinder block walls on the other. They didn't make it more than twenty yards before another pickup screeched to a halt in front of them. There were two gunmen in the back of it. They aimed their rifles but did not fire.

Bishop and Christina both turned only to find a black SUV blocking the other end. Transferring his weapon to his opposite hand, he reached into his pocket. He had been in Mexico all of five hours and already he'd got a teenager shot and himself cornered. If these assholes didn't kill him, Vance sure as hell would. He pulled out his iPRIMAL and entered the duress sequence. He was about to trigger it when one of the doors on the back of the SUV opened.

"Y'all should give up now. Nobody else needs to get hurt."

The accent caught Bishop off-guard; it was Texan.

"It's the guy from the farm," hissed Christina, her fists clenched.

The tall American walked forward a few steps and Bishop recognized the Stetson and the suit. The man on the other side of the truck was wearing mirrored aviators and clutching a pistol.

"That's the asshole who tried to rape me," she whispered.

"You got nowhere to go, pal. Why don't you just put that lead chucker down and we can talk about this like civilized human beings."

Bishop glanced over his shoulder at the men in the truck behind them. They were holding their weapons at the ready. "If I start shooting, your men are more likely to hit you."

The cowboy hat wearer was only twenty yards away. Bishop was confident he could drill him through the skull. He might even be able to get the drop on the rapist. But the guys behind would almost certainly gun him down.

"Now you're clutching at straws, pal. Anyway you play it this is going to end badly. You drop the weapon and we can talk it through. I'll have you on a plane back stateside before you know it."

"What about the girl?"

"Same deal."

"And the wounded kid?"

"We'll get him to a hospital."

Bishop couldn't see any other way out. He crouched and made to place the AK on the ground. The bellow of a V8 engine filled the air and he spun his head. There was a horrendous crunch as Emilio's red F250 smashed into the back of the pickup blocking the road. The two men in the rear were thrown through the air like rag dolls. Before they hit the ground Bishop fired a burst from his rifle. The bullets snapped through the space that the Texan's head had occupied a moment before. His second burst was aimed at his black-jacketed sidekick. The rapist was not as fast and clasped his face as he dropped to the ground.

"Get in!" Roberto screamed from the bed of the truck.

Bishop grabbed Christina and threw her up to the rancher. Then he leaped over the side. The F250 reversed, spun, and roared off down the road.

"We lost Carlos!" Bishop yelled over the buffeting wind.

Roberto took off his jacket and handed it to Christina. "I know. We're going to make those bastards pay."

CHAPTER 12

"Burro, have your men found that truck yet?" Pershing was in the back of the Chevy as it sped north on the highway back to the drone factory.

"No, sir, but they'll keep looking."

It was late and he knew if they hadn't found the truck by now it wasn't going to happen. "Forget it. Call them off."

He pulled his satellite phone from his jacket and dialed King's number as they pulled up at the sheds. The CEO of the security company answered in two rings. "Burning the midnight oil, huh, George. What's going on?"

"The guy with the journalist in New York. By any chance was he about five-eleven, well-built, and wearing a Yankees cap?"

"That's him. Why? Don't tell me he's turned up in Mexico."

"He sure has. Are we any closer to finding out who he is?"

"Not yet. We're chasing down the UN angle but it looks like it's fake. From the way he worked over our boys he's got to be former military, maybe a security contractor. He's not government or we'd know by now."

"We just caught one of the local resistance guys so I might have more for you by morning."

"OK, I'll pass that on. You need anything?"

"Yes, sir. I want to request extra support through our man in the CIA. Another two hundred grand would be useful in case he needs more motivation."

"I'll have it transferred to your operations account."

"And I'll let you know what I turn up."

"Good. If you need tactical support let me know. I can have Team 2 down there within seventy-two hours."

"Will do, have a good evening, sir." Pershing terminated the call and hopped out of the vehicle. Burro was waiting. The cartel killer had a bandage taped to his cheek and wore a scowl.

"Mr. Pershing, have you found out who that bastard is yet?" he asked as Pershing joined him under the florescent lights.

"Not yet. Let's ask our new friend."

A tractor started its engine, catching their attention. The bright green John Deere drove in through the sliding doors with the bucket high. The captured youth hung upside down from the bucket with his hands tied behind his back.

"Well isn't that just the prettiest sight." The tractor came to a halt in the middle of the shed. "All trussed up like a hog."

The teenager's eyes fluttered opened and he moaned.

"Burro, did you bandage his wounds?"

"Yes, Mr. Pershing."

"Good, we don't want him bleeding out anytime soon." Pershing opened the trunk of the Chevy and prepared himself an espresso. A minute later he walked to the tractor, glass in hand. "Hola!" He raised the coffee in a mock salute.

The captive's eyes were wide.

"What's your name, boy?"

"Cccccarlos," he stuttered.

Pershing sipped from the coffee. "Listen, son, I'm not a violent man. All I want is some information. If you tell me what you know, I'll let you go. Do you understand?"

Carlos nodded.

"The journalist, she had a friend. Who is he?"

"I, I, I don't know. Some guy from the UN."

Pershing took another sip. "Does he have a name?"

"Aden, his name is Aden." The boy sobbed.

"Just Aden?"

"That's all I know. I promise."

"Do you know why Aden is here?"

Carlos shook his head. "No, he never said."

He finished his coffee. "Are you lying to me, Carlos?"

"No, no, I promise, I'm not lying."

"The farmer, Roberto, what's he planning?"

"I don't know. I promise, I don't know."

He stepped closer. Their noses were almost touching. He smelled the chili on the kid's breath. "Carlos, do you know what that sick fuck, Burro, is going to do to you if you don't tell me the truth?"

Mucus bubbled from the boy's mouth as he sobbed.

"He's going to slice around your middle and pull your skin over your head. Then he's going to tie it with a piece of wire and you're going to suffocate slowly, in your own skin."

The youth made a feeble noise. It reminded Pershing of the bleat of a wounded deer.

"They want to blow something up at the mine. Stop the digging and the mine will close."

"When?"

Carlos shook his head and a fleck of mucus landed on Pershing's jacket. "I don't know, soon. They will go soon. The woman needs photos before she leaves."

Pershing took a handkerchief from his pocket and wiped the snot from his suit. "Thank you for your cooperation, Carlos." He walked back to the Chevy punching Howard's number into his phone.

"Do you know what time it is?" the CIA analyst whined when he picked up.

"Time for you to do some goddamn work," Pershing snapped.

"Hey man, I'm at home."

"Then you better get your ass back to the office. I want you to access the C4I4 footage and find that damn journalist. She was in town earlier today with a guy wearing a Yankees cap. He's going by the name Aden and I need to know everything about him."

"Is it an emergency? I can pull up the footage tomorrow."

"Yes, it's an emergency. This Aden guy beat seven shades of shit out of our boys in New York. Now he's with the journalist and a bunch of dirt farmers who are trying to work out how to shut down the mine. Run him through the database and put him on your target deck. We need to shut him down."

"Yeah, no worries, man. I'll just call my buddies at Homeland Security and borrow a couple of surveillance birds. Maybe they'll throw in a SEAL Team as well."

"You done?"

Howard stayed silent.

"Good. There's a ten K bonus for every day you get a dedicated line of Pred."

Howard gave a low whistle. "Now we're talking. I'll see what I can do. You got a preference for day or night?"

"Night coverage, my boys can handle it by day."

"You got any threat reporting I can use to sell this?"

"Course I do, the guy with the journalist. I think he's some kind of environmental terrorist. Probably looking to abduct American workers from the mine, or worse still, blow it up. I'll let you fill in the details."

"Details? Man, that's going to cost you an extra ten grand."

"Fine, just make it happen. Send me everything you've got on our Person of Interest."

"Will do."

"Have a lovely evening." Pershing hung up. He contemplated another espresso but thought better of it. He wanted a good night's sleep.

"Mr. Pershing, what do you want us to do with him?" Burro asked.

He knocked the grounds out of the coffee machine's group head onto the floor and ran the machine through. "Make an example of him. You people seem to be pretty good at that."

He finished packing and got into his SUV as Burro and his boys lowered their victim to the ground. They untied his chains from the bucket of the tractor and looped them over the tow ball on the back of a pickup. He started screaming and Pershing pulled the heavy door shut to block out the noise.

A moment later Burro hopped into the Chevy and they drove out of the shed onto the dirt road. The truck dragging Carlos followed. It was twenty-five miles to the mine. Pershing guessed the kid would last one at most. By the time they hit five miles his body would be a grubby piece of meat bouncing along the road. He sighed. These people were savages.

***

FORT BLISS, TEXAS

Howard pulled open the fridge and retrieved a can of energy drink. He popped the top as he walked out of the staff room, swiped the access door, and stumbled to his desk. He put the can down, logged in, and activated the application that linked him to the Chihuahua C4I4 network. Opening the search tool, he inputted Christina Munoz's biometric profile. In a few seconds the system had two matches. The state-of-the-art cameras in Chihuahua had captured high-resolution video of the attractive journalist.

Howard took a sip from his drink as he zoomed in on a recording of her walking away. She was wearing tight-fitting jeans and her butt looked awesome. He took a screenshot and hit print.

Scanning through the footage, he found the guy who was traveling with her, Aden. He was tall with an athletic frame, dressed in jeans, a T-shirt, and a casual jacket. Some kind of ex-military jock, Howard thought. He was probably already in her pants.

He edged the recording forward frame by frame until he had the best shot of Aden's face. He had aviator sunglasses on and a baseball cap. That was going to make facial recognition difficult. Still, it was worth a try. He exported the clearest image to his desktop. He opened a CIA database and imported the picture.

While he waited for the software to analyze the image he walked across to the printer station and picked up the screenshot of the journalist. As he waddled back to his desk he smiled. He was going to take some of Pershing's bonus to Vegas and find an ass like this in one of the strip clubs. A fist full of cash would make it his for the night.

A beep from his computer interrupted the sordid fantasy. He sat and checked the results of the search. "What the hell?" The database had returned over five thousand hits.

Howard opened the sorting parameters and tried to find one that might narrow it down. Under key words he entered Aden, terrorism, military, and environment. That left him with five results. He checked them but none looked like his man. He deleted Aden and searched again. Twenty hits. A couple of guys looked similar but nothing definitive. He deleted environment; three hundred hits. "You shitting me!" It was going to be a long night.

He decided to check the unknown results first, in case Aden had been caught on camera but never identified. It was a smart move; within seven images he thought he had a match.

The image was from Kiev, Ukraine, in 2012. It had been shared by the Ukrainian Security Service as part of a counter-terrorism cooperation program. According to the metadata, the single shot was from a terrorist attack on a nightclub. It was grainy, and at a bad angle, but to a trained eye the guy was almost certainly the same person. This time, however, he was wearing a chest-rig over his civilian clothes and carrying a suppressed submachine gun. A tall blonde man in a similar outfit stood next to him wielding a larger belt-fed weapon.

Howard shook his head and scratched down some notes. There was no way these guys were terrorists, he thought. They were more like well-resourced Tier-1 operators. He recognized both the weapons carried. The HK MP7 was a favorite of DEVGRU, as was the MK48 machine gun.

He checked the data associated with the image. There was nothing else on file. Not even a police report. He dragged the image into PowerPoint, and added the original picture from Mexico. He looked around, double-checking to see if anyone was in the office. It was well past midnight and the room was empty. He took a photo with his cell phone and emailed it to Pershing's private account with a few notes. After that he opened a CIA report template and started fabricating a document to convince Homeland Security to approve a line of surveillance from one of their Predator drones. His chubby fingers danced over the keyboard as he typed the title of the report.

Militant Environmentalist Planning To Strike US Mine in Chihuahua.

JACK SILKSTONE

CHAPTER 13

LASCAR ISLAND

Chen Chua closed his browser and stretched his neck. He had been sitting at his computer for three hours working on potential missions for the next PRIMAL targeting board. Scanning the internet and intelligence reports for extreme injustice was enough to darken anyone's mood. But someone had to do it and Chua was immensely proud of the impact his team was making.

In the last six months they'd enabled PRIMAL operatives to target sex trafficking in two countries, and brought an end to a civil war. Not a bad effort for a small intelligence cell, he thought. Still, working in an underground bunker was a little depressing. He decided he needed to go topside for a few hours off. A bit of mountain biking on a few of the trails and a swim would help reinvigorate him.

He left his desk and crossed the operations room, glancing at the huge screens bolted to the bare rock wall. He stopped in front of the personnel tracker. It showed the location of all of the PRIMAL operatives, each with their own icon. There was a dumbbell for Mitch in Alaska, a flower in Indonesia for Saneh, and a smiley face in New York where Mirza was. A chess piece was located in Northern Mexico; Bishop. He turned to the watchkeeper manning the operations desk. "Frank, is there some sort of glitch with the tracker?"

The former Para officer checked his computer. "No mate, I've got green lights across the board."

"Then why is Bishop in Mexico?"

Frank shook his head. "Not sure, I figured he might have headed down for some sun. Or, it might be linked to the work Flash did for Mirza. Something about a fake online profile and phone hack."

"Tell me this has something to do with the journalist?"

Frank shrugged. "Beyond me, boss. All I know is they were investigating a mining company and some kind of corporate fund."

Chua rolled his eyes. "You give that guy one job, one damn job. Frank, can you get hold of Bishop and patch it through to Vance's office."

"No problem. I haven't gotten them in trouble, have I?"

"No, Bishop's proven more than capable of doing that by himself." He spun on his heel and strode to the office of PRIMAL's Director of Operations. He rapped his knuckles on the opaque glass door and pushed it open. Vance was not at his desk.

"Hello, Chua," a deep voice sounded from the behind the door.

He pushed it open to find the PRIMAL director reclining in his leather armchair with a book. On the side table sat a steaming mug.

The bull-headed African American took off his reading glasses and rubbed the bridge of his nose. "What can I do for you?"

"Sorry to interrupt, Vance. I wanted to know if you knew anything about Bishop being in Mexico."

Vance's eyes narrowed. "Mexico?"

"That's what his iPRIMAL's saying. I've got the watchkeeper tracking him down."

The phone on Vance's desk started ringing.

"That should be him."

"Put it on speaker."

Chua pressed answer. "Bish, this is Chua. Vance is also here."

"Hi guys. I'm guessing this isn't a welfare call." Bishop's voice sounded distant.

"No it's not. You're a little further south than we originally discussed. You better just be buying Tequila and fireworks," Vance said.

"I can explain."

Vance raised one of his eyebrows and Chua shook his head.

"Is this linked to the journalist?"

"Yes, I met her like Chua wanted. The good news is she's not anywhere close to compromising PRIMAL."

"And the bad news?" asked Vance.

"The bad news is she was attacked by a bunch of thugs. Security contractors. I stepped in and—"

"And then you chased the rabbit down the hole," said Vance.

"She's on to something big. The guys who attacked us in New York are linked to some kind of dodgy security company with ties to a private equity fund."

"How does that link to Mexico?" asked Chua.

"The PE also has ties to a company called Resources and Environmental Development Group. They're running a big mine down here in Chihuahua. Chua's journalist was investigating them for running farmers off their land."

Chua muted their end of the call. "They've already done some digging into these guys. Mirza's been posing as an Indian mining developer."

"They don't mess about do they?" Vance gave him a nod and he un-muted the call. "Have you been able to verify any of her claims yet?"

"Sort of."

"Sort of? What does that mean?"

"We hit the ground earlier today and linked up with a local activist group."

"And?"

"And then we were attacked."

"Attacked? By who?"

"Cartel goons, they managed to grab one of the activists. These guys weren't messing around, Vance. They must have had surveillance on them from the get-go, or maybe they tailed us from town. I don't know."

"And you think they're tied in with the mining company?"

"The guy in charge had US contractor written all over him. Looked like a cowboy, he was wearing a bloody ten-gallon hat."

Vance frowned as he digested the information. "I want you to get everything you can to Chua's team. They're going to chase this down from our end. In the meantime, I want you out of Mexico."

"That's a bit of a waste, isn't it? I mean, I'm safe now. We're switching vehicles as we speak, then moving to a secure location outside of town. Now that I'm here, I may as well check out the mine."

"What do you think, Chua?"

"So long as Bishop thinks the risk is acceptable."

Vance sighed and got up from his armchair. "OK, get in and do a recon. But I want a full debrief first and if Chua assesses the risk as too high, then you're out of Mexico immediately."

"Roger."

"Bish, I'll call you back in five." Chua ended the call.

Vance reached over and pressed a button on the touch screen behind his desk. He selected the personnel tracker and studied it. "What do you think, bud? Bish chasing pussy again?"

"There is that, but if Mirza's going along with it they're probably on to something significant. I'll take a close look and get back to you."

Vance zoomed in on Bishop's location. He was on the outskirts of Chihuahua city in what looked like a car yard. "Have your analysts work up a target pack for presentation at the board. Look into the security company, the miners, and the fund."

"Will do."

"Oh, and get Frank to put Mitch on stand-by. If this turns out to be something big, Bishop will need his support."

Chua nodded. "So much for down time. I was going to hit the trails on my bike."

Vance shrugged. "Well, I wasn't enjoying the book anyway. Who needs fiction when real life is this exciting."

"Hey, I need sunlight."

"How about you take a day off next week? Get one of the

crew to chopper you and your bike up to the rim of the volcano."

He grinned. "That's not a bad idea. You should come, it's good exercise."

"No one needs to see me in lycra, bud. I'll be in the squat rack if you need me. Just try not to break your neck."

***

ALASKA

Mitch wore an ear to ear grin as he sped across the rolling arctic landscape. The sled's runners hissed in the thick snow as he was dragged along at twelve miles an hour by fourteen canine high performance athletes. The dogs, Siberian Huskies, were amazing creatures. He had researched them before the trip. They burned three and a half times the calories of a Tour De France athlete and had twice the VO2 capacity.

He had joined the musher, led by Sonny, yesterday at checkpoint Kaltag. He'd helped feed and prepare the dogs before they set out over the 82 miles to the next checkpoint in Unalakleet.

The dogs pulled the sled through a thicket of pine trees and down over a frozen creek. As they slid up the other side the sled hit a rock and flipped over on its side. Mitch was thrown into a snowdrift.

"Ho, ho, ho!" yelled Sonny in an attempt to get the dogs to stop. He managed to hold on to the sled as it skidded for another ten yards. "Stay, stay."

Mitch extricated himself from the snow and dusted himself off.

"You OK?" asked Sonny.

"OK? I'm having a bloody ball, mate." Mitch collected an armful of equipment that had been thrown clear.

Sonny flipped the heavily-laden sled back onto its runners. "This thing is seriously fast, Mitch. I'd wager we're in contention for a top-five finish. Can't thank you enough for putting it together."

Mitch had hand-built the sled from carbon composite and donated it to the musher and his team. As repayment he'd been invited to join them for a leg of the world's last great race. It was something he'd always dreamed of doing.

"I'm just happy to be a part of it, mate." He looked up to see the dogs pulling the sled away. "Although it appears that the team's off without us."

Sonny jumped into action. "Stay, stay!" he yelled as he chased the huskies.

Mitch grabbed the last of the gear and stumbled after him. He skidded and slid on the packed snow. "All they want to do is run."

"That's what they're bred for, eh."

Mitch climbed back into his seat at the front of the sled. "Any chance of me standing at the back later?"

"Sure. When we get out onto the flats."

The dogs started pulling as soon as they heard Sonny's voice. In a matter of seconds they hauled the four hundred pound sled back to its cruising speed. They climbed up a small rise, skirted a rocky outcrop and slid down into a narrow valley. There was not a cloud in the sky. The air was crisp and dry, the landscape pristine and untouched. Mitch loved every moment. So much that he almost missed his iPRIMAL vibrating inside his jacket. He slipped off one of his mitts and reached inside the heavily insulated parker. The message was short.

Possible mission pending. Be prepared to extract to NYC at short notice.

New York? What mischief was Bishop up to? He opened the mapping app. The GPS had his location as half way between the two checkpoints. At their current speed they would hit Unalakleet in six hours. In an emergency he could hitch a ride with one of the Iditarod Air Force planes and get there ahead of time. Then it was still a six hour flight to New

York. He sent a message to the watchkeeper.

Earliest time of arrival in NYC is 24 hours from now.

He stuffed the smart device back inside his jacket. Even if they recalled him, he was still going to get in another six hours of sledding. He smiled; at this stage, that was all that mattered.

***

NEW YORK CITY

Mirza left the hotel early, eager to see a few of the city's sights. A short walk to Hell's Kitchen and a climb up a set of wrought iron stairs brought him to the High Line.

The mile-long linear park was formerly an elevated train line that shipped freight in and out of the city. Earmarked for demolition until a group of local residents successfully lobbied for its development into a public space. Mirza thought the result was spectacular. He wandered along the narrow walkway enjoying sculptures, colorful murals, and views over the city streets.

After half an hour he sat on a bench and spent a few minutes studying the brightly colored mural on the wall opposite before opening a newspaper. He was dressed in a threadbare black jacket with brown slacks, and a scruffy tweed paddy cap. His mustache was gone, replaced by a day's growth. It was an inconspicuous look, an off-duty cab driver or a street hawker, another face in a city of eight million.

He was waiting for a call from Chua and knew exactly what it was about. The Bunker was now fully aware of Bishop's little sojourn down to Mexico. The discreet Bluetooth earpiece beeped and Mirza rocked his jaw from side to side to answer the call. "Good Morning, Chua, how are you?"

"I'm good, thank you. I see you're out enjoying the fine weather."

He smiled. PRIMAL's intelligence chief was thorough. He

would have checked Mirza's location indicator, then the local weather. "It's a beautiful day here." Mirza lowered his paper and watched as a fit Asian woman walked past with a pug. The little animal was wheezing as it pulled frantically at its leash.

"I'm envious. New York is my favorite city. How cool is the High Line?"

"Fantastic, I'm glad you recommended it."

"One of the best places to just hang out on a nice day. I like it more than Central Park."

"That's also on my list."

"Well, take the time to see it all now while you've got the chance. Flash has started getting email feeds from the hack you installed on Wesley Chambers' phone. MVI, GE, and RED are all linked together in this Mexican project. We're pulling the intel apart piece by piece, but first glance tells me the whole thing's dodgy."

"The Manhattan Ventures chairman, Pollard, didn't give anything up, but he certainly implied they had experience in dealing with non-compliant locals. Have you read Christina's article yet?"

"Yes, and I spoke to Bishop. He was attacked by cartel thugs as soon as he arrived in Mexico."

Mirza's jaw tensed. "Is he OK? Do I need to get down there?"

"He's fine. He and the girl have met with a local resistance element. They're going to recon the mine and get some imagery. My team's collating everything we have to present at the targeting board tomorrow. Until we get approval this remains a prelim op. If we get approval, Mitch will fly in and you'll both support Bishop."

An elderly couple walked toward Mirza and he rose, offering them the seat. "I really do think this is worth pursuing, but we need to tread carefully." He started walking. "These people are powerful and they have a lot at stake. If they got a look at Bishop in Mexico they're going to be suspicious."

"I agree. There's also a good chance your Indian cover was burned."

"I've already dropped it. Both Kestrel and Pollard mentioned their people were ex-government. Kestrel actually mentioned the CIA. I'm worried they might have active links, or worse."

"You think this could be a front for CIA operations?"

"Maybe."

"I'll look into it. See what Vance says. Shouldn't scare us off though. If these guys have done half the things that Christina has written in her article, then they need to be held accountable. We know they've tried to kidnap her on two separate occasions. CIA or not, I'm happy to expose corruption no matter who's the perpetrator."

"I don't think anyone's going to disagree with that." Mirza stopped at the railing and looked out over Hudson. A container ship was plowing its way through the brown water. "We just need to be careful."

"You pass that on to Bishop. He never likes to hear it from me. Oh, and if you're looking for a spot for lunch, there are some great places about a hundred yards from where you are. Take the next set of stairs down."

"Thanks for the tip."

"I'll check in with you once the targeting board is done. In the meantime, enjoy your vacation. Later." Chua ended the call.

He descended the stairs and contemplated ringing Bishop. No, Chua, would have already updated him. He'd wait to see what came out of his recon with Christina and the targeting board. In the meantime he'd enjoy some of the fine cuisine that New York had to offer. He had come a long way from the streets of New Delhi.

CHAPTER 14

CHIHUAHUA

Pershing's office at the mine was a bare-walled portable building that had been trucked in on the back of a sixteen-wheeler. He hated it. It was hot during the day, cold at night, and isolated him from what was happening on the ground. It was a necessary evil though, and he was forced to spend a good portion of his time in it working at his computer.

He fumed as he checked his email for the fourth time that day. Howard, that fat useless prick, had found nothing more on the man who'd escaped with the reporter and almost shot Burro through the face. All he had was the grainy photo from the Ukraine and the Chihuahua City C4I images. It wasn't much.

The CIA analyst hadn't even been able to come good with the Predator drone. He'd only managed to secure a one-off flight that spent a single hour over the mine before flying back to the border with nothing to report. Pershing sent a terse email to Howard, then used a secure communicator application to dial through to his boss, Charles King.

The call connected and King's shaved head appeared on screen. "George, did you get anything useful out of the kid?"

"Yes, I just flicked you an email. Seems our man goes by the name Aden. What's more he's currently in the planning stages to disrupt the mine."

King's face turned serious. "What do you mean? More protests?"

"No. I believe he intends to sabotage our operations directly. Sir, this guy is a serious threat. I've attached the images provided by our Company man. Check out the one from the Ukraine. I think you'll find it interesting."

There was a pause as King brought up the picture from his email. "This is all the CIA have?"

"That and the C4I4 images from Mexico. They're the same guy. My concern is that he's not acting alone. If he's linked to a protest action group he'll have support. And I'm not talking about dirt farmers with shotguns."

"No, they're tooled up all right. Do we know anything else? When was the photo taken?"

"2012. It's allegedly from a terrorist attack Aden was involved with. A big-time arms dealer in Kiev had his entire enterprise taken down."

"Alright, I'm going to initiate security protocols."

"I'll tighten things up here and push Langley for additional support. I'm still trying to get a drone."

"Right. Keep me posted." King terminated the call.

Pershing stared at the high-resolution C4I4 image of Aden for a moment. With the Yankees baseball cap and sunglasses the picture wasn't ideal. He printed off a copy, grabbed his Stetson from where it hung on the wall, and stepped out into the midday sun. He stood looking out over the mine site as he folded the photo and stuck it in his suit jacket.

His office was one of thirty portable buildings clustered together into a micro-city. They housed the accommodation, cookhouse, and recreation facilities of the mining crew and security personnel. Across the road were the vehicle maintenance sheds, secure gold storage vaults, the ore processing facility, and beyond that the tailings dams. A track wider than a dual-lane highway ran from the crushers and the refinery back into the mountains. That was the way to the pit.

The snarl of a high performance engine caught Pershing's ear and he walked to one of the maintenance hangars.

Burro and half a dozen of his men were watching mechanics put the final touches on four DeJong Special Ops Vehicles. Painted in flat desert tan, with off-road rally-spec suspension, 6.2-liter V8 engines, and 35-inch sand tires, the dune buggies were serious hardware.

One of the diesel mechanics wiped his hands on a dirty rag. "This one's good to go, boss."

Pershing dropped his hat on the workbench and walked

around the vehicle. He pointed at the fluorescent orange flag affixed to a ten-foot whip antenna. "What's with the damn flag?"

"Stops the trucks running you over."

Pershing snorted. "They ain't gonna catch this thing. Get rid of 'em." He grabbed the heavy steel roll cage with one arm and slid in through the open side. "Burro, get in."

As he waited for the lieutenant to climb in he gave the controls a once over, checking the GPS and a digital screen bolted to the dash. "This working?" he asked, pointing to the screen. It was the latest generation Remotely Operated Video Enhanced Receiver, or ROVER. The tablet-sized device could stream full motion video from a drone.

"It did last night, Mr. Pershing. I was able to see everything."

He nodded and thumbed the starter. The V8 roared to life. He let it idle for while then dropped the buggy into gear and eased on the accelerator.

The engine rumbled as they rolled out of the shed and turned out onto the wide stretch of unsealed road leading to the mine's pit. Once clear of the maintenance areas he stomped on the accelerator. The engine snarled and the buggy shot forward snapping their necks backward. It fish-tailed wildly as Pershing swung the steering-wheel back and forth.

He glanced across at Burro. The Mexican was clutching the side of the cockpit with white knuckles. He laughed and followed the track as it curved, cutting into the rock on both sides.

A massive dump truck appeared directly in front. He accelerated around it sending the buggy into a wild slide. "Wooo hooo!" he bellowed over the roar of the engine.

He spun the wheel and slammed on the brakes, bringing the buggy to a skidding halt. "Hell, yeah, that's fun."

Burro inhaled suddenly as if he had forgotten to breathe. The dust from the wheels swept over them and he coughed as it cleared.

They were at the entrance to the pit. From here the track

led down to a wide basin. It had once been a jagged mountain range but now was a gaping crater. Below them gigantic front-end loaders hacked chunks off the hillside and fed them into dump trucks. The trucks then made their way up the winding ramp, out of the pit, to the ore crushers.

Pershing cut the engine. "As soon as we get all the buggies running I want the men out patrolling."

"Day and night?" asked Burro.

"The mine perimeter by night and I want them pushing out into the desert by day. If they see anyone, they shoot them."

Burro nodded. "Can we get some night vision?"

"Negative, these buggies have blown the budget. You've got what you got." Pershing pulled the printed photo from his jacket and handed it over. "Make photocopies of this. I want everyone to see it."

Burro gently touched the bandage on his cheek. "I'm going to kill that bastard."

"No, I want him alive." He hit the starter button on the buggy, floored it, and sent it into a sliding U-turn. Dust rooster-tailed off the rear wheels and they sped down the track to the camp.

***

NEW YORK CITY

Casey Millwood had been working for Ground Effects Services for a little over six months. The CEO had poached him from his previous role, Head of Information Security, at a technology firm in Silicon Valley. He considered himself at the top of his game, one of the best in the business. However, in the last hour he'd come to realize there was someone out there more capable than he was.

On King's orders he'd run a complete security sweep over their entire phone fleet. The intensive search had taken five hours and uncovered nothing. All phones were accessing known databases, running their standard IP settings, and performing exactly as they should. None of the encryption systems had been manipulated and there were no external devices trying to access their network. When he'd reported this to King, the CEO ordered him to conduct an even more detailed search on the firm's five black phones. He had no idea who used them and had zero access to their email databases.

Casey ran the search again and found nothing other than a slightly high data usage from one of the handsets. Spurred on, he found a weather app installed on the device was using twenty percent more bandwidth than usual.

He opened the application and knew immediately he had hit pay dirt. He studied the code and realized the device was slowly replicating the entire encrypted email database, minus images and attachments, to an IP address outside their network.

He remotely shut down the phone. It took him another five minutes to track the IP address. It led him directly to a weather database. This guy was good. Whoever it was had hacked into the service provider and embedded the code directly into the weather provider's system. If he wanted to check where it was sending the data packets to he was going to have to do the same thing.

He picked up his phone. "Mr. King, I've found a compromise."

"Which phone?"

"Number five, sir. It was transmitting data but I've shut it down."

"Very good. Number five, huh? I'll deal with that clown personally. Now, can you trace the hack?"

"I might be able to but it's going to take time."

"Do you need more manpower? You can pick your own team."

Casey considered requesting additional support but his pride stopped him. "No sir, I can beat this guy."

"Guy? Do you already know who it is?"

"No, but he's good. Whoever did this has resources, and skill."

"That's interesting. I want a damage assessment on how

much information was compromised. However, your highest priority is to find out who did this and where they are. You got that?"

"Yes, sir." Casey shivered involuntarily as the call hung up. He almost felt sorry for whoever did this because when King found out who they were they were screwed.

***

FORT BLISS, TEXAS

Howard stood in front of the candy machine contemplating which of the delicacies his taste buds most craved. He was about to punch in the code that would release a Hershey bar when Everest startled him.

"Don't eat that crap, Howard. It'll mess up your energy levels. You need something low GI. Slow releasing to keep you going all day. Then you wouldn't need to drink that sugary energy drink."

Howard turned and found his superior holding an apple. Everest offered it to his analyst by holding it on the palm of his hand, like he was feeding a horse.

He took it. "Thanks, boss."

Everest smiled. "No problems. Look, I really appreciate the effort you've put into turning things around the last few days."

Howard caught him glancing at the freshly polished brogues that had been giving him blisters. The shoes were the most uncomfortable he'd ever owned.

Everest led him out the kitchen and down the corridor. "I wanted you to know that I've noticed. The report you submitted last night on the environmental terrorist threat to US interests in Chihuahua was first rate." He gave him a pat on the shoulder. "Keep it up."

Howard pulled a face as his boss strode back to his office. The man was clueless, he thought. The report he had submitted was completely fabricated. That was why it was good. It was almost one hundred percent fiction.

He walked over to the little boxes that housed their cell phones when they were in the secure area. On his phone was an email and missed call from Pershing. He walked out to the smoking area and returned the call.

"Why do you never answer your damn phone?" asked Pershing.

"I've told you before, I can't have it in my workspace. It's like you don't listen to anything I say. I've told you this at least three times."

"How about you holster that attitude, cowboy."

Howard bit his lip.

"What's going on with our surveillance? One hour is hardly worth getting out of bed for."

Howard clenched his fist. Fucking field agents. They had no idea how hard it was to get assets and good intel. They just snapped their fingers and expected everything served up on a platter. "We were lucky to get that. I had to do some creative work."

"Well you better get more creative because we're not just dealing with dirt farmers anymore." Pershing filled him in on the security breach and the hacking of the phones.

"You fucking kidding me, dude? Is your phone compromised?"

"Relax, this phone's fine. I wouldn't be about to raise my offer if it wasn't secure."

"Your offer?"

"I want dedicated assets looking at this; persistent surveillance and analysts. There's a hundred-K bonus in it once the threat is neutralized. That's on top of the extra ten grand retainer for the surveillance."

"A hundred, now that's some coin!"

"It is indeed. Sort it out. Do what you have to do." Pershing terminated the call.

Howard sat for a few seconds before he realized he was still holding the apple. He crunched into it as he contemplated the way forward. Now there was real evidence of a capable adversary, he had more leverage to push for a team of his own.

All he needed to do was fabricate some Source 88 reports and take it to his boss. The man already had a hard-on for his previous work. He looked at the apple like it was poison and tossed it over the fence. He would grab a candy bar on the way back past the machine, he was going to need the energy. But first he was going to have a smoke.

CHAPTER 15

LASCAR ISLAND

The PRIMAL targeting board was a monthly event that ultimately cost lives. Usually the lives on the line were those of despots, criminals, corrupt politicians, and the like. Scum and villainy, as the Director of Operations so eloquently put it. However, occasionally it was the lives of their comrades, the PRIMAL operatives that went into harm's way to set wrongs right and bring justice to dark corners of the world. It was in this meeting that targets were put forward for consideration and decisions were made as to who PRIMAL would bring to justice.

Vance and Chua were sitting at the conference room table waiting for Frank, the watchkeeper, to set up the video link to Abu Dhabi.

Frank activated one of the wall-mounted monitors, and the handsome Arabic features of PRIMAL's benefactor appeared on the screen. Stroking his manicured beard he studied something on his desk before looking up. "Gentlemen, how are you all?"

Vance leaned forward and spoke into the microphone on the table. "Our settings must be all messed up at this end, Tariq, because those green eyes of yours are looking particularly dreamy."

The CEO of Lascar Logistics broke into a broad smile. "It's not like you to offer a compliment, Vance. Does this mean you need more money?" He pretended to frown.

Despite funding nearly all of PRIMAL's operating costs, Tariq rarely involved himself in the day-to-day operations of the organization. However, like Vance and Chua, he did hold the power of veto over any mission. It was one of the controls that ensured they remained focused on delivering impartial justice.

"I wouldn't say no to more cash." Vance coughed. "But, on a more serious note, have you got today's target deck?"

Tariq held up a tablet. "Yes, I've had time to go over it in detail. It's an impressive piece of work. Chen, please thank your team for me."

Chua smiled. "Thanks, Tariq, I'll pass it on. Now, if everyone is ready, I'm going to summarize the developing operations and move straight on to the emerging time-sensitive issue."

Tariq nodded.

Vance folded his massive arms. "Go on."

Chua pressed a remote and a map appeared on another screen. "We're still developing intelligence on the following potential ops. In priority order. One, ongoing humanitarian violations by the Myanmar junta. Two, exploitation of test subjects by a pharmaceutical company in Angola. Three, a white supremacist gang operating out of Scandinavia, and finally, a Chinese backed poaching syndicate devastating the black Rhino population in Zimbabwe. He looked up from his notes. "Does anyone have any questions or objections regarding any of these collection operations?"

"Just one," Tariq asked. "I'm yet to read Mirza's report from Myanmar. I was wondering how agent recruitment there was progressing?"

"It's developing nicely. We have three potential Blades identified. My team's going through a comprehensive analysis and we'll select one in the near future."

"Good."

"OK, that brings us to our operation of opportunity."

"Ah yes," said Tariq. "Gentlemen, when are you going to learn that wherever you send Aden, he's going to find trouble? The man is a magnet for it."

Vance sighed. "Tell me about it. But, it's a bit cruel to keep him locked up here."

"Cruel for me, he'd drive me insane," said Chua. "I've been through a full debriefing with him, and in his defense, what he has uncovered is fairly significant in terms of injustice."

Tariq nodded. "From what I've read, I concur. If these people are indeed killing farmers and burning their homes, then we're obliged to scope an intervention."

Vance sat up in his chair. "I agree. But I'd like to take a very low-key approach to this operation. We should aim to target them at the corporate level. Expose the corruption and environmental issues, and bring the authorities to bear."

Tariq nodded from on screen. "Gentlemen, I have one major concern; what if this is a CIA operation? We might end up exposing PRIMAL to significant risk. Vance, what's your assessment on this?"

As a former CIA officer, Vance had an intimate understanding of how the agency worked. "My gut feeling is this isn't a CIA operation. The days of the Company running little cash ventures are long gone. In saying that, it's possible one or two of their officers are getting their hands dirty. So I agree that it poses a risk, and Mexico is the motherfucking badlands. So like I said, we need to play this one real careful. No mentoring local militias or any of the kinetic business."

A knock at the door interrupted him.

Chua checked who it was and exchanged some quick words. He opened the door and Flash, PRIMAL's resident digital intel specialist, entered.

Chua sat back down. "Gents, we've got more information coming in that has a direct impact on our decision here. Flash, the room is yours."

The stocky, shaggy-haired analyst looked around the room excitedly. "Hey, so hi, everybody. OK, this is pretty big. The hack that Mirza installed on one of the banker guys' phones. Yeah, well they found it, and they're trying to ping it back to us."

Vance wore a concerned look. "What does that mean?"

"It means they know someone's looking at them but don't know who. There's no way they can trace it back to the Bunker or anything like that. But they do know someone with serious capability is sniffing around."

"From what I understand, Flash, the hack was well hidden,"

Chua said. "Someone had to be doing some serious digging to find it."

"That's right. I backtracked the ping and the source is a Ground Effects Services office in New York. This is interesting because it confirms they're providing the IT security to MVI."

"MVI?" Tariq's voice came across the speakers.

"Yeah, they're the ones who funded the mining operation. Both MVI and GES have offices in the same building."

"No indication that NSA is involved?" asked Chua throwing in yet another three-letter organization.

Flash shook his mop of hair. "Nah, boss, this guy's good, but he's using commercial software. I've tried to hack into their server but they're running a very tight ship. If we want to get inside their system we're going to need to get someone, or something, physically inside the building."

"I think that's as good a place to start as any," said Vance. "I propose we bring Mitch down from Alaska and start gathering all the intel we can in New York. That way we can establish exactly who we're dealing with."

Chua nodded. "I agree. And once we get more info from Bishop about the mine, we can decide what course of action to take with him."

Tariq stroked his beard. "I just need a little clarification on who everyone is. RED is running the mine, GES is providing security, and MVI are the guys bankrolling the operation. Correct?"

"That's correct," Chua said.

"OK." He nodded. "I concur. Let's make it a priority to get as much intel as we can."

Vance thumped the table with the palm of his hand. "Excellent, let's get it happening. In 72 hours I want to know everything there is to know about these fucktards."

CHAPTER 16

CHIHUAHUA

The jolting of the truck woke Bishop. He found Christina nuzzled in his shoulder, still fast asleep. He checked his watch. Only an hour had passed since they'd left the outskirts of the city. Looking out over the tailgate, he was surprised to see the urban sprawl had been replaced with mountains and a dusty rutted track.

After they'd escaped from the Black Jackets, Roberto had taken them to a friend's car yard on the outskirts of town. Despite Emilio's protests, Bishop had paid cash to swap the battered F250 for a newer, blue, Dodge Dakota pickup. They had stayed overnight before heading off at the crack of dawn.

The blue Dodge pulled up outside a cluster of stone buildings and the four Mexicans got out of the cab. Bishop gently nudged Christina to wake her. "Hey, I think we're there."

He jumped over the side of the truck and helped her down.

Their destination was a modest ranch perched on the side of a low hill. It overlooked an inhospitable valley dotted with rocky outcrops, dry brush, and tall spiked plants. The farm buildings were all made of local stone and bare beams. Three small huts were clustered behind a main residence and a large square barn. Bishop guessed the ranch was set up as a bed and breakfast.

The front door of the farmhouse opened and an elderly gentleman wearing a plaid shirt and jeans appeared. He took one look at Roberto and his men and waved them inside.

Bishop wandered across to the barn and peered inside. There were stalls along one side, straw on the floor, and a storage room at the end. The musty smell of horses hung in the air. A whinny sounded from one of the stalls and a horse poked its nose out.

"Aden," Christina called from outside.

He walked back to find the Mexicans had returned.

Roberto pointed to the huts. "We can stay here for the next few days. They've given us two huts. The four of us will stay in the bunkhouse. Christina, you and Aden will have the other cabin."

"Hey, that doesn't sound fair."

"Do you and Christina want the bunkhouse and the four of us can share a bed?"

Bishop shook his head. "No, I just thought–"

"It'll be fine," Christina said as she gathered her bags from the truck and made her way to the cabin.

He watched her for a moment, then pulled his iPRIMAL from his pocket. He wasn't surprised to find there was no phone reception. It wasn't useless though; he could still access the stored data and the GPS worked. "How far are we from the mine?"

"About twenty miles," said Roberto as he grabbed his jacket from the truck. "But don't worry. We won't be walking. My friends have agreed to lend us horses."

"Horses? No one said anything about horses." He followed the rancher down to the cabins.

"If we go by road the Chaquetas will find us. If you want, you can walk, but it's a long way through the desert."

Bishop opened a mapping app on his iPRIMAL. "The mine doesn't appear on any of imagery."

Roberto looked confused. "How are you getting the internet out here?"

"The mapping data is cached." He pointed to their current location. "We're here. Where is the mine?"

"North, about twenty miles. We'll ride through a canyon, past the old gold mine, and across the desert till we hit a creek. Then we climb higher into the mountains."

Bishop traced the route with his finger.

"That's it there," said Roberto when a series of jagged peaks filled the screen. "That's monstruo. Now, please excuse me, I'm going to have a shower and organize dinner."

"When are we going to leave for the mine?"

"Tomorrow night. That gives you all day to get to know your horse."

Bishop sat on the rough-hewn bench out the front of his cabin and studied the mountain range Roberto had indicated. It was huge and surrounded by jagged terrain. He didn't like horses at the best of times but at night, on rocky ground, he knew it wasn't going to be easy. At least it was tactically sound. The horse was the perfect covert infiltration vehicle and it was unlikely a bunch of cartel thugs or security contractors would be patrolling the desert at night. Nope, only an idiot would be bumbling around out there on a glorified donkey.

***

NEW YORK

Mitch banked the Gulfstream and leveled out, lining up with the main runway at Westchester County Airport. He dropped the flaps, eased back on the throttle, and touched down with a gentle thud. The tower authorized him to taxi off the strip and onto the apron.

He spotted the buggy waiting for him. It had a rotating orange light on its roof. He followed it to a clear section of the apron and powered down the engines. He yawned as he pried himself from the pilot's seat and stretched his legs. It had been a six hour flight from Alaska. Grabbing his bags from the main cabin, he dropped the stairs and stepped out into the pleasant warmth of an afternoon spring breeze.

The guy in the buggy was waiting. "Welcome to Westchester County, Mr. Henderson."

Mitch dropped his bags in the back of the electric cart and shook the man's hand. "Thanks, mate. Is there anything I need to sort out?" He activated the remote control that closed the aircraft door.

"No, everything's good. If you leave me the keys I can have the jet refueled. Your office has arranged for a week's parking but we can extend that if you need it."

Mitch jumped into the passenger seat. "She's still got plenty of juice. I'll let you know if I'm going to stay any longer."

"Very good." The man started the cart and drove toward the hangars. "She sure is a beauty. We get a lot of jets here but not many 650s. Is she yours?"

Mitch laughed. "I wish. She belongs to a very wealthy businessman." He thanked the driver when they reached the office, signed the parking permit, and walked out the front of the small terminal. There was a yellow cab waiting at the curb. He threw his bags in the back and sat in the front passenger seat. He turned to the scruffy-looking driver. "What, no help with the bags? I hope you don't think you're getting a tip, champ."

Mirza gave him a big smile. "Mitch, it's good to see you."

"You too, mate."

Mirza pulled the taxi away from the curb and they drove out of the airport. "How was the sledding?"

"Shorter than expected but still a hell of a ride."

"Sorry about that."

Mitch gave a lop-sided grin. "Not your fault, mate. Tell you what, it's going to be good to get into the field. You, Bishop, and Saneh have been hogging all the fun recently. So, tell me, what's been going on?"

"Did Chua give you an update on Mexico and the phone hack?"

"Yep, I'm pretty much up to speed on everything except the target building."

"It's not going to be easy to infiltrate. I was invited to a meeting there two days ago. They've got twenty-four hour security and the building's thirty-six stories high."

"And the cover you used is blown, right?"

"Yes, I'd assume so."

"I'm guessing the guards are pretty switched on. Not your average bored mall cops?"

"Correct, and they have very tight IT security."

"Yeah, spoke to our man Flash about that. He's pretty

much in love with the guy that tried to ping his bug. Went on about it for at least twenty minutes. Good though, kept me awake on the flight down."

Mirza chuckled. "He's passionate, that's for sure. Look, if you want a nap now, we're at least an hour from the apartment in Manhattan."

He reclined the seat and closed his eyes. "Good idea. Once we get there I'd like to grab a bite to eat and get eyes on the target."

"We can use the cab if you want."

"You borrow it from a cousin?"

Mirza looked embarrassed. "Not all cabbies are Indian, Mitch."

"You did, didn't you!" He laughed. "That's ace. You've got the perfect cover."

***

Wesley Chambers gazed out the window of his office as he sucked the last drops from a bottle of Gatorade. He had a splitting headache, the result of necking back endless shots of Ciroc vodka the night before. Watching the procession of traffic flowing back and forth across the Brooklyn Bridge, he managed a smile. Last night had been fantastic; an associate had introduced him to two Victoria's Secret models and after a few drinks in the club they had reconvened to his boat for fun and games. The girl he'd ended up with was a goddess: tall, gorgeous, and with curves that could kill a man.

A knock at his door interrupted his sordid recollection. "Come in."

He spun around as it opened, expecting to see his pretty secretary, Clarissa, with another bottle of Gatorade. Instead, the shaved head and piercing gaze of Charles King greeted him.

"Working hard I see, Wesley."

The investment banker's eyes narrowed. "What do you want?"

King strode into the room and looked around. He spotted

the framed picture of Nemesis and smiled. "That's a fancy boat. Must be worth a pretty penny."

"More than you'll earn in a lifetime. I'm guessing this isn't a courtesy call. What do you want?"

King lowered his athletic frame onto the plush leather couch in the corner of the office. "I know you think I'm a pain, Wesley, most of you banker types do. All jacked up on your own importance." He folded his hands in his lap. "You bring in millions of dollars of investment, and that makes you super-important and super-powerful."

"Look Charles, I don't have time—"

"Shut the hell up and listen," King snarled.

He shivered involuntarily.

"I get it, people like you are vital to the company. It's the only reason you're still here. But, what you don't understand is in this business, there's a certain need for discretion."

"Cut to the chase. What are you getting at?"

King nodded at the smartphone sitting on Wes's desk. "Your phone, been having problems with it?"

"The piece of crap doesn't work."

"That's because I had it shut down."

"What the hell would you do that for? How the hell are our investors supposed to reach me? How am I supposed to work?"

King rose, walked across, and placed an identical device on the desk.

"I don't want a new phone, Charles. I want this one to fucking work. Get your people to fix it and get it back to me, ASAP."

King reached into his pants pocket. There was a click as his hand flashed. He punched a black knife through the old phone, pinning it to the polished teak desk. "You let that fat Indian prick hack your phone, you jackass. You've compromised our entire Mexican operation because you were off your head on blow."

He wished his office chair would open up and swallow him.

"Clean up your act, Wesley, otherwise you're going to find

out very quickly that Jordan Pollard has no time for you or your antics."

He managed a feeble nod as King pocketed his knife and left the office. He slumped back in his chair and wiped his brow with a handkerchief.

"Excuse me, sir." His secretary held up another bottle of Gatorade.

He beckoned for her to enter. His headache had become a whole lot worse.

***

Mitch paid the hawker and took a hefty bite of the hot dog. Disappointment washed over him as his teeth met and the bland processed meat touched his taste buds.

Mirza chuckled. "I told you. It's all a scam. Only the locals actually know where to get a decent hot dog."

"This tastes like rubber." He dropped the food into a trashcan.

They were on the street opposite the Pulvermach building, where both MVI and GES had offices. Mitch looked in through the window of a diner. "Feel like a hot choc?"

"Sure, why not. You might be able to get something better to eat."

The diner was empty and they took a window table. It offered them a good view of the foyer of their target building. Mitch picked up the menu as he studied the foyer. "You're not wrong, mate. It's going to be a high risk job to get in."

"The only ingress points are the ground floor or the roof. On the ground the CCTV and guards make it next to impossible to get in and out without being detected. The roof has a number of options: air-conditioning vents, fire escape, and a window cleaning gantry."

"You think any are workable?"

"Yes, however, getting onto the roof is a problem. Two options. One, vertical; helicopter or parachute. Two, lateral; rope on from another building. They all come with significant risk."

A waitress came over and asked for their order.

"I'll have the beef burger and a vanilla milkshake, thanks love," said Mitch.

Mirza ordered a hot chocolate. They waited till the waitress had returned to the counter before Mitch continued the conversation.

"So, Flash is positive he can't gain access without us physically getting into the actual server?"

"It's completely isolated. There are no links out. That's why we need to get in and plant a transmitter."

The waitress walked over and delivered Mitch's shake. "Yours will be a few more minutes, darling."

Both men contemplated the problem in silence. Mitch sucked on his straw as he watched the crowds walk past. He noticed a woman talking on her phone as she walked into the building. She nodded to the security guards, swiped her ID, and disappeared. He turned back to Mirza. "I think I've got a solution. Your cousin OK with us borrowing his cab again?"

***

FORT BLISS, TEXAS

Howard adjusted his tie and buffed his shoes on the back of his pants. This was the first time he had ever requested a formal meeting with the JTF director. He'd been working non-stop since speaking to Pershing and the intelligence package under his arm was extremely thorough. It contained false liaison reports, link analysis charts, and fabricated HUMINT from Source 88. If this wouldn't convince Everest, nothing would.

"Terrance, is that you?" the director asked from behind the door.

Howard took a deep breath. "Yes, sir." He tentatively pushed it open.

"Come in, son." Everest gestured to the chair in front of his desk. "I have to admit, this meeting request caught me a little by surprise." He smiled. "A good surprise, that is." He nodded at Howard's tie. "And you're wearing your own clothes too."

He sat and dropped the file on Everest's desk. Damn, he thought, he had not meant for it to seem so casual.

The director's gray eyebrows arched. "What's this?"

He swallowed. "It's an intel pack I've been working on for a while, sir."

Everest picked it up and started flicking through it. "Summary?"

"Sir, it outlines everything we have on an environmental terrorist who has links to an American left-wing journalist. They are planning to attack an American-backed mine just south of the border in Mexico."

If Everest's gray eyebrows were raised before, now they were trying to make contact with his receding hairline. "Really?"

"Yes, sir. We've got reporting that a mercenary known only as Aden is currently in Mexico conducting planning for an attack on the Barrio Del Rancho mine near Chihuahua. This guy's a bad ass, sir. He's professional, low key, and he's got skills. I received an email today from Ground Effects Services, the organization running security at the mine. One of their phones had been bugged by one of Aden's associates."

Everest held up the C4I4 image from Mexico. "This the guy?"

"Yes, sir, I'm calling him Objective Yankee."

Everest chewed his lip and flicked to the next image. "This picture." He stabbed his finger at the grainy picture showing Objective Yankee standing next to a tall blonde operative, both armed to the teeth.

"Yes, sir, in Kiev he was part of an attack on a nightclub owned by an arms dealer. Over twenty people were killed in that incident alone."

"Yes, seems to be a pretty serious threat."

"It is, sir."

"So what's all this about, Howard? I'm guessing you're not

140

here just to show me your good work. What do you need?"

"Sir, I would like to put together a tiger team to work on two projects."

"I'm guessing one of them is to deal with the Objective Yankee threat. What's the other?"

Howard realized he was leaning forward with his hands clenched together. He leaned back and tried to relax. "Confirming the identity of the new Sinaloa boss for Chihuahua. As you know, my source is telling me it's Ramon Ramirez, but we're still not sure. Once confirmed, I want to work up courses of action to engage him."

Howard could see the director's brain was working. The man chewed his lip as he stared into the distance. He pouted as he leaned forward. "Good initiative, Howard. I like it. I'll give you an additional analyst and a signals intelligence guy. You can work out of one of the operations rooms. Need anything else?"

"Yes, sir, I'd like a Predator to provide eyes on the mine at night. We know this guy's moving in for his recon. We might be able to catch him out."

"I'll check with ops. If we've still got hours this month you can have what's left. It's probably a better use for it than dawdling up and down the fence watching refugees hiding in the dunes."

"Excellent, sir, I won't let you down."

Everest's eyes narrowed. "If you do, you're done."

The color drained from Howard's face.

"I'm just messing with you. Get back to work."

Howard loosened his tie and wiped his hands on his pants as he escaped down the corridor. He contemplated ringing Pershing and passing on the good news but decided against it. He would confirm the availability of the Predator first, then head home to get some sleep.

***

CHIHUAHUA

After dinner, Roberto and the brothers, Miguel and Gerardo, lit a fire in a pit behind the cabins. They sat in a circle, watching the flames dance and smoking cheap cigars. Gerardo, the older of the two, had a guitar on his knee and was softly strumming a tune.

Bishop sat on a log at the edge of the group, staring out over the desert. It always amazed him how clear the stars were when you got away from the glare of the city. He zipped up his jacket to ward off the cool night air.

"If you are cold, you should sit closer to the fire," said Roberto as he offered Bishop a cigar.

"I don't smoke, thanks." He dragged his log a little closer to the flames.

"Has Christina already gone to bed?"

"Yes, I think all the excitement wore her out."

Roberto nodded as he puffed on his cigar.

Gerardo started humming as he played, and in a short while added lyrics to the tune. He had a rich baritone voice that filled the night air. Bishop knew enough Spanish to identify it as a love ballad.

He glanced down the hill to where Emilio was sitting by himself on a rocky outcrop. There had been no animosity from the old rancher, even though Bishop felt responsible for the capture of his son, Carlos.

"We chose to fight back," Emilio had said when he tried to apologize. "We all know what's at stake."

Bishop was lost in his thoughts for a moment, then rose from the log. "I'm going to turn in. I'll see you gentlemen in the morning."

"Goodnight, Aden, thanks again for your help," said Roberto.

The two brothers nodded in agreement and he left them at the fire. He pushed the door of the cabin slowly open and crept in.

"Aden, is that you?" Christina mumbled from the bed.

"Yes." He stripped down to his boxers and T-shirt and slid in under the blankets, trying not to disturb her. It was a small double bed and she nuzzled into his neck and swung her arm over his chest. She mumbled something incoherent before her breathing grew shallow and she fell asleep.

He lay there thinking about Carlos, and the predicament the farmers faced. It was obvious without help it was an almost hopeless cause. As he lay there listening to Christina's breathing and evaluating the situation, his eyes grew heavy.

***

NEW YORK CITY

The yellow New York taxicab stopped at the curb in front of the Pulvermach building. "How much longer do you need?" Mirza asked from behind the wheel.

"Just a few more seconds, then we need to go around again," Mitch replied from the back seat. The PRIMAL technician had used suction caps to string lengths of wire around the inside of the cab. They were plugged into a laptop, which he was studying intently.

It was the early hours of the morning and the streets were relatively quiet. New York might not sleep but it certainly slowed a little. The only vehicles on the roads were cabs, street sweepers, and garbage trucks. Mirza watched the traffic as he drummed his fingers on the steering wheel and hummed a tune. He glanced in the mirror and noticed a man in a suit staggering along the road. "Mitch, we've got another one." Two drunken businessmen had already tried to hail them.

"OK, OK, we're good. I just need you to circle the block once more."

Mirza started the cab, indicated, and pulled away from the curb. He drove down the street and turned, circling back around the block. "This is going to have to be the last time. If I drive past again the security guards may notice."

Mitch was still studying the laptop's screen. "Last time, I promise. I've pretty much got everything I need."

"Pretty much? We've been around five times."

"Yep, I've got it all, I've definitely got it this time. Let's go."

Mirza drove slowly along the road behind the office complex. "So how exactly does it work?"

"The antennas pick up all the Wi-Fi, Bluetooth, and cell phone networks operating in the area. When we drive around Flash's software uses triangulation algorithms to locate the source and map it out. Then all I need to do is work out which ones might give us a way of penetrating GE's network."

"And if there isn't one?"

"Then we have to go back to plan B. Parachuting onto the roof and sneaking in. But hey, that sounds like an operator problem not a technical issue."

Mirza grinned. "I thought you were looking forward to getting into the field."

"Parachuting and sneaking in through air vents is not field work." He patted his computer. "This is field work."

"Each to their own." Mirza drove across town toward the apartment they had rented. "So you sure you got everything?"

Mitch hunched over the laptop. "Yeah I think so, old man."

"Old man? Do you even know how old I am, Mitch?"

The geek looked up from his computer. "Just a term of endearment, mate. But now that you mention it, how old are you?"

"Older than you. So you should respect your elders and tell me what you've found."

"Can't argue with that. We've got bugger-all networks and a handful of devices. These guys are running a pretty tight ship. But, there are always kids that don't want to play by the rules. I've found a very faint Bluetooth signal coming from around the twentieth floor. It looks like a tablet device."

"How does that help?" Mirza asked as he turned down their street.

"Well, tablets use a lot of power and the easiest way to charge them is to plug them into a USB port, yeah."

Mirza shook his head. "A company like GE would definitely have locked out their ports."

"That's not a drama. Hacking around a locked-out USB

port is the easy bit. The hard part is going to be getting a Bluetooth transmitter close enough to upload a hack."

"And we're back to parachuting," Mirza said laughing.

"That's not as stupid as it sounds." Mitch closed his laptop. "What time do you think the closest hobby store opens?"

CHAPTER 17

CHIHUAHUA

Bishop tentatively approached his horse, dressed in a pair of jeans, cowboy boots, a plaid shirt, and a battered wide-brim hat. His mount, as he described it, was a dinosaur bred with a donkey and he was struggling to even get into the saddle let alone ride the Clydesdale-cross.

Christina sat astride her palomino watching with a broad smile. Like Bishop, she had borrowed some more appropriate clothing from the owners of the bed and breakfast ranch. "How can someone grow up in Australia and not know how to ride a horse?"

"Hey, I never rode a bloody kangaroo to school either. I grew up near the beach, not on a farm." He slipped his boot into the stirrup, reached up, and grabbed the pommel. With a grunt he hauled himself up.

As he did the horse twisted her neck, bared her teeth and tried to bite him. "Fuck you!" yelled Bishop as he slid his leg over the mare's back and managed to get his foot inside the other stirrup. "Did you see that? She tried to bite me."

Christina laughed. "I'd bite you too if you tried to mount me like that."

"I'd make sure I was wearing spurs."

Roberto was leaning against the fence and shook his head. "Twenty miles in the saddle is going to be rough on you and that horse."

"Tell me about it." Bishop took up the reins and held them like he'd been shown. His horse shook her head in objection. "You sure I can't ride different one?"

"Tinkerbell is the only one who can carry you," said Roberto.

"Come on. It's not like I'm heavier than you."

"True, but I'm not going to ride that one."

"Why not?" asked Bishop.

"Because she's a nasty bitch. Now try walking her around a bit."

Bishop dug his heels in slightly. "You hear that, Tink, everyone thinks you're a bitch." The horse braced herself on all four legs, lifted her tail, and proceeded to deposit the contents of her bowel into the dust. "Sweet mother of God." He tucked his nose into his armpit. "What do they feed this thing, refried beans?"

Christina rode her pony alongside Tinkerbell.

"She smells better than you, Mr. Rarely Showers. Now come on, big girl, let's go for a walk.

Tinkerbell made a snorting noise and followed Christina's mare. Bishop held the reins limply as she lumbered along. "This is more like it. Maybe I can just stay back here all day. The view's much better, hey Tink."

Christina looked back over her shoulder and gave him a smile.

At that moment Bishop realized for the first time in a while he actually felt relaxed. Last night had been one of the first in a long time that was dream free. He smiled, not sure if it was Christina or maybe just the fact he was in the wilderness.

They walked the horses into the desert for half an hour before turning back to the camp. Bishop was feeling more comfortable and Tinkerbell seemed to have accepted him.

Christina maneuvered her horse next to him. "Hey cowboy, how about we try a trot?"

He shook his head vigorously. "Nooo."

She pursed her lips seductively, slowed, and used her reins to slap Tinkerbell on the rump. "Come on!" she yelled urging them both into a fast trot.

Tinkerbell lifted her head and sprang forward as Bishop clung to the saddle's horn. His heart pounded as she broke into the equine equivalent of a jog. It was not anywhere near as bad as he was expecting. She seemed to glide over the ground effortlessly.

Christina laughed. "See, it's not hard."

They brought the horses back to a walk and returned to the ranch. As they passed through the gates Bishop noticed a dust trail as someone drove away in a pickup. Roberto and Emilio were leaning on a rail watching the truck disappear into the distance.

"Something's up," Bishop said as he directed Tinkerbell to the stables.

Christina jumped off her horse and took Tinkerbell's reins. "I'll take care of these two. You go see what's going on."

As Bishop walked to the two men, Roberto left Emilio and pulled him aside. When they were out of earshot he spoke. "They found Carlos."

"Where?"

"On the road to the mine. They dragged him behind a truck for miles. The only reason they knew it was him was because they found his boots."

Bishop felt as if someone had reached into his chest and torn out his heart. The weight that had lifted from his shoulders was back, with a vengeance. "God, I'm so sorry, Roberto."

"It's not your fault. This is a war and in war there will always be casualties."

He looked over at the wizened old rancher leaning against the rail. "Is Emilio alright?"

Roberto shook his head. "No, but it is to be expected. A man is not supposed to outlive his son. These people are brutal, Aden."

"They're animals."

Roberto handed him a battered .38 revolver. "When we go on the ride you should take this. I will take my shotgun."

"You don't have any ammunition for the AK?" The rancher shook his head.

Bishop checked that the cylinder of the heavy revolver was loaded. He felt naked without the body armor and assault rifle he usually carried on a PRIMAL mission. All they had was the pistol, shotgun, and Christina's Canon 5D camera. He shoved the revolver into his pants and walked slowly across to where

Emilio was staring into the desert.

"I'm sorry for your loss." He grasped the rail with both hands. "Your son was brave. He stood and fought when others fled."

Emilio turned to him, tears running down the creases of his weathered face. "You're a warrior, Aden. Why do you fight?"

"For justice."

"Then help me find justice for my son and for the families that have lost everything."

Bishop put his hand on the man's shoulder as he fought back his own tears. "I will."

***

FORT BLISS, TEXAS

Howard was the first to arrive at the operations room Everest had allocated to him. It came with all the computers, screens, and comms equipment a support team needed to run a field operation. They would not be directing operatives, but the gear would allow them to communicate with the crew of the Predator drone. The room also had a refrigerator he had stacked with cans of sugar-free energy drink. He was not counting on getting much sleep in the next few days and Everest's comment regarding sugar had struck a chord.

He sat at his new desk, put down his Starbucks Grande latte, and brushed the creases from his new chinos. Logging into the system, he projected his computer onto one of the screens on the wall. Then he opened the in-briefing he had prepared for his two new analysts.

This was the first time in his career he was going to be responsible for subordinates. He was feeling a little edgy. The knock on the door startled him and he almost tipped over his coffee.

Both his team members were waiting outside. He invited them in and they introduced themselves. Shelly, the all-source analyst, was a homely, middle-aged blonde who wore her hair in a pigtail. Ben, his signals analyst, was skinny, and in his mid-twenties.

It only took Howard five minutes to deliver the in-briefing before concluding. "Guys, in addition to this intel, we recently found out our target in Mexico is using the name Aden."

"So Objective Yankee's name is Aden?" Ben asked.

"Correct, however it may be a cover name."

Shelly sat at her desk and pointed at the big screen on the wall. "Howard, can you go back to his image, the one from Kiev."

"Sure."

The grainy image of Bishop and Kurtz standing side by side appeared. Both men were clad in black and heavily armed.

"That's the one. I was thinking, maybe we can track him down through the other guy. The shot of his face is a little better. If I had to guess, I'd say he's of Nordic stock, maybe Scandinavian."

"I ran him through the database but it didn't get a hit," said Howard.

"We should send out a Request for Information to our European partners. It might take a while but it will definitely broaden the network," she said.

"Good idea. Can you take care of that?"

Shelly smiled at him. "Sure thing, boss."

Howard sat a little taller in his chair. 'Boss', he could get used to that. He clicked to another image; a slide showing a timeline covering the next three days. "Guys, this is our allocation of Predator hours." He used his mouse cursor to point out red sections of the time scale. "We've got three blocks of six hours. They'll all be flown from around 2100 to 0300 hours in the morning." He advanced the slide deck to a map of the area around the mine. "We need to submit the areas that we want it to focus on, ASAP."

Ben stood and pointed to the rugged mountainous terrain to the east of the mine. "If I was going to approach this I'd infiltrate through here. Vehicles would be useless in that terrain so there's not much chance the guys from the mine will patrol it. If Objective Yankee is ex-military, he's going to know that."

Howard used his mouse to draw a box over the area. He'd read Ben's file, the skinny geek was also a National Guardsman who had completed two tours of Afghanistan. He knew what he was talking about. "You do up the Predator pack, Ben. Make it a priority."

"Roger. Also, is there a chance I can get the details of the hack the security guys found on their phone? If I can get it over to the NSA they might be able to pull the software apart and find out who programmed it. Might give us a better idea of who we're dealing with."

"I'll see what I can do. When you get time, I also want both of you to take a look at the Sinaloa cartel comms traffic and see if there's anything that might relate to the threat to the mine."

"You think they might be behind this?" asked Shelly.

Howard nodded. "Possibly. Whoever has hired Yankee is going to need some serious cash and, tell me if I'm wrong Ben, but the type of hacking we're talking about isn't cheap either."

"Yeah, it ain't cheap. Not when programmers are charging a grand an hour to build it. You're looking at least fifty or sixty hours to build something simple."

"Good to know."

"Have they identified how the hack got into their system?" Ben continued.

"Not yet. But as soon as they do, they're going to let us know. Now if you guys have got enough to get started, I'm going to get some fresh air." Howard gulped the last of his coffee, grabbed a can from the fridge, and swiped his way out of the room. He walked down the corridor, retrieved his phone from the storage cubicles, and headed outside.

The director caught him at the door. "How's it going, Terrance? You got everything you need?"

Howard gave him a broad smile. "Sure do, boss. The team's hard at work. I'm just going to grab a few minutes of fresh air." He felt Everest's hawk-like gaze pass over him. It lingered on the zero-sugar energy drink.

"OK then. I might drop by later on." He turned and

wandered back to his office.

Howard took a deep breath as soon as he was outside. He was never one for the outdoors but the fresh morning air seemed to be particularly invigorating today. He lit a cigarette, popped the can of energy drink, and placed it on the outdoor table. Then he fished out his phone and dialed Pershing's number. Source 88 was going to be a very happy man.

CHAPTER 18

CHIHUAHUA

They left the ranch just before dusk. Roberto on a muscular quarter horse called Tucson, Christina on the palomino, and Bishop on Tinkerbell, the flatulent brewery horse. For the first few hours Bishop enjoyed the ride. The sunset highlighted the barren landscape in shades of red as they rode across a hard-baked plain of stunted shrubs down into a shallow canyon.

By the time the sun disappeared his legs were in agony. Not just the muscles, but also the hair on the inside of his thighs. The constant friction between his jeans and the saddle felt like it had wrenched out every single one from its follicle. Between that and the constant eruptions of gas coming from Tinkerbell's rear, the novelty of the horse ride had well and truly worn off.

As the temperature dropped, they stopped to pull on jackets and rest the horses. Bishop dismounted with a sigh of relief, and walked bow-legged, trying to shake the fatigue from his legs.

"How you doing?" Christina asked.

He was trying to stretch out his calves. "I'm a bit stiff but doing OK."

"Thanks again for agreeing to come."

"I wasn't about to let you go alone, and I owe it to Emilio. After what they did to his son, I–"

Roberto interrupted them with a low whistle. "Hey, let's get going."

"Just a minute," Christina said as she adjusted her saddle.

When she was ready, they set off along the creek, twisting their way up the valley floor.

He was surprised at how much light there was in the desert. A sliver of moon shone down from the cloudless sky bathing everything in a soft metallic glow.

They plodded along the creek for a few more hours, Tinkerbell with her nose closely following Christina's horse's rear end. Long ago her ears had laid back against her skull as she decided that lugging Bishop's two hundred pounds through the desert was a drag.

She jerked her head up as Christina reined in her horse. In the moonlight Bishop saw Roberto had dismounted. He did the same, swinging out of the saddle, dropping to the sand. He groaned and stretched his legs. There was water flowing along a rocky creek a few yards away. Bishop reached into his pocket and pulled out a molasses candy. He had taken a handful of them from the barn. He put it on the palm of his hand and offered it to his mount.

Tinkerbell's ears shot forward as she caught a whiff of the candy. Her whiskers tickled his palm as she snuffled it up and chewed. She whinnied softly and nudged his hand with her nose. "Yeah, I've got you figured out, haven't I?"

He gave the horse a pat and led her to join the others. Roberto nodded at the bank. "This is called Digger's Canyon. There's an old gold mine up there." He pointed to the hill that rose into the night sky. "It's at least a hundred years old but you can still go inside."

"There's lots of gold in the hills?" Bishop asked.

Roberto shook his head. "No, it's all mined out. Now you have to take all the dirt and put it through machines, whole mountains smashed to pieces. Soon you will see."

He felt a tug on the reins and turned to find Tinkerbell trying to walk to the creek. Roberto grabbed his shoulder. "Don't let her drink here, it's poison."

"What?" Bishop handed the reins to the rancher and went down to the water's edge. He switched on the light on his iPRIMAL and could see the edges of the flowing creek were caked in a thick orange froth.

"That's terrible," said Christina as she crouched next to him and pulled out her camera. "Do you think it's safe for me to use my flash here?" she asked.

"Should be fine." He switched off his phone to conserve

the battery as she took a photo of the waste.

Bishop took his reins from Roberto. "How far down does it go?"

"All the way from monstrou down to the main river. There it's not so noticeable because there's more water. Come, we still have another hour to go before we reach the mine."

Bishop gave Tinkerbell another treat before climbing onto her back. The horse's ears were up and she sniffed the air inquisitively. He wondered if she smelled the pollution in the water.

Over the next hour they climbed out of the canyon and trotted along a plain at the base of the mountain. As they rode through rocky outcrops he noticed a glow emanating from behind the mountain range. He realized it must be the lights from the mine running twenty-four hour operations.

Roberto halted them at a creek junction and the base of the mountain. He pointed at the ridgeline silhouetted by the glow from the mine. "We go by foot from here." He jumped off his horse and led it to the water, letting it drink. "This creek is fed from a spring. It's clean, for now."

Bishop and Christina waited for his horse to drink its fill then took their turn. When all three horses were watered they tied them to an old gnarled tree. As Bishop looped Tinkerbell's reins onto the line the rancher had tied, she nudged him in the back and whinnied. He turned and scratched her forehead. "Typical woman, now you can't live without me." He gave her another treat and followed the others up the steep slope.

"This all used to be part of Emilio's farm," said the rancher as they climbed toward the mine's glow. "But now monstruo eats it all."

It took them over forty minutes to reach the crest. They heard the rumble of heavy machinery as they halted a few feet from the top.

"Make sure your flash is off," said Bishop.

Christina nodded and checked the camera, taking a few shots to check the settings.

"Stay behind us," he said as he followed Roberto to the

mine's edge. A few yards from the lip the rancher unslung his shotgun, dropped to his stomach, and snaked forward.

Bishop followed and was shocked at the scale of the operation as it came into view. Massive front-end loaders were lifting loads of rubble and loading gargantuan dump trucks. They rumbled across the mine pit like wheeled dinosaurs, shifting thousands of tons of earth.

Bishop waved for Christina to join them. Powerful floodlights illuminated the entire site and would make for good photos. Not only for Christina's article, but he would be able to send copies back to the Bunker for vulnerability assessment.

"It's huge," Christina whispered when she was next to him.

He replied in a normal tone. "It's OK, they're not going to hear us."

Christina snapped photos as Bishop studied the layout of the mine. There was no way Roberto and his men would be able to decisively sabotage the pit operation. With rocket launchers or explosives they might damage some of the gigantic trucks or loaders, but those could be repaired or replaced.

Roberto tapped him on the shoulder. "Guards."

The old-timer had a good eye. Bishop barely made out the weapons of the men standing next to a dune buggy. They all wore black jackets. "Chaquetas."

Bishop waited for Christina to finish photographing. "Roberto, is there a place where we can see the mine's camp?"

"We can follow the hill around."

"Let's check it out."

They scrambled back down the side of the hill and traversed the rocky slope. It gradually eased off after a few hundred yards. Bishop moved into the lead, pushing ahead to scout the way.

He crouched in the cover of an outcrop and scanned the camp below. A road ran through the center and on the near side was an accommodation and offices complex made from transportable buildings. On the other side was the mining infrastructure: a crushing plant, fuel depot, refinery, secure storage sheds for the unrefined gold, and huge water tanks, filled the level space.

Patrolling the perimeter were pairs of armed Chaquetas and Bishop's first thought was to switch on his iPRIMAL, call in an airstrike, and level the entire complex. However, there were no assets available, and Vance and Chua would never authorize that option..He watched as two more of the high-speed buggies rolled out from a shed. He was starting to feel uneasy at the amount of security. This number of guards, late at night, was overkill, unless they suspected an imminent threat.

A crunching of rock behind caught his attention and he turned to see Christina. "Where's Roberto?" he whispered.

She pointed further along the ridgeline. "Over there."

Bishop kept an eye on the two buggies. As they followed the track away from the mine, only their lights were visible, but it looked as if they were conducting a clearing patrol around the boundary fence.

Christina snapped a series of photos. Shielding the screen, she checked the exposure settings.

"How did they turn out?"

"Not great. We really need to come back during the day."

"No way, have you seen how many men are down there?"

The sound of the buggies was getting louder.

Roberto's gravelly voice sounded from behind them. "We need to get a move on."

Christina packed her camera away and all three pulled back from the ridge.

"If you're going to hit these guys, night time's the way to go," Bishop said as they scrambled down the rocky slope. "They've got no night-vision goggles or ground sensors. You could sneak in, sabotage, and get out."

"That's what I was thinking too," replied the rancher.

It took them twenty minutes to walk back down to where they'd left the horses. Tinkerbell greeted Bishop with a friendly neigh and he fed her his last molasses candy. They saddled up and Roberto led them back through the desert toward the canyon.

Bringing up the rear Bishop thought he heard something. He cocked his head and listened. Behind the squeak of leather and soft thud of Tinkerbell's hooves there was the faint drone of an engine. It was probably just the machinery at the mine.

CHAPTER 19

NEW YORK CITY

The cab was parked in a back alley with Mirza at the wheel. Once again, they had chosen to work in the early hours of the morning. There was less traffic on the road, it was dark, and the cab was one of hundreds prowling the streets.

He watched Mitch in the rear vision mirror. "You really think this is going to work?"

Mitch was holding what looked like a miniature flying saucer. The four-bladed multi-rotor had been purchased from a hobby store. He'd assembled it, made some modifications, and was now ready to soar between the Manhattan skyscrapers.

"Of course it's going to work. When has anything I've made ever not worked?"

"Well, there was that time in Libya…"

"That doesn't count. Bishop broke it before I even had a chance to get it off the ground." Mitch shook his head. "That guy's bloody lethal."

Mirza touched the screen of his iPRIMAL and checked Bishop's status. "He might be lethal but at the moment he's in the middle of nowhere with no support. We should be down in Mexico with him." The command and control app automatically updated Bishop's location via the iPRIMAL's GPS chip.

"We need to sort this hacking business first." Mitch made the final adjustments to the drone. "So you all good with your part?"

"Yes, I watch the tablet. Find the right Bluetooth device."

"Which is?"

Mirza picked up the tablet. A piece of tape was stuck to the bottom of it with the Bluetooth device's name. "Clarissa's Fab iPad."

Mitch gave a wry smile and shook his head. "I don't ever

want to meet Clarissa. I guarantee she's watched every episode of Sex in the City ten times. OK, what then?"

"Then I connect to it, and it will upload a patch."

"Correct, the key is we need to stay in range of the Bluetooth until the upload is complete. Once we do that, Flash will be able to use the iPad to access GE's network."

"When it's plugged into an isolated USB port."

"That's correct. Don't ask me how he can do it. I just build the toys, he writes the code. You ready?"

"Are you?"

"Born ready. If I can pilot a tilt-rotor I can pilot this thing." He opened the door of the cab, reached up, and placed the pizza-box sized drone on the roof. Once he was back in the cab he donned a pair of oversized goggles.

"You look like you're going scuba diving."

"Just drive."

Mirza smirked as he drove out the alley and parked the cab in a loading zone next to the target building. "We're in position."

Mitch was now seeing the world through the drone's camera. In his hands he held the radio controller for the device. He had a lot of experience with piloting full-size aircraft but never a hobby-sized copter. He thumbed the stick that controlled the power input to the four engines. "OK, I'm sending her up."

On top of the cab the little drone buzzed like an angry hornet and leaped off the roof, shooting into the air.

"Whoa, slow down, little lady." He slowed the ascent, rotating the copter till it faced the building. "OK, we're about five stories up. How we tracking?"

"No Bluetooth networks yet."

"OK." Mitch increased the throttle and it started climbing. It bucked wildly and darted forward. Through his goggles the building loomed. He pulled back on the stick, tipping the nose up. Now he was looking at the skyline. "Shit!" He dropped the nose and throttled back slightly.

The little aircraft came within inches of the glass building then dropped. Mitch managed to recover it by giving it more throttle. He decided it was better to play it safe and stuck to the middle of the alleyway. The quadcopter rocketed skyward climbing another ten stories in seconds. "How are we going now?"

Mirza was watching the screen intently. "Not seeing it."

Mitch gave it more power, climbing another half dozen stories.

"Got it. No, wait. No, it's gone."

Mitch brought the drone to a hover and held it in position. "Did we fly past?"

"Yep. It was there for a split second. Really weak signal, but it was there."

"OK, I'm lowering." He edged the stick back and the craft slowly descended.

"That's it, got it." Mirza stabbed the tablet with his finger. "Activating now." He watched as the Bluetooth transmitter on the drone tried to connect. "It's not connecting."

Mitch had plenty of experience flying helicopters between building and canyon walls. He knew how hard it was to fight the updrafts and cross winds in an aircraft that weighed over a ton. With a two-pound toy it was almost impossible. He inched close to the glass as the drone was buffeted by the wind.

"OK, nearly got it."

Through the tiny camera Mitch saw the glass wall was only inches away. The slightest touch would tear off a blade and send the copter spiraling down to the street.

"It's uploading," Mirza announced as the Bluetooth connection initiated and Flash's program automatically started transferring the data.

Mitch sighed. He finally felt like he had the feel of the little drone. A red indicator flashed in the corner of his goggle's virtual reality display. "Ah shit, bollocks."

"What? We're over half way."

"I'm almost out of power." The quadcopter had an automatic landing system once batteries reached a critical point. Mitch had disarmed it.

"Nearly there."

The PRIMAL technician knew once the red light was on he had no more than twenty seconds of power left.

High above them the little craft dropped a few feet.

"She's coming down." Mitch had the throttle stick pushed all the way forward. He turned off the camera to save power and tore off his goggles. Opening the car door, he peered up.

After a few seconds he spotted it, tumbling out of the sky. He ducked back into the cab as it thumped onto the asphalt. He jumped out, grabbed it, and dived back in. "Did it work?"

Mirza held up the tablet.

UPLOAD COMPLETE

***

FORT BLISS, TEXAS

Howard opened the email as soon as it hit his inbox. He had been waiting for the initial damage assessment from the IT security manager at Ground Effects Services. The report was brief and failed to mention any of the potentially incriminating activity the company had been involved in. But it did contain a picture of the man GES thought had installed the bug on one of their phones. Howard sighed. The perp was an overweight Indian and his face had been caught on a low-resolution security camera. He emailed the photo to Shelly and Ben. "Team, I've got a photo of another player. The guy who put the bug in the phone."

"Any details?" asked Shelly from her desk.

"I'll send you the report. He was using some bullshit cover story so it's probably no use."

"OK, I'll run it through the system anyway," she replied. The middle-aged analyst had spent the entire day trying to find something on Objective Yankee. As yet they'd been unable to identify him, or his tall blonde-haired associate who they were now calling Objective Red Sox. "Wow, Terry, this image is worse than the others."

"Yeah, I'm sorry, but it's all we've got." Howard rubbed his eyes and contemplated downing another can of energy drink. He checked his watch, the Predator was due online any minute. It would be in the air for three hours. After that they'd be able to get some rest. "Ben, how's our bird tracking?"

"Just came on-station."

One of the screens on the wall flickered and the imagery from the aircraft's powerful infrared sensor appeared. The terrain looked like something you'd expect to see from a Mars space probe. The ground was rugged and undulating with sporadic patches of dried grass and shrubs.

"They're going to start close to the mine and work their way out. That OK?" Ben was typing in a chat window to the crew of the aircraft.

"Sounds good. Let me know if they find anything."

"Boss, they want to know if they're looking for anything in particular."

Howard shrugged. "Tell them to keep an eye out for anything suspicious. You know, people, vehicles, that sort of thing. He watched the screen as the camera skirted the mine. The floodlights washed out the sensor, filling the screen with white so the operator slewed it further south.

"OK, they're holding at ten thousand feet," said Ben.

Howard returned his attention to the document he was reading on the Sinaloa cartel. Although he'd fabricated the links to Aden, it was actually possible there was some truth to it. The Sinaloa cartel was the biggest in the area and technically the Black Jackets were encroaching on their territory. However, Pershing had approached the Sinaloa and they'd shown little interest in working with the mine. As long as the Black Jackets were not impacting on their drug market, the Sinaloa was happy to keep them at arm's length. Despite what the media reported, the cartels actually preferred to avoid conflict. It was bad for business and attracted the attention of the authorities.

"Terry, we've got something," said Ben pointing excitedly at the screen. "Three people riding away from the mine on horseback."

Howard looked up with a jolt. He hadn't expected to pick up anything interesting, particularly on their first night of dedicated Predator support. Sure enough, there were three white-hot blobs on the gray background. As the camera zoomed in he easily identified them as people on horseback.

"That might be our man moving back from a recon," said Ben.

"Tell the Pred to stay on them." Howard pulled out his cell phone and held it under his desk. With the amount of contact Pershing was demanding he couldn't leave it outside the secure area. He sent a text to the GES contractor passing him the frequency for the aircraft's video transmission and a brief description of what they'd found.

A moment later the phone vibrated as a return message arrived.

Keep tracking them

***

CHIHUAHUA

Pershing was in his office when he received the text message. He'd been studying a map of the area and planning how he was going to push the last of the farmers off their land. When his phone had buzzed he thumbed a response, grabbed his hat and gun belt, and walked over to the equipment shelter. He found two of the Black Jackets leaning against a bench, one smoking a cigarette.

"Hey, pal, what have I told you about smoking in here?" The man stared blankly.

"Stub it out and find me Burro," Pershing snarled. He swore that most of these men had the intellectual capacity of a donkey. Grabbing hold of the roll-cage of one of the dune buggies, he slid into the passenger seat. He powered up the ROVER screen and inputted the frequency for the Predator drone. It took a few seconds before the full-motion video image appeared on the screen. Sure enough, there were three people on horseback riding away from the mine.

"You wanted me, Mr. Pershing?" said Burro.

Pershing gestured to the driver's seat of the buggy. "Get in, son." He adjusted the ROVER's screen so it displayed a map as well as a smaller view of what the camera was seeing.

Burro slid into the driver's seat. Pershing pointed at the map. "We've got some guests heading toward the old gold mine. I want you to take a couple of buggies out there and bring them in. Think you can handle that?"

Burro jabbed his finger at the screen. "We can use the old farm track and cut them off before the canyon."

At least this one had half a brain, he thought as he hauled himself out of the buggy.

Burro was already issuing orders before Pershing left the shed. As he crossed the road, V8 engines burbled to life. He watched as the off-road vehicles roared out of camp, heading toward the front gate and security post. He was about to return to his office when he changed his mind and walked across to his Chevy. Lifting the trunk, he turned on the espresso machine. It was a little late for caffeine but he had an inkling he was not going to be sleeping anytime soon.

CHAPTER 20

CHIHUAHUA

The effect of the molasses candy must have worn off because Tinkerbell was back to her usual miserable self. Her ears were laid back and she had resumed her position directly behind Christina's horse. Bishop yawned, he was happy with that as it didn't require any effort on his behalf.

In his mind he was trying to think through the options for supporting the ranchers in their fight against the mine. While the cartel thugs were protecting it, there was no way they could target it directly. They needed to neutralize the Black Jackets. Otherwise, PRIMAL would only be able to target the parent companies and that was unlikely to give the farmers the justice they deserved.

Tinkerbell's ears swiveled forward and she turned her head back. "I'm sorry, girl, this sugar daddy is all out of candy." She stopped walking and arched her head to look behind them.

He tugged on the reins. "Come on, Tink, we need to get home."

She refused to continue and Bishop was about to give her a kick when he heard the noise. He immediately recognized the engines of the dune buggies. "Go! They're coming!"

Roberto and Christina didn't need to be told twice. Their horses leaped forward and galloped. Tinkerbell still refused to budge.

"Come on, girl." He dug his heels in. Tinkerbell whinnied and broke into a canter. Ahead, he focused on a cluster of hills growing in size; the start of the canyon. Roberto and Christina's horses were barely visible in the gloom as they disappeared into the canyon.

The roar of V8 engines grew louder, echoing off the mountain walls. He glanced back. The buggies' headlights bounced across the desert, less than a hundred yards away.

In an instant, Tinkerbell went from a canter to a gallop. It was as if the ghosts of her forefathers, the war horses that carried knights into battle, were urging her on. Her hooves flashed as she thundered toward the canyon. Bishop clung to the saddle as the powerful animal unleashed her inner beast. He managed to glance back again. As unbelievable as it was, they were drawing away from the buggies.

The horse was breathing heavily when they hit the lip of the canyon but it didn't slow her. She thundered down to the channel the elements had carved into the valley floor, slowing only when she weaved between rocky walls and pillars of earth.

Headlights flashed and an exhaust echoed as one of the buggies dropped into the canyon. At that moment, Tinkerbell stumbled in a tight set of turns. Bishop was sent sailing through the air.

He slammed against a dusty bank, skidding along stones and dirt. It took him a few seconds to gather himself. By the time he staggered to his feet, Tinkerbell was disappearing into the darkness. He heard the buggy; it had slowed to maneuver through the tight terrain. His mind raced. With one buggy in the canyon, the other was free to race across the plain and cut them off. Christina and Roberto would never be able to outrun it. He only had one option.

He scrambled up the side of the shallow canyon, grabbing roots and fistfuls of grass as handholds. As he reached the top, he saw the buggy slide around the corner. "Here goes nothing." He sprinted across a narrow outcrop and leaped off a pillar of rock.

He hit the top of the buggy hard, slamming into the spare tire. The vehicle accelerated and he barely managed to cling to a nylon tie-down strap. The driver jerked the steering wheel side to side, trying to throw him clear. When that failed, he slowed.

Bishop was ready when the cartel thug running shotgun stuck a pistol and his head over the side of the roof. He smashed the man in the face with the heel of his boot, knocking him back down. The pistol went off, blowing a hole in the tire between his legs. The heavy-duty rubber started deflating with a hiss, leaving Bishop clinging to a loose strap.

He switched his attention to the driver. He hooked his legs into the strap, leaned down over the side, and grabbed the driver by the throat.

In hindsight, it wasn't the best move. The driver reacted by taking his hands off the wheel and grabbing Bishop's arm. At the same time he panicked and stomped on the brake.

The buggy skidded as it hit soft sand. With all four wheels locked it dug in and tipped on its side, catapulting Bishop through the air. Not again, he thought as he slammed into the ground. The buggy slid on its side, coming to a halt in the dust.

Bishop hauled himself off the ground. His shoulder ached but nothing seemed to be broken. He moved cautiously around the tipped over buggy, his .38 revolver in his hand. There was no sign of moment from the co-driver. He soon realized why; the man was crushed under the buggy, his neck at an unnatural angle. The driver was dazed and moaning but still alive.

He reached up and grabbed the side of the vehicle. It teetered on its side and he hung his weight off it. Sure enough it rocked toward him. He jumped back as it dropped onto its wheels with a thud.

Bishop checked the driver for weapons, unbuckled his safety harness, and dragged him clear of the wreck. He tore off the man's combat vest, found a pair of flexicuffs, and secured his hands with them. The dead co-driver also wore a chest rig and Bishop put it on. Now he had two AKs, a bunch of magazines, and three grenades. He threw the weapons and gear in the passenger foot well.

He climbed into the buggy and punched the starter button. As the engine coughed to life a screen attached to the dash flashed and lit up. He immediately recognized the ROVER tablet and knew this must have been how they'd been compromised. "Fuck!" he swore punching the dash. Now he was in the middle of nowhere, with no support, and a bloody drone overhead. The buggy's radio crackled and someone spoke in Spanish.

Bishop picked up the mike from where it dangled. He wondered if he should give them something to think about. It might force them to abandon the hunt and try to rescue their comrades. He thumbed the transmit button. "Hey fucktard, if you're looking for ball-bag and ass-wipe, you're shit out of luck. Cos they be dead motherfuckers."

The voice that replied was heavily accented. "You better hurry, mister Aden, because I'm going to kill your friends."

Bishop switched on the headlights and lit up the rock walls as he spun the wheel. As he raced out of the canyon and back up to the desert plain, he kept one eye on the ROVER screen. When it finally connected it showed two horses working their way along the twisting canyon. He eased off the accelerator as the buggy cleared the canyon and bounced into the desert. Spinning the wheel frantically, he searched for the tracks of the other vehicle. He found them and stomped on the accelerator, chasing the tracks that followed the side of the canyon.

A knocking sound from the back of the buggy was getting louder. The temperature gauge on the dash tipped into the red. "Shit!" Bishop hoped the engine had enough life left to catch the other buggy. He glanced across at the ROVER. The drone was still following Roberto and Christina. He estimated they were about five hundred yards ahead.

The knocking coming from the engine sounded like something was trying to escape from inside. Bishop backed off the accelerator, hoping to buy a few more minutes. A loud bang followed by intense hissing confirmed his worst fear, and the buggy shuddered to a halt. He checked the video feed. The other buggy had found a way into the canyon and cut off the riders. He squinted into the darkness and spotted a flash of headlights against the rocky hillside.

He looked down at the ROVER. The device was a ruggedized tablet, battery-powered with a power cable connected to the buggy. He tore the tablet from its cradle, ripping out the cables. Then he vaulted out of the buggy and grabbed an AK from the passenger's side.

Running as fast as he could, he stumbled as his eyes

struggled to adjust to the darkness. As he ran he stuffed the ROVER screen behind his stolen chest rig.

The boom of a shotgun echoed in the cold night air, followed by the bark of a rifle. Bishop slowed, walking steadily toward the gunshots, his AK held ready. As he reached the edge of the canyon the other buggy came into view, about a hundred yards away. In the glow of its headlights he spotted two figures loading a body into it. He raised the rifle. The vehicle took off in a cloud of dust and he resisted the urge to fire a burst and risk hitting the captive.

A moment later the buggy's taillights disappeared in the dust and he was left in the dark. Resisting the urge to scream out in rage, he slid down into the canyon and walked to where the buggy had been. He pulled out the ROVER and checked the screen. The drone was still above. The video feed was now centered on him.

Using the tactical light on his stolen AK, he looked around for a sign of anyone else. Nothing. He scanned the ground, hoping to find horse tracks or footprints. As he searched a strange sound penetrated the darkness. He jogged toward it and found Roberto's horse.

The quarter horse had been shot through the chest. His eyes were wide with fear and bloody red froth bubbled from his nose.

"Jesus Christ." He cocked the AK.

The horse tried to struggle to its feet as he approached. "Hey, steady boy," he said quietly, trying to reassure the animal as he raised the rifle.

As the single shot echoed off the canyon walls he heard a clatter of rocks from further along the canyon. He stalked silently in the darkness before reaching the creek. Thirty feet away he spotted the outline of Christina's palomino. The saddle was empty. He walked to the horse and grasped her reins. She nickered and nuzzled his shoulder. "Where is she, girl?"

There was a noise a little further downstream. "Christina, is that you?"

She appeared from behind a boulder and ran to him.

"Aden, thank God!"

He slung his weapon and she hugged him.

She sobbed into his chest. "They took Roberto."

He held her tight. "I know, and if we don't get moving they'll get us too. They've got a drone overhead; the only place we can hide is the old gold mine."

***

Pershing was leaning against the Chevy when he heard the buggy in the distance. The powerful headlights flashed at the bottom of the road to the mine and it screamed up the track toward him. He put one hand over the top of his coffee cup to keep out the dust as the buggy skidded to a halt. Burro jumped out, ran around to the other side, and reached into the space behind the seats. His co-driver joined him and together they pulled out a body.

Pershing sipped from his cup has he inspected the battered rancher who lay on the ground grimacing in pain. "Ah, Mr. Roberto Soto, I've been looking forward to having a chat with you." He nodded at Burro. "Where are the others?"

Burro shrugged. "That Aden bastard killed them."

"Not your minions, you damn retard. The other riders. Don't tell me that son-of-a-bitch is still out there." He placed his coffee cup on the tailgate of the truck and pushed back his jacket to expose the pearl-handled pistol in its intricate leather holster.

Burro swallowed, carefully considering his next words. "You're still following them with the drone. We just need more men."

He fixed him with an icy stare. "Well, how about you get it done then."

Burro nodded, and ran to the accommodation block.

Pershing placed his cup back in his Chevy before squatting down next to Roberto. He smiled. "I apologize for his behavior. Good help is kind of hard to find in these parts." He winked. "But you'd know all about that, wouldn't you?" He stood and opened the door to his office. "I'd be much obliged if you joined me inside."

Burro's co-driver jabbed Roberto with the barrel of his AK and nodded at the door. Pershing closed it behind the rancher and pointed to the metal folding chair in front of his desk.

Roberto watched warily as his captor circled around and sat behind his desk. "So, Mr. Soto. Can I offer you a drink of water?"

Roberto shook his head.

"Do you mind if I call you Roberto?"

There was no answer. Pershing had no doubt this was a hard man. He had dealt with idealists before: jihadists, communists, and fascists. They all crumbled when he started cutting off fingers. But men of the land, farmers and ranchers, they could be different. They toiled from dusk to dawn, and were used to physical pain. He knew with men like this you needed to use the full gambit of psychological tools in an interrogator's arsenal.

Pershing took off his hat and put it on the desk. "OK, Roberto, I'm guessing you had a chance to have a good look around. It's an impressive facility, wouldn't you say? I've got a platoon of cartel gunmen here and the full support of the authorities. This mine is here to stay, and any resistance is futile."

The rancher's cold gray eyes seemed to bore a hole straight through his head.

"If you're not going to talk, then this is going to be hard on you. Not just you, but your family too."

At the mention of his family the rancher's leathery lips thinned. Pershing thought he was about to speak.

A knock at the door interrupted them.

Pershing grabbed his hat. "If you'll excuse me, sir, business is calling." He opened the door.

"The men are ready, boss," Burro said. Behind him three pickups of armed Black Jackets were waiting.

"Good. Lock this sorry son-of-a-bitch in one of the spare offices and post a guard. Make sure he has water, food, and a bucket to shit in."

Burro turned and snapped out orders to two of his men. They looked disappointed as they jumped down from a truck. They would miss out on the hunt.

"OK, let's get this show on the road!"

CHAPTER 21

Bishop looked at the stars as he caught his breath. He knew it was futile to try and spot the drone. What they needed to do was hide from the aircraft's sensors, and the only way to do that here was to get underground.

They had reached the sandy area with the poisoned creek, Bishop running alongside as Christina rode her horse down the canyon. He fished his iPRIMAL from his pocket; hoping it had enough battery power to activate the emergency beacon. "Damn." The screen was cracked, he must have landed on it during a fall. He powered it up but the screen glowed blank.

He switched the device off and pointed at the hill to where Roberto had showed them the old gold mine. "We can't take your horse up there with us."

"What about the drone? She might lead them back to the farm," said Christina as she dismounted.

Bishop knew the safest option was to shoot the horse. But he couldn't bring himself to do it. "The drone will stay on us." He hung the horse's reins over the saddle and slapped her on the rump. "Go on, go!" he yelled clapping his hands. The beautiful Palamino took off down the canyon at a gallop. "Good luck, girl."

As they climbed the hill the rumble of engines grew louder. "That didn't take them long." He grabbed Christina by the hand and hauled her up the slope. "We need to move!"

He pulled out the ROVER and activated the screen. The drone was still fixed on them. He zoomed out and identified the old mine location. It was only a few hundred yards away. A worn trail to the entrance was on the overhead image. "Come on." He scrambled up the rocky incline. Behind him Christina struggled for her footing.

"I'm sorry," she puffed.

"Don't be sorry. You're doing great." The noise of the vehicles stopped, replaced by doors slamming and men shouting. "I'm going to scout ahead," he hissed. He climbed further and found a goat trail. In the moonlight he spotted the track the cartel guys would be using. He didn't dare to pull out the ROVER again. Even with the screen brightness turned down, it might give them away.

Christina caught up with him and he gave her a chance to catch her breath. As he watched the track he spotted the first figures approaching. "Christina, I need you to go first. This path leads to the mine. I'm going to slow these guys down."

She nodded and scrambled into the darkness.

Bishop knelt and waited half a minute before he closed one eye and lifted the AK. He fired a burst at the figures on the track below, then dashed after Christina.

Yelling filled the air followed by random gunfire. He smiled, it was the exact effect he was after. He jogged back along the track, pushing through waist-high grass. When he spotted Christina he knelt again.

A minute later he caught a glimpse of a dark shape approaching cautiously. He aimed and fired. A man cried out. He sprinted after Christina and almost ran into an old mining cart. She was crouched behind it. Bullets snapped through the air and the bark of automatic weapons reverberated off the hill.

Bishop kicked at the ground in front of the cart. His boot hit something hard and metal. "Railway tracks. Follow them into the mine."

Christina continued through the grass as Bishop waited by the cart. He took one of the grenades from his stolen chest rig, yanked out the pin, and tossed it into the darkness. He turned and ran after Christina.

The explosion shook dust and rocks from the hillside as he ran into the mouth of the mine. Christina had balked at the gaping black hole. He grabbed her arm. "We're dead out there. In here, we have a chance." Reluctantly she followed him into the darkness.

***

Pershing was waiting in the Chevy a few hundred yards

from the mine when Burro tapped on the window. He checked the time on the dash. It was four-thirty in the morning. He lowered the window. "Have you captured them yet?"

Burro was still puffing. "They're cornered in the mine."

"Have you sent anyone in?"

"No, Mr. Pershing, but there's nowhere for them to go."

He sighed. "So it should be very easy for y'all to go in and get them."

"OK." He turned to walk back.

Pershing opened the door. "Oh and Burro. Send someone to get explosives. If we can't get them out, we'll bury them in there."

"That's more like it." The cartel killer talked to one of the men at the trucks before heading back up the hill. A pickup started and drove off.

He watched for a moment then followed Burro, catching him halfway up the hill. "Did you lose any men?"

"Yes, just one. But it's OK, he was stupid."

They walked the rest of the way in silence. Pershing looked out to the east. In less than an hour the sun would start to rise, taking the edge off the frigid desert air.

When they reached the mine entrance they found men on both sides of the opening, some sitting on rocks, others with weapons pointed into the darkness. Every now and then one flashed the tactical flashlight mounted on his weapon.

"So who's going in there?" Pershing asked.

The men looked at each other.

He laughed. "So you're all chicken shit." He cupped his mouth and yelled down the hole. "Aden, you and Christina should come out now. If you stay in there you're only going to die." He paused. Hearing nothing, he continued. "I'm going to give you twenty minutes to consider your options. Then, if you don't want to come out we're going to come in."

Pershing turned to the men sitting on rocks watching. "What are you dumb shits doing? It's goddamn cold. How about you light a fire."

***

It was pitch black inside the mine. Bishop used the flashlight on the AK to light their way as they pushed deeper into the heart of the mountain. When they were a few hundred yards inside he activated the ROVER and placed it on the ground. Without a signal from the drone it was just a softly glowing panel. With the brightness turned down he guessed it would last at least a few hours.

Christina sat next to the glowing screen, wrapping her arms around her knees.

Bishop draped his jacket over her. "You heard the cowboy. They're going to send guys in here. We need to be ready." He unfastened all the pouches on his vest and performed a quick check of his equipment. Four full magazines remained for the assault rifle. He also had two grenades, a packet of cigarettes and a lighter, the ROVER, his damaged iPRIMAL, a watch, and his Gerber covert folding knife. He ran his fingers through his hair and cursed. He'd lost his baseball cap.

"Are we going to be OK?" she asked quietly.

He flashed her a confident smile. "Of course. I've gotten out of worse than this." It was not exactly a lie. Bishop had been in plenty of situations where death seemed imminent.

She swallowed. "OK. What do you need me to do?"

***

Pershing stood in front of the blazing fire warming his hands. He checked his watch. Twenty minutes had passed and he'd heard nothing from inside the mine. He turned to Burro. "I need two men to go in."

"Good luck with that, Mr. Pershing. Nobody wants to go in there."

He took out his wallet, peeled off a thick wad of hundred dollar bills, and addressed the group. "I've got two grand here. I'll give a thousand dollars to anyone who goes into that mine. When you get the Aden guy and his girl, I'll give you another nine each to match it."

The men started talking. He had their interest. Before long two of them stepped forward.

"Finally, among the sheep we have some wolves." He handed each man a thousand dollars. One of them refused the cash and spoke to Burro in Spanish.

The lieutenant translated. "He doesn't want the money, Mr. Pershing. He wants your pistol."

Pershing contemplated the request. The chrome pearl-handled .45 had been a gift from an oil tycoon who had appreciated some work he'd done. It was one of his most prized possessions. But hell, he could always buy another one. He slid the weapon out of its holster and handed it over. "It's a deal."

The two Black Jackets each chose a side of the three-yard wide tunnel and stalked forward, aiming their weapon-mounted flashlights down the passage. Powerful beams of light pierced the darkness.

When they were out of sight, Pershing turned to Burro. "You sure there's no other way out?"

Burro shook his head. "Pedro said he's been inside when he was a boy. There's only one way in and out."

"The guys inside have got ten minutes. If they haven't dragged them out by then, we're going to blow it."

***

The two gunmen were a hundred yards into the mine and had yet to see any sign of either the woman or Aden. They moved forward tentatively, the flashlights attached to their weapons bobbing in the darkness as they leapfrogged forward. It was a slow process, but it meant neither of them was exposed without a cover man.

"What's that? Can you hear it?"

The other man turned his head. He thought he heard a woman crying. They edged forward until they could see her in the soft glow of the ROVER screen.

One of them inched forward until his flashlight illuminated the woman. She was hunched over and sobbing.

She looked up with tears flowing down her cheeks. "You killed him," she wailed.

The man lowered his weapon.

Bishop's arms were burning. He'd held himself in position up on the tunnel's wooden scaffolding for over two minutes as the Black Jackets slowly searched down the tunnel. Christina played her part to perfection and when the men lowered their guard, Bishop swung down from the roof.

His feet hit one of the cartel thugs square in the chest sending him smashing into the wall. A weapon clattered to the ground. Bishop landed behind the second man. He transferred the blade pressed between his lips to his fist and punched it into the base of the man's neck driving it up into his brain. The body twitched as it collapsed.

Dazed from the blow, the first man feebly raised an arm as Bishop stabbed him in the heart.

He switched off the flashlights on the assault rifles. Only the glow of the ROVER screen remained.

"Are they dead?" Christina asked softly.

He stripped the equipment from the bodies. "They can't hurt you now." As he removed their jackets there was a clatter as something hit the ground. He picked up a .45 pistol. It was a custom job. Not something you would usually see in the hands of a low-ranking foot-soldier. He stuffed it in one of the empty pouches on his chest rig.

He dragged the pile of gear to Christina. He had selected the least bloody of the two jackets for her. "Put this on, you're going to need it."

She donned the oversized jacket and slung her Canon camera over it. As she adjusted the strap on the camera, she stopped and sniffed the air. "Aden, can you smell that?"

"Smell what?"

"It smells like something metallic. Like fireworks."

It took a split second for Bishop to recognize the smell of a burning fuse. He pulled Christina off the ground. "Run, run!"

He activated the light on his AK, grabbed her by the hand, and dragged her down the railway tracks deeper into the mine. As they ran Bishop flashed the light from side to side searching for a hole in the rock. Finally he found one. He shone the light into it then pushed Christina inside. He barely fit in behind her. "Block your ears and open your mouth." He wrapped his arms around her and they waited.

Minutes seemed to stretch into eternity. Then it started as a rumble and shudder. Dust and debris dropped from the ceiling and Christina whimpered.

Seconds after the initial rumble a roar like a freight train blasted past the opening, through the mineshaft. Christina's scream was cut off as the oxygen was sucked out. Then it was over and they could breathe again. Christina coughed in the dusty air. "What, what happened?"

"They blew the entrance."

***

Pershing held onto his Stetson as the rush of wind and dirt blew out of the mineshaft. It took half a minute for the cloud of dust to settle, then he dusted off his suit. "Check it." He waited as the men lit up the entrance to the tunnel with their flashlights. The explosive charge had done its work. The roof of the shaft had collapsed, completely blocking the entrance.

Burro laughed. "Nobody's getting out of there, Mr. Pershing."

He kicked the rubble and spotted something trapped under a collapsed beam. Kneeling down, he tugged it out from under the piece of wood and held it up. It was a battered New York Yankees cap. "I think that's the end of Aden."

He turned and walked back to where the men were sitting around the fire. He warmed his hands and looked out over the mountains to the east. A faint tinge of pink glowed on the horizon. "A good night's work, boys. Time to get back and find out what Mr. Roberto Soto knows."

The first rays of sunlight reflected off the mining camp's tin roofs as the convoy led by the black Chevy arrived. Pershing had the battered Yankees cap in hand when he strode across to one of the transportable buildings. There were two Black Jackets standing guard. "Open up, I need to talk to him."

Inside, Roberto was lying on a thin mattress in the corner of the room. His hands were shackled by handcuffs and a length of chain ran through them around one of the building's metal uprights.

Pershing grabbed a chair, spun it on one leg, and sat. He took off his Stetson, ran fingers through his thinning hair and placed the hat on his knee. "I hope I didn't wake you."

Roberto sat up and stared.

He tossed the battered New York Yankees cap onto the ground. "You recognize this? Belongs, sorry I should say belonged, to your buddy, Aden. Seems him and your pretty journalist friend had a little accident in the old mine out near Digger Canyon." Pershing watched the rancher's face for any sign of emotion.

Roberto glanced once at the hat, then returned his gaze to Pershing.

"I'm a reasonable man, Roberto. If you tell me who else is helping your little band of renegades, I'll give you the chance to talk them down."

The craggy-faced farmer remained silent.

"Here's the deal. If you work with me, I'll make it very lucrative for you and your friends. Convince the other farmers to leave their land peacefully, and I'll make sure you're generously rewarded." Still no response.

"Tomorrow, you and me are going out to the Veda farm. Perhaps then you'll reconsider your position on all of this. The mine's gotta expand, buddy, and those people are in the way of progress."

Pershing stood and put his hat back on. "I'll let you sleep on it." He was about to leave when the rancher spoke.

"You're going to pay for this."

He tipped his Stetson. "We all do in the long run." Slamming the door behind him, he headed to the accommodation block the Black Jackets used. He opened the door and stuck his head in. Burro was asleep in an armchair in front of the TV. "Hey, dip shit."

The Mexican woke with a snort and got out of the armchair.

"You want to make ten grand, son?"

Burro rubbed his eyes and nodded.

"I need you to find Roberto Soto's family."

"You want me to kill them? Extra ten."

"Not yet, just find them."

***

LASCAR ISLAND

Frank, PRIMAL's British watchkeeper, yawned as he finished a chapter of his book. He was three hours into a particularly uneventful shift in the Bunker, PRIMAL's command center. He glanced up at the personnel tracker and confirmed nothing had changed. The map was zoomed out to show the location of their personnel across the globe. Aleks was in Thailand tracking down Kurtz, the rest of his team were on a beach in Spain, Mitch and Mirza were in New York, Saneh in Bali, and Bishop in Mexico. He noted the icons were green, meaning the iPRIMALs had checked in recently. All except Bishop's. His was still amber.

"How thing's tracking, Frank?" Vance asked as he stepped out of his office. "Anything from Bishop?"

"No, the last location we got from him was four hours ago." Frank zoomed the map down to where the chess piece icon was hovering. Switching to satellite imagery revealed it was located in a deep canyon. "He's been powering down intermittently to conserve batteries. I'm expecting him to check in sometime soon."

Vance walked across and sat in the command chair. "How far is that from the mine?"

Frank activated the touch screen on his desk and measured

the distance. "About four, five kilometers."

"And they're mounted on horseback."

"Correct."

"Hell, he should have wrapped up his recon by now…" He paused. "When are Mirza and Mitch due down there?"

He checked his notes. "Tomorrow, they're finishing the New York piece at the moment."

Vance drummed his fingers against the leather armrest of his chair. "Couldn't hurt to push forward their infil. Can you ask Chua for an update on their op in Manhattan?"

He hit a button on his screen and connected to the intelligence chief's desktop. "Chen, Frank here, need a quick SITREP on Mitch and Mirza's job."

Chua's voice came in over a speaker. "They're almost finished. Flash is handling the hack from our end now."

"OK, thanks."

"Anything going on I need to know about?" asked Chua.

"I'll come have a chat in a few minutes," Vance boomed from his chair.

"Copy that."

Frank terminated the call.

"What gear is on the Gulfstream?" asked Vance.

He opened a menu on the tablet. "Fairly comprehensive loadout, boss. Clothing and armor for four, small arms, some tech gear, comms, sniper rifle, and some heavier stuff. More than enough for Mitch and Mirza to wage their own little war."

Vance grunted. "That ain't gonna happen. This is still an intel collection op, we're not getting sucked into a goddamn war."

Frank nodded. "Understood, boss."

"Good, now let's get them down there as soon as we can."

CHAPTER 22

CHIHUAHUA

Bishop switched off the AK's flashlight to see if there was any ambient light. Nothing. It was total darkness. There was just the sound of their breathing and the steady drip of water falling from the ceiling.

He wrapped his arms around Christina in an attempt to stave off the cold and reassure her.

"Are you afraid, Aden?" Her voice was low and soft.

He considered the question. Long ago he had come to terms with death, although he was not particularly thrilled with the current situation. "No, I'm not afraid."

She shivered. "Good, because I am."

They had emerged from their hole in the wall to a tunnel on the edge of collapse. A solid wall of rubble blocked the exit. They had pushed deeper into the mine but only a hundred yards further they reached the end. Other shafts split off from the junction but none of them tunneled very far into the rock.

"We're going to be OK."

"Do you believe in God, Aden?" Christina's voice sounded distant.

"I did when I was a boy."

"Why not now?"

"I guess I've seen a lot of things, things that make me think if we do have a god, he doesn't care."

"So what do you think will happen when we die?"

Bishop pulled her in close. "We are not going to die. Not here."

"Nobody knows where we are. The only person who even knew we were out here is probably dead by now."

"That's not true. What about Emilio? What about Miguel and Gerardo? They all know we're out here. They'll come looking for us."

"Let's be realistic. Even if they did come here, we're trapped." Her voice trailed off. "We're alone."

"There are others, Christina, others who'll notice I'm gone. They'll send people to dig us out."

"And how long will they take to get to us, Aden?" She started crying. Her body shook as she sobbed. "I'm never going to see my family again. I'm never going to see my sister or my niece. I'm never going to see my mom or my dad."

Bishop just held her tightly. After a few minutes she broke the silence. "Do you have any family, Aden?" She sniffled.

"My parents are both dead and I was an only child." He swallowed, almost choking on his words. "But I guess you might say I have a family of sorts."

"Who?" she whispered.

"The men and a woman I work with. We're a close team. We rely on each other and we understand each other. They're my family."

As they held each other it dawned on Bishop that if he didn't get Christina out of the mine he was going to be responsible for the death of another innocent woman. In the darkness his memories came flooding back. Karla, the teenager in Japan, Jess, the doctor in South Sudan, and the dream of Saneh shot dead on the ground. He didn't realize he was crying until he felt a tear run down his cheek. "No."

Christina jolted. "What?"

He released his hold on her and felt around for the AK. "No, we're not going to die in here." He activated the flashlight, illuminating the mineshaft. "There has to be another way out. An air shaft, a drainage tunnel, something." He flashed the light down one of the side tunnels. "Come on, we're sticking together."

Christina climbed to her feet and they explored the tunnel. The walls were solid rock. Bishop inspected them with the flashlight, looking for any type of opening. They searched every inch of the short tunnel.

"There's nothing here, Aden."

"Let's check the other end."

As they walked back down the tunnel Bishop stopped. He heard something over the sound of water dripping from the roof.

"Can you hear that?"

"What?"

"It sounds like running water." Bishop knelt down and put his ear to the floor. Sure enough he heard water rushing behind the rock. "Lots of running water."

"Why is that good?"

"This may be our way out of here." He reached for a metal bar he had found in the tunnel. He started smashing it into the floor and prying away chunks of stone.

"That's going to take a long time."

"I only need a small hole."

He managed to wedge the bar between two slabs of rock. Working the metal back and forth, he forced it down through the rock. When he pulled it out, the end of the bar was wet.

"The miners didn't dig any lower because there's an aquifer below. An underwater stream that probably leads to the river."

"Probably? What if it doesn't?"

Bishop took one of the grenades out of his vest. "Go to the end of the tunnel and wait for me around the corner. Put your hands over your ears and open your mouth, same as before."

He waited till Christina was clear and pulled the pin from the grenade. He wedged it six inches down with the handle jammed against the rock. Stepping back, he pulled the pin on another grenade. Reaching as far as he could he pushed it into the hole and released the handle. "One thousand." He sprinted away. "Two thousand, three thousand." He took cover with Christina. "Four thou…"

The explosion blew rock and dust through the air, and nearly deafened them.

Bishop tentatively approached the hole the explosion had blown in the floor. It was about two feet wide and shaped like a triangle. He shone the light from the rifle down the hole. There was a drop of about three feet then crystal clear water.

He used his knife to unscrew the flashlight from the

weapon.

"That looks like it might be a way out." He slung the AK before lowering himself into the icy cold water, flashlight in hand. Crouching, he shone the light down the stream. There was an air gap that ran for twenty yards before the rock ceiling met the water.

"Is there a way out?" asked Christina from above.

He shrugged. "It's not great, but it's all we've got. It might be a good idea if I go ahead. When I get out I'll come back for you."

She shook her head. "No way. If you die on the way out, no one will ever find me. I'll die alone in the dark." She lowered herself into the hole. "I'll take my chances in here with you."

***

Bishop checked his watch. They had been in the underground stream for over an hour, ducking underwater between the air pockets. Christina was shivering. The ice cold water had leached the heat from her body. First she had lost all feeling in her hands and now her speech had started to slur. Bishop knew if he didn't get her out soon he was going to lose her.

They'd only managed to move a few hundred yards downstream. The problem was he had no idea if and when the stream reached the surface. He didn't want to tell her, but it was highly likely they were not going to get out. He tried not to dwell on the thought, but it was a harsh reality that lurked in the darkness.

He considered going back to the mine. At least there they could get out of the water. He might even build a small fire from some of the snapped shoring. He pushed the idea from his mind. Christina would never make it.

Shining his flashlight at the cave ahead, he saw the ceiling had started to rise and the stream was widening and becoming shallow. He waded forward pulling Christina. They pushed through a gap and came out into a large cave. He climbed out of the stream pulling her from the water.

He hugged her. "I need you to keep moving, OK?" Her teeth chattered.

She nodded slowly then started marching on the spot.

"That's my girl. Keep moving, and wait here. I'm going check out where the stream goes."

There were tears in her eyes. "No, don't leave me."

Bishop hugged her. "I'll be back in a minute."

He shone the flashlight around the walls of the cave. It was roughly a dome, about thirty yards in diameter. A pocket of soft stone that had been slowly carved away by the ground water. He switched off the light. It was pitch black. There was also no breeze or any sign air was coming in from the outside.

He shivered and walked back to the stream. It disappeared through a hole in the rock. He was in no hurry to climb back into the freezing water but it was the only possible way out. He ducked down under the current and aimed the light downstream.

His heart skipped a beat. At the very edge of the light he saw a tinge of green. Photosynthesis needed one key component, sunlight. He turned off the light. Everything was pitch black. As his eyes adjusted he thought he saw the faintest spot of light through the water. He blinked. Was his mind playing tricks on him or was there actually a glow?

Turning he pushed back against the stream, activating the flashlight. The first thing he heard as his head broke the surface was Christina's frantic voice.

"Aden, ADEN!" she called from the water's edge.

"It's OK, I'm here." He shivered as he climbed out of the stream.

She latched on to him. "Don't go again. You left me in the dark"

He hugged her. "It's OK, I think I've found a way out."

She shook like a leaf as she clung to him. He grasped her face in his hands. Her cheeks were like ice. "We need to go underwater again. Can you do that for me?"

She shook her head. "I can't go back in there."

Bishop rested his forehead against hers and hugged her. "Christina, I'm not going to let you die here. I'm going to get you home to your family."

She shook her head. "No, no, I can't do it."

"It's OK, it's OK." He sat her down.

"Tell me, what's the story with your tattoo?" he asked, trying to keep her mind occupied.

"I, I had a birthmark when I was little. The other kids used to make fun of me. When I turned eighteen my mother took me to a tattoo parlor."

"That's one cool woman."

"Yeah, she is."

"I need to get you back to her, Christina."

She swallowed. "It's sad that you don't believe in God."

"I have my own beliefs."

"Like what?"

"I believe we get once chance at life. I'm trying not to make a complete mess of it."

Bishop put his AK aside and threw off his chest rig and jacket. He stuffed the chrome .45 in the front of his pants. Then he took the memory card from her camera and slipped it in his pocket.

"You're going to be fine," he said as he helped her out of her jacket. "I'm going to tie you to me, OK?"

She nodded.

He stripped the sling from the AK and wrapped it around both her wrists. "I need you to hold on to my belt." He looped the strap around his thick nylon belt. Now even if she let go he could still drag her through the water. "You just need to hold on and kick, OK?"

She nodded as he started running her through breathing exercises to expand her lungs. Then he leaned forward and kissed her gently on the cheek.

She managed a feeble smile.

Bishop turned toward the hole in the cave wall and counted. "One, two, and three." He put the flashlight in his mouth as he ducked underwater and swam forward with long powerful strokes. He felt Christina's hands pulling on the back of his belt as he swam. Stroke after stroke he powered forward towing her to what he hoped was safety.

Time seemed to slow as he used up the oxygen in his system. He exhaled slowly through his nose, keeping his strokes smooth. Christina let go of his belt. Then he felt the tug as the strap wrapped around her wrists jerked on the back of his belt. He knew she'd passed out as she went from being heavy in the water to dead weight. The flashlight slipped from his mouth as he struggled to maintain forward momentum. His lungs burned and he realized he had made a fatal mistake. He fought the urge to inhale as his body screamed for oxygen.

Then he saw it, a faint glow coming from ahead. It seemed so far away. In his mind he heard a long dead friend's voice. "Get the hell out of here, Bish." Ice had given his life for another, and drowning in a cave was no way to honor that sacrifice "Go! Get the hell out of here."

The underwater stream spat Bishop into a deep pool with light streaming from above. He pushed off the rock floor and dragged Christina to the surface. As his head burst through he sucked in air. The bright sunlight assailed his eyes. He fumbled for the clasp on his belt, managed to unlock it, and pulled it through, freeing Christina's hands. Then he rolled over, pulling her head to the surface. His boots made contact with the riverbed and he dragged her from the water.

The world spun and he collapsed next to her on the sandy bank. In a daze, he struggled to his knees and fumbled as he tried to check her pulse with his numb fingers. It was faint. Her lips were blue, her mouth half open. He turned her onto her side and green water drained from her mouth. Then he flipped her onto her back and started pumping her chest with his hands.

"Come on, Saneh, live!" he screamed as he forced down on her chest. Tears filled his eyes and he fought off dizziness as he counted out the compressions. Reaching thirty he gave her two breaths and started again. "Damn you, Saneh, you're not going to die. Fucking breathe, Saneh."

As he pumped down on her chest he heard the crack of her ribs. Her eyes flickered opened and she started coughing up mouthfuls of foul water.

Bishop turned her on her side as she coughed, then vomited. After a minute of constant hacking she lay back in the warm Mexican sun. "I thought I'd never see this again," she croaked.

He collapsed on the bank of the polluted river and closed his eyes.

"Aden," Christina whispered. "Who is Saneh?"

CHAPTER 23

Mitch checked the Gulfstream's heads-up display, confirming they were on target. The luxury jet was cruising at twenty-five thousand feet just north of the Mexican border.

Mirza was sitting in the co-pilot's seat, watching intently.

"You ready to take the stick yet, mate?"

Mirza wore a serious look as he reached forward and placed his hands on the yoke. "Ready when you are. Hands on." It was the first time Mirza had flown since training on the flight simulator back on the island.

"I'm handing over control in one, two, three. Hands off." Mitch released the controls and turned to Mirza with a grin. "There you go mate, you're flying."

Mirza smiled for a split second before turning serious again.

Mitch got out of his chair. "I'll leave the cockpit door open, mate. Just in case you have any problems." He walked into the luxurious cabin and sat in one of the armchairs. There was a laptop open on the desk in front of him.

PRIMAL's G650, nicknamed Sleek, was one of a number aircraft that had been heavily modified to conduct covert operations across the globe. The collection included: an Ilyushin-76 heavy transporter that doubled as a special ops support platform and gunship, a tiltrotor capable of flying long distances and landing vertically, as well as a number of helicopters and unmanned drones. Mitch had reconfigured and enhanced all the aircraft to meet their needs.

While the Il-76, or Pain Train as it was affectionately known, was his favorite, he really enjoyed flying the Gulfstream. He seriously doubted there was another aircraft this size anywhere in the world that had half as much capability. It had a comprehensive electronic countermeasures suite, a sophisticated intelligence collection capability, and the ability to deploy free-fall operators or airdrop specialist equipment.

Mitch opened the aircraft's control menu on the laptop and

activated the equipment delivery module. He double-checked the coordinates Chua's intelligence team had provided and activated the automatic dispatch program.

At the back of the aircraft, in what once was a baggage compartment, a tall gray object that looked like a coffin received the data and prepared itself for launch. Beneath it, a panel under the tail of the aircraft retracted.

Mitch watched the countdown. "Five, four, three, two, one... away." The program registered the parachute exploding from the top of the package, arresting its fall. Unlike a standard cargo chute, the ram-air chute was steerable. A GPS module and a tiny computer used electric motors to apply pressure to the canopy, steering it through the air. From twenty-five thousand feet, the precision cargo delivery system was capable of flying almost forty miles and landing within twenty yards of its target.

He shut the laptop and walked back to the cockpit.

"I felt it go," said Mirza as he waited for Mitch to retake his seat. "Handing over now."

They ran through the sequence again and he took the controls, immediately banked the aircraft north and commenced their descent. "We'll be on the ground in El Paso in twenty, across the border in an hour, and at Bishop's safe house just after sunset." He checked the iPRIMAL interface panel.

"Still no update from him?"

"No, nothing."

"He should have finished his mine recon by now.

He saw the worry on Mirza's face. "It's OK, mate, he's probably still out of battery. I bet he's shacked up with that journo."

***

Bishop glanced up at the edge of the canyon. The sun had disappeared behind the lip and they had barely made it a mile from where they had surfaced. If he remembered the terrain correctly, they were only a few miles from the mine, and a long way from help. Soon the temperature would drop and Christina's condition would deteriorate even further. In the hours after her near drowning Bishop had noticed troubling symptoms. Vomiting, dizziness, and an inability to control her body temperature indicated the water in the river might have poisoned her. His own eyes were sore and his skin was itching, but unlike Christina, he'd not ingested much of the polluted stream.

"Water," she croaked as she staggered along the canyon floor.

Bishop held her as they walked. "We can't drink it. It'll only make you sicker."

She shivered again. He pulled out his broken iPRIMAL and tried to turn it on. Nothing.

With a moan Christina collapsed against him. He helped her down to the ground where she dry retched. The sun was below the horizon now and it was only going to get colder. They needed a fire.

He gathered a handful of dry grass and quickly built a tepee of sticks around it. He emptied his pockets onto the ground. Somehow he still had both the folding knife and the chrome-plated colt. He ejected the magazine from the weapon and thumbed out a round. Using the knife, he pried the bullet from the brass casing. Then he trimmed a small piece of material from the bottom of his jeans and stuffed it into the cartridge.

He chambered the modified round and shot it into the sand. Picking up the smoldering piece of cotton with his knife, he transferred it into the heap of dry grass. It smoked and took light as he breathed gently on it. Within a few minutes he had a fire burning fiercely.

"You need to leave me," croaked Christina.

"No way. I didn't drag your ass out of that mine to leave you in the desert."

"Saneh needs you," she mumbled.

They enjoyed the warmth radiating from the fire for a few minutes before he got up to find more wood. As he searched, he found his thoughts wandering to Saneh. She was in Indonesia at a Yoga retreat. She would have no idea he was lost in the desert. If she did know, would she come? They had parted on bad terms and he wasn't sure it could ever go back to the way it was. His recklessness had probably cost him the only woman he had ever really loved. He shook his head and picked up another stick. That was all irrelevant now. His focus was on keeping Christina alive.

He was about to head back to the fire with an armful of sticks when he heard a noise. He dropped the kindling and drew his pistol. Stalking slowly along the bank he waited till his eyes had adjusted to the gloom. He heard the soft whinny of a horse and nearly cried out for joy. "Tinkerbell, is that you?"

The horse walked across, sniffed him, then nuzzled the side of his face. He took her reins and led her back to the fire. "Christina, look who I found."

He took the water bottle still hooked over the horn of the saddle and gave Christina a drink. She tried to gulp from it but he stopped her. "Just little sips." As she sipped he kicked out the fire.

"Had enough water?"

She nodded and handed him the bottle. He returned it to the horse and retrieved a blanket from where it had been tied behind the saddle. He draped it over her shoulders and helped her onto Tinkerbell's back. The stocky mare turned her head and sniffed Christina's leg. She whinnied softly when Bishop climbed into the saddle and held Christina in front of him.

Bishop gave her a gentle touch with his heels. "Come on girl, take us home."

She gave another whinny and started off along the creek bed.

***

Mirza was amazed at how easy it was to cross the border from Texas to Mexico. There was no check on the US side and the Mexican guards showed little interest in two men in a battered old Ford Bronco truck. He was thankful for that, because explaining what an Indian and a Brit were doing traveling together might have proven awkward. Although the cover story Mitch had developed was no less so. Allegedly he was the 'little spoon', whatever that meant.

Mitch was driving the truck at break-neck speed across a barren section of desert forty miles from the border. The lights bolted to the top of the truck lit up the sandy track for a hundred yards in front of them. The GPS app on the tablet attached to the dash counted down the distance from their destination.

"Thar she blows." Mitch slowed and turned off the track. The off-road tires crunched over dry bushes and shrubs as he pulled alongside the coffin-shaped equipment pod.

Mirza jumped out and started bundling up the gray parachute. He wound it around his arms and dumped it in the back of the Bronco. "How close was it?"

Mitch bent over the pod and unlatched a panel revealing a keypad. "Within ten yards. Best yet." He punched in a code and the container popped open revealing black gear bags.

Mirza loaded the bags while Mitch stripped the electronic guidance package from the pod and placed it on the back seat. The carbon fiber container would remain in the desert.

He took two Glock 19 pistols in paddle holsters from one of the bags. He clipped one onto his belt and pulled his shirt over it. Slamming the back of the truck shut, he joined Mitch in the cab and placed the second handgun on the console.

The technician was studying his iPRIMAL tablet. It was a larger version of the smartphones they all carried; a highly sophisticated battlefield management, intelligence, and communications system. He had preloaded it with imagery covering northern Mexico.

Mirza checked his pistol. "How far are we?"

Mitch activated the navigation function and slotted the device back into its cradle. "We'll be at Bishop's safe house within the hour."

CHAPTER 24

Roberto's eyes snapped open and he sat up as the door handle to his makeshift cell turned. One of the mine's workers entered with a tray and placed it on the floor.

Roberto recognized the man. He had been a farm hand that had labored for him over the summer. Now he was one of the few locals who had taken jobs at the mine; a move that had ostracized him from the small community.

The tray held a single bowl of white slop. Roberto locked eyes with the farm hand.

The man mouthed something. Roberto frowned, what was he trying to say?

Again, he mouthed the same word.

Roberto realized what he was saying. Message.

"I remember you," he said as the man turned to leave. "You helped me put out that fire at the Veda ranch."

The worker paused at the door with a confused look on his face.

"Yeah, that's right. You helped at the Veda ranch." He mouthed the next words. "Tomorrow, they're going to hit the Veda ranch."

The man nodded and disappeared. The door was locked and Roberto was left alone with the bowl of slop.

***

Bishop let Tinkerbell canter the last mile home. She seemed to understand the urgency of the situation. Her neigh woke the ranch before Bishop managed a shout. Lights snapped on in the ranch house, then the huts.

Everyone came out to meet them: the brothers Miguel and Gerardo, Emilio, and the ranch owner with his wife. Christina was pulled from his arms by strong hands and bundled inside the house to be tended by the rancher's wife. Bishop slid down from the horse and patted her on the nose. "Thank you, Tink!"

She gave a snort and tossed her head in the direction of the barn. She was ready for a feed.

Emilio took the reins from him. "Where is Roberto?"

Bishop shook his head. "They captured him."

The old man's shoulders slumped and he led the horse to the stable. It was the first time Bishop had seen the staunch rancher's will to fight defeated. He followed him into the barn and grasped him by the shoulder. "We'll make them pay for this, and if he's alive we'll do our best to get him back."

The old man turned to him, his eyes glossy. "First my son, now Roberto? We can't fight these people."

Bishop undid Tink's girth strap and slid the saddle off her back. "Yes we can." He peeled the saddle blanket from her back. She gave a shake and plunged her nose into the bag of oats offered to her by Emilio. "They don't know who they're dealing with."

He left Emilio to tend the horse and knocked on the front door of the house. The rancher met him with a grave face. He led him through to where Christina was propped up in bed. His wife was holding a mug of water and trying to get her to drink.

Christina managed a smile when she saw Bishop. "Hey," she croaked.

He leaned over and gently brushed a strand of hair from her face. He took the cup from the wife. "I'll watch her for a bit."

The woman nodded and left them together.

"How you doing, warrior?" he asked.

"I'm OK." She started coughing.

Bishop handed her a tissue from the nightstand. She struggled to hold it against her mouth. He knew she needed to get to a medical facility. "Hey, you did good today, kiddo. A weaker person would have called it quits, but you stuck it out. I'm proud of you."

She looked at him with weary eyes. "I hope Saneh realizes what a lucky woman she is to have your heart."

The comment was like a punch to his chest and he was lost for words.

The honking of a car horn snapped him out of it. "I'll be

back." He ran through the kitchen, past the rancher and his wife, to the front door. He cracked it open and peered through.

An old Ford Bronco was parked in front of the ranch. Emilio was standing a few yards off to the flank with his bolt-action rifle raised.

"No need for the gat, mate, we're friends of Aden."

Bishop instantly recognized the voice. "Mitch!" He pushed open the door and walked to the truck.

Mitch appeared from the driver's side of the vehicle, followed by Mirza who ran an eye over Bishop's disheveled appearance.

"What on earth happened to you?"

"I'll explain later. You got a trauma kit in the truck?"

"Of course. What's wrong? You hit?" Mirza asked as he opened the back of the Bronco and pulled out the medical supplies.

"Not me, the girl. I think she's got toxic poisoning." Bishop left Mitch to unpack the gear. He led Mirza back into the house.

Christina was still sitting up in bed.

"This is my friend, Mirza. He's a medic and will help you."

She looked at them, eyes heavy with malaise. "Hello."

"Hello, Christina. How are you feeling?" Mirza put a digital thermometer in her ear and took a reading.

"Sore and tired," she mumbled.

Mirza checked her eyes with a penlight. "Aden, we need to get fluids into her and get her to hospital in the next few hours." He unzipped the med kit and pulled out a giving set and saline bag. It took him only a few seconds to find a vein and insert the needle.

"The ranch owner's wife has offered to take her to El Paso," Emilio said, standing at the door.

Bishop nodded. "I think that's best."

"I'll let her know."

Christina coughed. "I don't want to go," she moaned.

He put his hand on Mirza's shoulder. "Can I have a few minutes with her."

Mirza handed over the fluids bag and stepped out of the room.

Bishop took her hand. "We've got to get you to a hospital, Christina. The water from the river has made you sick."

"But, you're not sick."

The corner of his mouth turned up in a half smile. "I managed to keep my mouth shut underwater."

Another fit of coughing wracked her body. "Promise me you'll get Roberto back."

"I'll do my best."

"No, promise me."

"I can't promise you that."

She glared at him. "You got me out of the mine, Aden. You can save Roberto."

He took her hand and kissed her on the cheek. "You just concentrate on getting better. I'll take care of everything here."

Ten minutes later Bishop watched the tail lights of the rancher's truck disappear down the track. Content that Christina was on her way to hospital, he walked across to where Miguel, Gerardo, and Emilio were smoking on the front porch of the bunkhouse.

Emilio looked up from cleaning a rusty bolt-action rifle. "Your friends, they are here to help?"

"They're here to see what can be done."

"What does that mean?" asked Gerardo.

"It means, if we can find a way to stop them, then we will. But, there are only three of us."

"No," said Emilio. "There are six of us."

Bishop nodded. "True. Now, I need to go and help set up our gear. I'll talk to you all in the morning. We'll come up with a plan to try and rescue Roberto."

"You need to sleep, Aden," said Emilio.

"I will." He strode back to the barn, stopping to pat Tinkerbell on the nose as he passed her stall on the way to the storage room.

Mitch and Mirza were already nearly set up. All the horse equipment had been piled at one end of the room, clearing space for the gear bags. Mitch had placed a laptop-sized satellite receiver outside. Cables ran through the window to a wireless router.

"So what happened out there?" Mitch asked.

Bishop sat on a step. "It all went to shit." He spent the next ten minutes filling them in on the events that had transpired since he had crossed the border into Mexico. When he was done both Mitch and Mirza wore concerned looks.

Mirza voiced his doubts first. "Sounds like they had surveillance on Christina from the start. Either that or one of the Mexicans is an informant."

Bishop shook his head. "No, I don't think there's a mole. The security at the mine is somehow hooked into US surveillance assets. I found a ROVER terminal in one of their buggies."

Mitch looked up from where he was studying his tablet. "It would probably be a Predator." His fingers danced across the glass touchscreen. "I'm bringing up the FAA network. If the birds are flying domestically they'll have had to submit a flight plan and run a transponder."

Bishop managed a wry smile. It was good to have Mitch on the team.

"Here it is." He laughed. "Real creative call sign, Pred South. The bird flew a mission in vicinity of El Paso last night for a period of eight hours. Looks like at about twenty-one thirty it wandered across the border into Mexico for five hours."

"You can't tell who it was working for?"

"No, it's a Customs and Borders bird, but that doesn't say much."

"It tells us enough. Whoever we're dealing with is linked into interagency assets. They're well resourced and supported. This is going to be a tough nut to crack. We need to continue a low-vis op. Collect all the intel we can and see what develops."

Mirza dropped a large black bag in front of Bishop. "Here's your gear."

He unzipped the bag. It contained all his basic loadout: rifle, pistol, chest rig, and a spare iPRIMAL.

"We don't seem to have much local support to work with," Mirza said.

"They mean well, but they're just farmers. With Roberto captured and Carlos dead, we've only got three guys."

"Yeah, and no offense, but Emilio looks like he's older than Jesus," Mitch said.

"Well, I owe him. When we were evading the Black Jackets, his son tried to help me…" His voice trailed off.

"And?"

"And they murdered him. Dragged him five miles behind a truck."

"Bloody hell." Mitch looked at Mirza and there was silence.

"Anyway, those cartel assholes will get their due." He reached into the pocket on his jeans. In among the sand and dirt was the SD card. "We got some photos of the mine. Security is real tight, heaps of cartel gunman. More bad guys than a Bond movie. Sorry, the card's pretty beat up."

"You'd be surprised at how tough they are. I'll send the pics through to the Bunker."

That reminded Bishop of the chrome .45 he'd been lugging around. He pulled it from his waistband and unloaded it. "I took this off one of the cartel guys in the mine. It's got an inscription."

Mitch inspected the weapon. "Wow, not your average pea shooter. I'll take some photos and send it through to Chua and the team. In the meantime, why don't you get some rest? Mirza and I will get things sorted here. Once we've checked in with the Bunker we'll work out a game plan. What's the security situation here?"

"The guys from the mine think we're dead. But they'll be interrogating Roberto, if he's still alive. We should run a sentry and move in the morning."

"I'll put a sensor on the road. Mirza and I will take watch and get the gear sorted."

"The ranch owner and his wife will have to find another place to bed down for a while. Can you make sure they get some cash?"

"Will do. Now, you get a few hours sleep."

"No, I'll do a shift." As Bishop stood his legs almost gave way. He placed a hand against the wall to steady himself.

"Bollocks you will," said Mitch.

"I think I might give you a once over before you get your head down," said Mirza as he reached for his medical kit.

Bishop sat back down. "You got anything in there that will help me sleep?"

Mirza took a few pills from the kit. "Here, an anti-inflammatory, and a sleeping tablet. In a few hours you'll be feeling a lot better." He started checking Bishop's vitals. "I'll put a bag of fluids on your arm while you sleep. You look dehydrated."

He exhaled slowly. "Whatever the doctor orders."

CHAPTER 25

LASCAR ISLAND

Flash leaned back in his chair and aimed his Nerf gun at the trashcan-sized robot that was cleaning the floor. His target was an empty soft drink can balanced on top. He tracked the robot as it navigated around a chair. It paused, almost as if it sensed the ambush. Slowly, it inched out from behind cover.

"I have you now," whispered Flash as he squeezed the trigger.

The dart sprang out of the gun with a loud clack, arced across the room, and hit the tin can with a soft clink. He leaped from his chair, pumping a fist, and hopping on one leg. "Yeah bitch, take that."

A beep from his computer interrupted his celebration. He dropped his stocky frame into his chair and spun to face the thirty-two inch screen. "Boom!" The tablet Mitch and Mirza had hacked was online. The receptionist who owned the iPad had finally plugged the device into a USB port to charge. Now, Flash had to bypass the lock out and gain access to the port itself. His fingers danced over the keyboard as he hummed a Steppenwolf song, Magic Carpet Ride. In a couple of minutes he had bypassed the security protocols and gained access to the GES network. He cracked his fingers, now the fun was going to start.

He accessed the local admin drive and went straight for the personnel files. Chua had instructed him to find out exactly who they were dealing with. He downloaded a folder containing the CVs for over a dozen employees. The PDF documents were small and unencrypted.

He scanned through the other folders but didn't find anything interesting. He grabbed a dozen invoices from the accounts folder then went for the mother lode, the email server. As expected, it was encrypted but that wasn't an issue.

The problem was choosing what files to download. He glanced at the interface in the corner of his screen that told him how much power the iPad had. He doubted the secretary would leave it plugged in once it was fully charged. It was at eighty percent and climbing. He grabbed a chunk of emails belonging to the CEO, Charles King.

He stopped browsing so the files could download faster. While waiting, he opened the CVs he had already copied. Just as he thought, most of the employees were ex-government. A range of gunslingers, cops, and intelligence types, not unlike the PRIMAL team. One file caught his eye; George Pershing's CV read like an action novel. Former 'State Department', he had served in some far-flung places. The photo in the corner of the document showed a middle-aged, lean-faced employee with a receding hairline. Was it the same guy Bishop had described? He remembered the engraving on the pistol Mitch had sent through. He searched the intel database and found the photo. The inscription read.

GHP Chad 2003

GHP, George Henry Pershing. He earmarked the file and checked the progress of the download. It was about halfway. He opened the accounts invoices he had downloaded and browsed through them. They were from a variety of clients ranging from oil companies to governments, and everyone in between. The company name on one of the files caught his eye, Dynamic Business Consulting. He went back to the CVs and searched them for the name. Yes, there it was. Pershing had worked for the same company after leaving government service.

He opened a browser and researched the company. It seemed to be a legitimate consulting firm, based out of Atlanta. Flash leaned back in his chair as he considered the information. It all seemed too convenient. The invoice from DBC to GES was a big one, nearly six million dollars for a team of security consultants.

He rocked forward to check on the download of files. Damn, the tablet had disconnected from the network. He shrugged, there were still a significant number of emails to decrypt and analyze. He dumped the files into a software program that Chua had procured from an NSA contact. It would take at least a day or two for the program to crack them all.

He typed a single line in a chat window to Vance. Dynamic Business Consulting, ever heard of them?

He knew the PRIMAL Director of Operations was at his desk because the reply came back almost immediately. Cover firm for the Company, why?

"Shit," mouthed Flash. GES had contracts with the CIA, and Pershing almost certainly had a background with the Company. He started to type a reply message when the door to his office swung open and Vance stormed in with Chua in tow.

"Is GE contracting to the CIA?" PRIMAL's Director of Operations asked.

"Yes sir, at least for some of their jobs. They were paid over six million from a front company earlier this year. And the cowboy guy that's going after Bishop, he's former CIA."

Vance leaned against the desk and folded his arms. Chua stood in the doorway.

"That raises the stakes."

The Chief of Intelligence nodded in agreement.

"Update Bishop, Mitch, and Mirza. They need to be aware we could be dealing with government level capabilities and assets. We need to gather as much intel on GE's activities as we can."

***

CHIHUAHUA

The thumping on his door woke Bishop from the deepest sleep he'd had in months. He groaned and glanced at his watch. The luminous hands told him it was four in the morning. He had only been in bed for a few hours. He turned on the light and noticed the needle had been removed from his arm.

Mirza opened the door with a mug of coffee in hand. "Morning!" he said cheerfully.

Bishop wiped the sleep from his eyes. "What's going on?"

"Emilio got a message from a local who works at the mine. Roberto's still alive."

"What, when?"

"A few minutes ago. Roberto passed a message that the men from the mine are going to attack a farm at dawn. Emilio's about to leave with the other two."

Bishop took the coffee. "Give me a sec to get dressed. Don't let Emilio leave."

"Will do."

He was over at the barn a minute later with mug in hand. Mitch, Mirza, and what remained of the autodefensa were already there. Like Bishop, the two PRIMAL operatives were dressed in jeans, plaid shirts, and jackets. Their combat equipment was laid out on the ground. The Mexicans were eyeballing the gear. "Emilio, any news on Christina?"

"She made it to the hospital safely."

"Good." He turned to his fellow PRIMAL operatives. "OK, team, what have we got?"

Mirza spoke first. "According to Emilio's man, Roberto is still at the mine. He's in OK health, but he's heavily guarded. He managed to pass us a message that the cowboy and his cronies are going to hit the Veda ranch this morning."

"OK, who's Veda?"

"Pablo Veda," Emilio explained. "He owns the last property standing on the southern side of the mine. Twenty acres. Lives there with his two sons."

"And do you trust this contact of yours? Who is he?"

The old man rubbed his eyes. "He's a ranch hand who took a job at the mine. A good worker, I trust him."

"Yeah, but what if he's working for the cowboy? What if this is a trap?"

"No, they have Roberto, and they think you're dead. They

think we are beaten. They will attack the Veda ranch." Emilio's lip quivered as he spoke. "I know Pablo. He will not leave his land. They'll have to kill him. If we do not help him then all will be lost. They will have won. My son will have died for nothing!"

Bishop glanced at his fellow PRIMAL operatives, then back to the ranchers. "Can you guys give us a moment alone."

Emilio nodded and gestured for the other two men to follow him outside.

"What did the Bunker have to say?" Bishop asked.

"We haven't run this past them, mate," replied Mitch. "We checked in with them a few hours ago. Chua's team has been burning the midnight oil. They've updated our intel files with a full breakdown of the Chaquetas cartel and the local Sinaloa branch. Chua also thinks they might have ID'd your cowboy. Ex-CIA geezer called…" He checked his iPRIMAL. "George Henry Pershing."

"Does Vance know him?"

Mitch shook his head. "No, according to his CV he started at the Company after Vance left. But that's not all they dug up. Seems GE has a number of contracts with the CIA."

"No shit. That would explain the Predator. Does that mean this is a CIA-backed op?"

Mitch shook his head. "No, Chua and Vance don't think so. We don't have any specifics for the CIA contracts, but they seem to be separate from GE's resources security side of things. They think this Pershing chump is calling in favors."

"And what's our tasking? Still just intel collection?"

"Yep. Vance has tasked us to identify potential opportunities to shut down the mine. He specifically said we're not to engage in any kinetic activity at this stage."

"If we shut down the mine but all the farmers are dead, that's a bloody waste of time," said Bishop.

"And Emilio is going no matter what we do," said Mirza.

"Then we need to go with him and convince this Veda guy to avoid a confrontation."

Mitch nodded. "Right, but what about your mate who got

captured? You want to request the CAT for a recovery op?" The CAT was PRIMAL's Critical Assault Team. Heavily armed operatives equipped with cutting-edge technology. A brute force instrument used when field agents required additional firepower.

Bishop sighed and shook his head. "Vance won't approve it for a civilian."

"So, what are our options?" Mirza asked.

"Well, the security at the mine is hardcore, and we've lost the element of surprise. If we're to have any chance at recovering Roberto we'd need to come up with something local to neutralize the Chaquetas. I'm keen to explore the Sinaloa angle."

"Play the cartels off against each other? That's going to be dangerous."

"Might be our only option." Bishop checked his watch. "Is all the gear packed?"

"Yep," Mitch replied. "And the Bunker's already scoped a suitable safe house for us closer to town."

"OK. Let's move on the Veda job. I want you both in overwatch. If this goes bad and we can't get the farmers to leave, you need to be able to lay down the smack and cover our withdrawal."

Mitch grinned. "We packed for just the occasion."

"Good, then gear up and let's roll."

CHAPTER 26

Pershing finished pouring an espresso and turned to his captive. "You sure you don't want one, Roberto? Great way to start the morning, gives you a real kick in the pants."

The rancher stared at him.

"No? OK." Pershing lifted the glass and sipped from it. "Looks like it's going to be a beautiful day. It's a real pity you don't want to help me save your friends down there." He gestured at the farmhouse half a mile away.

They were standing behind the Chevy, parked outside the front gate to the Veda ranch. In front of them Burro waited with four pickups full of his men. Beyond the trucks was the house. It sat at the base of the same hilly range as the mine. The geologist had told Pershing this particular area contained the richest deposit in the area.

The rumble of a large diesel engine caused the espresso glasses on top of Pershing's machine to vibrate. Glancing over his shoulder, he spotted a low-loader transporting a bulldozer. He slid the coffee machine away and closed the trunk. A car came out of the dust behind the truck, a police cruiser.

It slowed to a halt and an officer lowered his window. "Morning, Mr. Pershing."

He reached into his jacket, retrieved an envelope, and handed it to the cop. "Make it snappy, boys, I've got a lot of work to do today."

The officer and his partner nodded and drove off, passing under the tall wooden sign marking the entrance to the property. They turned on the lights and siren as they drove down to the farmhouse.

Pershing sipped his coffee as he watched. "I give them about three minutes. What say you, Roberto?"

In the distance the boom of a shotgun sounded.

"Might be a little less." He chuckled then knocked back his espresso.

The police car had stopped a few hundred yards down the

road. Pershing watched as it backed off the track and turned around. It accelerated toward them, slowed, and stopped alongside.

"I guess you miss out on that bonus, boys."

"Mad old bastard didn't even want to hear what we had to say," said the officer. "He deserves what he gets."

Pershing waved them on. "Much obliged for your attempt."

Once the police car disappeared down the road, Pershing pointed to Burro. "Your boys are up!"

***

Mirza adjusted the focus on the scope of his suppressed G28 marksman's rifle. He and Mitch had positioned themselves halfway up the hill overlooking the farm. Clad in the mottled grays and browns of A-TACS camouflage, they blended seamlessly with the arid surroundings. Bishop was down at the farm with Emilio and the brothers, trying to convince the Pablo Veda and his family to leave.

Mirza pushed the transmit button attached to the foregrip of the rifle. "Bish, we've got at least four truckloads of hostiles and a dozer moving down the road. We need to go now."

"I'm working on it."

Through his scope Mirza watched as the Black Jackets jumped down from the pickups and fanned out into two long lines. Every second man carried a rocket launcher slung across his back. He turned to Mitch who was lying behind a shrubby outcrop a few feet to his left. "I'll target the rocketeers. You hit the dozer first. Use HE. Engage on Bishop's word."

The Brit had a camouflaged MK48 machine gun pressed against his shoulder. Like Mirza's weapon, it sported a long cylindrical suppressor and an optic sight.

"Roger." Mitch lowered the machine gun and shouldered his PAW-20 grenade launcher. The futuristic-looking weapon was a bullpup, the magazine containing seven twenty-millimeter high-explosive grenades. It would make short work of an unarmored vehicle.

Mitch adjusted the range on the holosight. "Bugger me, that's a lot of bad fuckers. Are we going to be able to hold them off?"

"We have to." He thumbed the radio button. "Bishop, how are things tracking down there?"

The response was immediate. "Not good, mate. They don't want to leave. Standby to engage."

Mirza flicked the safety off his rifle. "Acknowledged."

***

Bishop ran a gloved hand through his hair and fought the urge to scream. The pig-headed farmer, Pablo Veda, and his two sons were refusing to abandon the farm. Even Emilio had been unable to convince him to budge. "Fuck!" He slammed his fist down on the kitchen table. "If we don't go now, we're not going."

Veda had a double-barrel shotgun under his arm. He was short, pot-bellied, and wore a look of fierce determination. He rattled off a few sentences in Spanish and disappeared into the lounge room of the homestead.

Emilio started to translate.

Bishop held up his hand. "I get the gist." Like the rest of the team, he wore A-TACS combat fatigues and an armored assault rig. An integrally-suppressed Tavor assault rifle was slung across his chest.

He followed Pablo through to the front of the house where his sons were waiting. The two teenage boys were poised with a pair of bolt-action varmint rifles. Great for shooting prairie dogs but of limited value in a gunfight. They had smashed out the glass in the windows and were crouched behind the stone walls. Bishop locked eyes with the youngest. The kid was terrified.

"Emilio, tell the boys to keep the trucks running."

Miguel and Gerardo had parked the Dodge pickup and the Bronco behind the house. Emilio had shown them a rough track that snaked out from behind the ranch. It was their planned exfil route.

He transmitted to the other PRIMAL operatives over the radio. "Team, it looks like we're staying." As he released the radio toggle, something that sounded like a freight train roared over the house.

"Rocket fired. Request permission to engage," replied Mirza.

Bishop took up a position at a window. He spotted the Black Jackets in a skirmish line only a few hundred yards away. Balancing the glowing red dot of his Trijicon on one of them, he took up the slack in the trigger. "Weapons free! I say again. Weapons free!"

***

Pershing shook his head as the rocket sailed over the building and disappeared into the distance. "Goddamn amateurs," he said to Burro. They had moved past the front gate, and were now standing next to the Chevy only a couple of hundred yards from the homestead.

He pointed at Roberto. "If you had helped, all this might have all been avoided."

The bark of an AK sounded from downrange. "And so it begins." He lifted a pair of binoculars to his eyes and focused on the extended line of Black Jackets. He frowned as one of the men toppled over. Had he tripped, or had the farmers managed to shoot him?

"Mr. Pershing. The dozer!" Burro yelled.

He focused his binoculars on the heavy earthmover following the gunmen. Puffs of smoke and angry flashes of flame sprouted from its bodywork. He watched in disbelief as the cockpit glass shattered and the driver flung open the door and leaped clear. Explosions rocked the metal beast as the dull thuds of grenades filled the air. The line of Black Jackets turned and fled. "Burro, what the hell is going on?"

A bullet ricocheted off the windshield of the Chevy, whistling away into the distance. "Look out!" screamed Burro as another bullet hit the truck.

"Everybody in," Pershing said diving into the front passenger seat as Burro forced Roberto into the back. One of his men ran around the other side of the vehicle and walked into a volley of bullets that almost tore him in half. Blood sprayed across the windows.

"Go, go, go!" yelled Pershing as the bullets rang on the vehicle's armor like hail on a tin roof. Heavy-caliber rounds chewed chunks from the laminate windshield as the driver spun the vehicle and accelerated through the open gate and down the road.

Behind them the Black Jackets were in full retreat. They left four dead men behind as they piled into their trucks and sped after the Chevy.

In the back seat, Roberto smiled. "How's that for a kick in the pants?" It was one of the few things he'd said since being captured.

Pershing scowled as he watched the old man in the rear vision mirror. He picked up his phone and started dialing.

***

Pablo and his sons wore broad grins as they walked back from the burning dozer. Mitch's grenades had set fire to the engine and cabin, turning it into a flaming pyre.

Bishop managed a halfhearted smile as Pablo grabbed his free hand and pumped it vigorously. He turned to Emilio. "He does know they're going to come back, right?"

The grizzled old rancher nodded. "He won't leave, Aden. His people fought for this land against the Americans. He will not give it up."

Bishop shook his head. By fighting off the cartel the PRIMAL team had further cemented Pablo's determination. So much for maintaining a low-vis op.

"No sign of hostiles," reported Mirza over comms.

"Roger," replied Bishop. "Pull back to the ranch. I've got a feeling we may have a Pred overhead soon."

"Acknowledged."

Bishop watched Miguel and his brother Gerardo load the bodies of the cartel men into the back of their pickup. All four had been killed by headshots. All four had been carrying SMAW-D bunker-busting rockets. The rockets were now lined up on the porch, alongside the dead men's assault rifles.

It didn't take Mitch and Mirza long to move down from their overwatch position. Bishop joined them in the kitchen where Pablo was brewing a pot of tea on a wood-fire stove. "Nice shooting, fellas." He gave Mitch a friendly punch on the shoulder. "Not a bad hit-out for our super geek."

"This mean I'll finally get some respect from you door-kickers?" Mitch asked.

Bishop looked at Mirza. "No!" they replied in unison.

There was silence as the reality of their situation overcame their temporary victory.

"How long do you think we've got?" Mirza asked.

Bishop sighed. "I don't know."

"We need to bug out. They're going to come back, and with more men."

"I know that. But I'm not abandoning these people to be slaughtered. So, we need to be ready to fight and we need as much warning as possible. Mitch, have you got anything that'll help?"

"Yeah, I can set a few sensors on the road in. We can also monitor the FAA network. If they re-task a drone to check us out we should be able to see what's going on."

"OK, if we can get a camera feed up we might be able to convince them to leave next time they approach."

"Yeah, I can rig an IR-triggered cam."

"Good. Mirza, I want you to show the farmers how to use the weapons the Black Jackets dropped."

Mirza's eyes narrowed. "Sure that's a good idea? It might make it even harder to get them to leave. They might think they have a chance."

Bishop sighed. "If they won't leave, we'll need every gun we can get."

"OK, I'll give them a quick lesson."

At that moment Emilio walked into the room. Bishop turned to him. "Are there any other farmers that'll help?"

He shook his head. "No, those who are willing are already here. The others are scared. But..."

"What? If you have any ideas share them."

"I know a man who can help us. But, he is Sinaloa."

Bishop shrugged. "The enemy of my enemy is my friend. How long will it take?"

"A few hours."

Bishop glanced at Mirza and Mitch. They all knew the odds were stacked against them. Both men gave a nod. "Let's set up a meeting."

CHAPTER 27

Sparks showered down from the cabin of the D7 dozer as the engineers welded steel plate over the windshield. Pershing watched from the floor of the workshop. He had ordered the engineers to armor the bulldozer and one of the smaller six-axle dump trucks. If those bastards at the Veda ranch wanted a war, he was going to bring them a blitzkrieg.

"Mr. Pershing, may I have a word with you?"

He turned to face the mine's operations manager, scowled, and turned back to the trucks. "What is it? Can't you see I'm a little busy."

The orange hardhat-wearing manager jerked his thumb at the truck. "What the hell do you think you're doing with my rigs?"

"Your rigs?"

"That's right, my rigs. You're in charge of security. I'm in charge of keeping this mine running, and to do that I need that dozer and that dump truck."

He sighed. "You can have them when I'm done."

"That's not the problem."

"Then son, what the hell is the problem?"

"You're wrecking them."

The scream of an angle grinder filled the shed as one of the workers started cutting firing ports in the thick steel sides at the back of the dump truck.

Pershing cupped a hand to his ear. "I can't hear you."

The mine manager shook his head and retreated to his office.

The phone in Pershing's pocket started ringing. He pulled it out, left the shed, and walked across to his own office. He had already tried to call his boss three times. Now, finally, he had a call back.

"George, what's going on?" Charles King asked.

"Sir, we've just been screwed, hard!"

"Explain."

Pershing outlined the events at the farm.

"Do you have any more idea who these guys are?" King asked when he was done.

He opened the door to his office. "They have to be linked to the Aden guy. They've got some serious hardware; HE, sniper rifles, the works."

"And what have you got? Fucking water pistols? We've spent a shit-ton equipping your little militia. Now put it to use and solve this problem."

Pershing threw his Stetson on the hat stand and slumped into his chair. "I will but we need more intel. Who are they? Who are they working for?"

"I'm sure your CIA buddies can find out what you need."

"They're still chasing down leads. Did we get anything from the follow up on the phone hack?"

"Dry hole. These guys covered their tracks. Look, just get this problem solved, George. I can't afford any fuck ups."

"Yes, sir." He paused. "There are only a handful of the bastards and I've got plans to deal with them. But..."

"But what?"

"It might be prudent to send a tactical team as a contingency. You mentioned Team 2 was available?"

"Shrek and his boys just finished up in the Congo. I'll get them down to you in 48 hours but it will come out of your budget."

"Understood. I'm heading into town now to rustle up some police support. I've got a Pred on-station tonight, then I'm going to hit it at daybreak. With a police tactical unit, fifty Black Jackets, and homemade heavy armor, we'll make short work of the dirt farmers and their mercs."

"Keep me posted."

"Will do, sir." Pershing hung up and tossed the phone on his desk. Running his hands through his thinning hair, he contemplated his planned assault on the Veda ranch. There couldn't be more than a few of the heavily-armed mercs defending it. If they were still there in the morning they were dead men. If not, well, the ranch still needed to be razed. It was the last property on the southern side of the mine that needed to be cleared and he wasn't about to let it stand in the way of progress.

A knock sounded on his door. "What is it?"

It swung open and Burro stuck his head in. He still had an adhesive bandage covering the wound on his cheek. "Sir, we're ready to go."

Pershing grabbed his hat. He would use the drive to Chihuahua to call Howard and convince him to ramp up intelligence support. They needed to know exactly who was targeting the operation and they needed to know yesterday. He frowned as he stepped outside and saw the dents in the side of his Chevy. Burro's men had cleaned the blood from it but the damage remained; a reminder that someone had bested him.

***

It was late in the afternoon and Bishop and Emilio were in the Bronco heading north. They had left Mitch and Mirza at the Veda ranch to prepare the defenses, while they attempted to garner support from the Sinaloa. The old man was driving as Bishop researched the cartel on his iPRIMAL.

They were the largest narco-trafficking organization in Mexico and one of the most ruthless. They also happened to be rivals with another faction that included the Chaquetas Negras. According to Chua's intel pack, the two groups were in an uneasy ceasefire. He finished reading and slid the device back into his jeans. He had changed out of his camouflage gear for the meeting.

"I want to thank you for this morning," said Emilio as he drove them along the highway. "You gave me the chance to hit back at the men who killed my son."

"Your boy was a brave man, and we're a long way from done when it comes to dealing out justice."

"I know, but this was a good start."

Bishop's iPRIMAL buzzed. "Excuse me." He answered the call and Chua's voice came through in his earpiece.

"Bish, this is Chua, I've got Mitch and Mirza online and Vance here with me. Acknowledge that you're in the car with a local resource?"

"That's correct. Did the boys update you on what went down today?"

Vance's deeper voice replaced Chua's. "Yes they did. I thought I told you to stay out of trouble."

"We weren't about to let them get slaughtered."

"Understood. Now, I'm just not sure that pulling in the Sinaloa cartel is a smart move."

"I'm willing to listen to alternatives. But we're running out of time. We've put a dent in the Black Jackets, and the Sinaloa might be willing to help finish them off."

"Yeah, but what if this turns into your Alamo?"

"I'm not about to let these goons get the drop on us. If we can't get the Sinaloa to help we'll convince the locals to withdraw."

"Understood. I've recalled the CAT as an additional measure. The boys will be flying to the island from Europe tomorrow. I've given permission for Aleks to continue looking for Kurtz. Kruger will be heading up the team." He paused. "Go ahead with your meeting, we'll assess after that. In the meantime, Chua's got some additional intel for you. I'll hand over to him."

"Roger." Bishop looked out across the desert. The sun was setting, bathing the harsh terrain in a soft orange glow.

"We've confirmed that our cowboy is George Henry Pershing, a former CIA officer now working for GE," Chua said. "Flash has researched the mining operation and it's probable it's not a CIA front. He's managed to crack the encryption on the emails he downloaded. It seems Pershing is providing information to the agency in exchange for intelligence support."

"That explains a few things," said Bishop.

"He's working with a number of local assets. One is a cartel lieutenant who goes by the name Burro."

"Yeah I know him. He tried to rape Chris."

"Uh huh. According to his police file, he's a nasty piece of work. In addition, Pershing has been paying bribes to a number of government officials including the Chihuahua Chief of Police. It appears GE was working in the area establishing contacts long before mining operations commenced. They also implemented a CIA contract to install a sophisticated CCTV network in Chihuahua city."

"Makes sense, a bit of advance force operations prior to the big push. Can you put a pack together on the police chief? If we can isolate Pershing from his support base we might find it easier to influence him."

"Already on it. Flash is still working through the data. He did want me to ask if Longreach meant anything to you."

"No, I don't remember hearing anything about it. Why?"

"It's mentioned a number of times in the emails. I think it might be a side-project GE is running with the Chaquetas."

Emilio slowed the truck and pulled off the main highway onto a side road. In the distance Bishop saw a large outcrop of trees; an oasis in the desert. "Team, I'm almost at my meeting. I'll open up a surveillance line. If for whatever reason this goes bad, Mitch and Mirza know the drill."

Vance's voice replaced Chua's. "Play it safe. Ask for their help. Offer nothing."

"Yeah, I got it. Out." He terminated the call, activated the device's stealth surveillance mode and slipped it into his pocket. The camera and microphone would continue transmitting despite no outward sign it was occurring. The Bunker would monitor the feed and alert Mitch and Mirza should things go bad.

As they drove along the sandy track the distant trees gained definition. Bishop spotted a fence and small building. "That it?"

Emilio slowed as they approached the high wire fence. The building was a guard post. Behind it a thick line of trees blocked observation of the estate. Bishop squinted as a bank of security lights flashed on. "Yes, we're here." The leathery old rancher wound down his window to talk to the guards.

The two smartly dressed men surprised Bishop. Their blue uniforms were pressed and the black assault rifles they held were brand new. Not what he expected.

Emilio turned back from the window. "They want to know if you are armed."

Bishop lifted his jacket to reveal his pistol.

The guard at the window nodded and spoke to Emilio in Spanish.

"They asked if you might leave it here. You'll need to get out."

Bishop stepped out of the truck. He ejected the magazine from his Beretta, cleared it, caught the ejected cartridge, and slipped it into his pocket. One of the guards took the weapon and issued him with a receipt. He got back in the truck and the men slid the security gate open. "That was all very civilized."

They followed the road through the trees and pulled up outside a hacienda. The residence was single-story, white, and had broad sweeping verandahs. As they stepped out of the truck onto the gravel driveway a pair of Rottweiler dogs appeared from the shadows and bolted toward them.

Emilio leaped back into the truck but Bishop held his ground. The dogs skidded on the gravel, jumping in a frantic attempt to lick his face. He laughed, pushing them off.

"Four thousand dollars each and all they want to do is lick people to death." The gravelly Latino-accented voice came from under the verandah.

Bishop extracted himself from the affection of the canines and walked over. "They're beautiful animals."

"Thank you. My son loves them. My name is Ramon." The head of Sinaloa operations in Chihuahua offered his hand.

He returned the firm handshake. "I'm Aden."

Ramirez was a short man. Bishop guessed he was about five-foot-three. He had a broad, honest face, a bushy mustache that hung over the corners of his mouth, and a thick mop of jet-black hair. Dressed in loose-fitting linen pants, leather sandals, and a light blue Miami Dolphins T-shirt, Bishop didn't think he looked like a narco kingpin.

"This is a lovely house," he said as they waited for Emilio to join them.

"Thank you. It was my father-in-law's. When he passed, he left it to my wife and now I get to enjoy the tranquility it provides." Emilio arrived and a broad smile spread across the cartel boss's face. "Emilio, it has been far too long." He grasped the rancher's shoulder. "Why do you not visit me anymore?"

"You married into crime."

There was an awkward silence before Ramirez spoke. "Things are changing. The Sinaloa gives more to the people now than the Mexican government."

Emilio shrugged. "We will see."

Ramirez turned to Bishop. "Please excuse my rudeness." He gestured toward the door. "Come inside and join me for supper."

The inside of the house was tastefully decorated with simple wooden furnishings, glazed terracotta tiles, and white-washed walls. Ramirez led them into the dining room where plates of food and bottles of beer had been laid on the table. His stomach grumbled, reminding him he hadn't eaten all day.

"Emilio tells me that you're here to help fight the Chaquetas," Ramirez said once they were seated.

Bishop ate a mouthful of flauta and wiped his chin with a napkin. "Yes, they've murdered a number of farmers and taken their land. That's the reason I'm here–"

"Why?"

Bishop looked confused.

"Why are you helping them? They're not your people. It's not your land. Why do you, an American, care what happens to a handful of ranchers?"

"Because I made a promise to someone that I'd help. Because sometimes doing the right thing is more important than anything else."

Ramirez seemed to consider the answer. "This is true. That is why the Sinaloa cannot help you."

Emilio thumped the table with his palm. "Why not? I

thought you wanted to help the people."

"We do. That is why we cannot start another war. We fight the Chaquetas and they will ask for help from the Juarez cartel. The peace is tenuous, and if it's lost then many, many Mexicans will die." He turned to Bishop. "You are a military man, yes? You understand that sometimes the good of the many outweighs the good of the few."

He could not fault that logic.

"But this doesn't mean I won't help. Any damage you do to the Chaquetas will only strengthen my position. Do you need weapons?"

He shook his head. "No, what we need are experienced fighters. We are a handful, standing in front of an army."

Ramirez shrugged. "I'm afraid that is the one thing I cannot give you. Explosives, weapons, information, these are things I can provide."

Bishop spooned some slow-cooked pork onto his plate. "In that case, what can you tell me about the Chaquetas' other ventures?"

"They are thugs. Guns for hire that other cartels use to do their dirty work. They have a base in Buenaventura, perhaps one hundred men, at the most. They're not heavily involved in smuggling."

"Nothing else, no recent ventures?"

Ramirez fixed Bishop with an intense glare. "Either you are very well informed or you're good at guessing."

"I just want to know my enemy."

"I get information from a contact in the police. He told me the chaquetas have purchased a farm near Nueva Piedras. I think they're going to try and grow their own marijuana."

"That's interesting." He ate another spoonful of pork. "By the way, this is delicious."

"My cook is one of the best. I'll have her pack some for your men." He pushed his chair back and rose. "I'm sorry to seem rude, but I promised my wife I'd spend time with the children tonight. Duty calls." He shook Bishop's hand and hugged Emilio. "If there is anything else you need, just ask."

He left them in the dining room.

Bishop finished his food and waited as the maid cleared the table. Emilio wore a heavy scowl. "The trip was for nothing."

"No it wasn't. We can use this information to hurt your enemies. And if we need more weapons, we know where to ask."

The maid reappeared with a cardboard box laden with plastic food containers. Bishop thanked her and carried the food out to the truck. He managed to stow it on the back seat before the slobbering dogs reappeared. He pushed them off and climbed back into the cab. "So what's the go, Emilio, you and Ramirez family or something?"

The rancher started the truck and drove them back to the guardhouse. "He's my nephew. He was a good boy, and then he married the daughter of a Sinaloa Lieutenant. I have not spoken to him since." He lowered his window and took Bishop's Beretta from the guards.

"That piece of information might have been useful prior to the meeting," Bishop said as he slipped the weapon back into its holster.

"You didn't ask." Emilio turned on the Bronco's headlights, drove through the gate, and accelerated down the track.

Bishop pulled out his iPRIMAL and wrote a few notes. Tomorrow would be a big day. In between babysitting the farmers and working out how to deal with the police chief, he'd investigate the Chaquetas' farming operation outside Nueva Piedras.

***

Pershing tossed his satellite phone on the car seat next to him and rubbed at his temples. It was long after sunset and Howard and his intel team were still no closer to identifying who was helping the Mexicans. The only good news from the fat bastard was the availability of a Predator. The drone would spend a few hours over the Veda ranch later tonight. Hopefully it would give him some insight into who was there. Not that it mattered. His army would crush them regardless.

His driver flicked on the indicator, and a moment later pulled the Chevy off the road into a gas station. They drove past the brightly lit service center and parked next to a silver SUV. Burro got out of the front passenger seat and walked around to the other car. A moment later he opened Pershing's rear door and Felipe Guzman peered in.

"So now you whistle and I come running," Chihuahua's chief of police snapped.

"You're the one who didn't want to talk on the phone. Now, quit your squawking and get in."

The senior police officer climbed in and pulled the door shut.

Pershing tossed an envelope into his lap.

"What's this for?" He pocketed the cash.

"It's for the SWAT team you're going to lend me for the Veda ranch tomorrow morning."

"SWAT? What the hell are you talking about? I've given you police officers already."

"I need tactical operators not donut-munching dimwits. I need your SWAT team first thing in the morning. If you've got an armored car, they're going to want that as well."

"Are you fucking kidding me?" He tossed the money back in Pershing's lap and grabbed the door handle.

"I lost four of my boys at the ranch today," Pershing said as he gripped the policeman's arm. "These farmers are running a goddamn illegal militia on your turf. They've got mercenaries training them, and now they've got automatic weapons."

Felipe shrugged. "I don't give a fuck. The more criminals you get killed the better."

"The guys we're up against will close the mine. You know what that would mean."

"What?"

"The gold dries up and there's no more cash. My people aren't gonna keep funding that fancy lifestyle of yours, Felipe."

The chief slid back into the seat and held out his hand. Pershing handed him the envelope. "How many men do you need?"

"At least twenty."

"They'll be there. But..."

"But what?"

"I want a cut of whatever you're doing out at Nueva Piedras."

"Come again?"

"You're not the only one with good intel. I don't want to know what you're doing, I just want a small cut. In return I'll make sure my people stay well clear."

"I just gave you fifty grand, Felipe." He contemplated the offer. "I tell you what; your boys show up tomorrow and help me capture the mercs, then I'll consider doubling it."

"My men will be there. You just remember who runs this town," the police chief said as he got out.

Pershing waited for him to drive off and Burro jumped back into the Chevy. They were ten minutes down the road when he finally asked the question he'd been pondering. "Burro, hypothetically speaking, how much would it cost to have that greedy son-of-a-bitch killed?"

The lieutenant grinned at him in the mirror. "I'd take care of him for free, Mr. Pershing. You want me to make it happen?"

He shook his head. "No, he's still useful. For now."

CHAPTER 28

Bishop's eyes flashed open and he sniffed. The smell drifting into the living room was delightful. He unraveled himself from a blanket and stumbled to his feet. He groaned, every inch of his body seemed to ache. Glancing out through the windows he saw it was still dark. There was still a faint flicker from the smoldering dozer. He noticed Mitch and Mirza's sleeping bags were already rolled up. He walked into the kitchen.

Emilio was sitting at the table with a mug of coffee in his hands. Pablo was in front of the stove, stirring the pot that had to be the source of the amazing smell.

He pulled a chair out from the table. "What's cooking?"

"Huevos a la Mexicana," said Emilio.

"Eggs Mexican?" guessed Bishop.

"Very good." Emilio poured him a mug of black coffee. "Your friends are outside."

Pablo put a plate of food in front of him. Bishop guessed why they were called Mexicana. The green bell peppers, tomatoes, and eggs represented the colors of the national flag. "Have they eaten?" he asked.

Emilio nodded. "They didn't want to wake you."

"Any luck convincing our friend to leave?"

He shook his head. "He says you will defeat the narcos. His sons are outside practicing with their new AKs."

"They're going to come back in force, Emilio. We won't be able to stop them, even with extra guns."

The rancher nodded. "I know. But, we can try."

Bishop quickly devoured the plate of food, strapped on his chest rig, and grabbed his Tavor assault rifle. He noticed three of the SMAW-D rockets they'd recovered from the cartel were gone. Mitch and Mirza would have taken them to their overwatch position. He placed the remaining launcher next to the door.

"Gracias," he said to Pablo and stepped out into the

darkness. He walked between the trucks, past a corral, and up a ridgeline. The moon was still above the horizon and it cast a silver light across the ground. As his eyes adjusted he moved faster, climbing quickly. When he arrived at the crest he stood silently, turning his head as he searched for the pair.

"Morning, Bish!"

He snapped his head in the direction of Mitch's voice. It had come from only a few feet in front of him. He gave a grunt as he crouched next to where his two comrades were sitting. Their camouflage made them almost invisible. "You guys enjoying the view?"

"Just keeping an eye on things," said Mirza.

"How long was the Pred on station?" Bishop asked Mitch as he took a seat.

"Two hours. Wouldn't have seen much. Just the vehicles."

"Good stuff, anything from the ground sensors?"

"No mate, all clear at the moment."

"Mirza, how did the training go?"

"I took them through the rifles and the machine gun. They're eager, but there's only so much I can do in a few hours."

"Yeah, thanks anyway."

They sat enjoying the silence for a few minutes. There were still stars in the sky, but a faint glow on the horizon meant dawn was not far away.

Bishop broke the silence. "We need to be prepared to remove the farmer and his boys, by force if required." He paused. "I really didn't want it to come to this."

"None of us did, Bish," said Mirza.

There was a red flash from the tablet at Mitch's feet and he picked it up.

"What is it?" asked Bishop.

"One of the sensors is going off its tits. I think it might be faulty." His fingers danced over the screen. "Oh, you've got to be kidding." He passed the tablet across to Bishop. Mirza leaned over his shoulder.

The screen showed a still from the tiny infrared camera

Mitch had strapped to a fence post three miles down the road. It was another bulldozer. Steel plate had been welded on all sides of the earthmover. Now it was a mobile pillbox.

"Faaaaark!" exclaimed Bishop. "We don't have the firepower to take that down. The rockets we captured aren't even going to dent it." The SMAW-D rockets had thermobaric warheads designed for bunker-busting; they were not armor-piercing.

"It gets worse." Mitch showed another photo, this time of an armored dump truck bristling with rifle barrels.

"We need to pull out," said Bishop. "Send those images to my iPRIMAL. I'll show them to Pablo."

"Mitch and I'll cover you," Mirza said. "If we can't stop them we'll withdraw back to the farm." He cupped a hand to his ear. "You hear that?"

In the distance they heard the clanking of the dozer.

"We've got twenty minutes till dawn," said Mirza.

"We'll be gone in ten." Bishop skidded down the slope back to the farmhouse.

***

Pershing had his driver pull over in the cover of a small ridge, two thousand yards from the farm. He was not going to make the same mistake twice. When his blitzkrieg was underway he planned to walk up the rise and observe through a pair of binoculars. "Any of you gentlemen want a coffee?" he asked Burro and the police tactical commander.

The two men were eyeing each other off like a pair of junkyard dogs. It would have amused Pershing had he not needed them to work together to clear the ranch. He had his armored vehicles ready to go as well as the two police pickups jammed with SWAT operators. All he was waiting for were his buggies.

"Yeah, Mr. Pershing." said Burro.

The police officer shook his head. "My boys can have this wrapped up in half an hour if you let us go now."

"Patience." He stamped coffee into the press and prepared an espresso for Burro. "You're not dealing with dirt-poor autodefensa, these people have professional help."

The officer adjusted his thigh holster. "How do you mean?"

Burro took his cup. "They've killed a fair few of my men, hombre."

"That wouldn't be very hard, would it?"

Pershing finished another pour and took a sip. "Gentlemen, gentlemen. We're all friends here. All of you are getting paid. There's plenty of money and plenty of killing to go around." He savored the freshly brewed espresso shot. "There's no change to the plan. Burro and his boys will punch in with the dozer and the dumper. They will draw fire and suppress. Then SWAT will move through from the flank and clean up whoever's left. We'll use the buggies to cut off any squirters."

The policeman thumped his chest plate with his fist. "My men should go behind the dozer. We won't need your fire support."

"You may well not. But it's better to be safe than sorry, and while I'm paying the bills, I get to make the plans." He smiled. "That clear?" He turned to Burro. "Where the hell are those buggies, son?"

"They'll be here soon. We should start without them, before it gets too light."

Pershing considered the suggestion. The longer they waited the more likely the occupants of the farm would be ready and waiting. "OK, let's go."

Burro issued a command into his radio and the dozer started clanking forward. The armored dump truck filled with Black Jackets crunched through its gears as it followed. The police pickups waited for their commander then moved off to the flank.

Behind, Pershing heard the throaty roar of the V8 dune buggies. He smiled as he walked up the rise, his plan was coming together.

***

Bishop bolted down the hill. He leaped over rocks, skidded in the scree, and fell three times before reaching the bottom. Sprinting across the field to the house he burst in through the back door. The kitchen was empty. He pushed open the door to the living area. The farmer and his sons were crouched behind the smashed-out windows. The AKs taken from the dead cartel men were held ready.

"They are coming," said Emilio. He was covering the other set of windows with Miguel and Gerardo.

"Yes, and this time we can't stop them. We need to go." He held up his iPRIMAL and showed them the photo of the armored bulldozer.

Emilio translated for the pig-headed rancher. Pablo looked at the screen, mumbled something, and shook his head. He aimed his AK back out the window.

"He will not leave. He says you can blow it up again."

"Then Pablo is going to die here with his sons."

The clanking of the dozer was audible now along with the roar of its powerful diesel engine. Bishop glanced out the window. Dawn was upon them, the sun rising directly behind the beast as it trundled closer. He thumbed the transmit button on the side of his rifle. "Hit them with everything you've got."

The telltale thunk of a high-explosive round from Mitch's PAW-20 echoed off the mountains. Pablo looked out the window eagerly and watched as the grenades slammed into the dozer, obscuring it in dust and flame. The men in the house cheered. But, the dust settled and the armored tractor still approached.

"Bish, we're taking fire," Mirza transmitted. There was a roar as one of the rockets they'd taken from the dead gunmen streaked down from the hillside and slammed into the dozer. Another two rockets streaked through the air, this time hitting the armored dump truck. The heavy beast shrugged off the blows and lumbered on. Mitch and Mirza had expended their entire HE arsenal without stopping either of the homemade tanks.

Bishop fought the urge to fire at the earthmover. He knew the bullets would be wasted. As he aimed, the dump truck moved out from behind it and accelerated forward. When it was a hundred yards away it turned broadside to the house. The side of the truck bristled with rifle barrels.

"Get down!" yelled Bishop as bullets smashed into the building, splintering wood, and shattering glass.

One of the farmer's sons gave a grunt and fell to the floor. The others cowered as Bishop took a smoke grenade from his vest and flicked it through the open window. Ignoring the cracks of bullets around him, he grabbed the wounded teenager by the collar and dragged him into the kitchen.

"Bish, we're taking heavy fire. Withdrawing to you," transmitted Mirza.

"Roger, one of the lads has taken a hit to the chest. He's in the kitchen. I need you to stabilize him and get everyone in the trucks. Bishop propped the boy against the stone wall. He felt around his back. There was a small exit wound. It was bleeding but not heavily. The kid was lucky; the 7.62mm full metal jacket round had punched clean through.

Emilio crawled into the kitchen. "Is he alive?"

Bishop tore a field dressing from his vest and handed it to him. "I need you to hold this on both sides of the wound."

Mitch's British accent came over the radio. "Bish, mate, you've got cops closing in fast. They're trying to flank you." His suppressed machine gun snapped in the background.

"Roger. Keep hitting them. I'll have a crack at the dump truck." Bishop grabbed the last SMAW-D and dashed out the back door. He armed the rocket launcher as he sprinted behind a water tank, the slung Tavor bouncing against his chest as he ran.

Shouldering the rocket launcher, he leaned around the corner. The dump truck filled his sights. He squeezed the forward safety and thumbed the red button. The weapon thundered and the rocket hit the rear wheels of the truck with a boom. Bishop dropped the tube and sprinted back as the police SWAT unit spotted him. Bullets kicked up dust as he skidded around the corner.

As he caught his breath, he saw Emilio and Mirza lifting the wounded teen into the back of the Bronco. Mitch ran past him, skidded onto his front and started firing the machine gun at the advancing police.

"Pablo, we're leaving!" Bishop screamed. The rancher looked defeated as he climbed into his truck with his remaining son. Emilio and Mirza were already in the Bronco. Miguel and Gerardo were waiting in the blue Dodge pickup.

Bishop leaped over the tailgate into Pablo's pickup. He thumped the roof of the cab and they took off.

"GO, GO, GO!" screamed Bishop as the old house started to shudder. The other two trucks followed, Mitch jumping in the back of the Dodge pickup after firing a long burst.

With a roar the building collapsed as the dozer smashed its way through the rancher's home. Bishop braced his feet against the tailgate as the truck accelerated. He shot at the earthmover out of frustration.

"That was a tad close," Mitch's voice came through over the radio.

***

The trucks raced across the paddocks leaving the bulldozer and the cops in their dust. The Bronco led, Emilio at the wheel. They bounced across the field, following a narrow track that wound through the hills and would eventually join the road to town.

Bishop thumbed his radio. "How's the kid doing?"

"If we can get him to a hospital within the next few hours he'll live," said Mirza.

"How's everyone else?" He took a few seconds to check himself over. He had all his gear and no bullet holes.

Mitch replied first. "Some wanker shot a hole in my pants. An inch higher and I'd have lost my old fella."

Mirza laughed as he tried to report. "I'm fine. You OK, Bish?"

He tipped his head to the side and looked out from the bed of Pablo's pickup. He thought he heard the roar of an engine. "I'm good." He squinted down the road behind them. Were they being followed? Bullets cracked through the air as a dune buggy appeared through the cloud of dust. "Boys, we've got company." Bishop raised his Tavor and fired a few shots as they slid around a corner. He caught a glimpse of a second buggy. "Two hostiles on our six."

Another burst of fire smashed out the rear window of the truck. He swiveled around to check the rancher was OK. Pablo gave him thumbs-up through the shattered glass. Bishop turned his attention back to their pursuers. Firing accurately was impossible as the Bronco was swerving back and forth. He tore one of the HE grenades from his rig, yanked the pin, popped the handle and lobbed it in the air. It detonated showering one of the buggies with shrapnel. The driver slammed on the brakes and it disappeared in the dust.

The track they followed grew narrow and began to snake its way through the hills. The trucks were forced to slow and in a few seconds the high performance buggies roared back into sight. Bishop managed to trigger off a wild burst before an assault rifle wielding co-driver blasted the pickup. There was a loud bang as one of the truck's tires exploded. To his credit, the farmer didn't stop and managed to maintain control of the swerving truck.

Bishop fired another burst before his Tavor ran dry. He ripped off his empty mag and rammed a fresh one home.

"Bish, we're going to drop back on your right hand side," Mitch transmitted.

The road was barely wide enough for two vehicles. The rancher was keeping the truck straight but once the flat tire shredded it would be all over. "OK go, go, go!"

The Dodge in front of him pulled over and braked hard. Mitch was in the bed of the pickup with the MK48 machine gun. He knelt with the weapon braced against his shoulder. His biceps bulged as he hammered the buggies.

One driver was killed instantly. The buggy slammed into the

side of the hill and cart-wheeled off the road. The other driver swerved and accelerated toward Bishop's truck. It hit with a crunch, shunting the pickup to one side and almost throwing him out. At the same time the co-driver fired a burst through the cab.

Mitch retaliated with a long burst directly into the buggy's engine bay. Bishop tossed his last grenade over the tailgate. It bounced on the bonnet of the crippled assault vehicle and dropped into the cockpit. The two trucks raced ahead as it detonated behind them. The burning buggy shot off the road and down into a canyon. A muffled explosion echoed through the hills.

Pablo brought his truck to a halt. Bishop jumped from the back and wrenched open the door. The rancher was slumped over the steering wheel, his torn shirt a mess of blood and gore. The bullets, mangled from hitting the truck, had slashed through his torso inflicting horrendous wounds. Bishop was amazed he was still alive.

Mitch jumped down from the Dodge. "Is he OK?"

Bishop shook his head as he pulled a morphine-injector from his vest and jabbed it into the man's leg to ease the pain.

A bullet snapped through the air and Bishop glanced down the road. Pickups bristling with black jacketed gunmen were closing in.

Mitch shouldered the MK48 and sent a volley of rounds in their direction. "We've got to go, mate!"

Bishop punched the side of the truck. There was no way the farmer was going to survive. The floor of the cabin was already slick with his blood. The old man reached out and grabbed his shoulder. He looked into Bishop's eyes and whispered, "Go."

Mitch's machine gun rattled as he opened fire again. "C'mon Bish!"

He tore himself away from the dying man and leaped into the bed of the Dodge. He screamed with rage as he fired the Tavor back down the track. Mitch jumped in behind him and the big Dodge took off, the others in the Ford Bronco following.

Bishop watched in disbelief as Pablo's shot-up truck wobbled after them. It gained speed but could not keep up. They raced around a turn into a narrow pass cut through the rock. The damaged truck appeared again, skidded sideways, hit the sheer rock wall, and flipped. It came to a screeching halt, wedging itself in the narrow pass. Bishop couldn't believe it. The old man, in his last moments, had blocked the route, enabling them to escape.

Tears ran down his cheeks and he slumped against the cab of the blue truck. He swallowed and glanced at Mitch.

The Brit's eyes were misty. He wiped them with his sleeve. "So much bloody dust."

CHAPTER 29

Pershing surveyed the battlefield with a critical eye. The farmhouse had been completely demolished but not without cost. The dump truck was a blackened wreck, three of Burro's men were dead and another half-dozen had blast injuries, two of the cops were wounded, and for what? There was not a single body to be found. The farmer, his sons, and whoever was helping them had got away clean. "Burro, what's going on with those buggies?"

The Black Jacket had his radio pressed to his ear. "They're out of range."

He spat in the dust as the police SWAT commander left his vehicles and approached.

"How are your men?"

The policeman wore a scowl. "They'll live. We want our money. We're leaving."

Pershing took off his hat and ran his fingers through what was left of his hair. "The job isn't finished." He gestured toward the house. "You didn't kill anyone."

The officer held up a brass cartridge. "This is a blackout round. We saw camouflaged men with heavy weapons. American Special Forces. We're not going to fight men like that."

"They're not American. They're goddamn mercenaries and your boss sent you here to stop them."

"My orders were to report to you for a job." He tipped his head in the direction of the crushed house. "Looks to me like the job is done. Now, I've got men that need medical attention and we're leaving. So, pay me our damn money."

Pershing tossed him a thick envelope. "Tell your boss he's not getting his bonus." He walked off, took his satellite phone from his pocket and dialed the GES operations center at their facility in Virginia. Someone answered the phone after two rings. "It's Pershing. I want an update on the status of Team 2."

"Standby."

He watched the police trucks drive off as he waited.

"Sir, Team 2 is consolidating here. We expect them to be moving to your location within the next twenty-four hours."

"Twenty-four hours?"

"That's correct, sir."

He terminated the call and dialed King. "Sir, I need Team 2 in location as soon as possible."

"What's going on down there?"

"Nothing I can't handle. I just need people I can trust."

"Got it. Hang tight, help's on the way." King ended the call.

Pershing glanced over his shoulder. The trucks Burro had sent after the buggies had returned.

"Hey, Mr. Pershing. The boys got one of them."

He strode over to the trucks.

"Over here." Burro dropped the tailgate.

Lying in the back was a stocky, pot-bellied farmer. A spreading pool of bright red blood dripped off the tailgate. Pershing turned to Burro. "What about the others?"

The cartel lieutenant asked his men.

"They got away. They blew up the buggies and escaped."

The veins in the side of Pershing's head throbbed as he clenched his jaw. He pointed to the ground between the house and the smoldering dump truck. "Throw him down there. I want fuel, and I want a tire."

The mortally wounded farmer moaned as the Black Jackets pulled him from the truck and dragged him along the ground. They dumped him in a heap.

"Bring me the other one," said Pershing.

They pulled Roberto from the Chevy and stood him in front of the dying man.

"No, no." Tears ran down his cheeks as he recognized Pablo Veda. The rancher was an old family friend.

"You could have stopped this. You could have convinced them to pack up, take the money and go. But instead you wanted to fight. You wanted to take me on." Pershing leaned in close to Roberto's face. "Now y'all get to see what happens when you fuck with progress."

The Black Jackets propped up the dying man and placed a tire over his head. He collapsed as they drenched him in fuel. Burro lit a cigarette and passed it to Pershing.

"No, don't do it," Roberto pleaded. "He's already dying. Let him be."

"You tell me who's helping you and I'll let him die peacefully."

Roberto glared, shaking his head.

He shrugged and flicked the cigarette at Pablo.

The fuel ignited with a soft whoosh. The semi-conscious rancher was so far gone that Pershing doubted he felt a thing. That was unfortunate. A writhing, screaming mass of flame may have loosened Roberto's tongue. He studied Roberto's face. He showed no emotion as he watched his friend burn.

Pershing had seen men like this before. You could beat them, bribe them, and threaten them, but they never broke. He needed to find something the man truly valued. He needed to find his family.

***

It took them an hour to get to their next safe house. Emilio drove them along back roads as Mitch monitored the FAA app for a Predator mission. It was all clear but they had doubled back and checked for a tail anyway.

The property on the outskirts of Chihuahua had been selected by Chua's team in the Bunker. They had analyzed a number of commercial spaces that suited their needs and concluded that the warehouse was the best fit. It had room to park the vehicles inside, and contained accommodation, a kitchen, and offices.

Bishop dropped his chest rig on the floor of the kitchen and activated an iPRIMAL tablet. He stabbed the screen with a gloved finger and opened the target pack Chua had sent him. It was a file on the Chihuahua police chief containing biographical details, key associates, and his relationship with

Ground Effects Services, Pershing's parent company.

He was struggling to put his anger aside. Not only had they lost Pablo, but the farmer's youngest son was fighting for his life in hospital. Mirza's skill in stabilizing him was the only reason he had made it that far. Emilio had driven the boy and his brother into Ciudad Juarez for medical treatment. Whether or not he would live was now in the hands of the local health system.

"What have we got?" Mirza asked as he dropped his gear next to Bishop's.

Mitch sat cross-legged on the floor and started cleaning his machine gun.

Bishop's forehead crinkled as he studied the information on the screen. "It's the pack on the Chief of Police. Got a lot of detail considering the timeframe."

"So he's tied in with the mine?"

"Yes, the links are a bit loose at the moment but this might be a way to get to Pershing."

"It explains the SWAT team at the farm."

He continued to read. According to the Bunker's analysis of the GES financial records, they'd received a significant payment from a CIA shell company for an IT project in Chihuahua. Chua's intelligence team had linked the dates of the invoice to a media release on the rollout of a sophisticated CCTV system across the city.

"Mitch, what do you know about Cognitive systems?" asked Bishop.

"Tech firm based in California. They specialize in recognition algorithms and surveillance. Mexico City rolled out their CCTV analysis system, state-of-the-art."

"GE had the contract to install it in Chihuahua."

"Then you can guarantee the CIA is pulling the data."

"Can you use it to track people?"

"Sure can. You get a picture of the target and the facial recognition gear will follow them from camera to camera."

Bishop felt sick as he remembered the CCTV cameras at the scene of the riot in Chihuahua city. "They would have had

Christina's photo. The CIA would have passed the details to Pershing. Shit, we led them straight to Roberto. We got Emilio's son killed." He tossed the tablet on the bench and slumped against the wall.

Mirza grasped his shoulder. "We don't know that, Bish."

He shook the hand off. "Carlos, Pablo and his son, Christina and Roberto. Karla…" Bishop's voice trailed off.

Mirza's tone hardened. "You can't beat yourself up every time someone gets killed. It's Pershing who's responsible, not you."

"I'm going to make that bastard pay in spades. It's our turn to hit back. That fucker's been one step ahead of us the whole time." He picked up the tablet again. "Mitch, can you hack that Cognitive system?"

"Yeah, you get me into the server room and I can give Flash access. The problem will be getting inside."

Mirza flicked through the police chief's intelligence pack on his iPRIMAL. "Flash has access to the GE personnel files. He should be able to put together an ID card. They put the system in so they probably perform maintenance."

"Mirza, you're a dead set genius," said Bishop. "We get access to the system and…" He held up the tablet. The screen displayed a photo of the police chief. "We can track this guy and grab him. Then we convince him to cut his support for Pershing, and wring him for information."

"He might know what Longreach is. Has Chua worked it out yet?"

Bishop continued to scan over the target pack. "Don't think so."

"Could be drug related," offered Mitch as he pulled a cleaning rod through the machine gun's barrel. "I thought of something else too. If we want to trash the mine, we're going to need a shitload of bang."

"And anti-armor rockets," added Mirza.

"Yesterday it was intel collection only. Now we're going to blow the mine?" He shook his head, suppressing a grin as he took his phone from his pocket. "I'm guessing Emilio's nephew can supply exactly what we need. It's time to hit back."

CHAPTER 30

The police headquarters in Chihuahua City was a modern construction of polished concrete, exposed metal beams, and a high glass-walled entrance. It would have been more at home in Silicon Valley.

Mitch walked up the stairs to the foyer and felt a little intimidated by the constant stream of law enforcement officers coming and going. Dressed in a polo shirt, slacks, and a smart pair of leather shoes, he stood out from the uniformed personnel but they paid him no attention. Over his shoulder he carried a backpack loaded with his tablet, laptop, and a soft case filled with tools. Everything you would expect to find in the bag of an IT technician. If it was not for his bulging arms he might have been mistaken for a nerd.

He walked to the reception desk and smiled at the policewoman through the ballistic glass. "Hola, do you speak English?" he asked in a terrible American accent.

She smiled. "Yes, how can I help you?"

He pushed his ID card through the gap beneath the glass. "I'm from GE. Here to upgrade the C4I4 software." Mitch almost grimaced at the sound of his accent. Bishop had tried to school him in the art but he didn't have an ear for it. Well, he was committed now.

"I'm sorry, I don't know what that means." The woman turned and spoke to another officer. A third man, in civilian clothing, came over and spoke to them before approaching the glass.

"Hello, you are here to fix the computers?"

Mitch nodded. "Yeah, sort of. I'm here to update the software on the biometric recog system."

The man's face was blank.

"OK, yeah I'm here to fix the computers."

"Yes, you wait here. We will send someone down to see you." He pointed at the waiting area.

Mitch sat and picked up a magazine. It was in Spanish. He

thumbed through the pictures.

"Excuse me."

He looked up and saw an overweight man dressed in a suit and tie, sporting a full beard.

"I was told you are here to fix our computers? I'm the head of IT."

Mitch stood and shook his hand. "Hi, I'm Bruce from GE."

The man smiled. "Oh, you must be here for the Cognitive system." He handed Mitch a visitor's pass.

"That's the one, partner. We've got a new patch, speeds up searches by twenty percent."

His smile turned into a frown. "Your people usually do that remotely. Have there been any problems?"

"No, not at all. We just like to get out on site every now and then to check things over, and make sure our clients are happy. Don't worry, it doesn't cost you anything."

The IT manager looked relieved. "Well in that case, let me show you to the server room."

Mitch followed him to the elevator. "So, have you had any problems with the system?"

"No, it's been very good."

That's right, thought Mitch. The CIA would want it to work perfectly.

The manager led him out the elevator and down a corridor to a security door. He swiped the key access and they entered the server room. Mitch shivered; the air-conditioning was running full bore to keep the room at an icy fifty-three degrees.

"This is the Cognitive rack here."

Mitch gave it a once over then pulled out his laptop and plugged it in.

"How long do you think this will take?"

He keyed in a few commands. "About twenty minutes." He rubbed his hands together. "It's a bit colder in here than outside. Is there any chance you can whistle me up a coffee?"

The manager nodded and left the room. Mitch pushed in an earpiece and wirelessly tethered it to his laptop. "Flash, can you hear me?"

There was a slight delay as the signal bounced seven and a half thousand miles and back again. "I've got you loud and clear, bro, and I've got access to the system."

He watched as code raced across the screen of his laptop and heard Flash humming.

The door beeped and the IT manager appeared with a disposable cup filled with black coffee. "Hey thanks, bud." Mitch took a sip from the beverage. He was more of a tea kind of guy but no one seemed to drink it in the Americas.

The manager peered at the laptop screen. "No problems?"

"No, everything seems good. I'm just running a diagnostic, then I'll upload the patch."

"OK, well, I'll be back in about ten minutes, yes."

Mitch gave a broad smile. "Should be all done by then. Thanks for the coffee."

Once he was out the door Mitch transmitted to Flash. "The IT guy here looked straight at the screen, mate. Is he going to be able to read any of this?"

"Hell no. Would be like asking Chua to check out my code. That man wouldn't know ASCII from BASIC."

"I'm going to tell him you said that."

"He knows it. OK, I'm in. I've got access to the Cognitive database and the real-time feeds."

"First things first, you need to get Christina and Bish off the system. Then we need to track down the Chief of Police. We want full pattern of life." Mitch could hear Flash's fingers racing over the keyboard.

"Hey slow down, big fella. It's not often I get a man inside the bad guy's server room. Now, while you're there you might be able to patch the police email server into the Cognitive server. That'll give me full access to everything the dirty cops are up to."

Mitch glanced at his watch. "OK, but I've only got a few minutes at most."

"No problem. Use the cable from your laptop. The email rack should be labeled."

He moved down the aisle of servers searching for the email

database. The servers were numbered not named. "Flash, they've got numbers stuck on them."

"OK, wait a sec." Flash's fingers were racing again. He was not sure if it was possible but it sounded as if he was typing even faster. "Got it. You're looking for rack number three."

He examined the labels. Three was directly opposite the one they were working on. "Found it. He plugged the cable into an empty LAN port and connected the other end into the Cognitive server. "It's in. You've got to hurry, Flash. I can't leave this cable hanging halfway across the room."

"Yeah, yeah, keep your panties on."

The security door beeped and opened. Mitch reached across and put his hand on the plug in rack 003. The IT manager had the door open but was talking to someone in the corridor. "Hurry up!" he whispered.

Just as the manager pushed open the door Flash gave him the OK. Mitch yanked the cable.

"How's it all going?" the man asked.

"Good, I'm all done. The system's purring like a kitten." Mitch unplugged the cable and stashed it in his backpack. He slid his laptop inside and slung it over his shoulder. "I think you're going to be very happy with the increase in performance."

The manager returned his smile. "Very good. Now, I've got to go to a meeting. Do you mind showing yourself out?" he asked as he guided Mitch out of the server room and shut the security door.

"Sure thing." He offered the man his hand. As they shook he realized his palms were sweaty. He turned and walked down the corridor to the elevator. It took him to the ground floor where he made a beeline for the exit.

"Hey, stop!"

Mitch froze, his heart in his mouth. He turned around slowly.

"You need to hand in your security pass."

He walked across to the desk and handed over the pass. "Sorry, I forgot." He turned and strolled out the doors, down the steps, and hailed a taxi.

"We should definitely do this more often," said Flash through the earpiece. "I could get used to this sort of access."

"Go fuck yourself," replied Mitch. "Remember I'm a geek like you, mate, not an operator."

"Well, I'm not sneaking around in Mexico with a machine gun." Flash chuckled. "Anyway, I've wiped all links to the team. It's going to take us a few hours to get the intel Bish wants. I'll check in later."

A cab pulled up and Mitch got in. He gave the driver a slip of paper with an address. They drove three blocks before pulling over. He paid the man, walked through a park, and got in the blue Dodge pickup waiting on the other side.

"We good?" asked Bishop as he pulled out into the traffic.

"Good to go, mate."

"Excellent. Emilio's back from his nephew's and he's got everything we need. Bishop glanced at his iPRIMAL. The device was directing him to their new safe house, the empty warehouse on the outskirts of town.

"So, we're in business then."

Bishop nodded. "Let's take these bastards down."

***

Howard and his team had been working on Objective Yankee for three days but were no closer to identifying him or any of his associates. Pershing was calling every few hours and his boss, Everest, was demanding results. He figured he had a day to dig up a lead or the director was going to shut him down. Once that happened his resources would disappear and Pershing would cut off the payments.

He slammed a fist down on his desk. "How the fuck can these people simply not exist? They're running around killing cartel guys and no one knows who the hell they are."

Ben, his signals analyst was trawling through phone activity in vicinity of the mine. Shelly, the all-source analyst was on her lunch break.

Howard loosened his tie and waddled over to the bar fridge in the corner of the room. He popped a can of zero-sugar energy drink and took a hefty swig.

The door to the room opened and Shelly entered. "Any luck, boys?"

"No," mumbled Ben.

"Nothing," added Howard.

She sat at her workstation and got back to work.

The sound of fingers tapping away at keys was the only noise in the room as Howard stared at the wall. Shelly looked at him from over her screen. "Hey, Terry."

"Yeah"

"I've got some good news."

"You won lotto and we can all go home?"

"Not that good. The BfV got back to me about that information request." She referred to the Bundesamt für Verfassungsschutz, Germany's internal security agency.

Howard put his drink down and remained seated as he scooted his chair around to her desk. "Did they get a hit?"

"Yeah, that tall guy, Objective Red Sox, is one Wilhelm Jaeger, a former police officer and GSG 9 operator."

"No shit. So what's the go, has he gone rogue?" He leaned over her shoulder to read the email.

"No further information. If we want more details they're going to have to get a court order and put in a formal request to the German Federal Police."

"Did you search for the name in our database?"

Shelly nodded. "Yes, we've got nothing."

He rolled back to his desk and took another sip of the energy drink. A formal request for information was a big deal and would take the Germans days to get the required paperwork through. It would have to come from Everest so he needed to get moving. He adjusted his tie. "Can you print off what we've got? I'm going to have to go and see Everest."

***

Pershing took the memory card from Burro and slotted it into his laptop. The pictures that appeared on the screen were a little fuzzy but they served his purpose. "Good work, son. Now go and get me that piece of shit rancher."

Burro nodded and left the office. He hit print on the photos while he waited.

When Roberto was dragged in, Pershing winced. His face was battered and swollen, one eye completely closed over. He almost regretted letting the Black Jackets take out their frustrations on the prisoner. They had lost over a dozen of their comrades to the ranchers and mercenaries in the last week and Roberto had borne the brunt of their anger.

"Burro, can you get Mr. Soto a glass of water please." Pershing tipped back in his chair. "At first I thought that kid was a bit of a waste of time. Got to admit, he's really coming into his own."

The rancher stared at him with his jaw clenched.

"Still, that's not why we're here. I'm going to give you one last chance to tell me where the rest of your buddies are at."

Burro reappeared with a glass. He put it on the desk in front of Roberto. The rancher never even looked at it. He just stared at Pershing.

"Look, I understand. I grew up in an area not unlike this on a ranch not too different from yours. It was a hard life. Pop was tough and he would have fought tooth and nail had someone tried to take his land. But, it wasn't worth shit and when he died, he died a poor man. You tell me where your friends are and I'll give you twice what your land's worth. You ask Burro, I'm good for it."

The lieutenant nodded. "You sure are, Mr. Pershing."

Roberto pursed his lips and it looked like he was going to talk. But, instead he spat on the desk.

He sighed. "I didn't want it to come to this." He turned over the printed pages and pushed them to the other side of the desk. "But if you don't tell me where they are, the people you love are going to suffer."

He watched Roberto's face as he looked down at the

photos of his wife and children. The images had been taken at a shopping mall in Juarez. His stony glare softened and tears flowed from both of his eyes. One corner of Pershing's mouth turned up in a sinister smirk.

CHAPTER 31

Bishop laid plastic sheeting on the unfurnished office floor and taped it in place. He stood back and admired his handy work as Emilio brought in a metal chair and placed it in the middle of the room. "Thanks Emilio."

The old rancher stared at him for a moment.

"What's up?"

"You work for the UN?"

Bishop nodded. "That's right."

"What about the other two?"

"No, let's just call them security consultants. We go back a long way and they owe me a few favors."

"Mercenaries."

"Yes, except they're not getting paid."

"There's lots of gold at the mine. Maybe they could steal it?"

"That's not necessary. It belongs to your people, not us."

"Then why would they help us?"

Bishop grasped him by the shoulder. "Because not everyone in the world is a wolf, Emilio, some men are sheepdogs."

He walked into one of the bedrooms where Mitch was working on his iPRIMAL tablet. The team had made it off-limits to Emilio and his men. "How's it going?"

"Great, the boys in the Bunker have used the system's license plate identifier to track the police chief's movements. By working back through the archives they've ID'd his favorite brothel. He visits the Loco Poni most nights." He brought up a map of the city and showed Bishop the location.

"Excellent, we'll grab him there. What time does he usually go?"

"Between seven and ten. I can let you know as soon as he leaves the office. Flash has given me remote access to the system. If he turns right he's on his way home. If he turns left he's on the way to the titty bar."

"Let's hope he's in the mood for a little jiggy jiggy." Bishop left Mitch to monitor the system and joined Mirza in the living room. The PRIMAL operative was showing Miguel and Gerardo how to use the RPG-7. At Bishop's request they had received two of the rocket launchers from Emilio's cousin in the Sinaloa Cartel. "How many rockets they give us?" he asked.

"Only six," Mirza replied.

"Should be enough to take out that dozer. What about bang?"

"A lot. At least two hundred pounds of PowerGel in the back of Emilio's truck." Mirza left the two farmers with the unloaded RPG. "Bish, do you have a minute?"

"Sure, mate. Let's jump in with Mitch." He opened the bedroom door and pulled it shut behind them. "What's up?"

"I think we need to request additional support from the Bunker. We can't hit the mine with just the six of us."

He nodded. "I've already spoken to Vance about deploying the CAT. Some of the boys are still getting back from Europe but he reckons he can get them here ready to roll in forty-eight hours. We're going to wait till then to hit them."

"OK, good. And he's supportive of a kinetic solution now?"

"After what happened at the Veda ranch, he agrees there's no alternative. If we can come up with a sound plan involving the CAT, he'll green light it."

"Looks like our man's got a hard-on," whooped Mitch.

"What?" asked Mirza.

"The Chief of Police," said Bishop. "He's heading to his favorite bang bar." He clapped his hands. "Let's go pick him up."

***

Bishop looked out the window as Emilio parked the truck outside the address for the bar. "You sure this is the right place?" he asked. It was a squat, three-story building, with no windows. The cinder block walls were painted bright yellow and glowed under the streetlights.

"Yeah mate," said Mitch. "That's the chief's car over there." He pointed at the silver SUV parked down the street.

"And he's alone?"

"Well, probably not now. But he arrived alone."

"Right." Bishop checked his Beretta and holstered it under his jacket. He double-checked the TASER and auto-injector in his pocket. "I'm good to go. Everyone ready?"

"I'm ready," said Mirza.

"Me too," said Emilio.

"Good, let's keep this tight and fast."

They got out of the truck and approached a solid metal-clad door. Emilio buzzed the intercom and spoke to the voice at the other end. They talked for a good minute, the conversation sounding heated.

"What's the problem?"

"He says it's a private club. I told them you're very wealthy American miners. He's gone to ask his boss if it's OK."

They stood outside for a few more minutes before the intercom hissed and the voice returned.

"OK, they want two hundred US to let you in."

"What? That's robbery. OK, fine."

"They want to see the money."

Bishop pulled his wallet from his pocket and pulled out a wad of cash. He waved it in front of the camera on the intercom. Finally, the door clicked and Emilio pulled it open. They walked into a foyer where they were welcomed by a scantily clad hostess and a stocky, barrel-chested thug.

The bouncer held out his hand. "Two hundred dollar."

Bishop smiled and held out the wad of notes. As the guard reached for it he dropped the cash, grabbed the man's hand, and twisted it. A sharp kick knocked him off his feet and a moment later he was face down on the floor, hands bound with flexicuffs.

"Keep an eye on him, Mitch." Bishop pocketed the cash.

"Easy as pie." Mitch dragged the bouncer into the cloak room.

Emilio showed the terrified hostess a picture of the Police

Chief, asking in Spanish where he was. She shook her head. Bishop pulled back his jacket revealing the Beretta. She nodded and led them up a staircase to the second floor.

"What a shit hole," he said as they walked down a dimly-lit corridor with thick red carpet and brightly colored doors on either side. The air was thick with the stench of cigarettes and booze.

Mirza scrunched up his nose. "I seem to find myself following you into lots of places like this."

"Hey, if you want to hunt monsters, you got to go into the lair."

The girl stopped in front of a bright orange door. Bishop waved her out of the way and listened. It sounded like someone was filming a porno. He pulled a balaclava over his face and drew the TASER. Mirza did the same, drawing his pistol.

Emilio grasped the girl by the shoulder.

Bishop turned the handle and pushed the door open with his boot. Facing him was a naked, hairy, overweight man thrusting behind a curvaceous blonde. The girl screamed as he walked in. The policeman dove for the pistol he had thrown on the floor with his pants.

The twin probes from Bishop's TASER caught him in the side of his flabby torso and he went down hard. Bishop knelt and jabbed the auto-injector into his neck. The convulsing mass of fat and hair went limp, sprawled on the floor.

"OK boys, gift wrap that hairy turd for special delivery." Bishop gestured for the girl to grab her clothes and sit in the corner. Emilio brought the hostess in and told them to sit together.

Mirza grimaced as he pulled the unconscious man's legs together and wrapped tape around them. "How come I get all the unsavory jobs?"

Bishop grinned from where he was covering the door with his Beretta. "Hey, at least the TASER killed his boner."

"Thanks, real nice." Mirza finished taping his hands then pulled the bedspread from the mattress. "Emilio, help me wrap him up."

They rolled him in the blanket and taped it securely.

Bishop kept an eye on the corridor. "OK, guys, let's go."

Emilio and Mirza carried the bundle and Bishop led them out to the corridor, pistol drawn. A side-door opened and a half-dressed client appeared. Bishop aimed the Beretta. "Fuck off, yeah." The man's eyes widened and he retreated back into his room.

At the bottom of the stairs Mitch was waiting with a backpack slung over his shoulder. He pulled out a black nine-inch rubber dildo and waved it around. "I found a few props to help with the interrogation."

Bishop shook his head. "You're a fucking weirdo, Mitch. Give us a hand with this guy."

They carried the bundled up police chief outside and dumped him into the bed of the truck. Mitch stayed in the back with the prisoner while the others piled into the cab.

"That went well," said Mirza as he pulled off his balaclava.

"About time we had a win," replied Bishop as they drove back to the safe house.

***

The Chief of Police for Chihuahua was strapped naked to a metal chair in an empty room. His head was bowed, unconscious, and if he were not tied securely, would have slumped to the floor. Bishop pulled his balaclava down, picked up a bucket of ice-cold water, and dumped it over the naked prisoner. The man's head snapped up and he gasped for air, his eyes wide. "Wakey, wakey, champ!"

The chief started yelling in Spanish so Bishop slapped him. "Hey, hey, I know you speak English, so how about you wise the fuck up and start talking, yeah!"

"Do you know who I am?" spat the policeman. He strained against the tape holding him to the chair.

"I certainly do, Comandante Felipe Guzman. I know exactly who you are. I know where you work, I know where you live, and I know all about your little deals with Mr. George Henry Pershing."

Felipe shivered. "You stupid fucks. You don't know who you're messing with. Pershing is CIA, he's going to eat you for breakfast."

"Is he? That what he told you? Well I've got news for you, mate. He's as CIA as the pope is Mexican."

"Who are you working for, the Sinaloa?"

"I'm the one who's going to ask all the questions, Felipe. Now, how long have you been on the take from Pershing?"

"I'm not telling you anything."

"That right? What's your wife going to say when she finds out you're banging whores?"

"You think my wife gets a say in what I do? This is not America where the men are weak and the woman is boss. I fuck whoever I want to fuck."

"Oh, so you're a big man are you? Because from where I'm standing things aren't looking so big."

Felipe stared at a spot on the wall. Bishop had predicted this would happen. Threats were never going to work. Mexican society was centered on the image of the macho man. The strong male whose hacienda was his castle, and he was the lord. He already knew he'd have to get a little creative.

"OK, so this is what's going to happen, Felipe. You're going to tell me exactly what I want to know or things are going to get... interesting." He took a syringe out of his pocket and removed the safety cap. He showed it to the policeman then slid it into his arm and depressed the plunger.

Felipe fought against the tape. "What the hell is that?"

"Don't worry, it's nothing dangerous. Just a muscle relaxant and some Viagra." Bishop leaned in close. "You can feel it can't you? A warm fuzzy feeling, all your muscles relaxing, except one. But that's not a muscle is it?"

"What, what are you doing to me?"

"I'm not going to do anything to you. But my friend is. I'm just going to video it and send it to all your police buddies. Or maybe I'll just put it on the internet for all the perverts to jack off to." He opened the door. It took every ounce of his discipline not to burst out laughing. "Tell me, Felipe, are you familiar with the expression, I'm going to make a playground out of your ass?"

Mitch stood in the doorway wearing a gimp mask and a pair of cut-off denim shorts. His muscular, hairy chest was strapped into a harness with a steel ring in the middle. He was holding a giant black rubber dildo.

"What the hell?" screamed the bound man.

Bishop used his knife to cut the tape holding him to the chair. "It's OK, Felipe. You seem to be already enjoying this."

The policeman looked down at his raging boner.

"Nooo, you can't do this. You can't." Already his voice was slurring as the drugs kicked in.

"Then tell me what I want to know." Bishop knew he had him cracked. "Pershing's operations. I know about the mine, what else is there?"

"Nueva Piedras. Something going on out near Nueva Piedras. But I don't know what it is."

"You can do better than that."

Mitch strode over and caressed Felipe's leg with the dildo.

"Off highway 45, a wheat farm. They bought a wheat farm. I promise that's all I know." The police chief whimpered.

"You sure? Because if I find out you're lying, things are going to get real weird in here."

"I promise, I promise."

"Good, now there's one more promise I need you to make."

"Anything, just keep him away from me."

"The support for Pershing stops now. He gets no more police support. No more SWAT. No more officers. If he calls you, you don't answer. If he drops by your office, you deny him access. As far as you're concerned he no longer exists. Because if you don't comply, you're going to appear all over the internet."

"I promise, I promise."

Bishop turned away. "OK boys, try not hurt him too

much." He left the room as Mirza entered with a camera and a look of disgust.

He fought the urge to laugh as he returned to their operations room. While he was cross-referencing the new information, Mirza and Mitch would take some risqué video of the chief for insurance. Then they'd dress him in a set of coveralls and dump him close to his home. Apart from the video, the only trace remaining from the operation would be footage caught on the city's CCTV surveillance system. That was no concern; now that Flash had access to the server the recordings would simply be deleted.

CHAPTER 32

Mirza crouched at the edge of an irrigated field and scanned the sheds through a pair of binoculars. He was dressed in his camouflaged combat rig complete with a carbon nanotube helmet and a face wrap. A suppressed Tavor had replaced his sniper rifle.

He squinted at the floodlights that illuminated the cluster of sheds. He hit the transmit button on the foregrip of his weapon. "Bish, I've got a lot of vehicle and personnel movement out here."

"Roger, can you confirm what they're doing?" Bishop and Mitch were a few hundred yards behind him, in a dry irrigation channel.

"Negative. I'm going to have to get closer."

"OK, keep us posted."

He crouched low and moved through the waist-high grass with his weapon held tight in his shoulder. The terrain in every direction was dead flat. Perfect for agriculture as the heavy machinery could trundle across it watering, harvesting, and sowing. However, the lack of cover made it difficult for a covert approach. It was dark but he wasn't worried about being spotted by night vision equipment. The floodlights at the sheds would make it impossible for them to effectively employ any light amplification technology. He was more concerned with a roving patrol.

When he was a few yards from the edge of a crop circle, he dropped to his stomach and snaked forward to the limit of the thick green grass. He could see a pair of Black Jackets patrolling around the sheds as workers used a forklift to unload crates from the back of a flat-bed truck. The words on the side of the boxes were stenciled in Chinese. The truck blocked his view into the shed. He waited till the guards had disappeared around the corner of the building, then dashed from the edge of the grass to a stack of crates on the side of the concrete pad.

The forklift snorted as it jockeyed forward, pushing its forks in under a heavy crate. It lifted the load effortlessly and the driver backed it through the open doors into the shed.

Mirza slipped from the crates to behind the truck to get a view inside. He glimpsed more men inside the shed, dressed in coveralls. They seemed to be working on a production line. He watched as one man took a fiberglass wing out of a crate. Behind that, two more were unloading a pallet filled with plastic-wrapped bricks. They could only be one thing, drugs.

The sound of the forklift's engine warned him of its return. He slipped around the side of the truck and dashed back to the crates. "Bish, it's a drug distribution node," he whispered.

"Roger, how many shooters?"

"At least four guards and another five workers wearing coveralls. They're building some kind of aircraft."

There was silence as Bishop evaluated the situation. Mirza listened as the tractor unloaded another crate. By his calculations the guards should have circled the shed by now. He peeked around the side. He was right; they were standing at the open door smoking.

His earpiece beeped. "OK, Mirza, we're going to take the joint down. Mitch and I will move to the edge of the field. Meet us there."

"You sure that's a good idea? We're supposed to be gathering intel."

"We will be once we control the site."

Mirza recognized the tone of his friend's voice. Bishop had made up his mind and there would be no convincing him otherwise. At least, this time, the enemy didn't out-number them ten to one.

"Acknowledged. Be aware I have two hostiles twenty yards from my position. Once they move on I'll meet you."

"Roger. Moving now."

Five minutes later all three PRIMAL operatives were lying at the edge of the field peering through the grass.

"What do you reckon, Mirza?" whispered Bishop.

"We leave Mitch here to provide cutoff and cover the road. We take down the roving guards then sweep the sheds."

"Sounds good."

Mitch was armed with the suppressed 7.62mm MK48 machine gun. He wore a backpack filled with extra belts of ammunition.

The two guards finished another lap and strolled into view. The forklift had also finished unloading the flatbed and the driver started the truck's engine. "Let's wait till he goes," said Mirza. He watched as the truck made a three-point turn and disappeared down the road. "I've got the guy on the left."

"Ack," said Bishop.

"On three. One…" He took up the slack in the trigger as he exhaled and balanced the red dot on his target's head. "Two, three."

They fired in perfect synchronization, the .300BLK subsonic rounds barely audible. The heads of both guards exploded, spraying brain matter against the shed's sheet-metal wall as their bodies toppled.

Mirza led, moving swiftly across the loading slab with his Tavor ready. He paused, waiting for Bishop's hand on his shoulder to confirm he was ready. Then, he swung into the shed. He scanned left and right. A gunman filled his sights and he doubled tapped center of seen mass. An AK barked and bullets punched through the side of the shed. Bishop's Tavor snapped and another target dropped.

Mirza angled down the wall of the shed. He hit another guard with a double tap to the face. He caught a glimpse of another diving behind the pallet of cocaine bricks. Swiveling at the waist, he pumped rounds into the pallet. Cocaine exploded into the air as he kept firing. "Covering."

"Moving." Bishop strode smoothly across the factory floor and closed in around the pallet. He fired a rapid series of shots. "Target down."

Mirza swiveled his attention back to the other men in the shed. One of them had thrown down his weapon and was cowering behind a crate. The others had their hands in the air. "Get on the ground!" he yelled. At least one understood English, dropped to his knees, and lay down. The others followed his lead.

"Cover me," he said as he pulled a bundle of cable ties from his rig. He secured their wrists then checked their pockets for weapons and phones. By the time he was done there were five men secured on the floor and a collection of cell phones in his dump pouch.

Bishop strode forward covering the detainees. "Mitch, target is secure. I'm going to call Emilio and his boys forward."

With the gunfight over, Mirza finally had a chance to look around. The shed had been set up as some sort of drone factory. There were at least six completed aircraft in a line against the wall. He left Bishop to guard the prisoners and took a quick look. He'd been taking flying lessons with Mitch so could identify the basic characteristics of the miniature aircraft. They were twin-boom pushers with wingspans of about three and a half yards. They were fitted with what looked like the engine from a weedeater. "Bish, these things would be able to carry at least thirty pounds of cocaine each."

"Pretty clever little setup."

He knelt down and tapped the wing. "They're made out of fiberglass. I doubt any of the air traffic radars would even register this."

"Looks expensive. Pershing and his buddies are going to be real pissed when we blow it up."

Mirza's earpiece beeped as Mitch transmitted, "Lads, Emilio is inbound. We also got a ping from the sensors we left at the bed and breakfast ranch. Pershing and his thugs are hitting it now."

He watched as Bishop's face hardened. "Roberto must have compromised the old safe house. That means he's still alive."

"Or was when they got the info out of him."

***

Pershing jumped out of the Chevy and strode to the front door of the homestead. Burro met him in the empty kitchen. "No one?" he asked.

"Nada, Mr. Pershing. That dog lied to you again."

Pershing looked around the empty room. It was completely devoid of personal items. "Did you check the barn?"

"Yeah, no horses, just shit."

He frowned. "No, they were here. They knew we would come." The Predator flight over ranch had also reported nil activity. It wasn't surprising. If he were running the autodefensa he would have abandoned his safe houses as well.

"They'll have other places. Roberto will help us find them." Pershing expected Team 2 to arrive tomorrow. He would give 'Shrek' Cameron, the team leader, carriage of hunting down the enemy. That would allow him to concentrate on securing the mine and chasing up Howard's German lead. He was going to pull on every thread until this entire clandestine organization unraveled. However, there was a card he could play without Team 2. "Burro, give me your phone."

The lieutenant handed over his Nokia.

He stomped back to his truck.

"Mr. Pershing, what do you want us to do with this place?" Burro yelled after him.

"Burn it." He yanked open the rear door of his SUV. Roberto was sitting with his hands cuffed, his face a blackened mess of bruises and scabs. "There's no one here, Roberto."

"They were here," he croaked. "I don't know where they've gone."

Pershing almost felt sorry for the man. "Uncuff him," he said to the Black Jacket guard. When the rancher's hands were free he tossed the phone into his lap. "Ring one of your autodefensa pals."

Roberto's hands shook as he picked up the phone. He gave Pershing a defiant look.

He sighed. "Look, pal, you got two choices. You call your friend and your family lives, or you don't and…" He watched as Roberto slowly entered the phone number. When it started ringing he grabbed it. "Thanks."

"Hola."

"Hola yourself. You speak English?"

There was a pause. "Yes."

"Good, listen very closely. This is a message for you and whoever's helping you. I want you to come to the mine. I want you to hand over your guns. I'm going to give you ten grand US each and release your buddy, Roberto. Then, you're going to leave my operations the hell alone. You tell your mercenaries it's the same deal for them. You comply before noon tomorrow, or I'm going to kill Roberto and I'm going to kill his family. Then I'm going to hunt all of you down and kill you and your damn families. OK." He terminated the call. "Cuff him. If he gives you any trouble cut his throat." He slammed the door and turned to watch the ranch burn.

***

Bishop concluded briefing his plan. He had outlined it on the concrete floor using, by his estimate, about a hundred grand worth of cocaine to build the model. The team was gathered around him, except for Miguel who was covering the road with Mitch's machine gun.

"So that's it. We know Pershing is going to kill Roberto and you can guarantee he's going to know we've crashed this place within a matter of hours. But, if we make the first moves, we'll maintain the element of surprise. We can finish this now. Anyone have any questions?"

Emilio was squatting next to the model. Tools and odds and ends placed on piles of cocaine marked key locations in the mine. He chuckled to himself and looked up at the PRIMAL operatives. All three wore matching equipment: fatigues, chest-rigs, and weapons, everything camouflaged in matching A-TACS. "I like this plan. It is crazy for someone from the UN." He winked. "We are going to destroy monstruo and the Chaquetas."

"That's the idea." Bishop knew there was no way old Emilio still believed his UN cover story.

The rancher stood. "How did you know the location of the Chaqueta's base?"

"I know people who know things. What I don't know is Roberto's location in the mine."

"I will check with the boy who's working there."

"Excellent." He turned to Mirza and Mitch. "You guys want to take this offline?"

Both men nodded.

"Emilio, Gerardo, can you give us a minute?"

"Of course," Emilio said. The two Mexicans wandered over to the corner of the shed where the prisoners were sitting.

Bishop waited till they were out of earshot. "I already know what you're going to say, Mirza. But, if we wait for the CAT to get here, Roberto's going to be dead. They're still at least twenty-four hours away. The only other option is we try stalling, maybe call him back."

Mirza shook his head. "No, that's too risky. Your deception will work well. Now that the police chief won't be answering Pershing's calls, this is a good plan."

Bishop felt a smile tugging at the corners of his mouth. He turned to Mitch. "What do you think, mate?"

Mitch shrugged. "Hey, I reckon we owe it to Roberto. That tosser Pershing is going to kill him unless we surrender, and that sure as shit isn't happening on our watch."

Mirza glanced at his watch. "Well, we better get to work. We've got eight hours till sunrise."

"You sure about this?" asked Bishop.

The Indian operative nodded. "Like Mitch said, we owe it to the farmers. You just need to convince Vance."

"Might be better if we don't tell him."

Mirza raised his eyebrows.

"OK fine, I'll call him now."

CHAPTER 33

Pershing woke when someone started bashing on the door of his room. The flimsy material vibrated, making it sound like the entire transportable building was about to collapse. "Cut it out, damn it. I'm awake." He checked the time on his phone. It was 0520 in the morning. "What do you want?"

"Mr. Pershing, it's me, Burro. The drone base, it's under attack."

The fog of sleep instantly lifted, pushed away by a surge of panic and adrenalin. He grabbed his robe, slung it on, and wrenched open the door. "What the hell are you talking about?"

Burro held his phone up so Pershing could hear the gunshots and yelling. "It's Javier, he says they're under attack. They're holding out, but he needs help."

"Who's attacking? Police? Narcos?"

Burro spoke briefly into the phone. "He thinks it's the Sinaloa."

Pershing conducted a quick tactical evaluation in his head. If he sent his quick reaction force, the mine would be down on men, but that would be mitigated by the arrival of Team 2. They were due in this morning.

"Burro, send three pickups and twenty men. Tell them to protect the facility and take at least one prisoner for questioning."

"Yes, Mr. Pershing, I'll go myself."

"No, I want you to stay here."

He sat back down on the bed and rubbed his temples. The leak must have come from the police chief. Felipe wasn't answering his calls. Damn, he should have cut him in on Longreach. That greedy chili choker must have sold him out to the Sinaloa.

***

Mitch glanced down at the iPRIMAL strapped to his forearm. The time displayed was 0558 hours. "Where the hell are they?" He looked across at Miguel who was lying a few feet away. The Mexican shrugged and kept watching the track that led from the main road. "Trust me to get partnered with the only guy on the team that doesn't speak English."

They were laying on the roof of an equipment shed a half-mile from the drone factory. Mitch was in full combat gear with a Tavor assault rifle and Miguel had an AK. It had been nearly thirty minutes since they had forced one of their Black Jacket prisoners to make the call to their boss, and Mitch was keen to be off the roof by the time the sun peeked over the horizon.

Miguel pointed down the road. "Mirá."

He didn't know what the word meant but got the gist of it. Headlights turned off the main road and moved down the track toward them. He raised a thermal imager and could easily make out three pickups filled with gunmen. "It's them." He activated an app on his phone. All five connections were green. His finger hovered over the screen as he watched the trucks approach. When they reached the fencepost he was using as a marker, he tapped the device.

The ground beneath the convoy erupted as a series of five charges detonated. The explosives launched the trucks skyward, ripping them apart. He watched with the imager as passengers and chunks of metal were sent hurtling through the air like children's toys.

"Bloody hell!" Mitch had not laid the charges. It had been Mirza's responsibility. The Indian must have packed at least another twenty pounds of fertilizer and diesel around each bomb.

As the dust settled they climbed down from the roof. He placed his assault rifle in the back of the farm's ATV and climbed in. Miguel jumped into the passenger's seat and they drove back to the main sheds. He tried not to dwell on the fact he had just vaporized at least two dozen men. "Gents, ambush has been sprung. Moving back to the release point. Standby for aircraft launch in five," he transmitted over his Bluetooth headset.

Bishop and Mirza both acknowledged the message.

Mitch drove the cart into the well-lit main shed. The prisoners were gone, locked in the transportable accommodation block behind the hangars. He pulled up next to the UAV launching ramp where the first aircraft was positioned. There were three more sitting ready next to it.

His laptop was already plugged into the drone's control system and he double-checked the destination coordinates he had programmed. Happy they were correct, he armed the payload on the first drone, and closed the maintenance hatch with an electric screwdriver. He hand cranked the prop. The little engine caught on the first spin and buzzed to life, filling the shed with noise. He hit the catapult release button and the hydraulic ram shot the aircraft out through the open doors and into the brisk morning air. "First bird is airborne and on her way to the target," he transmitted before resetting the hydraulic ram.

Bishop responded first. "Roger. We're standing by."

Mirza was next. "I have eyes on target two."

Miguel helped him lift the second aircraft onto the catapult. With a thirty-pound load in its cargo hold, it was not light.

"Bird two is on the ramp and ready to go. Let me know when you want it."

This time it was Mirza who responded first. "Green light from me."

"Green light here too," confirmed Bishop.

Mitch spun the prop and reached down to hit the catapult release. Once this one was gone there was no turning back, they were at war. "Bird two is airborne."

**

Raphael Cardenas liked to think of himself as a connoisseur of fine things. His villa on the outskirts of the Mexican town of Buenaventura was a decadent display of luxury. Every day, workers tended to the swimming pool and elaborate gardens. Inside, an interior designer had spared no expense at modernizing the mud-brick construction with marble, polished wood, and boutique furniture.

The two hundred year old hacienda had been purchased, renovated, and decorated with funding from the mine project. That single operation had turned his small gang of criminals into a militant cartel overnight, allowing him to hire more fighters, buy more guns, and partner with the bigger Juarez cartel. Now, with the commencement of Pershing's drone flights, he was about to move into the lucrative business of narcotics smuggling. Soon, he would be in a position to wrestle territory from the Sinaloa.

Cardenas sat on the balcony of the upper story of the hacienda in his robe. An early riser, the cold did not bother him. He always took breakfast at daybreak, enjoying watching the sun rise over the desert. One of his servants brought him a tray with a newspaper and a glass of orange juice. He unfolded the paper and started reading.

He was on the second page of the sports section when a faint buzzing caught his attention. He frowned and lowered the paper. Was it a wasp? No, the noise was getting louder. It sounded like an airplane. He stood at the rail to see who was disturbing the serenity of the morning.

In the distance he spotted a speck. The aircraft was approaching directly. For a second he wondered if it was one of the American spy planes. No, it was flying low, and he wasn't important enough for that. It had to be some idiot in his light aircraft going for a joy flight. He had half a mind to grab the gold-plated AK from his room and give the moron a burst to send him on his way.

He sat back at the table and opened up the paper. He tried to ignore the sound but the droning was getting louder and louder. "Ay Dios mío!" As Cardenas dropped the paper he caught a glimpse of the gray drone before it slammed into the hacienda.

The fiberglass wings snapped clean off as it penetrated the

western wing of his home and detonated. The shock wave from the explosion threw Cardenas from his chair and part of the roof collapsed on top of him. Tiles and wood pinned him to the floor and he struggled against them. The air was filled with dust and smoke, burning his lungs as he fought for breath. He heard voices. "Here!" he yelled. "I'm here!" Hands pulled the wreckage from him.

"We've got to get out of here, boss," said one of his Black Jackets. "The place is on fire."

Cardenas let the man guide him through the wreckage and out across the lawns to the garage. When they were clear he turned back to watch his pride and joy burn. The entire west wing of the building had collapsed and was ablaze. If the drone had struck twenty yards to the right it would have killed him. He clenched his jaw. He knew whose work this was. "Get as many men together as you can, we're going to the mine."

***

Pershing shoveled the last of the omelet into his mouth and washed it down with a glass of water. He could say one thing for the Mexicans; they ran a tight ship in the camp kitchens. Every meal was delicious. He took a sip from his espresso and reached for his phone. He had waited till seven to ring King. Not for fear of waking his boss, he did not want to interrupt his run. He dialed the number and waited for him to pick up.

"George, what's up? Shrek and his boys arrived yet?"

"Not yet, sir. I expect them within the hour. I need to let you know that Longreach is under attack. I've dispatched the Black Jackets to find out what's going on."

"Do you know who?"

"I've got my suspicions. I think the Chief of Police may have sold us out to the Sinaloa."

There was a pause before King responded. "What are you going to do about it?"

"I'm thinking it's time he was replaced. His second-in-command is our man through and through."

"Very good, authorized. If Longreach is compromised, so be it, just as long as it doesn't blow back on the mine. Have the CIA tracked down Objective Yankee or any of his associates?"

"Howard has identified a potential link in Germany. Once he has more information I'll pass it along. Looks like they're some kind of international mercenary outfit."

"Sounds like wannabe A-Team assholes. As soon as the details firm up, let me know. They're going to find out very quickly it doesn't pay to mess with professionals."

"Yes, sir, I've got a local here that was working with them. I want to move him to one of the rendition facilities."

"That's going to take some effort, leave it with me. That all?"

An explosion shook the walls of the transportable office.

King chuckled. "Sounds like you're getting a bit too close to the blasting there, George. I'll leave you to it."

He hung up and dashed out of the office. The scene that greeted him was one of complete chaos. The equipment sheds were burning, thick smoke hung in the air, and miners ran from their accommodation in all directions.

"What the…" A buzzing sound filled the air and he looked up, catching a glimpse of a small gray drone. It disappeared behind the sheds. A devastating explosion shook the ground and a fireball rolled into the sky. It had hit the fuel dump. He spotted the mine manager running through the smoke. "Where the hell are you going? Get those goddamn fires out."

The man stopped and stared at him. "Yes, sir." He ran toward the fires.

Pershing opened the door of his SUV and grabbed the radio mike. "Burro, where the hell you at?"

"I'm here, Mr. Pershing."

He glanced over his shoulder. The cartel leader had an assault rifle in his hands and his combat vest on. "What happened to the men who went to the factory?"

Burro shook his head. "They're not answering."

His phone vibrated. Howard could pick the best times. He answered. "Unless you can get me a fucking SEAL team, I don't have time to talk to you."

"What?"

"I'll get back to you." Pershing terminated the call and turned his attention to Burro. "How many men you got right now?"

"Only ten, Mr. Pershing. All the others went to the drone farm."

"Get them ready. I think we're about to be attacked."

***

Mirza's camouflaged combat fatigues blended in perfectly with the rocky slope overlooking the mine's camp. He was laying between two boulders with his HK marksman's rifle trained on the camp's front gate. The laser rangefinder built into the scope read four hundred meters to the security checkpoint. Well within range.

"Both drones struck the mining facility. Equipment sheds and the fuel farm are burning," he reported.

Mitch's voice responded. "Roger, last bird is ETA four minutes."

Mirza used his rifle's digital scope to snap a picture of the burning facilities and transmitted it to the others.

Bishop replied within seconds. "Good work, guys. Mirza, send SITREP on security."

"I've only seen a couple of guards at the front gate."

"Roger. Once that final bird hits we're moving in to get Roberto." He was waiting a short distance from the mine with Emilio and Gerardo in the Dodge.

"I'm poised to provide surgical fire support," reported Mirza as the buzz of the third drone filled the air. "Mitch, your bomb is early." He watched as the little gray aircraft swooped over the top of the hills. The PRIMAL technician had removed the parachute system so when the drone reached its destination it simply dove into the mining infrastructure. Thirty pounds of PowerGel exploded in an angry ball of flame.

"Direct hit on the processing plant. Bishop, you are good to go." He swiveled the rifle to cover the security checkpoint. Smoke now obscured most of the camp and he wished he had a thermal scope.

CHAPTER 34

Bishop jumped in the back of the pickup, followed by Gerardo. He thumped the top of the cab with his fist. "Let's roll."

The Dodge roared and took off up the winding dirt road toward the mine. Bishop stood in the bed of the truck with a MK48 machine gun poised on the roof. The rubber caps on the bipod legs held it firm as they raced up the road toward the security checkpoint.

When they were three hundred yards short Emilio slowed, giving Bishop a stable firing platform. The MK48 snarled as he blasted the guardhouse with 7.62mm rounds. With the Black Jackets dead or cowering, Emilio accelerated and Bishop ducked behind the cab.

The big truck hit the gate, buckling it with a clang. It clung to the front of the bullbar as they smashed through. At a T-junction, Emilio turned right and the gate dislodged, dropping beneath the wheels. The track was a service route that followed the fence line. It snaked in behind the accommodation block where Emilio's contact had reported that Roberto was being held.

Bishop braced himself against the cab, racked the action, unclipped the top cover, and switched out the box of ammunition for a new one. As they pulled up alongside the accommodation buildings he handed the machine gun to Gerardo and unslung his Tavor assault rifle. "Cover me."

Emilio stayed with the truck as Bishop jumped out followed by Gerardo. Adrenalin surged through his veins but he forced himself to remain calm, moving cautiously through the rows of transportable accommodation.

He knew Roberto was supposed to be at the guard's accommodation but all the buildings looked the same. They moved through the rows of prefabricated buildings, looking for armed guards. Nothing.

His earpiece crackled and Mirza reported. "Bish, two black

SUVs have arrived at the front gate. They're blocking your exfil."

"Damn!" The plan had been to recover Roberto and get out by now. "Black Jackets?" After the drone strikes he expected the Chaquetas Negras to come after Pershing, but not this quickly.

"Negative, they look like contractors." The iPRIMAL strapped to his arm vibrated and he glanced down at the image received from Mirza's digital scope. Two black armored Chevy Suburbans and a handful of heavily armed gunmen had taken up defensive positions at the entrance to the mine.

"Roger, I'm still trying to find Roberto. Keep me posted." He moved over to where Gerardo was kneeling with the machine gun. "We're going to start searching these buildings. I'll lead."

***

Pershing drove in alongside two identical-looking black Chevys. Team 2 were waiting; the six operators had secured the demolished gates to the mine. As he stepped out of his truck a hulking brute with a shaved head and a goatee greeted him. The GES team leader was wearing a heavily-laden chest rig. Tattooed muscular arms burst from his tight T-shirt as he gripped his folding stock FAL battle rifle.

"Shrek, damn good to see you." Pershing shook his hand.

"What the hell is going on here?"

"We've been hit by mercenaries."

Shrek gave a whistle. "Looks like you got fucked hard."

"You could say that. They hit us with indirect fire first then shot their way in." He pointed to the bodies strewn around the bullet-ridden guard box.

"What's the plan?

"I need you to hold here. It's the only way out."

"Will do." Shrek issued orders to his men and they started pulling black Pelican cases from their trucks and unloading heavy weaponry.

Pershing nodded approvingly as an M240L machine gun and a Milkor grenade launcher appeared. One of the men handed him an AR carbine and a ballistic vest.

"It's amazing what you can bring across the border when you work for the right people," said Shrek. He signaled to two of his men and they set up defensive positions on the high ground overlooking the road. Another of his men blocked the exit with one of the armored SUVs.

"So, where are they?" the Team 2 commander asked as he surveyed the mine's camp with a pair of binoculars.

"They'll be in the accommodation block. We've captured one of their men and they want him back."

"And where are your indigenous guys?"

Pershing reached inside the SUV and grabbed the radio mike from the console. "Burro, report your location."

"I've got my men at the accommodation, Mr. Pershing."

"Hang tight, I'll send two of my guys in to back you up. I want you to work with them to hunt down any intruders."

"OK, Mr. Pershing."

Shrek nodded. "Mikey, Chris, clear through the accommodation area. The Mexicans wearing the Black Jackets are ours. You're looking for some guy called Burro."

"Copy that." The two operators jumped into one of the Chevys and sped off.

Pershing pressed the radio handset. "Burro, my boys are moving to you now. They're in a black SUV. Tell your men not to shoot at 'em."

"OK, Mr. Pershing. I tried to call the others at the drone farm again but they aren't answering."

He took a deep breath. "Forget about them. I want you to kill anyone in the mine who isn't supposed to be here. We'll block the exit, no one gets out."

***

Bishop kicked open the flimsy door to one of the accommodation buildings. Moving swiftly he checked the rooms. They were empty. There were over a dozen more buildings to clear.

As he rounded a corner he almost collided with two miners dressed in florescent safety vests and hard hats. They threw their arms in the air.

"Don't shoot, eh." The miner had a Canadian accent.

"Where's the prisoner?"

"Over in the guard's accommodation."

"Where's that?"

The man pointed across the road. "Behind the gym."

"Thanks. I'd get out of here if I was you. Tell your buddies."

The miner nodded and ran in the opposite direction.

Bishop's eyes were stinging from the thick black smoke that hung in the air. He coughed as he dashed across the road with Gerardo in tow. Behind the building marked GYM he saw an armed gunman standing next to an open door. A Black Jacket. A second man appeared dragging Roberto out of the building by his cuffed hands.

The first guard went to raise his weapon and Bishop gave him a third eye. The man leading Roberto dropped his AK and threw his hands up.

"Turn around!" He shoved the guard back through the open door, kicking his legs out from under him. With Gerardo covering he searched his pockets and found the keys to the cuffs.

"Roberto, you OK, mate?" Bishop said as he unlocked the cuffs and placed them on the Black Jacket.

"Yes. But I can't walk far." The rancher's voice was hoarse.

"We're going to get you out of here." He thumbed the transmit button on a UHF radio attached to his chest rig.

"Emilio, we need a pickup at the other end of the accommodation."

"OK, coming now."

Bishop pressed his iPRIMAL and transmitted to Mirza, "I've got Roberto. We're heading to the truck now."

"Acknowledged. Be aware, you've got one vehicle

inbound."

"Can you cover us?"

"Negative, I've still got limited visibility."

"What's the exfil looking like? The gate open?"

"It's blocked, at least four guys, heavily armed. You've got a chance if I suppress them. There's no other way out."

"Let's do it," Bishop transmitted as left the building with Roberto. The blue Dodge pickup barreled around a corner and screeched to a halt with Emilio at the wheel.

Gunfire sounded and bullets lashed the gravel and whistled through the air. Bishop sprinted behind the pickup and fired a volley of rounds in the direction of their attackers.

Dropping to the ground, he looked under the car and caught a glimpse of a gunman's boots. Tilting the Tavor sideways he snapped off a shot, dropping the man. Another series of shots finished him off. He changed the mag and out the corner of his eye glimpsed two gunmen wearing tan chest-rigs off to his flank. As he hit the bolt release time seemed to slow. The lead man had a bead on him. The ground between them exploded into dust and they skidded to a halt, backpedaling away. They dove out of sight and Bishop glanced over his shoulder.

Gerardo gave him a grin and fired another burst from the MK48. "Covering!" he screamed. Behind him Roberto was limping to the truck. Bishop ran up and threw him over his shoulder. He lumbered back to the vehicle, threw Roberto into the back, and leaped in after him.

Gerardo fired another burst as he ran. More gunmen appeared from the buildings. He reached the truck and tossed the machine gun in the back. As he clambered over the side one of the operators with a tan chest-rig snapped off a shot. Gerardo's head exploded, spraying Bishop in gore. The corpse seemed to cling to the vehicle for a moment before dropping into the dust.

"Fuck! GO, GO, GO!" Bishop screamed to Emilio as he slewed onto the shooter and emptied his magazine.

The truck lurched forward. He slid into the bed, grabbed

the MK48 machine gun, and rested it on the tailgate. They sped through the mine's camp and swung onto a service road, turning toward the mining operations area and gaping open-cut pit. As they left the camp, Emilio slowed and yelled out the window. "Where to now, Aden?"

"Go, just go."

He pressed the transmit button. "Mirza, Gerardo is down. Roberto is injured. Can we still exfil?"

"Negative, Bish. More vehicles have joined the party. There's no way you'd get past."

An image appeared on his iPRIMAL. Five vehicles had pulled up a hundred yards short of the front gate and two-dozen Black Jackets had dismounted.

"Shit."

Emilio brought the truck to a halt at the edge of the mine's pit. Bishop stood up in the tray and surveyed the terrain. The road turned off to a ramp that wound down into the expansive hole. There was no way out. All sides were dominated by sheer cliffs.

"Bish, there's some sort of standoff. The Black Jackets don't look friendly," Mirza transmitted.

"You reckon you can get them shooting, like we did in Japan?"

"I'll see what I can do. You need to find a place to hide."

Bishop had other ideas. His eyes fell on one of the huge yellow front-end loaders parked at the bottom of the pit and he banged on the roof of the truck. "Take us down there!" he yelled to Emilio.

***

Mikey and Chris had returned as the five-vehicle convoy stopped a hundred yards short of the gate. Despite being shot in the chest-plate, Chris was combat effective and took up a firing position.

Shrek passed his binoculars to Pershing.

"Cardenas," Pershing said as he focused on the distinctive

Conquest Knight armored SUV. The Chaquetas boss's vehicle was surrounded by four smaller trucks. Assault-rifle wielding gunmen were aiming their weapons at the mine's security checkpoint.

At first he had thought the Black Jackets had sent reinforcements to help, but now he wasn't so sure. Especially when Burro wasn't answering his radio. The handset in his vehicle crackled and he walked over to it. Finally.

"Burro, where you at?"

"This is Raphael Cardenas," came the reply.

"Raph, it's good to see you here. I'm having a little issue with the local farmers."

"I don't give a fuck about your issues. You know what your fucking issue is? You tried to kill me and you failed. That's your fucking issue."

Pershing glanced at Shrek who wore a bemused expression. "Listen, I don't know what the hell you're talking about. Take a look at the smoke coming from the mine and you'll see I've been attacked as well. You come up here and I'll show you who tried to kill you."

"No, I will not. I want you to give me access to the gold storage. I will take gold as compensation, then–" Cardenas's demands were interrupted by a series of shots cracking through the air. The radio went dead.

"What the fuck?"

A second later the Mexican gunmen opened fire and all hell broke loose. Bullets crashed into the SUV blocking the gate, ricocheting off the ballistic glass and the armored plate.

The response from Team 2 was controlled and aggressive. As Pershing dropped to the ground, the M240 started firing bursts from the high ground.

"You really pissed these fuckers off." Shrek wore a broad grin.

Pershing shook his head. "Someone did." He fired a series of rapid shots at the armored Conquest Knight.

"Hey, boss. You might have better luck with this." One of Shrek's men handed him a Milkor grenade launcher. Pershing grabbed the oversized six-shooter and unfolded the stock. He had trained on the weapon but never fired it in anger. He flicked off the safety, shouldered it, and centered the red dot on the black armored truck. The launcher kicked and he watched the grenade sail through the air and score a direct hit.

"Bang on, nice!" shouted one of the men.

Gunfire from the Black Jackets tapered off as the M240 sent them scurrying for cover. The cartel vehicles started reversing, attempting to distance themselves from the onslaught. As the Conquest Knight backed up Pershing hit it with the other five grenades. He laughed as the truck reversed haphazardly with one of its front wheels ablaze.

***

From the bottom of the mine's pit the sounds from the battle at the gate were muted. Bishop ignored the gunfire and focused on the yellow L-2350 front end loader towering above him. He'd never seen anything like it. A gargantuan 258-ton tractor as large as a two-story house, the loader was designed to work with the equally massive dump trucks. The four wheels were three times his height, and at the front a gaping black bucket looked like it could swallow a bus.

"Leave the truck, let's get on to this thing," he told Emilio and Roberto. They climbed the ladder on the side, managing to get Roberto into the back of the cabin. Emilio stood guard on the rear deck, wielding the MK48 machine gun, an RPG rocket launcher slung across his back.

In the driver's seat, Bishop frowned as he tried to make sense of the mass of buttons and switches. The central touch screen was blank, as were the video screens around the top of the cockpit.

He searched the cabin for a user guide or a start-up checklist. A booklet was wedged in the side of the front console and he flicked it open. There was a diagram showing what all the buttons did. He identified the start-up sequence, flicked some switches, turned a dial, and hit the ignition button.

Behind him the huge diesel engine rumbled to life. The touchscreen in the cabin lit up as the beast came alive. Around the sides of the cabin, flat screens displayed camera feeds from around the tractor.

His earpiece crackled. "Bish, it worked. I got them fighting but it's going to go on for a while," Mirza transmitted. The shots in the background were louder through the radio.

"Roger, can you get to the entrance to the pit? I've stolen one of the loaders. We'll pick you up on the way through."

"The contractors are pounding the cartel guys. They've got heavy weapons."

"Yep, and now I've got the world's biggest Tonka tractor."

As the engine warmed, he left the cockpit and walked out to the sloped back of the loader. A guardrail ran around the edge of the engine housing which was about the same size as the entire Dodge truck. Emilio had the machine gun resting on the rail and was staring in the direction of the gunfire.

"All good?" Bishop yelled over the rumbling exhaust.

The rancher gave a thumbs-up. Bishop responded with a reassuring smile and ducked back inside the cockpit. He checked on Roberto, huddled behind the driver's seat. "You OK, mate?"

The rancher's one good eye opened and he nodded.

"Right, it's time to get us out of here." He cracked his knuckles and settled into the driver's seat. "OK, big girl, let's see what you can do."

He pulled back on the joystick that controlled the bucket and it lurched into the air with a whine. He positioned it so it was just off the ground. According to the booklet the joystick on the other side controlled the steering. As he pushed the accelerator the loader snorted and trundled forward. He moved the steering joystick and the loader changed direction.

"Bish, I'm on the move. Will be at the top of the pit in the next few minutes," Mirza transmitted.

"Ack. It's going to take a while to drive this thing up from the bottom." Bishop aimed the massive digger at the ramp that wound its way from the floor of the pit to the road five levels above. It looked narrow. He got the front wheels onto the ramp. "Holy crap." It barely fit, with only a few feet free either side. He gave the loader a little more power and started climbing. He made slight adjustments with the joystick as he watched the camera feeds around the tractor.

"Oh shit." He overcorrected as they came close to the edge. The bucket clipped the wall of the pit tearing into rock. A gentle push on the joystick brought it back to the center and they ascended the winding ramp.

After what seemed like an eternity, he crested the pit and eased on the brakes. He searched the rocky slopes. A camouflaged shape materialized from among the boulders at the side of the road. It was Mirza. With his rifle slung across his back, he ran to the ladder and scaled the side of the loader. When he reached the cockpit Bishop gave him a nod. "Right, let's smash some shit!"

CHAPTER 35

Pershing crouched behind his truck as he watched a drone feed on a ruggedized tablet. One of Shrek's men sat across from him piloting the battery-powered quadcopter. It was flying over the Chaquetas Negras contingent. What was left of the cartel had sought cover behind a small hill.

"How many left?" asked Shrek.

"At least twenty. What I wouldn't give for some air support," replied Pershing.

"Well, we got the next best thing. Crack out the fireworks, boys."

A black case was dragged from the back of an SUV and the lid unsnapped. An operator pulled a 60mm M6C mortar from the box. He connected the base plate and sighted it as another man unloaded a crate of bombs.

"You guys pack for everything," said Pershing.

Shrek checked the drone feed. "Range 260 meters. Charge one, HE load."

He watched as the contractor tore all but one of the charge rings from a mortar bomb and slid it down the tube.

"Fire!"

The operator thumbed the trigger and the round left the tube with a thump. Pershing watched the screen intently. The cartel gunmen had gathered around the armored truck and the SUVs. Cardenas was giving his orders. There was a flash and a dozen of them disappeared in a cloud of dust. The sound of the explosion rolled over the hill.

"Smack on, boys. Time to shake and bake these fuckers."

The mortar team loaded another round, this time the bomb had a yellow ring around it. They fired, then reloaded and fired again.

Clouds of white smoke and burning phosphorous erupted among Cardenas and his men. The smoke and dust engulfed them all.

"Ceasefire!" Shrek yelled after ten bombs had dropped on

the stricken Chaquetas.

On the drone feed Pershing could see some of the vehicles were ablaze. Only one managed to escape down the road. The Conquest Knight wasn't moving. He glanced across the hill and watched as a white cloud plumed into the sky. Screams echoed in the distance.

Shrek pulled two long green tubes out of his vehicle. "You want the honors, George?"

Pershing nodded, taking one of the AT4 anti-armor rockets. They crested the hill until Cardenas's big Conquest Knight came into view. Both hefted the rocket launchers to their shoulders, and fired.

One of the rockets missed, detonating in the distance. The other impacted the luxury armored vehicle square on. There was a flash and black smoke joined the still burning white phosphorous.

Pershing smiled. "I reckon you boys just earned yourself a bonus." The sound of a diesel engine caught his attention and he turned in time to see a mammoth front end loader smashing its way through the accommodation buildings. "What the hell?"

**

Bishop slapped the touch screen in frustration. He had the accelerator planted to the floor and according to the digital display he was moving at a snail's pace of ten miles an hour. At least the accommodation buildings weren't slowing him down. One after another they folded like cardboard under the massive bucket.

The loader gradually gathered momentum, powering up the service road to the front gate. From his vantage point he had witnessed the last of Team 2's battle with the Chaquetas Negras cartel. The three black SUVs at the front gate were in a defensive formation with what appeared to be a mortar team. A couple of hundred yards down the road he saw the other group of SUVs was ablaze. Burning corpses littered the ground around them.

Bishop angled toward the vehicles at the front gate, raising the bus-sized bucket to deflect any gunfire.

***

Pershing reloaded the grenade launcher and fired a volley of grenades at the loader. Four of the rounds detonated harmlessly in the immense bucket. The fifth hit a tire, with zero effect. "More rockets!" he yelled.

"All out." Shrek surveyed the scene of destruction and looked back at his five men. He gave them a signal and they started loading gear into the trucks. "George, we need to haul ass."

He knew Shrek was right. Even with rockets, this fight was a lost cause. Without the local guard force, his small team couldn't secure the mine. He spat in the dust. "Let's go."

As he turned and hurried to his vehicle, the loader's bucket lowered and he spotted the driver at the controls of the monster. They locked eyes and the man he knew as Objective Yankee extended his middle finger. "Son-of-a-bitch, I buried you!" he exclaimed.

He watched in disbelief as the tractor crushed another building. A high-velocity round cracked through the air, snapping him into action. Wrenching open the door of his SUV, he jumped in the driver's seat. Shrek and his team had already loaded and tore off down the mountain road. He glanced in the rear vision mirror and clenched his teeth as the huge loader continued to rumble toward him. Spinning the wheels, he accelerated after the others.

***

Out the corner of his eye, Bishop saw Mirza run to the side of the cabin. The PRIMAL sniper balanced his HK on the handrail and gestured for Bishop to drop the bucket further. As it lowered Mirza fired another series of rapid shots at the three fleeing SUVs. Bullets glanced off the rearmost vehicle's armored glass as it sped down the mountain road. "Mirza, RPG."

"Way ahead of you, Bish."

He glanced to the opposite side. Emilio had the rocket launcher shouldered and fired at the last SUV.

The rocket left the tube with a boom and hit the Chevy's back window. The HEAT warhead failed to detonate and glanced off the laminated bulletproof glass.

Focused on the contractors, Bishop missed seeing the Black Jacket who ran across and jumped onto the loader's side ladder.

The cockpit shook as Emilio reloaded and launched another RPG at the fleeing vehicles. The rocket flew a few hundred feet, hit the road and exploded. The convoy rounded a corner and disappeared.

"Let's make sure they've got nothing to come back for," Bishop said as he toggled the joystick and swung the tractor toward the refinery and smelting works. Black smoke hung over the structures from the fuel dump that was still burning.

Out the corner of his eye he spotted a hand reach up from the side ladder and grab Emilio's leg. The rancher lost his balance and fell, striking his head on the rail. He lay still as a black-jacketed Mexican climbed onto the platform.

Bishop recognized him. It was the cartel lieutenant called Burro. He wore aviator sunglasses and had a wicked scab on his cheek. Bishop snatched his pistol from his holster and fired it. In the confines of the cabin the noise was deafening. The bullet struck the safety Perspex on an angle, ricocheted, and smashed into a control panel.

Burro smirked as he drew his own pistol. Bishop leaped from the chair and shoulder charged the door. It sprung open, hitting the would-be assassin. The gunman fired as he stumbled backward. The bullet punched through the door. A splinter of plastic lodged in Bishop's hand and he dropped his Beretta. With his other hand he grabbed Burro by his vest. A sharp pull smashed the young Mexican's face into the doorframe. He cried out and stumbled backward, aviator sunglasses knocked off his face. Bishop stepped over the dazed Emilio and kicked the pistol from his attacker's hand.

The cartel lieutenant's face switched to a mask of hatred as he recognized Bishop. "The Yankee, you're supposed to be dead."

Bishop smiled. "And you're about to be. Funny that."

Burro pulled a knife from his vest. "Fuck you, gringo."

The loader shuddered and Bishop almost lost his balance as a wheel dropped off the side of the track. They were heading for a huge ore crushing structure.

Burro sprang at Bishop, slashing with his knife.

He slipped the blow and struck Burro in the face, sending him reeling back.

The tractor started turning back to the road and Bishop glanced at the cockpit. Mirza had climbed in through the door on the other side and was at the controls.

Burro attacked again, this time stabbing wildly. Bishop sidestepped and backpedaled as his assailant pressed home the attack, stabbing and slashing.

He countered with a series of blows. Burro blocked the attacks, smiling as he danced from foot to foot.

A shot rang out and the smile dropped from the cartel lieutenant's face as he clutched his side. The knife dropped to the deck.

Bishop pulled the wounded man close by the lapels of his jacket and heaved him onto the railing that ran around the back of the earthmover.

Burro's eyes went wide as he toppled backward. He screamed as he bounced against the huge tire, then disappeared from sight. Two seconds later a bloody smear appeared on the tire as the wheel turned.

He looked back. Emilio was clutching the cartel lieutenant's pistol. "That's for my son." The old rancher staggered, on the verge of collapse.

Bishop reached out and steadied him.

"Bish, when you get a second, it would be great if you could show me how to turn this thing off," yelled Mirza from the cabin.

"Turn it off? No way, I'm just getting started."

***

A half hour later, Bishop brought the gargantuan front end loader to a halt, reached across, and hit the kill switch. He lowered the bucket and dumped the remains of the mine's gold storage vault onto the track. Then he climbed out of the cab and down the ladder to the ground.

"'Bout time you finished, you've been having way too much fun with that thing," Mitch said. He was leaning against the only transportable building that had not been flattened. Bishop shot him a broad smile. "You finished your environmental assessment yet?"

"My main concern is the cyanide tailings. I've locked the holding dam off, but if it's not removed in the next six months or so, it's going to leak into the water supply."

Bishop pointed to the pile of rubble in the bucket. It glinted as the midday sun hit it. "There's a shit-ton of gold in there. Roberto should be able to afford a clean-up crew."

"Bloody hell." Mitch walked over to inspect the load. Even unrefined, the gold bullion bricks were an impressive sight.

"Keep your grubby paws off it," Bishop said as he walked over to the office. He stuck his head in through the open door. "How are our patients?"

Mirza was inside treating Emilio and Roberto's injuries. He had them sitting on office chairs. Emilio had a bandage over his right eye with a cold pack pressed to it. Roberto had a bag of fluid running from a hat stand into his arm. "They're going to be fine. By the way, I found something of yours." He nodded at the desk. Next to Pershing's laptop was a battered New York Yankees baseball cap.

"No shit." He stepped into the room and retrieved the hat.

"Thought that might make your day."

Bishop grinned and put it on. "Almost makes up for missing George Henry Pershing."

Roberto shook his head. "No, you showed him. He won't

be back."

"You know what, mate, we couldn't have done this without you. Your team did well." His voice lowered. "I'm sorry we lost so many." Gerardo's body was outside in the bed of Emilio's truck. He would be buried on his farm alongside his ancestors.

"Better to die on your feet than live on your knees, Aden."

He took a card from his wallet and handed it to Roberto. It had a phone number and a non-descript email address on it. "I want you to let me know if the Black Jackets, or Pershing, or anyone else tries to put you on your knees again."

The battered and bruised rancher nodded and took the card.

There was a honk outside and Bishop stepped out to see a pickup pull up with Miguel at the wheel. "I think your backup has arrived."

There were five men in the bed of the truck. Farmers armed with shotguns and rifles. Down the road was a line of more trucks. Miguel had done well. After helping Mitch launch the aircraft he had gone to the town to rally support.

He watched as Emilio took the surviving brother aside and told him of Gerardo's death. His heart lurched as the man dropped to his knees and wept. Emilio wrapped an arm around his shoulders and held him.

A honk of a car horn sounded and he turned to see two silver BMW X5s driving up the road. The luxury SUVs passed the procession of farmers in their pickups and pulled up alongside the office. Heavily armed men spilled out and formed a loose perimeter.

Mitch gripped his machine gun and eyed them suspiciously.

Bishop approached as a short man in a gray suit stepped out. "Mr. Ramirez, I didn't think you were going to come."

The Sinaloa kingpin's bushy mustache lifted as he gave a broad smile. "How could I not? Your message was so intriguing." He marveled at the sheer scale of the destruction that had been wrought on the mine. Almost every building had been flattened and black smoke still billowed from the fuel dump. "You certainly have been busy."

Bishop nodded. "All in a day's work." As he stepped forward, one of the men made to stop him.

Ramirez pushed past his bodyguards. "You know, you killed Cardenas, the head of the Chaquetas Negras Cartel."

"Yeah, his boys found themselves a bit outgunned."

Ramirez's eyes narrowed. "Who are you people? You come down here and destroy the Chaquetas. You blow up their drug warehouse, you burn their mine to the ground."

"I guess you might call us justice. We're leaving these people under your protection, Ramirez. The gold from this mine belongs to them. The land belongs to them. Families will be compensated, lives rebuilt, and the miners won't be allowed back. That clear?"

The Sinaloa boss nodded. "It will be as you say. You have my word."

"Good, because we'll be watching, and if I have to come back, I'll bring more than just two of my buddies."

Bishop turned and walked to the Ford Bronco. Mitch had already packed the last of their gear from the safe house.

"I could really use men like you," yelled Ramirez. "Together we could shut down the Juarez cartel. You would make a lot of money."

"Just keep your word, and pray you don't see us again." He climbed into the truck and waited for Mitch and Mirza to join him. He started the engine and they drove up the road and out the gate.

"Why do I get the feeling this isn't over?" said Mitch as they headed down the winding mountain road.

"Because it isn't. We still need to find Pershing and shut down GE for good. We'll cache the gear in the desert and head back to El Paso. I'm thinking a steak at a restaurant, and a soft bed in a hotel. We can do our full debriefing with the Bunker tomorrow."

"So you've already back-briefed them on what happened at the mine?" Mirza asked.

"Ummm. I just let them know we don't need the CAT anymore."

"You didn't tell them about our plan did you?" said Mirza.

"Well, not exactly. I mean, they knew we were going to do a recce. I just didn't…"

Mitch shook his head. "You're out of control."

"Hey, it was a good plan. We played the cards we were dealt and it worked out for the best."

"Yeah, well now I'm pretty keen to play my hand with that bell-end, Pershing," said Mitch.

"Me too," added Mirza.

"That makes three of us."

CHAPTER 36

EL PASO, TEXAS

Christina placed her few belongings into a plastic bag and walked out of the hospital. It was late afternoon and she had spent the better part of the day waiting for the doctors to approve her release. Finally, a handsome young resident had handed her a box of antibiotics and signed the necessary document. It was not until she looked at the box on her way out that she realized he'd scribbled his phone number on it.

She squinted as she stepped out into the sunshine.

"Where do you think you're going, miss?"

There he was, leaning against a signpost with his battered Yankees cap pulled low. "Aden!" She blushed as she realized how excited she sounded.

"There's a diner around the corner. You mind if I buy you a coffee?"

She hugged him. "Sure thing."

"What was the last thing you remembered?" he asked as they walked.

"You saving my life. I've got a faint memory of another man being there. Dark, angular features, some kind of doctor."

He chuckled. "A doctor, he'll like that."

"So who was he?"

"A friend from work."

"From the UN?"

They arrived at the diner and sat at the only curbside table.

"Yeah. I told him where we were going and when I missed a check-in he got in contact with Emilio."

"OK. And Roberto?" she asked hesitantly.

Aden took off his hat and rubbed at his temples. She noticed the flecks of gray and the bags under his eyes.

"We rescued him yesterday. He sends his regards. Wanted me to tell you that you're welcome to visit when things settle down."

"What, how?" Relief washed over her face.

A waitress interrupted them and he ordered a burger and a shake. Christina ordered a coffee.

When the waitress was gone she leaned across the table. "How did you save him?"

"With the help of some friends." Bishop reached into the pocket of his jacket and tossed something on the table. It landed with a thud.

Christina did not believe her eyes. It was a solid lump of gold the length of her thumb. "Where did you get this?"

"The mine's back in the hands of the rightful owners."

"You mean you kicked out RED and the cartel?"

He winked. "Well, I'd like to take all the credit but the truth is Emilio and his guys did the heavy lifting." He filled her in on some of the details until their order arrived. Christina sipped her latte as she watched Bishop wolf into his burger.

"You haven't told me the whole story, have you?".

He neglected his food for a moment to pass her a memory stick. "I took the liberty of including photos and a few emails on here. You might find them interesting." He used a napkin to wipe ketchup from his chin. "The only caveat is you can't release the story till I give you the OK. The guys behind the mine are serious players and I'm not done with them yet. Which brings me to another point." He took out his wallet, extracted a credit card, and handed it over. "This card has thirty grand on it, a black account in the Cayman Islands. The pin number is your birth date." He took a long slurp from his shake. "I need you to disappear till we wrap this up. You got anyone you can stay with?"

Christina was expecting something like this. "Yeah, I've got a friend in South Africa. She's a photographer with a wildlife film company."

"OK, good. I've arranged for a passport to be sent to a safe deposit box at LAX." He handed her a slip of paper. "Here are the details. My email's there also if you need to contact me."

She took it and gave a knowing smile. "Forgot your UN

business cards again?"

"Yeah."

"Am I going to see you again?"

"Of course. I love Africa; I'll come visit you when this is all done."

She smiled. "You should bring Saneh."

He looked away and she regretted the comment. "Hey, I'm sorry."

"It's OK, I'm good." He waved for the bill. "Want to share a cab to the airport?"

"I haven't booked a flight."

He glanced at his watch. "If you want it, there's a business class seat booked in your name on the seventeen hundred to LAX."

She laughed. "You think of everything."

"I try." He paused. "Hey, Christina, when you write this, I'd really appreciate if you don't mention me, or any of my friends. We'll lose our jobs if we're implicated. Not to mention the fact we've made ourselves some powerful enemies."

"I can do better than that. I'll send you a draft before it goes to print. But, you have to promise to come to Africa."

He reached out and shook her hand. "It's a deal."

She held his hand and smiled. "Thank you so much for everything you've done. For saving my life, and for helping Roberto."

He looked down at the remains of his burger and mumbled, "Any man would have done the same."

"I'm not sure if she knows it, but Saneh is a very lucky woman."

Bishop ignored the comment. "You ready to go?"

***

Less than two miles from Bishop and Christina, Terrance Howard knocked back his fifth can of energy drink for the day. All morning he'd been unable to reach Pershing, he had no UAV support, and the caffeine coursing through his body wasn't helping his anxiety.

"Terry, I've got a satellite image!" yelled Ben.

"Get it up on the big screen."

It took the analyst a few seconds to transfer the high-resolution shot. When it appeared on the main screen Howard nearly had a heart attack. The mine's accommodation and administrative buildings appeared to be flattened. The entire facility was destroyed. The mining infrastructure was on fire with thick black smoke trailing into the desert.

"Whoa, that's not good," said Ben.

"No shit!" He grabbed the phone on his desk and dialed Pershing, for the sixth time.

It rang once before being answered. "What?"

"I'm looking at the mine. Dude, it's fucked up!"

"You're pretty damn observant. Aden and his buddies hit us hard."

"You OK?"

"What the fuck do you think, Howard? Billions of dollars have just gone up in smoke and I've been left holding my dick."

Howard swallowed.

"You better have called me with answers, because if I go down for this, I'm dragging you under with me."

"Look, um…"

"I thought as much. You've got three-fifths of fuck all haven't you?" He paused. "You find me Aden or it's all going to come out in the wash and you'll end up in a supermax sharing a cell with an angry ass-fucker called Maurice." Pershing terminated the call.

Howard stared at the satellite image as he contemplated the severity of the situation.

Ben clicked to another shot. A different angle revealed a row of huge dump trucks, all on fire. "So, what the hell happened out there?"

"Objective Yankee is what happened. We need to put everything we've got into an intel pack. This needs to go to the top."

***

Bishop saw Christina off at El Paso International, then took a cab to Horizon airport. Ten minutes out of town, the privately owned airport was the preferred location for private jets.

He walked across the tarmac to where the PRIMAL Gulfstream was parked. The aircraft's tail number had once again been changed. More of Chua's counter-intel procedures. He walked up the stairs and stuck his head into the cockpit. "Where we off to, fellas?"

"Jamaica, mon," said Mitch in his best rasta accent.

"Jamaica?"

Mirza glanced back from the co-pilot's seat. "Vance's orders. He's redirected us there to meet with Chua."

Mitch finished his preflight checks and started the turbofans. The whine of the powerful engines filled the cabin. Bishop went back and secured the door before returning. "So, anyone going to tell me what the hell is going on?"

Mirza shrugged. "We don't know much more than that. Got a message from the Bunker directing us to Norman Manley airport in Jamaica. Chua and a few others are already in location. They're establishing a forward operating base. The CAT is still on the island with the rest of the team. Once we're airborne I'll check in and find out more."

"Roger." Bishop moved back to the cabin and strapped himself in as they taxied out onto the runway. He yawned as the plush leather seat embraced him. Within seconds he was dozing, head back, mouth open. He stayed that way as the turbines screamed and the jet rocketed down the runway. They were at cruising altitude when a gentle shake woke him.

"You're drooling on my leather seats," said Mitch.

"We there yet?" Bishop frowned as he spotted Mirza sitting in the chair opposite reading the Gulfstream's flight manual. "Um, who's flying the jet?"

"Autopilot, mate. We're about five minutes from beginning

our descent." Bishop glanced at his watch. He'd been asleep for nearly an hour and a half. "I thought we were going to check in with Chua?"

"He called already. Going to brief us once we hit the ground. In the meantime, if you can please return your seat to the upright position, raise your window shade, reach down and grab your panties, because Mirza is putting this bird on the ground. One way or another."

Mirza gave him a cheesy grin and thumbs-up. He followed Mitch back into the cockpit.

"Hey, wait a minute. Mirza, he's only just started learning to fly. This is a bloody expensive jet!" Bishop was about to unbuckle his seat belt when the jet banked hard throwing him against the arm of the leather recliner. "You ball-bags." He laughed as he wrenched his belt tight.

With only a few abrupt corrections the landing was smooth and they taxied toward a hangar nestled in a freight handling area. Bishop stared out the window at the rusted iron walls as the jet came to a gentle halt. The cockpit door opened and Mirza appeared wearing a broad smile. "Very nicely done," Bishop said as he opened the door and lowered the stairs.

"I've got a good instructor."

"Steady on, you'll give the pommy bastard a big head."

Mitch appeared wearing a baseball cap proclaiming 'WORLD'S BEST PILOT'.

Bishop shook his head as he walked down the steps. "Too late."

They knocked on a side door and a full minute passed before a lock was drawn and PRIMAL's slightly-built intelligence chief greeted them. "Welcome to Forward Operating Base Kingston. Come on in."

"Not quite five-star is it?" Bishop said as they entered the old hangar. Light streamed in through rusted holes in the curved tin roof. The air was heavy with an earthy stench that reminded him of mushrooms.

"No, but it'll do. I'll give you the tour." Chua took them across the empty hangar floor to the back, which was jam-packed with Pelican cases, crates, and black bags. To the side was a line of stretchers and bedding. In a small corner office they found Flash. Chua's offsider was connecting a network of laptops.

"I can't believe Vance let you off the island."

Flash flipped him the bird. "Good to see you too, dick-lips."

He sat on a desk. "So you guys going to bring me up to speed?"

Chua sat on his metal chair. "There's a detailed team briefing at 2100 but I'll give you a quick heads-up. We've decrypted the emails Flash lifted from GE and we've uncovered some pretty heavy stuff. They're essentially the action arm for Manhattan Ventures and Investments. MVI raise capital and invest in highly speculative, unethical ventures. They send in GE to do the groundwork and maximize profit through force. Essentially they're the opposite of Tariq and GE is their version of PRIMAL."

"Making Pershing my ultimate nemesis."

Chua nodded. "Yep, and we haven't even touched the sides of what these guys are up to. We know they've also got CIA black contracts, but those are compartmented from the MVI side of things. As for MVI, well they've just finished establishing a rare-earth mine in DRC, and we've uncovered a new operation down in Venezuela."

"Well, we can scratch their Mexican aspirations."

"Good work; both Vance and Tariq wanted me to pass on their thanks. You'll be happy to know they've made it our top priority to bring the entire organization down."

Bishop got up from the desk. "These fuckers have tried to kill me twice. There won't be a third. I'll see you at the briefing." Leaving the office, he heard a voice that made his heart lurch.

"Aden." Saneh Ebadi's long hair bounced as she strode toward him. The former Iranian operative's striking features were stern as she came to a halt a few feet from him. "You had us worried there for a while, soldier." Her face softened and she managed an ever so slight smile. "I'm glad you're safe."

She looked radiant. The Indonesian yoga retreat had left her with a golden tan that accented her hazel eyes.

"Thanks. Hey, I was wondering if you'd heard anything from Aleks?"

She shook her head. "No, the last I heard he was still looking for Kurtz somewhere in Asia."

"Oh, so no sign of Kurtz yet."

"I think he's going to need some time."

"Yeah, well if you hear anything let me know."

She reached out and touched his arm. "Look, we're going to be working together on this one. Are you OK with that?"

He nodded. "Yeah, no problems. I just feel sorry for Pershing and his buddies at GE."

"Why is that?"

"Because after what they did in Mexico, I'm going to crush them."

"No Aden, we are going to crush them together."

"I like the sound of that."

CHAPTER 37

GES TRAINING AND OPERATIONS FACILITY, VIRGINIA

Charles King held on to his baseball cap as the silver Eurocopter EC175 flared and touched down on the grass landing zone. Once it powered down he approached, pulled back the sliding door of the luxury chopper and waited for the sole passenger to alight.

Jordan Pollard, chairman and majority stakeholder of MVI, stepped down from the helicopter, straightened his suit, and followed King's direction to the ATV parked next to the helipad.

They were on Ground Effects Services' 2500-acre training and operations facility located in southern Virginia. The sprawling complex housed four weapons ranges, an urban warfare facility, a driver-training course, rappelling towers, and a dense vegetation training area. It also had a fenced-off black-ops staging facility complete with a Sensitive Compartmented Intelligence Facility.

"Charles, how's the family?" Pollard asked as King started the buggy and they drove past the shooting ranges.

"They're good, sir. Sandy has put on a bit of a spread for us. The boys are still at camp."

"She's an amazing cook. I can't wait."

With his cap, black polo shirt, and tan cargos, King looked more like a security guard than the CEO of Ground Effects Services. They drove in silence through a densely forested area until they reached a security checkpoint. Black uniformed guards carrying AR carbines recognized both men and waved them through. They pulled up in front of a modern home that was modeled on the old plantation manors common in the area. It had red brick construction, with tall white columns either side of the door and a row of gabled windows on the upper level.

Pollard gripped the ATV's roll cage and groaned as he pulled himself from the buggy. "Damn knee." He hobbled after King and followed him into the study where he lowered himself into a leather recliner.

"So what in God's name happened down there?"

King poured him a tumbler of whiskey, neat, then walked across to a panel on the wall and activated a communications jamming system. "We were attacked by a team of highly trained, enabled, and motivated mercenaries."

"What brings you to that conclusion?"

"They armed the ranchers, did a recon on the mine, targeted the Chaquetas Negras, shut down Longreach, and then they destroyed the mine. If I didn't know better, I would bet my money on it being an ODA mission."

"Do you have any idea who they are?"

King nodded. "The CIA is calling the ringleader Objective Yankee. He's the guy Pershing tried to kill and he appears to have been involved in terrorist activities for a few years now. We've got a lead on one of his associates. A German national, former GSG 9. I'm sending one of my men to Germany to track him down."

Pollard got out of the chair and walked to the window. It was tinted, covered in a reflective film designed to scramble the beam of a laser listening device. He gazed at the trees thirty yards away. "How much information do these people have on us?"

"It's hard to say. We can assume they got most of Wesley's emails from his phone."

Pollard grunted. "That idiot. What does he know about the agency contracts?"

"Nothing."

"So, you don't think they've been compromised?"

"No, sir."

"What about Venezuela?"

"It's possible, but highly unlikely."

Pollard continued to stare as he sipped the whiskey. He

spoke softly, "This little problem in Mexico has cost me a lot of money. And when I say a lot, I mean well over a hundred million. So you can understand that I am a little angry about it. In fact you might say I am furious."

King swallowed.

The chairman turned from the window and fixed him with an icy stare. "So, what I want to happen is this. I want the people who are responsible found. I want them killed and I want their families killed. I want every living trace of them removed from the face of the earth."

"Yes, sir."

"Your man Pershing, where is he?"

"He's at a safe house in Texas with one of our tactical teams."

"And what's your opinion on his performance?"

"He's one of our best men, sir."

"Are you saying he isn't responsible?"

"None of us saw this threat coming. It was a wildcard. We've been targeted by professionals."

"Reel him in then. I want him to take point on this. He's been at the firing end; he knows what these people are capable of. Give him all the resources he needs, but if he screws up again, he's done. You understand?"

"Yes, sir."

"I already spoke to the Contracting Director. The analyst that Pershing was working with will be moved to the facility here. The CIA is taking this attack on US interests very seriously. They've agreed to foot the bill for the investigation. You will be taking the contract."

"Very good, sir."

"These people are going to find out what happens to people who fuck with me, Charles. My lawyers are going to sue the Mexican government under the Free Trade Agreement." He pointed at him. "And you're going to kill the men who attacked us." He placed the tumbler on the table and headed toward the door. "Now let's have lunch. Did your wife make that potato salad I had last time I was here? Goddamn, it was delicious."

***

Keep reading for a preview of PRIMAL Nemesis.

AUTHOR'S FINAL WORDS

When I first started writing this series, I did it entirely for me. It was therapeutic sending my operatives around the world taking down scumbags and dealing out justice. But, along the way a lot of people joined me on this journey. They email, instagram, tweet, Facebook, and leave reviews telling me how much they love the series and its characters. You guys are now the reason I write. So let me know what you think so I can continue to grow and learn as a writer. Leave a review and spread the word.

In case you didn't know, Reckoning is the first in a trilogy that pits the PRIMAL team against their deadliest enemy yet. The next book is PRIMAL Nemesis and if you keep turning the pages you'll see I've included the first chapter. If you want to keep up to date with the latest missions you can join PRIMAL here.

Back to it.

JS

JACK SILKSTONE

EXCERPT FROM PRIMAL NEMESIS

PROLOGUE

CARACAS, VENEZUELA

Antonio gripped the flagpole with both hands and waved it furiously. The bandana obscuring his face hid a broad grin. In the last few minutes the ranks of the university demonstrators had swelled from hundreds to thousands. There was now a sea of brightly colored flags swaying as the army of students surged toward Altamira Square. Calls for free elections, less corruption, and more security filled the air as they surged forward as one. There was energy around them that gave Antonio hope. Hope that they could force change on a government bloated with corruption and nepotism. Hope that they could make a real difference.

He passed the flag to a supporter and fished his smartphone from a pocket in his jeans. The Twitter message he'd sent from an anonymous account had been retweeted over four thousand times. Word had spread and more and more demonstrators were joining the revolution.

The twenty-year-old student was one of a handful organizing the demonstrations. A leader in the secretive Movimiento Estudiantil, or Student Movement, his job was to use social media to rally thousands of students to key points around the city. They were always one step ahead of the police, the military, and the colectivo gangs. Of the three the colectivo politically motivated militias were by far the most dangerous. Lacking the discipline of the government agencies, they had already badly beaten dozens of young demonstrators. But even they couldn't stop what had been started. The revolution had gained too much momentum. The government would be forced to listen.

"Antonio, Antonio." One of the other protest organizers, Camilla his girlfriend, tugged his sleeve. The petite brunette held up her phone. "The police are rallying at the square."

"OK." He checked his own device. Numerous tweets warning of an imminent police response were filling his news feed. The colectivos were also starting to gather their forces. It was time for the leadership of the Movimiento to disappear. The demonstration would continue without them. He sent a message to the other leaders. They would meet tonight to plan the next round of demonstrations and evaluate their tactics.

He took his girlfriend by the hand and led her out of the crowd and down a side street.

"I feel terrible leaving them," she said once they were clear of the turmoil.

He pulled the bandana from his face. "We can't risk being arrested. Who'll organize the demonstrations if we're captured?"

"True." She remained quiet as they walked down the street heading back to where they had left their bicycles.

Antonio unchained them. "We'll meet tonight at your place. The others will be there as well." He leaned across and kissed her. "We're doing the right thing, you'll see. Go home and study. Venezuela needs doctors." He mounted his bike and rode in the direction of his house.

The noise of the demonstration grew softer as he cycled away, replaced by the wail of sirens as a column of police cars raced past him. He suppressed a grin. By the time the police arrived most of the demonstrators would have already left. Only the hardliners would remain, those looking for a fight.

He pulled his bicycle up in front of his house and checked his messages as he climbed the stairs to the small residence. He had confirmation that all five of the Movimiento leaders would be at tonight's meeting. That was good news because they would have a guest attending, a member of the Voluntad Popular Party. The big players were starting to take notice of their growing influence.

***

"Boss, you might want to check this out." Pete, the team's intel specialist was sitting in front of an array of screens in the corner of an old sugar warehouse.

James 'Jimmy' Scott, the leader of 'Team 1', hauled himself off a tattered couch and ambled over to the makeshift intel center. It was 2000 hours on a Friday night and his five Ground Effects Services contractors hadn't seen any action for over a week. "You got something useful this time fucktard?" he said as he stuck his Tom Selleck-inspired mustache over Pete's shoulder.

The geek had half a dozen windows open across the three screens. He knew it all went over Jimmy's head. The former DEVGRU operator was a door-kicker through and through. "I've been monitoring about fifty different accounts across Twitter and Facebook. These kids are smart; they keep closing them down and opening new ones just before each riot. But they haven't been smart enough to switch devices. They're using the same IP and IMSI addresses."

Jimmy shrugged. "That sounds great, dweeb. What the fuck does it mean?"

"It means I can find them once we get the bird in the air."

"OK, so let's get it up." He turned and yelled across the warehouse. "Hank, job's on!"

An oil-stained operator turned from under the bonnet of one of the team's vehicles. The self-trained mechanic was constantly working on the battered van they used to move discreetly around Caracas. Their black SUVs rarely left the warehouse. Hank was also responsible for maintaining and preparing their helicopter drone for flight.

Pete uploaded the individual device identifiers into the drone as Jimmy and Hank disappeared through the doors at the back of the warehouse. Located on the outskirts of Caracas, the facility served as the team's forward operating base as well as a hangar for the drone. They had made it as comfortable as they could, partitioning off an area to sleep, and arranging three moth-eaten couches around a television. One corner of the dusty floor space had been converted into a makeshift gym with kettle bells, an Olympic bar, rowing machine, and rings hanging from an exposed rafter.

The communications data for the targets had finished uploading by the time the roar of a helicopter engine emanated throughout the high-ceilinged building. A minute later the noise faded into the distance. Jimmy strode into the room and switched on the television. Hank went back to working on the van.

"Do we get anything other than goddamn soccer on this thing?" Jimmy tossed the remote on the equipment case that served as a coffee table.

"I can hook something up after I finish here," said Pete as he double-checked the waypoints he'd programmed. One of his screens displayed the navigation software for the drone.

"Focus on the intel shit dick-wad." Jimmy jumped off the couch and made his way across to the gym.

Pete glanced across as the team leader stripped off his shirt revealing heavily-muscled shoulders with intricate tattoos running down to thick forearms. He dragged an empty crate across to the rings so he could reach them. At five-foot-five, he was the shortest of the six contractors. Something none of them dared to heckle him about.

Jimmy grunted as he grasped the rings and hauled his compact frame toward the ceiling. Pete as focused back on his screens. He was the only non-shooter and as a result was treated as a second-class citizen. He didn't mind though, as he knew that he was getting paid significantly more than Jimmy and any of the operators. GES valued his skills.

Two of his screens now displayed the feed from the million-dollar Schiebel Camcopter 100 that flew above the city in the darkness. He kept the aircraft under a thousand feet and monitored its flight path. A pulsing icon indicated its progress along the route. A small box in the bottom of the screen showed the view from the helicopter's forward-looking infrared camera. Except for a handful of passenger jets in the vicinity of the airport, the night sky over the Venezuelan capital was empty. Since he'd already entered the details of the phones he was targeting, all he needed to do was fly the aircraft in search patterns until the onboard systems located one of them. Depending on how large the search pattern was it could take hours or it could take minutes.

He glanced back at the gym. Jimmy was doing some kind of hardcore circuit that involved pull-ups, burpees, and swinging a kettle bell around his head. Fucking operators, he thought. A tone sounded and one of the screens flashed a warning. A cluster of red dots had appeared on the map. "Boss, I've got a hit! Three of the handsets just pinged in the same location."

Jimmy dropped from the rings and swaggered over. He leaned forward, dripping sweat on the keyboard. "How far is that?"

Pete grimaced, wiped the sweat with his sleeve, and plotted a route on the map. "Five minutes or so."

"Hell yeah, let's hit it." He turned away from the screen, cupped his hand to his mouth, and yelled, "Gear up, boys, we're rolling!"

***

The Movimiento leaders had agreed to meet in Antonio's girlfriend's ground floor apartment. Located in an affluent suburb, it was nicer than the other options that included a dormitory and his tiny flat. When they arrived he greeted the other four leaders and directed them to the living room where Camilla had laid out drinks and snacks.

One of the students filled a glass with water. "When are we expecting the Voluntad representative?"

Antonio checked the time on his phone. "Any minute now."

"We should think about making these meetings earlier." The young man yawned. "I've been studying all day and need some sleep."

They made small talk, discussing the day's successful demonstration and the pending exam period. All five were students from the Central University of Venezuela, in their early twenties, altruistic, and focused on forcing change on the government.

There was a knock on the door and the room fell silent. Antonio opened it a crack.

"Is this the Movimiento?" a woman's voice asked.

"Yes it is, please come in." He opened the door.

The visitor was middle-aged, curvaceous, and dressed in a gray pencil skirt, heels, white blouse, and a jacket. Her features were soft and she had full lips that broke into a bright smile as she entered the room.

The rest of the group rose as Antonio introduced the guest. "Ladies and gentlemen, I would like to introduce Caitlin Bracho from the Voluntad Party."

After the formalities were complete he invited her to speak.

"First of all, I want to thank Antonio for inviting me here today. Secondly, I want to thank you all for your ongoing work. Without your support, our own cause would be so much more difficult, if not impossible."

The group exchanged smiles as she continued. "Every time the students of Caracas, your friends, your supporters, head to the streets and protest, we send a clear message to the government. A message of intolerance when it comes to crime, corruption, and inequality." Her voice rose in intensity. She spoke with a rhythm, like a beating drum calling the tribes to war. "My party needs people like you to continue your work. To be the resistance, to fight the fight, and let Maduro and his cronies know we will not let them continue to rape this country and grow fat while others starve."

"We will fight," declared Antonio, his hand clenched in a fist.

"We will fight!" echoed the other members of the group.

The sound of a heavy thud against the front door startled Antonio and he jumped to his feet. Wood splintered as the lock gave way and the door burst open.

His girlfriend screamed as a hulking brute wearing a balaclava burst into the house. He brandished an extendable baton in a raised hand and wore a pistol on his hip. More men charged in behind him.

"Run, it's the colectivo!" he screamed as he tried to slam the living room door. The baton flashed down on his shoulder, smashing his collarbone. He screamed in agony and hunched over on the ground trying to protect his face.

Through a haze of tears he watched as the intruders savagely beat everyone, including the political representative. The searing pain in his shoulder pulsed and he vomited as his girlfriend was dragged from the living room by her hair. She screamed hysterically until a gloved hand clamped over her mouth. Her assailant was short but powerful. She didn't stand a chance. Antonio staggered to his feet and managed to snag a handful of the thug's shirt, tearing the fabric. The last thing he saw before someone smashed the back of his head was the intricate tattoo emblazoned on the man's forearm; a dragon clutching a trident.

***

RESTON, VIRGINIA

Charles King lifted a glass of champagne from the waiter's tray and raised it to his lips. He sipped as his wife chatted to someone whose name he should probably have remembered. They were attending a gala hosted by his boss, Jordan Pollard. The former US Army Brigade commander turned investment banker was the majority shareholder in the security company King ran, Ground Effects Services.

He sighed and ran a hand over his shaved head. He hated these events and thought they were a veritable smorgasbord of self-absorbed assholes who only attended because Pollard's wife Caroline spared no expense on food, alcohol, or entertainment.

The phone in his pocket vibrated and he subtly tried to check it. His wife shot him a frown. He shrugged and answered the call. It was Jimmy, the GES Team Leader in Venezuela. Listening, he walked to a quiet corner of the ballroom. After a few seconds, he replied, "I'll get back to you." He left his glass on a table and moved across to where Pollard was talking to an elderly couple.

Well into his sixties, his boss still cut a lean figure in his tuxedo. With his wavy gray hair and chiseled jaw, many women still found him attractive. Charming and engaging, he was ever the perfect host. Not many knew how utterly ruthless the man was.

He waited for a break in conversation before speaking. "Sir, do you have a moment?"

Pollard fixed him with cold gray eyes before turning back to the couple. "If you will excuse me." He tipped his head for King to follow and strode between his guests, through a door, into an empty corridor.

"Having a good time, Charles?"

"Yes, sir."

"Liar. You hate these things as much as I do. But, we do what we must to keep our women-folk happy." The joviality in his voice dissolved. "Now, is this about the debacle in Mexico? Tell me you've tracked the bastards down."

"No sir, we're still working on that. We've got a very strong lead on Objective Red Sox."

"The German, Wilhelm or something?"

"Yes, the intel team is now set up in our facility. We'll find him in no time." He glanced down the corridor, confirming they were alone. "I just had a call from Team 1. They dealt with a resistance group tonight and inadvertently captured a member of an opposition party."

"Do they have a name?"

"Yes, it's Caitlin Bracho."

Pollard walked away and made a phone call. The conversation lasted thirty seconds before he pocketed the device and turned back. "Have her disposed of."

"Sir, don't you think that's a little extreme? I mean, she's a politician. They can intimidate her, release her, and create the required effect."

Pollard fixed him with a stare. "Are you getting cold feet,

Charles?"

"No, sir, I just think it's unnecessary and risky."

"Don't get all self-righteous on me. What do you think your boy down in Mexico was doing? Handing out candy?"

"These aren't dirt farmers, she's a political leader. There could be blowback."

"Just make it happen."

He clenched his jaw. "Yes, sir."

"Good. Your boys are doing solid work down there." The corner of his mouth curled back in a snarl. "But they would want to be after your utter failure in Mexico."

"Pershing will find the men responsible for destroying the mine."

"He'd better, or he's done." The man's hard features softened. "Well, I guess we should get back to the gala."

"I need to call my man back."

"Text him."

He punched the message into his phone and sent it to Jimmy.

"Did you get a chance to try the lobster rolls?" Pollard asked when he was done.

"I did, they're amazing. Caroline always puts on the best spreads."

"That she does. I'll talk to you tomorrow, Charles."

"Yes, sir." King walked across to where his own wife was finishing her conversation.

"What was that about?" she asked.

He grabbed another glass of champagne. "Oh, nothing. Just something we've been tracking."

She put her arm around his waist. "Nothing too important, I hope."

"Just administrative issues. Have you tried the lobster rolls? Jordan recommends them."

**

RIO DE JANEIRO, BRAZIL

Kurtz drummed his fingers against the steering wheel of the rented minibus. Behind him the three other members of the rescue team were arguing whether now was the right time to move. He couldn't make out exactly what they were saying, just snippets. His hearing was yet to recover from a recent blast injury.

They had been watching the under-age brothel for the better part of a week. The seedy establishment was tucked away in one of Rio's wealthiest suburbs. Frequented by policemen, sex-tourists, government officials, and businessmen, it serviced the depraved needs of the rich and powerful. Everyone knew it was there. No one cared. Except, that is, for the small team of men in the bus.

The lanky German had been working with the Break Away organization for a little over two weeks. The not-for-profit's mission was to help rescue children from sexual slavery. Children who'd been kidnapped and forced into a life of pain and misery. Children like the three pre-teen girls being held in the brothel they were staking out.

Kurtz rubbed his unshaven jaw and slapped the steering wheel. "So are we doing this or not?" he asked loudly.

The leader, Brian, was a retired policeman from Kentucky. His voice wavered as he replied, "Yes, yes, we're ready. But, let's go over the plan again."

"Nein, we've been over it enough," said Kurtz. "The plan is good, it's simple, ja. We get in, we get the girls, and we get out. Then we take them away. Now is the time, we know there's no one there, just the caretaker."

"Yes, you're right," said another American. The other two volunteers in the back of the minibus were also former policemen. Like Brian, they were dressed in slacks and polo shirts. Kurtz, the most recent addition to the team was the youngest by at least ten years, and as such he had been relegated to the position of driver.

"OK, so we're going now, ja."

"Yes, let's go." Brian's reluctance was understandable.

Previously these raids had been left to the local authorities. The expatriate team usually only conducted the initial recon, identifying under-age brothels by posing as potential clients. However, the police had refused to act this time and it was only at Kurtz's urging they had decided to conduct the raid themselves.

Kurtz checked the mirrors as he pulled out from the curb. It was early morning and the quiet leafy streets were empty. In half an hour it would become busy as people drove their children to school and headed off to work. By then the team would be long gone.

He turned the minibus into a laneway between two rows of townhouses. The brothel used a nondescript back door that allowed patrons a discreet means of slipping back to their cars. He braked gently when they were opposite.

One of the retirees in the back slid the door open and stepped down to the street. He grabbed the door handle to the building and tried to yank it open. It wouldn't budge. "I can't get it open," he yelled.

"Let me try." Brian jumped out the front of the vehicle and joined the other two men on the street. He pushed them aside and grabbed the handle. It still wouldn't budge. "Damn, it's locked." He shook his head. When he'd visited the brothel during the recon phase he'd simply walked in. Posing as an American sex-tourist, he'd been welcomed and shown the girls.

"Dummkopfs," mumbled Kurtz as he climbed out of the driver's seat. In the back of his mind he wondered if the brothel had been tipped off and knew they were coming. He made a quick assessment of the door and identified that it swung inward. "Get out of the way." He kicked hard directly below the handle. There was a crunching sound as the lock tore from the jamb and it swung open with a crash. "One of you stay with the van," he said as he stepped into the corridor.

He felt naked without his armor and a weapon. It was an alien feeling for the former PRIMAL operative. Break Away, a not-for-profit organization, had a policy of never carrying weapons. In fact this was their most aggressive mission in their two year history.

Brian pushed past him and lumbered up a set of stairs. "This way." He reached the top and grunted as a baseball bat thudded into his chest.

So much for one caretaker, thought Kurtz as he spotted the youth who'd hit Brian. The kid with the bat wore a crazed expression and his eyes bulged from his head like an insect. He raised the bat and was about to deliver a killing blow when Kurtz leaped into action.

He jumped over his colleague and raised an arm to deflect the bat. It stung as it glanced off his forearm away from Brian's skull. With a grunt he thrust his knee forward. Ribs snapped and the kid collapsed to the ground gasping for air. Kurtz grabbed the bat and left him spluttering and whimpering on the tattered carpet. With the bat in hand he strode down the corridor. A door secured with a padlock barred the way. The lock sheared off with a single blow.

What he saw when he entered broke his heart. Huddled together on a single stained mattress were three young girls. They were dressed in ill-fitting lingerie, their faces smeared with makeup and tears. Kurtz collapsed against the wall and lowered the bat, his eyes misting with tears of his own.

The Americans entered the room. One of them shrugged off a backpack and handed the girls tracksuits. "We're here to take you home," the man repeated over and over, in Portuguese.

Kurtz stepped back into the corridor and found himself face to face with another gangster. The muscular assailant lunged with a knife. He managed to deflect the blow but the attacker reacted even faster, lashing out with a kick that knocked his bat to the ground.

The knife-fighter saw he was outnumbered and backpedaled down the corridor, the knife extended in front of him.

"Schweine," Kurtz hissed between his teeth as he strode forward and lunged. He grabbed the wrist of the knife-wielding hand and fired a savage punch at the man's face. It connected with a crunch. Driving forward with murderous rage, Kurtz struck again and again splitting the man's eyebrow open and pulverizing his cheekbone. The knife dropped to the ground and he delivered a devastating front kick. The force of the blow knocked the man backward and sent him sprawling on the carpet.

Kurtz picked up the bat and was about to finish him when Brian called out. "Come on, we need to go."

He turned and saw the others had the girls and were ushering them down the stairs. He gave the two injured gangsters a cursory kick and followed. When he got to the minibus one of the others was already in the driver's seat. He jumped into the passenger seat and slumped in the chair.

Glancing in the rear-view mirror he stared directly into the eyes of one of the rescued girls. Emotion choked him and tears welled up again. The little face smiled and Kurtz looked away. Catching one of the other volunteers staring at him he took a deep breath and struggled to contain himself.

An hour later Kurtz was back in his room at a cheap hostel. He'd managed to slip away from the rest of the men who were celebrating in a local bar. The girls were safe, handed over to a local agency who would work with the authorities to return them to their families.

Kurtz should have felt good; he'd saved the day and the girls were safe. Job well done, as Bishop would have said. He clenched a fist as his thoughts turned to his former teammates. It had been over a month since he'd abandoned them in Tokyo. A month filled with self-loathing, self-doubt, and heavy drinking. He grabbed the bottle of rum on the nightstand and took a swig. "Fuck Bishop and fuck PRIMAL," he mumbled as he wiped his mouth on his sleeve. He fell back onto the hard mattress and wept. "I'm sorry, Karla, I'm so sorry."

***

Buy PRIMAL Nemesis at www.amazon.com

JACK SILKSTONE

BOOKS BY JACK SILKSTONE

PRIMAL Inception
PRIMAL Mirza
PRIMAL Origin
PRIMAL Unleashed
PRIMAL Vengeance
PRIMAL Fury
PRIMAL Reckoning
PRIMAL Nemesis
PRIMAL Redemption
PRIMAL Compendium
PRIMAL Renegade
SEAL of Approval

ABOUT THE AUTHOR

Jack Silkstone grew up on a steady diet of Tom Clancy, James Bond, Jason Bourne, Commando comics, and the original first-person shooters, Wolfenstein and Doom. His background includes a career in military intelligence and special operations, working alongside some of the world's most elite units. His love of action-adventure stories, his military background, and his real-world experiences combined to inspire the no-holds-barred PRIMAL series.

jacksilkstone@primalunleashed.com
www.primalunleashed.com
www.twitter.com/jsilkstone
www.facebook.com/primalunleashed

Made in the USA
Middletown, DE
15 July 2017